賴世雄 圖解英文法

Preface 序

　　常有讀者向我反應，英文文法好難、好複雜，在學時讀不通，出了社會想要進修還是卡關。於是我召集了本公司的編輯群，以最好讀、最好懂為出發點編纂本書。書籍內容包含必懂的 20 大文法重點共 84 小節，特點如下：

1　使用化繁為簡的寫法，由淺入深以表格、圖像條理化複雜的文法觀念，讓讀者看完秒懂。

2　文字搭配圖片，加深印象，學習效果也更好！對於英文相關考試如升大學、全民英檢、多益、雅思、托福等皆適用。

3　例句為非常生活化的內容，讀者可把例句記熟，直接應用於日常生活中！

4　每一小節之後，我們為讀者設計多樣化的練習題，立即測驗可知學習成效。

　　最後希望大家能藉由此書大大提升英文實力，祝大家學習成功！

User's Guide 使用說明

★ 以 表格 及 圖像 ，將複雜的文法觀念化繁為簡！

冠詞所指的是「冠」在名詞前面的限定詞（限定詞指限定名詞某些意思的詞類）。
冠詞有不定冠詞與定冠詞之分：

種類		用途
不定冠詞	a、an	與不限定的單數可數名詞搭配使用
定冠詞	the	與特定的單數或複數可數名詞、不可數名詞搭配使用

例句		
Please hand me a book. 請遞給我一本書。 （未限定哪一本，即任何一本皆可）		Please hand me the book. 請遞給我那本書。 （有指名特定的某一本書，非任何一本）

★ 生活化 的例句簡單易懂又好記！

have 作助動詞的用法
❶ 形成完成式

句型	**現在完成式** has / have + 過去分詞
	過去完成式 had + 過去分詞
	未來完成式 will have + 過去分詞

例句	Linda **has saved** some money. 琳達存了一些錢。
	My parents **had** already **eaten** dinner when I got home. 我回到家時我爸媽已經吃過晚餐了。

⭐ 重要文字或例句搭配 圖片 ，學習成效更好！

❶ 不定冠詞（a、an）

使用 a 或 an 的時機
❶ a 用在字首發音為子音的單字前

說明	單字發音若為子音開頭，要搭配 a 使用。請注意，即使某單字字首為母音字母（如 u），但實際發音為子音時，仍要使用 a。

例字	a camera ［ˋkæmərə］ （一臺相機）	a uniform ［ˋjunəˏfɔrm］ （一套制服）
	a film ［fɪlm］ （一部影片）	a university ［ˏjunəˋvɝsətɪ］ （一間大學）

⭐ 每小節後有 練習題 ，隨即演練加深印象！

＼ 即時演練 ／

一、請勾選下列套色單字的正確種類。

① This house is big.   □ 普通名詞   □ 專有名詞

② Mom is in good health.   □ 具體名詞   □ 抽象名詞

③ Lily bought some bread.   □ 可數名詞   □ 不可數名詞

二、請寫出下列單字正確的複數形。

單數形 VS 複數形		單數形 VS 複數形	
① chair	_____	⑥ tooth	_____
② watch	_____	⑦ child	_____
③ lady	_____	⑧ sheep	_____
④ guy	_____	⑨ potato	_____

Contents 目錄

Chapter 1

形成句子的基本要素

1-1　詞類

英文單字依其在句子中的作用，共分為八類，稱為 **八大詞類**，分別是：**名詞、代名詞、動詞、形容詞、副詞、介詞、連接詞**及**感歎詞**。

八大詞類

1　名詞

作用	泛指人、事、地、物。

例句

Hank is a **student**.
漢克是學生。

2　代名詞

作用	代替名詞。

例句

Mary has a cat. **She** feeds **it** too much.
　　　　　代替 Mary　　代替 a cat
瑪麗有隻貓。她餵牠太多食物了。

3　動詞

作用	表示動作或狀態。

例句

The boy **kicked** the ball.
　　　　 表示動作
男孩踢了球。

The restaurant **is** full.
　　　　　 表示狀態
餐廳客滿了。

4 形容詞

作用 修飾或描述名詞或代名詞。

例句 Diana is wearing a **pretty** dress.

黛安娜穿著漂亮的洋裝。

He is **nice**.

他是好人。

 5 副詞

作用 修飾或描述動詞、形容詞、其他副詞或修飾全句。

例句 The woman walked **slowly** to the man.

女子緩慢地走向男子。

Kate is **quite** smart.

凱特蠻聰明的。

Those people are talking **very** loudly.

那些人講話非常大聲。

Fortunately, no one got hurt in the accident.

幸好沒人在此事故中受傷。

 6 介詞

作用 置名詞前，表示地方、時間、因果關係等。

例句 I usually stay **at** home **on** Sundays.
我通常週日會待在家。

Daniel is still **at** school.
丹尼爾還在學校。

This restaurant is famous for its sandwiches.
這家餐廳以其三明治而聞名。

7 連接詞

作用 連接單字、片語或子句。

例句 Ella and Eva are twins.
艾拉跟伊娃是雙胞胎。

Do you want a glass of water or a cup of coffee?
你想要一杯水還是一杯咖啡？

The runner won the race and broke the record.
這名跑者贏了比賽並打破紀錄。

Harry just turned 20, so he is old enough to vote.
哈利剛滿二十歲，所以他可以投票。

8 感歎詞

作用 表示感歎、驚訝、憤怒等情緒。

例句 Wow! You look amazing!
哇！妳美呆了！

What! Are you kidding me?
什麼！你在開玩笑嗎？

 深 度補充

有些單字可作不同詞類使用

例句 Clara always has a smile on her face.
克萊兒總是面帶微笑。（此處 smile 作名詞）

Charlie is smiling.
查理微笑著。（此處 smile 作動詞）

This is my backpack.
這是我的背包。（此處 This 作代名詞）

This backpack is mine.
這個背包是我的。（此處 This 作形容詞）

\ 即時演練 /

請勾選下列套色單字的正確詞類。

① I don't have any money. ☐ 名詞　☐ 代名詞
② That was a nice meal. ☐ 名詞　☐ 代名詞
③ Please open the window. ☐ 動詞　☐ 形容詞
④ The window is open. ☐ 動詞　☐ 形容詞
⑤ Tom speaks English well. ☐ 形容詞　☐ 副詞
⑥ My favorite color is blue. ☐ 形容詞　☐ 副詞
⑦ Eddie is kind and friendly. ☐ 連接詞　☐ 介詞
⑧ I don't like to drive at night. ☐ 連接詞　☐ 介詞
⑨ Hey! What are you doing? ☐ 感歎詞　☐ 名詞
⑩ Those shoes are dirty. ☐ 形容詞　☐ 代名詞

解　　答				
① 名詞	② 代名詞	③ 動詞	④ 形容詞	⑤ 副詞
⑥ 形容詞	⑦ 連接詞	⑧ 介詞	⑨ 感歎詞	⑩ 形容詞

1-2　片語

片語是由**兩個或以上的單字**形成的詞組。由於片語本身無「主詞-動詞」之關係，因此單一片語不具有構成句子的條件 (有關「句子」之說明，請參考 1-4)。相對地，句子可由多個片語形成，如下：

例句分析	My mom	will drive	her own car	to the mall.
片語	名詞片語	動詞片語	名詞片語	介詞片語
功能	名詞	動詞	名詞	副詞
譯	我媽媽會開自己的車去購物中心。			

常見的片語種類

1 名詞片語

說明　名詞片語通常是由限定詞 (如 a、an、this、my 等) 搭配名詞而形成的。名詞片語在句子中可作主詞、受詞、補語或同位語。

例句
My bag is over there.　我的袋子在那裡。(名詞片語作主詞)

Someone ate the last piece of cake.
有人吃掉最後一塊蛋糕。(名詞片語作動詞 ate 的受詞)

Sam is the only child in his family.
山姆是家中唯一的小孩。(名詞片語作主詞補語)

Yushan, the highest mountain in Taiwan, is magnificent.
臺灣第一高峰玉山很壯觀。(名詞片語作同位語)

2 動詞片語

說明　動詞片語是由主要動詞與助動詞 (包括一般助動詞如 be 動詞和情態助動詞如 can 等) 並用所形成。

例句
Mike is laughing at his sister.
麥克在嘲笑他妹妹。

The prize was given to a 12-year-old girl.
獎項頒給一名十二歲女孩。

3 形容詞片語

說明 泛指用來修飾名詞或代名詞的片語。形容詞片語有下列常見形態：

1 形容詞組成　　　　　　　**4** 不定詞片語

2 副詞搭配形容詞　　　　　**5** 分詞片語

3 介詞片語

 Taylor is a **tall**, **handsome** man.
泰勒是一名高大又英俊的男子。

This dish is **too spicy**.
這道菜太辣了。

The dictionary **on the sofa** is Ken's.
沙發上面的字典是肯的。（介詞片語作形容詞修飾名詞 the dictionary）

Now is not a good time **to make a joke**.
現在不是開玩笑的好時機。（不定詞片語作形容詞修飾名詞 a good time）

The woman **waving at me** is my mother.
對我揮手的女士是我母親。（分詞片語作形容詞修飾名詞 The woman）

4 副詞片語

說明 泛指用來修飾動詞、形容詞或其他副詞的片語。副詞片語有下列常見形態：

1 副詞組成　　　　　　　　**3** 介詞片語

2 名詞 + 介詞 + 名詞　　　**4** 不定詞片語

 The man runs **very slowly**.
這男子跑得非常慢。

I prefer talking to people **face to face**.
我比較喜歡跟別人面對面聊天。

I'll meet Abby **at the train station**.
我會在火車站跟艾比碰面。（介詞片語作副詞修飾動詞 meet）

Rita asked me **to lend her some money**.
麗塔請我借她一些錢。（不定詞片語作副詞修飾動詞 asked）

5 介詞片語

 說明 泛指由介詞引導的片語，常搭配名詞或代名詞作該介詞的受詞。介詞片語在句子中常作形容詞、副詞或名詞。

CH
1

1-2

片語

| 例句 | The notebook **on the desk** is mine.
書桌上的筆記本是我的。
（介詞片語作形容詞，修飾名詞 The notebook） | |

Daisy saves her money **in the bank.**
黛西把錢存在銀行裡。（介詞片語作副詞，修飾動詞 saves）

6 不定詞片語

| 說明 | 不定詞片語通常指由 to 引導的片語，具有名詞、
形容詞或副詞的功能。 |

| 例句 | **To travel around the world** is my dream.
環遊世界是我的夢想。（不定詞片語作名詞） |

Do you want something **to eat**?
你想要吃點東西嗎？（不定詞片語作形容詞）

Vicky went back to her room **to do her homework.**
維琪回到房間寫作業。（不定詞片語作副詞）

7 分詞片語

| 說明 | 泛指由現在分詞 (V-ing) 或過去分詞 (V-ed) 引導的片語，
通常在句子中作形容詞用，修飾名詞或代名詞。 |

| 例句 | The man **performing on stage** is my friend.
舞臺上表演的人是我的朋友。 |

The cat, **frightened by the loud noise,** is shaking.
貓被巨大聲響嚇到，瑟瑟發抖著。

8 動名詞片語

| 說明 | 泛指由動名詞引導的片語，通常作名詞使用，可在句子中作主詞、受詞
或補語。 |

| 例句 | **Using social media** can be a waste of time.
使用社群媒體有時很浪費時間。（動名詞片語作主詞） |

My friends enjoy **playing board games.**
我朋友喜歡玩桌遊。（動名詞片語作受詞）

Matt's only interest is **watching movies.**
麥特唯一的興趣就是看電影。（動名詞片語作主詞補語）

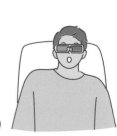

請勾選下列套色片語的正確種類。

① I exercise **on a daily basis**.	☐ 介詞片語	☐ 不定詞片語	
② Rick **is watching** TV.	☐ 副詞片語	☐ 動詞片語	
③ **One of my sisters** is married.	☐ 名詞片語	☐ 形容詞片語	
④ Who is that man **over there**?	☐ 形容詞片語	☐ 副詞片語	
⑤ My goal is **to win first place**.	☐ 分詞片語	☐ 不定詞片語	
⑥ Mr. Lin arrived **too early**.	☐ 副詞片語	☐ 形容詞片語	
⑦ **Eating lunch** is important.	☐ 分詞片語	☐ 動名詞片語	
⑧ I hope **to see you again**.	☐ 介詞片語	☐ 不定詞片語	
⑨ Ivan is still lying **in bed**.	☐ 副詞片語	☐ 形容詞片語	
⑩ The boy **sitting there** is Ben.	☐ 分詞片語	☐ 動名詞片語	

解　答
① 介詞片語　② 動詞片語　③ 名詞片語　④ 形容詞片語　⑤ 不定詞片語
⑥ 副詞片語　⑦ 動名詞片語　⑧ 不定詞片語　⑨ 副詞片語　⑩ 分詞片語

1-3 子句

子句是包含主詞(如 I、my brother 等)與動詞的相關詞組。子句依據結構可分為 **獨立子句** 與 **從屬子句**,而從屬子句又可依功能分為**名詞子句、形容詞子句以及副詞子句**:

依結構分類	依功能分類
獨立子句	
從屬子句	名詞子句
	形容詞子句
	副詞子句

以下依上列分類分項闡述:

獨立子句

 說明　獨立子句又稱主要子句,是可獨立存在且語意、句構完整的句子。

 例句　I arrived at the train station.
我抵達火車站。

The train was late.
火車延誤了。

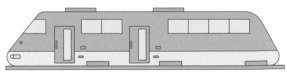

 深 度補充

連結兩個獨立子句

 說明　由於獨立子句可單獨存在,故連結兩個獨立子句時不宜直接使用逗號,而應採取下列方式:
1 使用標點符號(句點或分號)隔開。
2 使用對等連接詞(如 and、or、but)連結。

→ I arrived at the train station, the train was late. (×)

= I arrived at the train station. The train was late. (○)

= I arrived at the train station; the train was late. (○)

= I arrived at the train station, **but** the train was late. (○)

我抵達了火車站,但火車延誤了。

從屬子句

從屬子句又稱附屬子句,是由從屬連接詞 (如 because、if、since 等) 或關係代名詞 (如 who、which、that 等) 引導的子句。從屬子句的語意不完整,故無法單獨存在,必須依附獨立子句方能形成完整的句子。

If you are hungry, you can eat this pizza.

如果你肚子餓可以吃這份披薩。

This is the dress **that I wore to the party.**

這件是我穿去參加派對的洋裝。

從屬子句依功能分類

1 名詞子句

在句子中作名詞的子句,用於作為句子中的主詞、受詞、補語或同位語。

I don't know **what we are having for dinner.**

我不知道我們晚餐要吃什麼。(名詞子句為動詞 know 的受詞)

2 形容詞子句

在句子中作形容詞的子句,用於修飾句子中的名詞或代名詞。

I really like the jeans **that my sister gave me.**

我真的很喜歡我姊送我的牛仔褲。

11

3 副詞子句

說明 在句子中作副詞的子句，用於修飾動詞或整個獨立子句。

例句 The boss likes John because he is an efficient employee.
老闆喜歡約翰因為他是個工作有效率的員工。

＼ 即時演練 ／

請勾選下列套色子句的正確種類。

① Although Arthur is very wealthy, he is not happy at all.
　□ 獨立子句　　　　　　　□ 從屬子句

② Sam will go to bed after he finishes his homework.
　□ 獨立子句　　　　　　　□ 從屬子句

③ I like movies that are funny and exciting.
　□ 名詞子句　　　　　　　□ 形容詞子句

④ When I grow up, I want to become a teacher.
　□ 形容詞子句　　　　　　□ 副詞子句

⑤ I can't understand what you're saying.
　□ 名詞子句　　　　　　　□ 副詞子句

解　答
① 獨立子句　② 從屬子句　③ 形容詞子句　④ 副詞子句　⑤ 名詞子句

1-4 句子

句子是具有主詞與動詞的一群相關詞組,且能夠獨立表達完整意思。句子依照結構可分為**單句、合句、複句以及複合句**。依照功能則可分為**直述句、疑問句、祈使句以及感歎句**:

句子類型	
依結構	單句
	合句
	複句
	複合句
依功能	直述句
	疑問句
	祈使句
	感歎句

以下依上列分類分項闡述:

❶ 依結構分類

句子類型
❶ 單句

說明	單句 = 獨立子句
例句	Claire likes classical music. 克萊兒喜歡古典音樂。

❷ 合句

說明	合句 = 獨立子句 + 獨立子句

例
句

Emma enjoys swimming, but her boyfriend is afraid of water.

艾瑪喜歡游泳，但她男朋友卻很怕水。

3 複句

說
明

複句 = 獨立子句 + 從屬子句

例
句

You should study hard if you want to pass the test.

如果你想考試及格，應該要用功讀書。

4 複合句

說
明

複合句 = 獨立子句 + 獨立子句 + 從屬子句

例
句

Although Martin is old, he still has a sharp mind and he is in great shape.

雖然馬丁年紀大了，他的思緒仍清晰，身體也很硬朗。

2 依功能分類

句子類型

1 直述句

說
明

直述句又稱敘述句，為陳述事實或現象的句子。

例
句

Exercising is good for your health.

運動對你的健康有益。

2 疑問句

說
明

用於詢問或質疑的句子，主要為可用 Yes / No 回答的一般疑問句與以疑問詞（如 where、why、when、what、which、who、how）起首的特殊疑問句兩類。

例
句

Do you have any brothers or sisters?

你有兄弟姊妹嗎？

Where does Amy live?

艾咪住在哪？

❸ 祈使句

| 說明 | 表示命令、禁止、請求等的句子，通常會省略句子主詞（You）並以原形動詞開頭。 |

| 例句 | Run faster!
跑快一點！

Be quiet!
安靜！

Please open the window.
請打開窗戶。 |

❹ 感歎句

| 說明 | 表示驚訝、感歎等強烈情緒的句子。 |

| 例句 | How lovely you look!
妳真美！

What a beautiful day!
真是美好的一天！ |

請勾選下列句子的正確種類。

① Shelley is my colleague, but I don't like her. ☐ 單句 ☐ 合句

② The car that I borrowed from Ken broke down, so I need to call a mechanic. ☐ 複句 ☐ 複合句

③ May is learning a foreign language. ☐ 單句 ☐ 複句

④ Chris is in good health because he eats a balanced diet. ☐ 合句 ☐ 複句

⑤ Can you tell me when your plane will arrive? ☐ 直述句 ☐ 疑問句

⑥ Make sure to pay the bills before this Friday. ☐ 疑問句 ☐ 祈使句

⑦ The angry dog always barks at me when I walk by it. ☐ 祈使句 ☐ 直述句

⑧ What a smart boy you are! ☐ 祈使句 ☐ 感歎句

解　　答

① 合句　　② 複合句　　③ 單句　　④ 複句　　⑤ 疑問句

⑥ 祈使句　　⑦ 直述句　　⑧ 感歎句

Chapter 2

主詞

Chapter 2　主詞

2-1　主詞的形式

句子或子句中的主詞通常是用於表示主體或執行動作者。一般常見的句型中，通常是以**名詞**作主詞。但除了名詞之外，還可用**代名詞**、**動名詞 / 不定詞片語**、**名詞子句**、**名詞片語**等作主詞。以下分項闡述：

1 名詞作主詞

The movie was boring.
這部電影很無聊。

The restaurant is fully booked.
這間餐廳被訂滿了。

2 代名詞作主詞

We will host a party this weekend.
我們這週末要主辦派對。

I have a test tomorrow.
我明天要考試。

3 動名詞 / 不定詞片語作主詞

英文的句子中，動詞不可直接作主詞，須變成動名詞或不定詞片語才可作主詞用。以動名詞片語作主詞通常表示已知的事實或曾經做過的經驗。不定詞片語作主詞時，則通常表示意願、目的或未完成的事。

Listen to music makes me happy.（×）
→ Listening to music makes me happy.（○）
聽音樂讓我很開心。

Buy a house of my own is my goal.（×）
→ To buy a house of my own is my goal.（○）
我的目標是買自己的房子。

名詞子句作主詞

 英文的句子或問句不可直接作主詞用，須變成名詞子句才可作主詞用。

 That Mary didn't recognize me was embarrassing.
瑪麗沒有認出我讓我很尷尬。

Where the old man lives is a mystery.
這位老先生的住處不得而知。

Whether we will win or not is still uncertain.
我們是否會獲勝仍無法確定。

5 名詞片語 (= 疑問詞 + 不定詞) 作主詞

 一般的名詞片語 (即「限定詞 + 名詞」之形式，如 a book、my book 等) 是常見的主詞形式。但另一種由疑問詞與不定詞片語形成的名詞片語亦可作主詞使用。此類主詞可視為由名詞子句簡化而成的。

Where we will meet Roger has not been decided.
(名詞子句作主詞)

→ **Where to meet Roger** has not been decided.
(名詞片語作主詞)
(我們) 要在哪裡與羅傑見面還未決定。

What we will do will be discussed later.
(名詞子句作主詞)

→ **What to do** will be discussed later.
(名詞片語作主詞)
(我們) 要做什麼晚點會討論。

一、請根據中文提示，在下列空格中填入正確的內容。

① 學英文 (learn English) 很有趣。
提示：使用動名詞片語作主詞

_____ is fun.

② 去年發生的事 (what happened last year) 已經被遺忘了。
提示：使用名詞子句作主詞

_____ has already been forgotten.

③ 去歐洲念書 (study in Europe) 是我的計畫。
提示：使用不定詞片語作主詞

_____ is my plan.

二、請根據提示，改寫下列句子。

① How you should handle the problem depends on you.
提示：使用名詞片語作主詞

_____

② When we will leave for the airport is up to our parents.
提示：使用名詞片語作主詞

_____

③ Whether we will go has not been decided yet.
提示：使用名詞片語作主詞

_____

解　答

一、 ① Learning English
　　 ② What happened last year
　　 ③ To study in Europe
二、 ① How to handle the problem depends on you.
　　 ② When to leave for the airport is up to our parents.
　　 ③ Whether to go has not been decided yet.

Chapter 2　主詞

2-2　虛主詞

一般情況下，英文句子必須有主詞。有時，句子會使用虛主詞以取代真主詞。
代名詞 **it** 與 **there** 是常見的虛主詞。

❶ it 作虛主詞

用以取代真主詞

說明

在下列情況下，往往會出現主詞過長的情形，故可用虛主詞 it 代替，置
於句首，而被代替的真主詞則置於句尾：

❶ 動名詞片語作主詞

❷ 不定詞片語作主詞

❸ 名詞子句作主詞

注意

作真主詞的動名詞片語移至句尾時，通常會改為不定詞片語。

例句

Listening to music makes me happy.
→ **It** makes me happy **to listen to music.**
聽音樂讓我很開心。
(It 取代動名詞片語作虛主詞)

To buy a house of my own is my goal.
→ **It** is my goal **to buy a house of my own.**
我的目標是買自己的房子。
(It 取代不定詞片語作虛主詞)

That Mary didn't recognize me was embarrassing.
→ **It** was embarrassing **that Mary didn't recognize me.**
瑪麗沒有認出我讓我很尷尬。
(It 取代名詞子句作虛主詞)

2 there 作虛主詞

用以表示「有」

說明 There is / There are 可用以表示一個地方有某人、事、物，或某事物、某情況存在著，中文常譯成「有」。There is 後須接單數可數名詞或不可數名詞，There are 後面則須接複數可數名詞。

注意

There is / There are 中的 there 並非表示「那裡」之意，故不應將 There is / There are 譯成「那裡有」。若要表示「那裡 / 這裡有」，則應在句尾加上副詞 there 或 here。

例句 **There is** a glass of milk on the table.
桌上有一杯牛奶。

There are bears in the mountains.
山區有熊出沒。

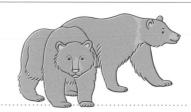

There was a fire (over) there.
那裡發生了火災。

There are some books (over) here.
這裡有一些書。

 **深** 度補充

There is / There are 與 has / have

說明 There is / There are 以及 has / have 的中文常翻譯成「有」，但兩組之間的意思與用法有所區別：

1 There is / There are 所表示的意思為「存在著」或「發生著」。There 本身即為主詞，其後接續的名詞可表人、地、事、物等。

2 動詞 has / have 所表示的意思則為「擁有」或「具有」，故其主詞通常為有生命的人或動物。

例句 **There is** an old lady in the middle of the street.
馬路中間有位老太太。

The old lady **has** a dog with her. The dog **has** a short tail.
老太太身邊有隻狗。這隻狗有一條短尾巴。

一、請根據提示,改寫下列句子。

① That we won the game is true.
   It _____

② Working with Tom is exhausting.
   It _____

③ To travel around the world is my dream.
   It _____

二、請根據中文提示,在下列空格中填入正確的字詞,每格限填一字。

① 轉角處有一間郵局。
   _____ _____ a post office on the corner.

② 那裡有數隻乳牛。
   _____ _____ some cows over _____ .

③ 這位貌美的女子有金色長髮。
   The beautiful woman _____ long, blonde hair.

④ 這裡有個「禁止吸菸」的標誌。
   _____ _____ a "No smoking" sign _____ .

⑤ 我明天早上有個重要的會議。
   I _____ an important meeting tomorrow morning.

解　答

一、① is true that we won the game.

② is exhausting to work with Tom.

③ is my dream to travel around the world.

二、① There; is / was

② There; are / were; there

③ has / had

④ There; is / was; here

⑤ have

Notes

Chapter 3

名詞、冠詞 與 代名詞

Chapter 3 名詞、冠詞 與 代名詞

3-1 名詞的分類與單複數形

名詞 泛指人物、地名、事物、概念等等的字。常見的分類有下列幾種：

名詞
- 依特殊性： 普通名詞 VS 專有名詞
- 依是否具有形體： 具體名詞 VS 抽象名詞
- 依是否可計數： 可數名詞 VS 不可數名詞

除了上列分類之外， 集合名詞 亦為一種常見的名詞種類。

以下依上列分類分項闡述：

❶ 普通名詞 VS 專有名詞

普通名詞
定義 「普通名詞」是指一般具體的人、事、物。

例字

apple（蘋果）

house（房子）

friend（朋友）

book（書）

table（桌子）

用法

❶ 有的普通名詞是可數名詞，如 table（桌子）單數可寫作 a table（一張桌子），複數可寫作 two tables（兩張桌子）；有的是不可數名詞，如 air（空氣）、water（水）、beauty（美）。

❷ 普通名詞若為複數可數名詞，須採用複數形（如字尾加 s 或 es 等）。

例句

My **friend** gave me an **apple**. 我的朋友給我一顆蘋果。

Kate put some **books** on the **table**. 凱特把一些書放在桌子上。

	專有名詞

定義 「專有名詞」是指特定的人、地、事物時所使用的名稱,包括月分、週名、節日、人名、職稱、頭銜、作品名、品牌名、地名等。

例字
December(十二月) ──────────▶ DECEMBER
Monday(星期一) ──────
Christmas(聖誕節) ──────
Mary(瑪麗)
Captain Hook(虎克船長)
Mr. Smith(史密斯先生)
Hamlet(《哈姆雷特》)
Nike(耐吉)　　Paris(巴黎)

DECEMBER						
MON	TUE	WED	THU	FRI	SAT	SUN
1	2	3	4	5	6	7
8	9	10	11	12	13	14
15	16	17	18	19	20	21
22	23	24	25	26	27	28
29	30	31				

特殊字詞

Mom / Mother(指稱自己的媽媽)　　Dad / Father(指稱自己的爸爸)

用法
1 專有名詞的第一個字母,通常須大寫。
2 專有名詞前通常不加冠詞 a、an 或 the。
3 專有名詞通常無複數形。

例句
Christmas falls on December 25th each year.
每年十二月二十五日是聖誕節。

Mary met Mr. Smith last month in Paris.
瑪麗上個月在巴黎認識了史密斯先生。

 度補充

	專有名詞轉成普通名詞使用

說明 專有名詞通常為不可數名詞,但在某些情況下可作普通名詞使用,此時可有單複數形式。

例句
There are two Jennys in my class.
我的班上有兩位叫珍妮的人。

A Ms. James is waiting for you.
有個詹姆士小姐在等你。

What do you usually do on Sundays?
你星期日通常都做什麼?

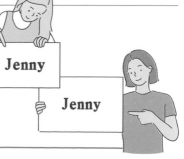

② 具體名詞 **VS** 抽象名詞

具體名詞

定義 「具體名詞」是指可以用五官（眼、耳、鼻、口、舌）感受到的有形體的人、事、地、物等。

例字

color（顏色）

rain（雨）

cake（蛋糕）

face（臉）　→　←　sound（聲音）

party（派對）

用法
1 有的具體名詞是可數名詞，有的是不可數名詞。
2 有的具體名詞是普通名詞，有的是專有名詞。

例句
The sound of the rain calms me.
下雨的聲音讓我心情平靜。

Tim bought a cake for Gina's birthday.
提姆買了一個蛋糕慶祝吉娜的生日。

抽象名詞

定義 「抽象名詞」是指非形體的事物，包括性質、人格特質、狀態、想法、信仰或概念等。

例字
beauty（美）　　　love（愛）
confidence（自信）　knowledge（知識）
courage（勇氣）　　power（力量）
happiness（幸福）　money（金錢）
friendship（友誼）　music（音樂）

health（健康）　wealth（財富）

注意

有形體的「錢」應用 bill（紙鈔）或 coin（硬幣），皆為可數名詞：

a one-dollar bill　　　two one-dollar bills
（一張一美元紙鈔）　　（兩張一美元紙鈔）

a coin　　　two coins
（一枚硬幣）　　（兩枚硬幣）

而抽象名詞 money（金錢）指的是「錢」的抽象概念，故為抽象名詞，且不可數。

用法

1 抽象名詞前通常不加冠詞，但要指特定的事物時，可加定冠詞 the。
2 抽象名詞通常無複數形。

例句

Knowledge is power.
知識即力量。

When will you return the money that you borrowed?
你什麼時候會還錢？

3 集合名詞

集合名詞

定義｜「集合名詞」指一群有關係的人物、事物集結而成的群體、類型或單位。

例字

family（家庭）	band（樂隊）	group（群，組）
cast（全體演員）	jury（陪審團）	class（班級）
media（媒體）	club（社團；俱樂部）	crowd（群眾）
committee（委員會）	public（公眾）	community（社區；群體）
society（社會）	staff（全體員工）	police（警察）
team（隊）	crew（全體船員／機組員）	

CH
3

3-1

名詞的分類與單複數形

29

| 用法 | ❶ 通常集合名詞視為整體時，其後使用單數動詞；視為個體時，則有複數形，且其後使用複數動詞。
❷ 有些集合名詞無複數形，但其後單複數動詞皆可使用，如 public（公眾）。
❸ 有些集合名詞僅限使用複數動詞，如 police（警察）。 |  |

 例句

The **family** comes from Taipei.
這家人來自臺北。(指「整體」，視為不可數名詞)

My **family** are all teachers.
我的家人都是老師。(指「個體」，視為可數名詞)

On the whole, the **public** is / are against the new policy.
整體而言，民眾反對新的政策。

The **police** are investigating the crime.
警察正在調查這起犯罪案件。

The family

❹ 可數名詞 VS 不可數名詞

可數名詞

 定義

「可數名詞」顧名思義是可以計數的名詞。

 例字

 **bicycle**（腳踏車）	 **gift**（禮物）	 **television**（電視）
 **magazine**（雜誌）	 **frog**（青蛙）	 **skirt**（裙子）

用法

1. 可數名詞有單數、複數之分。
2. 單數可數名詞前面須置冠詞（a、an、the）、指示形容詞（如 this、that）、所有格（如 my、his、her）、數詞（如 one、first）或量詞（如 each）。
3. 複數可數名詞前面不可置不定冠詞 a、an。
4. 複數可數名詞前面置定冠詞 the 時，表示所指的為特定的人或事物；若不置 the，則是泛指一般的人或事物。

 例句

The bicycle was a gift from my father.
這輛腳踏車是我爸爸送的禮物。（為特定的腳踏車）

Skirts are in fashion now.
裙子現在很流行。（泛指一般的裙子）

不可數名詞

 定義

「不可數名詞」通常指不可分割的事物或概念。

 例字

food（食物）	tea（茶）	soup（湯）
air（空氣）	bread（麵包）	milk（牛奶） ⟶
water（水）	paper（紙）	ice（冰）

 用法

1. 不可數名詞無單複數之分。
2. 不可數名詞使用時，須與單數動詞搭配。
3. 不可數名詞前面通常不加冠詞，但若要指特定的事物時，可加定冠詞 the。
4. 不可數名詞雖不可計數，但仍可在前面加上「單位」（如 a piece of）或「量詞」（如 some、a little）來表示數量。

 例句

The food in this restaurant is good.
這間餐廳的食物很棒。

Humans cannot live without air.
人類沒有空氣無法生存。

Please give me some water.
請給我一點水。

Kevin is drawing on a piece of paper.
凱文在一張紙上畫畫。

 說明 有些名詞可作可數名詞，亦可作不可數名詞使用。但使用時字義通常會有些微不同。

 例句 We made **a fire** by the tents.
我們在帳篷旁生了火。(fire 表「火堆」，為可數名詞)

My dog is afraid of **fire**.
我的狗很怕火。(fire 表「火」，為不可數名詞)

Mary has many **troubles** to deal with.
瑪麗有許多麻煩事要處理。(trouble 表「麻煩，問題」，常為可數名詞)

The naughty children are in big **trouble**.
調皮的孩子們倒大楣了。(trouble 表「困境」，為不可數名詞)

不可數名詞轉成可數名詞使用

 說明 有些不可數名詞傳統上被認定為不可計數的名詞，僅可搭配單位或量詞使用來表示數量。但實際在口語會話中已普遍出現作可數名詞的用法。如 coffee (咖啡) 可作可數名詞，此時表示 a cup of coffee (一杯咖啡)。

 例句 I would like to order **two coffees**, please.
我想點兩杯咖啡，麻煩你。

Who wants **a tea**?
誰想要喝杯茶？

❺ 如何形成可數名詞的複數形

規則變化

❶ 一般可數名詞

 說明 直接在字尾加 s 即可。

 例字
book ▸ books (書)   cat ▸ cats (貓) ⟶
farm ▸ farms (農場)   student ▸ students (學生)
desk ▸ desks (書桌)   truck ▸ trucks (卡車)

2 字尾為 ch（或 tch）、s（或 ss）、sh、x、z

| 說明 | 此時直接加 es。 |

例字

church ▸ churches（教堂）   brush ▸ brushes（刷子）
witch ▸ witches（女巫）   box ▸ boxes（盒子）
bus ▸ buses（公車）   waltz ▸ waltzes（華爾滋舞）
dress ▸ dresses（洋裝）

例外

stomach ▸ stomachs（胃）   quiz ▸ quizzes（小考）

3 字尾為子音 + y

| 說明 | 此時去 y 改為 ies。 |

例字

hobby ▸ hobbies（嗜好）   baby ▸ babies（嬰兒）
city ▸ cities（城市）   party ▸ parties（派對）
fly ▸ flies（蒼蠅）   story ▸ stories（故事）

4 字尾為母音 + y

| 說明 | 此時直接加 s。 |

例字

boy ▸ boys（男孩）   key ▸ keys（鑰匙）
day ▸ days（日子）   toy ▸ toys（玩具）
essay ▸ essays（短文）   way ▸ ways（方式）

5 字尾為 f 或 fe

| 說明 | 此時去 f 或 fe 改為 ves。 |

例字

elf ▸ elves（精靈）   life ▸ lives（生 / 性命）
knife ▸ knives（刀子）   thief ▸ thieves（小偷）
leaf ▸ leaves（葉子）   wife ▸ wives（妻子）

例外

belief ▸ beliefs（信仰）   safe ▸ safes（保險箱）
chief ▸ chiefs（首領）   roof ▸ roofs（屋頂）

6 字尾為子音 + o

 說明　此時直接加 es。

 例字

echo ▶ echoes (回聲)	potato ▶ potatoes (馬鈴薯)
hero ▶ heroes (英雄)	tomato ▶ tomatoes (番茄)

例外

cello ▶ cellos (大提琴)	memo ▶ memos (備忘錄)
piano ▶ pianos (鋼琴)	photo ▶ photos (相片)
kilo ▶ kilos (公斤)	logo ▶ logos (標誌)

可加 s 或 es 的字

mosquito ▶ mosquitos / mosquitoes (蚊子)
tornado ▶ tornados / tornadoes (龍捲風)
volcano ▶ volcanos / volcanoes (火山)

7 字尾為母音 + o

 說明　此時直接加 s。

 例字

bamboo ▶ bamboos (竹)	tattoo ▶ tattoos (刺青)
radio ▶ radios (收音機)	video ▶ videos (影片)
studio ▶ studios (工作室)	zoo ▶ zoos (動物園)

不規則變化

1 改變母音

 例字

foot ▶ feet (腳)	mouse ▶ mice (老鼠)
goose ▶ geese (鵝)	tooth ▶ teeth (牙齒)
man ▶ men (男人)	woman ▶ women (女子)

2 外來語的複數形

 說明　源自拉丁文、希臘文或其它語言的字通常會保留原來的複數形。

 例字

analysis ▶ analyses (分析)	basis ▶ bases (基礎)
crisis ▶ crises (危機)	bacterium ▶ bacteria (細菌)

datum ▸ data (資料)

medium ▸ media / mediums (媒體)

phenomenon ▸ phenomena (現象)

3 單複數同形

<table>
<tr><td rowspan="2">例字</td><td>aircraft (飛機)</td><td>series (系列)</td><td>deer (鹿)</td></tr>
<tr><td>sheep (綿羊)</td><td>offspring (子孫)</td><td>species (物種)</td></tr>
</table>

注意

deer 的複數形也可為 deers，但很罕見。

4 其他不規則變化

例字　child ▸ children (小孩)　　　ox ▸ oxen (公牛)

　　　person ▸ people (人)

（深）**度補充**

單複數意義不同的名詞

說明　有些名詞在字尾加上 s 或 es 之後，並非形成該字字義的複數形，而是成了含另一個字義的名詞。

例句
- content (內容)
  - contents (內容物；目錄)
- glass (玻璃杯)
  - glasses (眼鏡)
- good (好處)
  - goods (貨物)
- mean (平均數)
  - means (方法)
- manner (態度)
  - manners (禮貌)
- spirit (精神)
  - spirits (心情)

一、請勾選下列套色單字的正確種類。

① This **house** is big.　　　　　☐ 普通名詞　　☐ 專有名詞

② Mom is in good **health**.　　　☐ 具體名詞　　☐ 抽象名詞

③ Lily bought some **bread**.　　　☐ 可數名詞　　☐ 不可數名詞

二、請寫出下列單字正確的複數形。

單數形 VS **複數形**　　　　　　　　**單數形** VS **複數形**

① chair ＿＿＿＿＿＿＿　　⑥ tooth ＿＿＿＿＿＿＿

② watch ＿＿＿＿＿＿＿　　⑦ child ＿＿＿＿＿＿＿

③ lady ＿＿＿＿＿＿＿　　⑧ sheep ＿＿＿＿＿＿＿

④ guy ＿＿＿＿＿＿＿　　⑨ potato ＿＿＿＿＿＿＿

⑤ wolf ＿＿＿＿＿＿＿　　⑩ belief ＿＿＿＿＿＿＿

解　答

一、① 普通名詞　② 抽象名詞　③ 不可數名詞

二、① chairs　② watches　③ ladies　④ guys　⑤ wolves
　　⑥ teeth　⑦ children　⑧ sheep　⑨ potatoes　⑩ beliefs

Chapter 3　名詞、冠詞 與 代名詞

3-2　名詞與冠詞的關係

冠詞所指的是「冠」在名詞前面的限定詞（限定詞指限定名詞某些意思的詞類）。

冠詞有**不定冠詞**與**定冠詞**之分：

種類		用途
不定冠詞	a、an	與不限定的單數可數名詞搭配使用
定冠詞	the	與特定的單數或複數可數名詞、不可數名詞搭配使用

例句

Please hand me a book.
請遞給我一本書。
（未限定哪一本，即任何一本皆可）

Please hand me the book.
請遞給我那本書。
（有指名特定的某一本書，非任何一本）

以下依不同種類的冠詞分項闡述：

❶ 不定冠詞（a、an）

使用 a 或 an 的時機

❶ a 用在字首發音為子音的單字前

說明　單字發音若為子音開頭，要搭配 a 使用。請注意，即使某單字字首為母音字母（如 u），但實際發音為子音時，仍要使用 a。

例字

a camera
[ˈkæmərə]
（一臺相機）

a uniform
[ˈjunəˌfɔrm]
（一套制服）

a film
[fɪlm]
（一部影片）

a university
[ˌjunəˈvɝsətɪ]
（一間大學）

2 an 用在字首發音為母音的單字前

 說明　單字發音若為母音開頭，要搭配 an 使用。請注意，即使某單字字首為子音字母（如 h），但實際發音為母音時，仍要使用 an。

例字

an apple
[`ˈæpl̩`]
（一顆蘋果）

an idea
[`aɪˈdɪə`]
（一個想法）

an hour
[`aʊr`]
（一個小時）

an office
[`ˈɔfɪs`]
（一間辦公室）

an umbrella
[`ʌmˈbrɛlə`]
（一把雨傘）

3 若有修飾語，視不定冠詞後的修飾語而定

 說明　不定冠詞與名詞之間若有修飾語（如形容詞），須依據上述規則：若不定冠詞後的修飾語字首發音為子音，使用 a；若字首發音為母音，則使用 an。

 例字

a small [smɔl] apple（一顆小蘋果）
a blue [blu] umbrella（一把藍色的雨傘）

an interesting [`ˈɪnt(ə)rɪstɪŋ`] film（一部有趣的影片）
an honest [`ˈɑnɪst`] person（一個誠實的人）

4 若為縮略字，視字首的發音而定

 說明　不定冠詞後若為縮略字（即取用相關詞句中每個字的第一個字母而成的單字，如 US 為 United States 之縮略字），須依據上述規則：若該縮略字之字首發音為子音，使用 a；若字首發音為母音，則使用 an。

 例字

a CD
[`ˌsiˈdi`]
（一片光碟）

a TV
[`ˌtiˈvi`]
（一臺電視）

a UFO
[`ˌjuɛfˈo / ˈjufo`]
（一架飛碟）

a US [`ˌjuˈɛs`]
citizen
（一位美國公民）

例字	an ATM [ˌetiˈɛm] （一臺提款機）		an FBI [ˌɛfbiˈaɪ] agent （一名美國 聯邦調查局探員）	
	an HR [ˌetʃˈɑr] department （一個人資部門）		an ID [ˌaɪˈdi] card （一張身分證）	

不定冠詞的意義

1 表示「一個」（= one）

 Josh saw a movie last night.
喬許昨晚看了一部電影。

I need to buy a belt.
我得買一條腰帶。

2 表示「(普遍的) 全體 / 同類」

 A cat can be very different from a dog.
= Cats can be very different from dogs.
貓可能跟狗相差甚遠。

3 表示「每一……」（= per）

 The rent is NT$8,000 a month.
房租是每個月新臺幣八千元。

I exercise twice a week.
我每週運動兩次。

4 表示「相同的」（= the same）

 Birds of a feather flock together.
物以類聚。 —— 諺語

5 表示「某一個 / 位」（= a certain）

 Do you know a Mr. Green?
你認識一位格林先生嗎？

CH
3

3-2

名詞與冠詞的關係

6 表示「像……的人／物」(= one like)

 John wishes to become a Bill Gates.
約翰想成為像比爾‧蓋茲一樣的人。

2 定冠詞 (the)

定冠詞的意義

1 表示先前已提過的人或事物

 通常初次提及某人或事物且其為單數可數名詞時，會用不定冠詞 a 或 an，但後續再提及時使用定冠詞 the 即可，因為已清楚表明所指之人或事物為何。

 There is a boy in the classroom. The boy is reading a book.
教室裡有個男孩。這位男孩在讀書。

Gary has a brother and a sister. The brother is a teacher, and the sister is a doctor.
蓋瑞有一個哥哥跟一個姊姊。他哥哥是老師，姊姊是醫生。

2 表示名詞的特定性

 名詞後若接片語或子句加以說明或修飾此人、事、地、物，使此名詞具有特定性時，通常應搭配定冠詞 the 使用。

The pictures on the wall are nice.
牆上的畫作很好看。

Charlie is the person who stole your money.
查理是偷你錢的人。

注意

並非所有以片語或子句修飾的名詞都應搭配 the，應視該名詞是否具特定性而定。

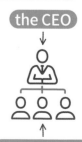

This man is the CEO of our company.
這位男士是本公司的執行長。
（執行長通常僅有一位，具特定性）

This man is an employee of our company.
這位男士是本公司的員工。(為眾多員工之一，未具特定性)

3 表示名詞的獨特性

下列類型的名詞常搭配定冠詞 the 使用以表示其獨特性：

1 在某範圍內獨一無二的人、事、地、物 (如太陽、月亮、某國總統)。

2 有順序、名次之分的人、事、物，通常搭配序數詞 (如 last、first、second、third 等) 使用。

3 與形容詞 only(唯一的)、same(相同的)或 very(正是)搭配使用的名詞。

The moon is so bright tonight.
今晚的月亮真亮。(僅有一顆月亮繞著地球公轉，具獨特性)

The president is making a speech.
總統正在演講。(國家僅有一位總統，具獨特性)

Sarah was the first student to finish the test.
莎拉是首位完成測驗的學生。
(首位完成測驗的學生僅有一人，具獨特性)

The only language that I know is English.
我只會英文。(唯一會的語言代表僅有一個，具獨特性)

4 表示最……或較……的人、事、物

下列情況常搭配定冠詞 the 使用：

1 表示在某比較範疇內最……的人、事、物，通常搭配最高級形容詞使用。

2 表示兩者之間較……的人、事、物時，通常搭配此比較句型使用：
the + 形容詞比較級 + (of the two)

Jim is the tallest person in the class.
吉姆是班上最高的人。

Rachel is the smarter of the two students.
瑞秋是兩位學生之中較聰明的。

深 度補充

定冠詞與專有名詞

1 the + 姓氏複數，表示全家人

The Smiths just moved next door.
史密斯一家人剛搬到隔壁。

the + 國家名稱

例字
the United States (of America)（美國）
the United Kingdom (of Great Britain and Northern Ireland)
（英國，大不列顛及北愛爾蘭聯合王國）
the Republic of Korea（大韓民國，南韓）

比較

以下字之前不加定冠詞 the：

America（美國）　　　　　　Britain（英國）
Korea / South Korea（韓國，南韓）

 the + 山脈 / 群島 / 水體

例字
the Alps（阿爾卑斯山脈）　　the Red Sea（紅海）
the Bahamas（巴哈馬國 / 群島）　the Nile（尼羅河）
the Pacific (Ocean)（太平洋）

定冠詞搭配形容詞

說明
定冠詞 the 可搭配形容詞使用，會形成下列四種狀況：

 泛指有某狀態或特性的一群人，視為複數名詞。

2 指一名特定的人（依上下文來判定）。

3 指全體國民，視為複數名詞。

 指抽象的事情、現象或概念等，視為單數名詞。

例句
The rich (= Rich people) are not necessarily happy; the poor
(= poor people) are not necessarily sad.
富人未必幸福；窮人未必悲傷。（泛指富人與窮人）

The deceased had no friends or family.
此逝者沒有任何親友。（指該名逝者）

The Japanese are known to be polite.
眾所皆知日本人很有禮貌。（指全體日本人）

The supernatural is often difficult to explain.
超自然現象通常難以解釋。
（指抽象的超自然現象）

3 零冠詞

零冠詞（即不加任何冠詞）的使用時機

1 複數可數名詞表示泛指或總括

例句
Wendy likes to read books.
溫蒂喜歡看書。

Dogs are man's best friend.
狗是人類最好的朋友。

2 不可數名詞無特定性

例句
Time flies (like an arrow).
光陰似箭。—— 諺語

Peter drinks coffee every morning.
彼得每天早上會喝咖啡。

3 稱謂、頭銜

例句
Sir, is that your wallet on the ground?
先生，地上的錢包是你的嗎？

Prince William will give a speech now.
威廉王子現在要發表演講。

4 語言、學科、運動、遊戲

例句
I understand Chinese and English.
我懂中文與英文。

My father teaches history in high school.
我父親在高中教歷史。

Henry will play basketball with his friends after school.
亨利放學後會跟朋友打籃球。

Grandpa is good at chess.
爺爺很會下棋。

5 三餐等：breakfast（早餐）、brunch（早午餐）、lunch（午餐）、dinner（晚餐）

例句
Some people skip breakfast in the morning.
有些人早上會不吃早餐。

What do you want for lunch? 你午餐想吃什麼？

by + 交通工具 / 方式

例句

I go to work **by bus** every day.
我每天搭公車上班。

This package will be sent **by air**.
這件包裹會空運寄出。

Sarah made her dress **by hand**. 莎拉手工製作她的禮服。

\ 即時演練 /

一、請在下列空格中填入 a 或 an。

① Jane is _____ teacher.

② Mom gave me _____ orange after lunch.

③ Tom is talking to _____ angry customer.

④ Shawn wants to buy _____ new TV.

⑤ There is _____ small island in the middle of the lake.

二、單選題

① The train travels at 250 km _____ hour.
(A) a   (B) an   (C) the   (D) ✕

② Do you want to have _____ dinner together?
(A) a   (B) an   (C) the   (D) ✕

③ Canada is _____ large country.
(A) a   (B) an   (C) the   (D) ✕

④ _____ sun rises in the east.
(A) A   (B) An   (C) The   (D) ✕

⑤ My best subject in school is _____ math.
(A) a   (B) an   (C) the   (D) ✕

解 答				
一、① a	② an	③ an	④ a	⑤ a
二、① B	② D	③ A	④ C	⑤ D

Chapter 3 名詞 、 冠詞 與 代名詞

3-3 名詞與數量詞的關係

❶ 數詞

數詞為限定詞的一種，常置於名詞前面，用來表示名詞的數目或順序。

數詞可分為 基數詞 與 序數詞 兩種：

數詞	作用	例字			
基數詞	用於計數	one	一	seven	七
		two	二	eight	八
		three	三	nine	九
		four	四	ten	十
		five	五	twenty	二十
		six	六	hundred	百
序數詞	用於排序	first	第一	seventh	第七
		second	第二	eighth	第八
		third	第三	ninth	第九
		fourth	第四	tenth	第十
		fifth	第五	twentieth	第二十
		sixth	第六		

> **註** 在使用序數時，一般要加上定冠詞 the 或是所有格。

> **例句**
> Mr. and Mrs. Lin have two girls.
> 林先生與林太太有兩個女兒。
>
> Jenny is the second child in her family.
> 珍妮是她家中排行第二的小孩。

數詞 + of + 名詞

> **說明** 「數詞 + of」可用於表示某特定人、事、物的數量或次序。

例句 Judy is **one of** my close friends.　茱蒂是我的好朋友之一。

Nine of the students failed the test.
學生之中有九位考試不及格。

Henry was **the first of us** to find a job.
亨利是我們之中第一位找到工作的人。

 深 度補充

「the / 所有格 + 序數詞」之例外

 說明 序數詞前面原則上應置定冠詞 the 或是所有格。
但表示「又……」時，可搭配不定冠詞 a 或 an。

 例句 This is **the third** cup of coffee I've had today.
這是我今天喝的第三杯咖啡。

Mary just had **her second** baby last week.
瑪麗上個禮拜剛生了第二胎。

Rick tried **a second** time.　瑞克又試了一次。

❷ 量詞

量詞也是限定詞的一種，是用來表示量或程度的字詞，通常置於名詞前面。量詞須視搭配的名詞為單 / 複數可數名詞或是不可數名詞使用，大致上可分類如下：

常見的量詞			其後的名詞分類
each（每個的）	every（全部的）		單數可數名詞
many（許多） few（很少）	a few（數個） several（一些）		複數可數名詞
much（許多） little（很少）	a little（些許） less（更少）	least（最少）	不可數名詞
any（任一） some（有些） a lot of / lots of（許多）	all（所有） enough（足夠的）	plenty of（充分的）	複數可數名詞 / 不可數名詞

 例句 Each child will receive a present.
每個小朋友都會收到一份禮物。

It took us several days to finish the project.
我們花了數天的時間才完成計畫。

Mom added a little salt to the soup. 媽媽在湯裡面加了點鹽。

Some friends are coming over. 有些朋友要過來。

Can you lend me some money? 你可以借我一點錢嗎？

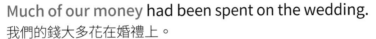

量詞 + of + 名詞

說明 「量詞 + of」可用於表示某特定人、事、物的一部分。

例句

Each of us has a specific job to do.
我們每一位都有特定的工作要做。

Many of my friends are married.
我有很多朋友已經結婚了。

Much of our money had been spent on the wedding.
我們的錢大多花在婚禮上。

The student could not answer any of the questions.
這位學生不會回答任何一個問題。

Rick ate all of the food on the table. 瑞克吃光桌上所有食物。

 **度補充**

比較 few、a few 以及 little、a little

說明 few 與 little 置名詞前使用時，意味著僅擁有或存在極少量，或表示缺乏某事物，有否定語意。相對地，a few 與 a little 置名詞前使用時，則意味著擁有或存在些許，或表示數量足夠。

例句

I have few friends.
我朋友很少。

I have a few friends.
我有一些朋友。

| I have **little** money. | I have **a little** money. |
| 我沒有什麼錢。 | 我有一點錢。 |

＼ 即時演練 ／

一、單選題

① Who was the _____ person to go to space?
   (A) one　　　　　(B) first

② There will be _____ people at the meeting tomorrow.
   (A) five　　　　　(B) fifth

③ Chris has been to _____ countries around the world.
   (A) many　　　　　(B) much

④ Jane opened a window to let _____ air in.
   (A) each　　　　　(B) some

二、請根據語意在下列空格中填入 few、a few、little、a little。

① My relative is staying with us for _____ days.

② Don't worry. We still have _____ time.

③ That company's products are always great. That's why they get very _____ complaints.

④ We need to go to the supermarket. There is _____ food left in our refrigerator.

解　　答
一、 ① B　　　② A　　　③ A　　　④ B
二、 ① a few　　② a little　　③ few　　④ little

Chapter 3 名詞、冠詞 與 代名詞

3-4 同位語

同位語本身為名詞、名詞片語或名詞子句，通常置於另一個名詞、代名詞或名詞片語之後，有補充或說明的功用。同位語有分 限定 與 非限定 兩種：

同位語分類	作用	是否使用逗點
限定同位語	加以限定或指名，為必要資訊	否
非限定同位語	為額外補充資訊，不影響語意	是

以下依上列分類分項闡述：

❶ 限定同位語

定義 | 限定同位語主要的作用為限縮或加以說明所修飾的人、事、地、物。

用法 | ❶ 限定同位語為句子中的必要資訊。去掉限定同位語會影響句子的語意，使得所限定的內容失去特定性。
❷ 限定同位語使用時通常不會搭配標點符號。

例句 | We **students** are excited about the field trip.

我們這些學生很期待校外教學。

I really like the book *The Lord of the Rings*.

我很喜歡《魔戒》這本書。

My friend **George** is a good person.

我的朋友喬治是個好人。

2 非限定同位語

 定義

非限定同位語是針對所修飾的人、事、地、物,提供額外的非必要資訊。

用法

1 非限定同位語為句子中的附加資訊。去掉非限定同位語並不會影響句子的語意。

2 非限定同位語使用時通常應搭配標點符號,最常使用的為逗號,有時也可使用括號或夾注號 "—"。

 例句

Mount Everest, the highest mountain in the world, attracts many climbers.

世界第一高峰聖母峰吸引許多登山者。

Mr. Lin, my neighbor, is an elementary school teacher.

我的鄰居林先生是國小老師。

Jane Miller (an 18-year-old student) won the contest.

珍・米勒(一名十八歲學生)贏得這場比賽。

Paris—the capital of France—is also called the City of Light.

巴黎 —— 法國首都 —— 又稱「光之城」。

請以同位語的方式將下列句子合併

① John is studying abroad.
John is my cousin.

② Shakespeare's play is a classic.
The play is called *Romeo and Juliet*.

③ Vicky got a new pet dog.
The dog is named Lucky.

④ Mr. Brown announced a new company rule.
Mr. Brown is our CEO.

⑤ The disease affected our lives for many years.
The disease was COVID-19.

CH
3

3-4

同
位
語

解　答

① John, my cousin, is studying abroad.

或 My cousin(,) John(,) is studying abroad.

② Shakespeare's play *Romeo and Juliet* is a classic.

③ Vicky got a new pet dog, Lucky.

④ Mr. Brown, our CEO, announced a new company rule.

或 Our CEO(,) Mr. Brown(,) announced a new company rule.

⑤ The disease COVID-19 affected our lives for many years.

Chapter 3 名詞、冠詞 與 代名詞

3-5 人稱代名詞

人稱代名詞可用來代替人、事、物。人稱代名詞有三種人稱：**第一人稱**指「說話的人」或「自己」；**第二人稱**指「說話對象」；**第三人稱**指「被提到的人、事、物」。人稱代名詞會依數量、性別與格而有所差異：

			主格	受格	所有格
第一人稱	單數		I	me	my
	複數		we	us	our
第二人稱	單數		you	you	your
	複數				
第三人稱	單數	陽性	he	him	his
		陰性	she	her	her
		中性 / 無性	it	it	its
	複數		they	them	their

❶ 依主格、受格、所有格分項闡述

① 主格

說明　句子中，主詞與主詞補語須使用主格。作主格的人稱代名詞有下列幾個：I (我)、we (我們)、you (你；妳；你們)、he (他)、she (她)、it (它；牠)、they (他們；它們；牠們)。

例句　I am a student.
我是學生。(此處 I 為主詞)

You are late.
你 / 妳 / 你們遲到了。(You 為主詞，
應視上下文判斷為「你」、「妳」或是「你們」)

It is **he** who is hungry. 肚子餓的人是他。(此處 he 為主詞補語)

It is a puppy. 牠是一隻小狗。（此處 It 為主詞）

It is **they** that won the game. 在比賽中獲勝的是他們。
（此處 they 為主詞補語）

❷ 受格

說明 句子中，動詞與介詞的受詞須使用受格。下列為作受格的人稱代名詞：
me（我）、us（我們）、you（你；妳；你們）、him（他）、her（她）、it（它；
牠）、them（他們；它們；牠們）。

例句 Please come and visit **us**.
請來看看我們。（此處 us 為動詞 visit 的受詞）

Danny is angry because his friend lied to **him**.
丹尼很生氣因為他朋友對他說謊。（此處 him 為介詞 to 的受詞）

Mary was waving at me, but I didn't see **her**.
瑪麗在跟我揮手，但是我沒看見她。
（此處 her 為動詞 see 的受詞）

Stir the coffee before you drink **it**.
喝咖啡前攪拌一下。（此處 it 為動詞 drink 的受詞）

These cookies are fresh. I just baked **them**.
這些餅乾剛出爐。我才剛烤好。（此處 them 為動詞 baked 的受詞）

❸ 所有格

說明 人稱代名詞所有格是用以表示「所擁有的」，其後必須接名詞，故可視
為形容詞使用，因此又稱「所有格形容詞」。人稱代名詞所有格有下列
數個：my（我的）、our（我們的）、your（你的；妳的；你們的）、his（他
的）、her（她的）、its（它的；牠的）、their（他們的；它們的；牠們的）。

例句 **My** father is a doctor. 我父親是醫生。

What is **your** name? 你／妳的名字是什麼？

The little girl finished **her** homework.
那位小女孩完成她的作業了。

The restaurant is famous for **its** desserts.
這間餐廳的甜點很有名。

Parents should take care of **their** children.
家長應該要好好照顧他們的小孩。

代名詞 they、them、their 視為單數使用

說明
傳統上，they、them、their 僅被視為複數第三人稱，但近年英美母語人士漸漸開始在口語會話及非正式寫作上也將它們視為單數使用。使用時機大致有下列兩種：

1 用於代替性別不明確的人或群體，常與不定代名詞 each（每個）、everyone（每個人）、anyone（任何人）等搭配使用。

2 用於代替性別認同不受限於男性或女性的人。

例句

Each child is special. **They** should be free to develop **their** own hobbies and interests.
每個小孩都很特別。他們應該能自由地發展自己的嗜好與興趣。

Everyone has **their** own ideas about the project.
每個人對於這個計畫都有自己的想法。

Anyone is welcome to come to the party. **They** can also bring **their** own food.
任何人都可以參加派對。他們也可以自己帶食物。

2 代名詞 it 的常見用法

1 代替先前提過的事物

例句

I started saving money last year. My sister is doing **it**, too.
我去年開始存錢。我妹妹也在存錢。

Taipei is a convenient city, but **it** is full of people.
臺北是個便利的城市，但人太多了。

I can't find my pen. Have you seen **it**?
我找不到我的筆。你有看到嗎？

2 表示時間、日期、距離或天氣

例句

What time is **it**?　現在幾點？

What day is **it**?　今天是星期幾？

How far is **it** to the museum?　到博物館有多遠？

It is getting cold.　天氣越來越冷了。

3 it 作虛主詞

說明 代名詞 it 可置句首，代替句子後面的內容，或後面的真主詞。

句型

It is ... +
$\begin{cases} \text{不定詞片語 (to + V)} \\ \text{that 子句} \\ \text{動名詞片語} \end{cases}$

例句 **It is** nice to meet you.　很高興認識你。

It is true that the child is talented.
這名小孩有天賦是真的。

It is no use crying over spilt milk.
為了打翻的牛奶而哭沒有用 / 覆水難收。── 諺語

4 it 作虛受詞

說明 代名詞 it 可置一些不完全及物動詞後，作該動詞的虛受詞，代替句子後面的實際受詞。以下是此用法常用的不完全及物動詞：

make（使……是……）

take / think / consider（認為……是……）

believe（認為 / 相信……是……）

find（認為 / 發現……是……）

句型

主詞 +
$\begin{cases} \text{make} \\ \text{take} \\ \text{think} \\ \text{consider} \\ \text{believe} \\ \text{find} \end{cases}$
+ it... +
$\begin{cases} \text{不定詞片語 (to + V)} \\ \text{that 子句} \end{cases}$

例句 The boss **made it** clear that this meeting is important.
老闆清楚表示這場會議很重要。

Larry **took it** for granted that his friends would always help him.
賴瑞認為他的朋友總是會出手幫忙是理所當然的。

I **find it** hard to solve this problem.
我認為這個問題很難解決。

句型

It is + {
名詞 (片語)
介詞片語
副詞 (片語 / 子句)
} + that + ...

例句

It is Sam that is getting married.
要結婚的人是山姆。

It was with your help that I was able to finish the work.
因為有你的幫助我才能完成工作。

It was because John was lazy that he was fired.
約翰是因為懶惰所以被開除了。

\ 即時演練 /

一、請根據中文提示，在下列空格中填入正確的代名詞。

① 荷莉住在我隔壁。

Holly lives next door to _____.

② 你的房間必須隨時保持乾淨整潔。

_____ room must always be kept clean and tidy.

③ 蒂娜看到一件不錯的洋裝並買了下來。

Tina saw a nice dress and bought _____.

④ 吉姆很少見到安妮，但他們會藉電子郵件保持聯絡。

Jim rarely sees Annie, but _____ keep in touch by email.

⑤ 我的妹妹生病了，所以她去看醫生。

My sister was sick, so _____ went to the doctor.

二、單選題

① _____ was dark outside when Charles arrived home.
(A) I   (B) You   (C) It   (D) They

② You should not let your daughter watch that movie; it might scare _____.
(A) he   (B) him   (C) she   (D) her

③ _____ was lucky that no one was hurt in the accident.
(A) It   (B) He   (C) She   (D) You

④ Put the dishes there, and I'll wash _____ later.
(A) them   (B) their   (C) it   (D) its

⑤ Emily found _____ easy to learn a new language.
(A) me   (B) you   (C) them   (D) it

解　答

| 一、 | ① me | ② Your | ③ it | ④ they | ⑤ she |
| 二、 | ① C | ② D | ③ A | ④ A | ⑤ D |

Chapter 3 名詞、冠詞 與 代名詞

3-6 所有格代名詞

所有格代名詞可用來取代「**人稱代名詞所有格 + 名詞**」。所有格代名詞的主要作用是為了避免名詞重複出現，並使句子更加簡潔。所有格代名詞會依人稱、數量、性別等而有所差異：

			所有格代名詞
第一人稱		單數	mine
		複數	ours
第二人稱		單數	yours
		複數	
第三人稱	單數	陽性	his
		陰性	hers
		中性 / 無性	its
	複數		theirs

所有格代名詞的用法

1 可作主詞、受詞或補語

說明	所有格代名詞可作主詞、受詞或補語，且所有格代名詞的主格與受格同形。當主詞時，其後動詞單複數要依主詞的單複數決定。

例句	Irene's hair is dark brown. **Mine** (= My hair) is light brown. 艾琳的頭髮是深棕色。我的是淺棕色。（Mine 作主詞） Ella found her scarf, but Gary couldn't find **his** (= his scarf). 艾拉找到她的圍巾，但是蓋瑞找不到他的。（his 作受詞） This book is **mine** (= my book), not **yours** (= your book). 這本書是我的，不是你的。（mine、yours 作主詞補語）

2 of + 所有格代名詞

 說明 使用「of + 所有格代名詞」時，可與不定冠詞（a、an）、指示形容詞（this、that、these、those）或數量詞（one、ten、some、a few、many 等）並用，但不可與定冠詞 the 並用。

 句型
$$\left.\begin{array}{l}\text{不定冠詞}\\\text{指示形容詞}\\\text{數量詞}\end{array}\right\}+ \text{名詞} + \text{of} + \text{所有格代名詞}$$

 例句 Grace is **a good friend of mine**.
葛瑞絲是我的一位好朋友。

These students of yours are smart.
你的這些學生很聰明。

Some clothes of hers were bought on the internet.
她的一些衣服是在網路上買的。

 度補充

人稱代名詞所有格 + own

 說明 所有格代名詞也可用「人稱代名詞所有格 + own」來表達。此處 own 為代名詞，表示「自己」。

 例句 That's not my parents' car. It's **my own**.
= That's not my parents' car. It's **mine**.
那不是我爸媽的車。是我的。

所有格代名詞 its 鮮少使用

 說明 its 可作所有格代名詞，亦可作人稱代名詞所有格，但英美母語人士鮮少將 its 作所有格代名詞使用。

 例句 The puppy doesn't know that this ball is **its**. (劣)
→ The puppy doesn't know that this ball is **its ball**. (佳)
→ The puppy doesn't know that this ball is **its own**. (佳)
這隻小狗不知道這顆球是自己的。

單選題

① The car next to _____ looks very fancy.
   (A) our   (B) ours   (C) we   (D) my

② These are not my sister's gloves. _____ in her room.
   (A) His are   (B) His is   (C) Hers are   (D) Hers is

③ My phone doesn't work, so my neighbors let me use

   _____ .
   (A) they   (B) them   (C) their   (D) theirs

④ Gordon is a distant relative of _____ .
   (A) I   (B) me   (C) my   (D) mine

⑤ Don't use my toothbrush. Use _____ own.
   (A) your   (B) yours   (C) you   (D) its

解　答

① **B** 理由 ours = our car

② **C** 理由 Hers = Her gloves = My sister's gloves，為複數故其後動詞應用複數動詞 are。

③ **D** 理由 theirs = their phone = my neighbors' phone

④ **D** 理由 of 之後應接所有格代名詞，形成「不定冠詞 + 名詞 + of + 所有格代名詞」的句型。

⑤ **A** 理由 your own = your (own) toothbrush

Chapter 3 名詞 、 冠詞 與 代名詞

3-7 反身代名詞

反身代名詞是結尾為 -self（表示單數）或 -selves（表示複數）的代名詞，常用來表示「（某人）自己；親自」之意。反身代名詞不宜獨自作主詞使用。反身代名詞的形態視主詞的**人稱**、**數量**與**性別**而定：

				反身代名詞
	第一人稱		單數	myself
			複數	ourselves
	第二人稱		單數	yourself
			複數	yourselves
	第三人稱	單數	陽性	himself
			陰性	herself
			中性 / 無性	itself
		複數		themselves
無 / 未知				oneself

❶ 反身代名詞的用法

❶ 反身用法

說明　通常句子中的主詞與受詞為同一人或同一事物時，及物動詞或介詞的受詞可用反身代名詞取代。句中動詞若為授與動詞（即有間接受詞、直接受詞兩種受詞的及物動詞），反身代名詞可作間接受詞。

例句　Be careful! You may hurt **yourself**.
小心！你可能會傷到自己。（yourself 為動詞 hurt 的受詞）

Kevin thinks of **himself** as the smartest person in class.
凱文自詡為班上最聰明的人。（himself 為介詞 of 的受詞）

| 例句 | Hannah is teaching **herself** Japanese.　漢娜在自學日文。
（herself 為授與動詞 teach 的間接受詞，Japanese 則為直接受詞） |

2 強調用法

| 說明 | 反身代名詞可置主詞、受詞或補語之後，亦可置句尾，有強調的作用，表示「(某人)本身／親自」。在此用法下，反身代名詞為所修飾的名詞、代名詞的同位語。 |

| 例句 | I **myself** made this cake.
= I made this cake **myself**.　我親自做了這個蛋糕。
I saw the movie star **himself**.　我見到了那位電影明星本人。
It is the queen **herself**.　這正是女王本人。 |

3 表示某人獨自或獨力進行某事

| 說明 | 反身代名詞常與介詞 by 並用，形成 by oneself 的慣用語，有兩種意思：
1 表示單獨、某人獨自一人，意思與 alone (單獨地) 相近。
2 表示某人獨力進行某事。 |

| 例句 | The old man lives **by himself**.　那位老先生自己獨居。
I can't do everything **by myself**.　我沒辦法獨自一人做所有事。 |

2 常見的反身代名詞慣用語

1 behave (oneself)　守規矩

| 例句 | The mother told her children to **behave themselves**.
那位母親告訴她孩子要守規矩。 |

2 devote / dedicate oneself to + 名詞 / 動名詞　奉獻 / 致力於……

| 例句 | The rich gentleman **devoted himself** to helping the poor.
這位富有的紳士致力於幫助窮人。 |

3 enjoy oneself　玩得愉快

| 例句 | We are all **enjoying ourselves** at the party.
我們在派對上都玩得很愉快。 |

4 help oneself to...　自行取用 (食物)

| 例句 | Please **help yourselves** to the food.
請自行取用食物。 |

5 make oneself at home 　　當自己家 / 請不要拘束

例句 Don't be shy. **Make yourself at home.**
別害羞。就當自己家。

6 occupy oneself with... 　　使自己全神貫注於 / 忙於……

例句 Amy likes to occupy herself with books in her free time.
艾咪喜歡在空閒時看書打發時間。

7 rid oneself of... 　　除去 / 拋棄……

例句 Luke wanted to rid himself of his fears.
路克想要消除自已的恐懼。

＼ 即時演練 ／

單選題

① The small children are not old enough to look after ＿＿＿＿＿＿.
(A) myself 　　(B) yourselves 　(C) itself 　　(D) themselves

② Mandy bought ＿＿＿＿＿＿ a new computer to celebrate her success.
(A) herself 　　(B) hers 　　(C) himself 　　(D) his

③ I ＿＿＿＿＿＿ designed this dress.
(A) me 　　(B) my 　　(C) mine 　　(D) myself

④ You have to solve this problem by ＿＿＿＿＿＿.
(A) myself 　　(B) yourself 　(C) himself 　　(D) itself

⑤ We helped ＿＿＿＿＿＿ to the drinks at the party.
(A) our 　　(B) ours 　　(C) ourselves 　(D) us

解　答

① D 　理由 主詞為第三人稱複數 the small children。
② A 　理由 主詞為第三人稱單數陰性 Mandy。
③ D 　理由 主詞為第一人稱單數 I，為強調用法。
④ B 　理由 by oneself 表「獨自」，且主詞為第二人稱單數 you。
⑤ C 　理由 help oneself to... 表「某人自行取用……」。

3-8　指示代名詞

指示代名詞用於指明一定的人或事物。下列為常見的指示代名詞：

		指示代名詞
單數		this　（這個）
		that　（那個）
複數		these（這些）
		those（那些）

this、that、these、those 的用法

1 表示與說話者之距離

說明

this、these 表示與說話者距離較近的人或物，that、those 則表示與說話者距離較遠的人或物。

例句

This is my alarm clock. **That** is yours.　這是我的鬧鐘。那個是你的。

Those are my children, and **these** are my sister's.
那些是我的孩子，這些是我姊姊的。

2 口語會話中使用

說明

下列兩種口語會話情境經常使用指示代名詞：

1 介紹他人時：介紹一人時使用 this，介紹兩人或以上時則使用 these。

2 電話會話中表明自己身分時。

例句

This is my best friend, William.　這是我最要好的朋友威廉。

These are my colleagues, Sarah, Ben, and Wendy.
這些是我的同事莎拉、班及溫蒂。

Sarah　Ben　Wendy

Hello. **This** is Eric. May I speak to Mark?
你好。我是艾瑞克。請問馬克在嗎？

3 this 與 that 可代替句子或子句

 this 與 that 可用來代替前面出現的句子或子句,以避免字詞重複。

John forgot about the date. **This** made Gina very angry.
約翰忘記要赴約了。這讓吉娜非常生氣。

I can't believe John forgot about our date.
That made me very angry.
約翰忘記我們的約會真是令人難以置信。
那讓我很生氣。

4 that 與 those 可代替同一句中提過的名詞

 同一個句子中,若有重複出現的名詞,可以用 that 或 those 取代。該名詞之後須有介詞片語、分詞片語或形容詞 (子句) 等修飾語。

 The color of my hair is different from **that** of my brother's.
我頭髮的顏色跟我哥哥的不一樣。

These products are better than **those** (that) we made last year.
這些產品比我們去年做的好。

5 those 泛指有某特質或特徵的人

 those 與關係代名詞 who 並用形成 those who... 的句型時,表示「……的人」,泛指擁有某種特質或特徵的人。此時亦等於 people who...。

 Those who are interested in this job can call us.
= People who are interested in this job can call us.
對此工作有興趣的人可以來電。

 深 度補充

指示代名詞的問與答

 指示代名詞 this、that、these、those 可在 be 動詞開頭的是非問句中使用,形成 Is this / that...? 或 Are these / those...? 的句型。但回覆時應使用第三人稱代名詞 he、she、it、they,而非 this、that、these、those 回答。

例句	A Is **this** your water bottle? B Yes, **it** is. / No, **it** is not. A 這是你的水壺嗎？ B 是的 / 不是。	A Are **those** your friends? B Yes, **they** are. / No, **they** are not. A 那些人是你朋友嗎？ B 是的 / 不是。

＼ 即時演練 ／

請根據中文提示，在下列空格中填入正確的指示代名詞。

① 我需要買新鞋。這雙蠻舊的。

I need to buy new shoes. _____ are quite old.

② 請用你自己的杯子。這個是我的。

Please use your own cup. _____ is mine.

③ 那些人是你的父母嗎？

Are _____ your parents?

④ 馬路對面的那間是茉莉的房子。

_____ is Molly's house across the street.

⑤ 這位是本公司的新人。

_____ is our company's newest employee.

⑥ 我的兒子終於找到工作了。那讓我很開心。

My son finally found a job. _____ made me very happy.

⑦ 臺南的天氣可能會跟臺北的差異甚大。

The weather in Tainan can be very different from _____ in Taipei.

⑧ 我喜歡與和善又親切的人相處。

I like to be around _____ who are nice and friendly.

解　答				
① These	② This	③ those	④ That	⑤ This
⑥ That	⑦ that	⑧ those		

Chapter 3 名詞、冠詞與代名詞

3-9 不定代名詞

不定代名詞通常用於表示不明確或未明定的人、地、事、物。不定代名詞大致上可依照其為單數、複數或可為單數 / 複數而分類：

	不定代名詞	搭配之動詞
單數	another、each、either、neither、one、other	+ 單數動詞
	everyone、everybody、everything	
	someone、somebody、something	
	anyone、anybody、anything	
	no one、nobody、nothing	
複數	both、few、many、several	+ 複數動詞
不可數	little、much	+ 單數動詞
單數 / 複數	all、any、more、most、none、some	+ 單數 / 複數動詞

以下將用法相近的不定代名詞歸納闡述：

❶ one、ones、another、other、others

one、ones

1. one 可代表單數可數名詞，來代替敘述中不特定的人或物，以避免名詞的重複，而 ones 則代表複數可數名詞。
2. one 也可表示「任何人」。

one（為單數可數名詞時）+ 單數動詞
ones（為複數可數名詞時）+ 複數動詞

I want to change this dress to a larger **one** (= dress).
我想換更大件的洋裝。

例句

Harry is the **one** who <u>wants</u> to go swimming.
想去游泳的人是哈利。

One should never take advantage of others.
永遠都不該占他人便宜。

....

Your shirts are old. You should buy new **ones** (= shirts).
你的襯衫很舊。你應該買新的。

There are so many books here. Which **ones** <u>are</u> your sister's?
這裡有很多書。哪些是你姐姐的書？

another、other、others

用法

句子中，若範圍沒有限定 (即「非限定」) 時，可使用 another 以表示「(非限定的) 另一個」。相對地，若句子中範圍有限定 (即「限定」) 時，則可使用 the other 表示「(限定的) 另一個」。其分類如下：

	非限定	限定
單數形	another (另一個)	the other (另一個)
複數形	others (其他)	the others (其餘)

例句

Ruby doesn't like this doll. She wants **another**.
露比不喜歡這個洋娃娃。她想要另外一個。
(此處 another 未限定要哪一個洋娃娃)

Josh likes to help **others**.
喬許喜歡幫助他人。
(此處 others 表未限定的其他人)

....

Benny raised one arm and then **the other**.
班尼舉起了一隻手，又舉起另一隻。
(此處 the other 指班尼兩隻手的其中一隻)

Annie is taller than all **the others** in her team.
安妮比她球隊裡的其他人都高。
(此處 the others 指隊伍裡除了安妮之外的其他人)

the other

one

不定代名詞 another、other 與 others 常用於下列句型：

❶ one... the other... 一個……另一個…… （限定的兩者）	
❷ one... another... the other... 一個……一個……另一個…… （限定的三者）	
❸ one... another... 一個……另一個…… （非限定的兩者）	
❹ some... others... 一些……另一些…… （非限定的兩群）	
❺ 數詞... the others / the rest... 若干……其他 / 其餘……	

例句

❶ Mr. Lin has two sons. One is a teacher, and the other is a police officer.
林先生有兩個兒子。一個是老師，另一個是警察。

❷ Mr. Lin has three daughters. One is a lawyer, another is a writer, and the other is a doctor.
林先生有三個女兒。一個是律師，一個是作家，另一個是醫生。

❸ Hobbies vary from person to person. One might enjoy jogging, while another might love swimming.
嗜好因人而異。有人可能喜歡慢跑，有人則可能喜歡游泳。

❹ Hobbies vary with people. Some might enjoy jogging, while others might love swimming.
嗜好因人而異。有些人可能喜歡慢跑，有些人則可能喜歡游泳。

❺ There are five exchange students. Two are from Canada, and the others are from the UK.
有五位交換學生。兩位是來自加拿大，而其他人是來自英國。

❷ both、either、neither、all、any、none

	不定代名詞	
	兩者	三者 (或以上)
全部	both	all
任一	either	any
全無	neither	none

both、all

 用法　both 表示「兩者都」，all 表示「全部」。

 句型　both (為複數可數名詞時) + 複數動詞

　　　all (為複數可數名詞時) + 複數動詞

　　　all (為不可數名詞時) + 單數動詞

 例句

Henry has two sisters. Both live in Taipei.
亨利有兩個姊姊。兩位都住在臺北。

All were happy with the results.
所有人都對結果很滿意。

All that I want is peace and quiet.
我想要的就是平靜而已。

either、any

 用法　either 表示「兩者中任一」，any 表示「三者 (或以上) 中任一」。

 句型　either + 單數動詞

　　　any (為「any + 複數可數名詞」時) + 複數動詞

　　　any (為「any + 不可數名詞」時) + 單數動詞

 例句

I don't care whether you serve coffee or tea; either is fine.
我不在乎你上咖啡還是茶；兩個都可以。

例句 I need some coins. Are there **any** in your purse?
我需要一些硬幣。你的錢包裡有嗎？

I want some water, but there isn't **any** left in my bottle.
我想喝水，但我的瓶子裡沒了。

neither、none

 用法 neither 表示「兩者皆不」，none 表示「無一人 / 物」。

 句型 neither + 單數動詞

none（為「no + 複數可數名詞」時）+ 複數動詞

none（為「no + 不可數名詞」時）+ 單數動詞

 例句 I tried to convince Paul and Karen, but **neither** trusts me.
我試圖要說服保羅與凱倫，但他們兩人都不信任我。

All the guests are in the dining room, but **none** are sitting down.
所有賓客都在飯廳，但沒有人坐著。

Sarah wanted more soup, but there was **none** left.
莎拉還想喝湯，但已經沒了。

❸ every-、some-、any-、no- 相關不定代名詞

以下列舉由 every-、some-、any-、no- 形成的不定代名詞，可用於代表未定的人、事物、地：

	人	事物	地
every-（所有）	everyone、everybody	everything	everywhere
some-（某）	someone、somebody	something	somewhere
any-（任何）	anyone、anybody	anything	anywhere
no-（無）	no one、nobody	nothing	nowhere

1 以上不定代名詞須搭配單數動詞使用。

2 -one 與 -body 結尾的不定代名詞同樣可以用來表示「人」，且通常兩者可互換使用，但普遍認為 -one 為較正式的用法，-body 則較常用於口語會話中。

3 否定句中只能使用 any- 開頭的不定代名詞。no- 開頭的不定代名詞本身已經有負面的意思，故不可在否定句中使用，以免造成雙重否定的情形。

Everyone agrees that Dan is a good boss.
大家都同意丹是個好老闆。

I have something important to tell you.
我有重要的事要告訴你。

I don't want to see anyone.
我誰都不想見。

There was nowhere to sit.
沒有地方可以坐。

深 度補充

every-、some-、any-、no- 相關不定代名詞搭配 else

every-、some-、any-、no- 開頭的不定代名詞可與副詞 else 搭配。else 表示「其他」或「另外」。

Sam ordered a salad because everything else was too expensive.
山姆點了一份沙拉因為其他東西都太貴。

That's not my wallet. It must belong to someone else.
那不是我的錢包。一定是別人的。

Do you want anything else?
你還想要其他東西嗎？

Only Gina knows how to speak Korean. No one else can do it.
只有吉娜會講韓語。其他人都不會。

everything、anything、nothing 與 but 並用的句型

1 everything but...   所有東西除了……
2 anything but...   除了……外，任何都是 / 可以……
3 nothing but...   除了……外，其他都不是 / 不要……

例句

Eric will eat **everything but** the cake.
除了蛋糕之外，艾瑞克所有東西都會吃。

Eric can give his friends **anything but** money.
除了錢以外，艾瑞克可以給他朋友任何東西。

Eric wants **nothing but** ketchup on his hot dog.
除了番茄醬之外，艾瑞克不想加其他東西在熱狗上。

4   many、much、(a) few、(a) little、most、more、several、some

many、much

many 與 much 皆表示「許多」或「多數 / 量」。兩者的差異在於 many 可代表複數可數名詞，much 則代表不可數名詞。

many（為「many + 複數可數名詞」時）+ 複數動詞
much（為「much + 不可數名詞」時）+ 單數動詞

Many regard this song as a classic.   許多人認為這首歌是經典。

Much has been reported about the event.
關於這起事件已經有很多新聞報導。

(a) few、(a) little

few 與 little 皆表示「極少數 / 量，幾乎沒有」，a few 與 a little 兩者則表示「一些」。(a) few 與 (a) little的差異在於 (a) few 可代表複數可數名詞，(a) little 則代表不可數名詞。

few（為「few + 複數可數名詞」時）+ 複數動詞
little（為「little + 不可數名詞」時）+ 單數動詞

Lots of students take the test every year, but few pass it.
每年很多學生參加此考試，但只有少數幾位及格。

Little is known about other planets.
關於其他星球大家知道的很少。

most、more

用法 most 表示「多數者」，more 表示「更多」。

句型 most (為「most + 複數可數名詞」時) + 複數動詞
most (為「most + 不可數名詞」時) + 單數動詞

more (為「more + 複數可數名詞」時) + 複數動詞
more (為「more + 不可數名詞」時) + 單數動詞

例句 Some of the glasses are broken, but most are still in good condition.
有些玻璃杯破了，但大部分都狀況良好。

We saved a lot of money, but most was lost in the fire.
我們存了很多錢，但大部分在火災中燒成灰了。

Many people are at the party already. More are coming later.
已經有很多人到派對現場了。晚點會有更多人來。

We are waiting until more is announced.
我們在等待更多消息宣布。

several、some

用法 several 與 some 皆表示「一些」或「幾個」。用以取代複數可數名詞時，several 與 some 可互換使用。但僅有 some 可用於取代不可數名詞。

句型 several (為「several + 複數可數名詞」時) + 複數動詞

some (為「some + 複數可數名詞」時) + 複數動詞
some (為「some + 不可數名詞」時) + 單數動詞

例句 I haven't seen all of the actor's films, but I've watched several.
這名演員的電影我沒有全部都看過，但有看過幾部。

If you want to read this writer's books, there are several in the library.
如果你想讀這位作家的書，圖書館有幾本。

Some say that happiness is the key to success.
有人說快樂是成功的祕訣。

例句
If you want more tea, there is still **some** in the kitchen.
如果你還想喝茶,廚房裡還有一些。

⑤ each

each
用法   each 用於表示「各個」,強調個別的狀況。
句型   each (為「each + 單數可數名詞」時) + 單數動詞
例句   There are three college students in this room. **Each** is working on the homework.   房間裡有三名大學生。每個都在寫功課。

＼ 即時演練 ／

一、請根據中文提示,在下列空格中填入正確的不定代名詞。

① 我有兩隻狗。一隻是黑色的,另一隻是棕色的。

I have two dogs. _____ is black, and _____
is brown.

② 你們當中五個人留在這裡。其餘的人跟我走。

Five of you stay here. _____ _____
follow me.

③ 才能因人而異。有人可能擅長烹飪,有人則可能擅長作畫。

Everyone has different skills. One may be good at cooking,
while _____ may be good at painting.

④ 有三種蛋糕。一種是巧克力,另一種是草莓,還有一個是椰子。

There are three kinds of cake. _____ is chocolate,
_____ is strawberry, and _____ is coconut.

⑤ 有些人喜歡在城市居住,有些人則偏好住在鄉下。

Some like to live in the city, while _____ prefer living
in the country.

二、請圈選出正確的不定代名詞。

① (One / Ones) must be polite to others.

② I just finished one drink. I think I'll have (another / others).

③ Two runners competed in the race. (Both / All) finished at the same time.

④ Of the two answers, I don't think either (is / are) correct.

⑤ Ben and Jerry were both at the meeting; neither (was / were) absent.

⑥ No one (was / were) there.

⑦ Please don't put (nothing / anything) on the table.

⑧ (Nobody / Anybody) likes George because he is mean.

⑨ Many (say / says) that this book is the author's best work.

⑩ Not (many / much) is known about the celebrity's childhood.

⑪ Tim's stories are interesting, but (few / little) are true.

⑫ Little (was / were) revealed about the incident.

⑬ All customers were male, and (much / most) were between the age of 20 and 30.

⑭ If you need money, I can lend you (some / several).

⑮ There are four chairs on sale. Each (cost / costs) NT$300.

解　答

一、 ① One; the other　　　　② The; others / rest

　　 ③ another　　　　　　　④ One; another; the other

　　 ⑤ others

二、 ① One　② another　③ Both　④ is　⑤ was

　　 ⑥ was　⑦ anything　⑧ Nobody　⑨ say　⑩ much

　　 ⑪ few　⑫ was　⑬ most　⑭ some　⑮ costs

Chapter 4

動詞

Chapter 4 動詞

4-1 完全不及物動詞

完全不及物動詞是不需要補語或受詞就能完整表達語意的動詞。以下介紹完全不及物動詞的用法：

1 主詞 + 完全不及物動詞

 說明
完全不及物動詞常置於主詞之後，不須額外加其他詞類即可表達完整語意。

 例句
The man shouted.
這名男子大叫。

Something happened.
有事情發生了。

2 主詞 + 完全不及物動詞 + 副詞（片語／子句）

 說明
完全不及物動詞之後可接副詞、副詞片語或副詞子句等，以修飾該動詞。

 例句
The man shouted loudly.
       副詞
這名男子大聲喊叫。

Something happened to the poor boy.
        介詞片語作副詞
那位可憐的男孩出事了。

Daniel cried when the dog barked at him.
       副詞子句
這隻狗對丹尼爾吠叫時，他就哭了起來。

(深) 度補充

不及物動詞 + 介詞 + 受詞

說明
基本上，不及物動詞不可接受詞，但有些不及物動詞可與介詞並用，形成片語動詞，此時就可以有受詞。但實際上此受詞是該介詞的受詞，而非動詞的受詞。

例句
Everyone was laughing the silly boy. (×)
→ Everyone **was laughing at** the silly boy. (○)
大家都在嘲笑這位傻傻的小男孩。

＼ 即時演練 ／

句子重組

① yesterday / It / raining / was

_____ .

② right now / clearly / I / think / can't

_____ .

③ next to / sat / Jenny / me

_____ .

解　答

① It was raining yesterday
② I can't think clearly right now
③ Jenny sat next to me

4-2　不完全不及物動詞

不完全不及物動詞又稱連綴動詞。此類動詞本身意思不完全，因此無法單獨存在，其後須接名詞、形容詞等，以補充句子之語意。此類補充語是用來補充主詞，故稱為**主詞補語**（subject complement，常寫作 SC）。常見的連綴動詞如下：

分類	常見的連綴動詞
be 動詞	be、am / is / are、can / will / must be 等
表示「變成」的動詞	become、turn、get、grow、go、fall
表示「仍然維持」的動詞	remain、stay、keep
表示「似乎」的動詞	seem、appear
知覺動詞	look、sound、smell、taste、feel

以下依上列分類分項闡述：

 be 動詞

be 動詞之意義

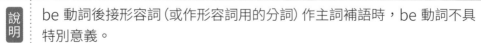

1 表示「是」

說明	be 動詞後接名詞（或動名詞、不定詞、名詞子句、名詞片語等）作主詞補語時，be 動詞有「是」的意思。
例句	Eric is a student. 艾瑞克是學生。

2 不具意義

說明	be 動詞後接形容詞（或作形容詞用的分詞）作主詞補語時，be 動詞不具特別意義。
例句	Penny is pretty. 潘妮很漂亮。

3 表示「在」

 說明

be 動詞後接地方副詞或地方副詞片語（即「介詞 + 地方名詞」）作主詞補語時，be 動詞有「在」的意思。

 例句

James is there.
詹姆士在那裡。（此處 there 為地方副詞）

One of my old friends was in town.
我有個老朋友在城裡。（此處 in town 為地方副詞片語）

❷ 表示「變成」的動詞

1 become + 名詞 / 形容詞

 例句

Martin asked me how to become a better student.
馬丁問我如何成為更好的學生。

When John won the lottery, he became rich.
約翰中樂透，變得有錢了。

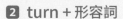

2 turn + 形容詞

 例句

Ruby's face turned pale when she heard the news.
露比聽到消息時，臉色變得蒼白。

The leaves have turned red already.
樹葉已經都轉紅了。

3 get + 形容詞

 例句

My parents are getting old.
我父母年紀漸大了。

With more practice, you will get better.
多多練習你就會進步。

4 grow + 形容詞

 例句

As the lights turned dark, the audience grew quiet.
隨著燈光變暗，觀眾也變得安靜。

Sam grew tired of his life in the countryside.
山姆厭倦了鄉村的生活。

5 go + 形容詞

例句
The milk has **gone** <u>sour</u>.　這牛奶已經酸掉了。
The company **went** <u>bankrupt</u>.
這間公司破產了。

 6 fall + 形容詞

例句
The baby finally **fell** <u>asleep</u>.　小嬰兒終於睡著了。
Harry **fell** <u>ill</u> after working nonstop for weeks.
哈利連續工作好幾個禮拜之後生病了。

❸ 表示「仍然維持」的動詞

1 remain + 名詞 / 形容詞

 例句
Jimmy and I **remain** <u>friends</u> after all these years.
多年後吉米與我仍是朋友。

You should **remain** <u>seated</u> until the plane comes to a full stop.
你應坐著直到飛機完全靜止。

2 stay + 名詞 / 形容詞

 例句
I hope we can **stay** <u>friends</u> after graduation.
希望畢業後我們仍是朋友。

The soldier **stayed** <u>calm</u> despite the dangerous situation.
儘管情況危險，這名軍人仍保持冷靜。

3 keep + 形容詞

 例句
The little boy **kept** <u>still</u> when his mother was cutting his hair.
小男孩的媽媽在幫他剪頭髮時，他保持靜止不動。

❹ 表示「似乎」的動詞

seem / appear (to be) + 名詞 / 形容詞

 說明
seem 與 appear 皆可用於表示「似乎」，之後通常用不定詞片語 (to be + 名詞 / 形容詞) 作主詞補語，但 to be 可省略。

注意

seem 與 appear 不可用於進行式,即無「be 動詞 + seeming / appearing」的形式。

例句

Mr. Smith **seems** (to be) a nice person.
史密斯先生似乎是個好人。

Joyce **seems** (to be) happy.
喬伊絲看起來很開心。

Your idea **appears** (to be) a good solution.
你的主意似乎是個好解方。

The young man **appeared** (to be) calm and relaxed during the interview.
這位年輕人在面試過程中看上去泰然自若。

❺ 知覺動詞

❶	look	看起來……
	sound	聽起來……
	smell	聞起來……
	taste	嚐起來……
	feel	感覺起來 / 感到……

⎰ + 形容詞

例句

You **look** nice in that dress.
妳穿那件洋裝看起來很美。

The food **smells** good.
這食物聞起來不錯。

You should try this dish. It **tastes** great!
你該試試看這道菜。味道很讚!

❷	look	看起來像……
	sound	聽起來像……
	smell	聞起來像……
	taste	嚐起來像……
	feel	感覺起來像……

⎰ + like + 名詞

CH 4

4-2

不完全不及物動詞

83

| 說明 | 知覺動詞後不可直接接名詞作主詞補語，若要與名詞並用，須先置介詞 like，表示「像」，之後的名詞作其受詞。 |

| 例句 | Stella **looks like** a princess in her wedding dress.
史黛拉穿著結婚禮服看起來就像公主。

It **sounds like** a good idea.
聽起來是個好主意。

What happened last night **felt like** a dream.
昨晚發生的事彷彿是場夢一般。 |

❸ feel（感覺起來，感到）**+ like +** 動名詞　　想要……

| 例句 | I **feel like** dancing.
我想跳舞。 |

 度補充

look、smell、taste、feel 亦可當及物動詞

| 說明 | smell、taste、feel 三個知覺動詞亦可當完全及物動詞，即後面可直接搭配名詞作受詞。此時意思均有改變： |

注意

look 若要作及物動詞，則須與介詞並用，形成片語動詞。

| 句型 | **look at / into / over +** 名詞　　看 / 調查 / (快速) 檢查……

$\left\{\begin{array}{l}\text{smell}\\\text{taste}\\\text{feel}\end{array}\right\}$ **+** 名詞　　聞……
　　　　　　　　　嚐……
　　　　　　　　　摸……；感受…… |

| 例句 | John **looked at** his newborn baby happily.
約翰幸福地看著他的新生兒。

I **smell** something burning.
我聞到有東西燒焦了。

I can **taste** garlic and pepper in this dish.
這道菜裡我嚐到大蒜跟胡椒的味道。

George put his hand on his wife's belly to **feel** the baby.
喬治把手放在他太太肚子上來感受寶寶的動靜。 |

句子重組

① one of / William / my good friends / is

_____ .

② looks / necklace / expensive / That

_____ .

③ The children / getting / are / tired

_____ .

④ remains / The woman's name / a mystery

_____ .

⑤ because of the war / became / The soldier / a hero

_____ .

⑥ surprised / seems / to see me / Amy

_____ .

⑦ feel / I / jogging / like / today

_____ .

⑧ and / fell silent / her face / Jane / turned pale

_____ .

⑨ This beer / like / juice / tastes

_____ .

⑩ in class / awake / Albert / stay / can't

_____ .

CH
4

4-2

不完全不及物動詞

① William is one of my good friends

② That necklace looks expensive

③ The children are getting tired

④ The woman's name remains a mystery

⑤ The soldier became a hero because of the war

⑥ Amy seems surprised to see me

⑦ I feel like jogging today

⑧ Jane fell silent and her face turned pale

⑨ This beer tastes like juice

⑩ Albert can't stay awake in class

Chapter 4 動詞

4-3 完全及物動詞

完全及物動詞是加了受詞之後，即可完整表達意思的動詞。受詞的形式有下列數種：

1 名詞當受詞

 例句
Penny **loves** chocolate.
潘妮喜歡巧克力。

2 代名詞當受詞

 例句
Sam is my classmate, but I don't **like** him.
山姆是我的同學，但我不喜歡他。

3 名詞片語當受詞

 例句
I don't **know** what to do now.
我不知道現在要做什麼。

4 名詞子句當受詞

 例句
The boy **believes** that Santa Clause is real.
這位小男孩相信聖誕老人是真的。

5 不定詞（片語）當受詞

 說明
以不定詞片語作受詞的及物動詞通常是用於表達某種願望或企圖。此類常見的及物動詞如下：

want（想要）	**hope**（希望，想要）	**desire**（渴望）	**expect**（期望）
wish（想要）	**long**（渴望）	**aspire**（渴望）	

> **注意**
>
> 動詞 anticipate 亦表「期望」，但通常是用動名詞作其受詞。

 例句
Beth **wants** to learn English. 貝絲想要學英文。
I **hope** to see you again soon. 希望可以盡快再見到你。

6 動名詞（片語）當受詞

 說明
並非所有及物動詞均可用動名詞或動名詞片語作受詞。常以動名詞（片語）作受詞的動詞有下列數個：

consider (考慮)	risk (冒險)	deny (否認)
enjoy (喜歡)	suggest (建議)	admit (承認)
dislike (不喜歡)	recommend (建議)	finish (完成)
practice (練習)	quit (停止，戒除)	anticipate (期望)
avoid (避免)	imagine (想像)	

例句

The boss is **considering** hiring another employee.
老闆在考慮再僱用一名員工。

Chuck **suggested** driving to the destination. 查克建議開車去目的地。

＼ 即時演練 ／

句子重組

① finished / reading this book / Mariah

_____.

② David / how to solve / doesn't know / this problem

_____.

③ tomorrow morning / arrive / I / expect to

_____.

④ the car / washed / yesterday / I

_____.

⑤ knows / No one / where Eric is

_____.

⑥ herself / Daphne / introduced

_____.

解　答

① Mariah finished reading this book
② David doesn't know how to solve this problem
③ I expect to arrive tomorrow morning
④ I washed the car yesterday
⑤ No one knows where Eric is
⑥ Daphne introduced herself

Chapter 4　動詞

4-4　不完全及物動詞

不完全及物動詞為一種及物動詞，但此類動詞加了受詞之後，意思仍不完全，需要加受詞補語（object complement，常寫作 OC），才能完整表達語意。以下分別介紹受詞補語的形式，以及常見的不完全及物動詞：

① 受詞補語的形式

1 名詞作受詞補語

例句

Many students consider Ms. Johnson the best teacher.
　　　　　　　　　　　　受詞

許多學生認為強森老師是最好的老師。

2 形容詞作受詞補語

例句

I find this story enjoyable.
　　　受詞

我覺得這個故事很有趣。

3 現在分詞（片語）作受詞補語

例句

The police officer saw a boy sitting by himself in the park.
　　　　　　　　　　受詞

警察看到一名小男孩獨自一人在公園坐著。

4 過去分詞（片語）作受詞補語

例句

Mark had his suit dry-cleaned yesterday.
　　　受詞

馬克昨天把他的西裝拿去乾洗了。

5 原形動詞作受詞補語

例句

Wendy's mother let her watch cartoons after dinner.
　　　　　　　　　受詞

吃完晚餐後，溫蒂的媽媽讓她看卡通。

CH
4

4-4

不完全及物動詞

89

6 不定詞片語 (to + V) 作受詞補語

例句
My boss encouraged me to share my ideas.
　　　　　　　　　受詞 ↰
我的老闆鼓勵我分享我的想法。

 7 介詞片語作受詞補語

例句
Liz's manager turned her into a popular celebrity.
　　　　　　　　　受詞 ↰
麗茲的經紀人將她變成很受歡迎的名人。

2 常見的不完全及物動詞

(1) 使役動詞

 1 let

說明
let 表「讓」，有允許某人做某事的意思。受詞後可接原形動詞或介詞作受詞補語。

句型
1 let + 受詞 + 原形動詞
2 let + 受詞 + 介詞

例句
Mom won't let me go to the party.
媽媽不讓我去參加派對。（原形動詞作受詞補語）

George let the dog in. 喬治讓狗進來。（介詞作受詞補語）

 2 make

說明
make 表「叫；逼」，有迫使某人做某事的意思。其後的受詞須接原形動詞作受詞補語。make 表「使」時，則須接形容詞或名詞作受詞補語。

句型
1 make + 受詞 + 原形動詞
2 make + 受詞 + 形容詞 / 名詞

例句
My parents made me take piano lessons after school.
我爸媽逼我下課後去上鋼琴課。（原形動詞作受詞補語）

Listening to this song makes me happy.
聽這首歌讓我心情愉悅。（形容詞作受詞補語）

This experience made me a better person.
這個經驗使我成為更好的人。（名詞作受詞補語）

3 have

 說明

have 之受詞為「人」且搭配原形動詞作受詞補語時，有請某人做某事之意。若受詞為「人」且搭配現在分詞作受詞補語，則表使某人做某事。have 之受詞為「事物」且搭配過去分詞作受詞補語時，have 有「讓」或「使」之意。

 句型

1 have + 受詞（人）+ 原形動詞
2 have + 受詞（人）+ 現在分詞
3 have + 受詞（物）+ 過去分詞

 例句

I'll **have** a mechanic fix my car tomorrow.
我明天會請技師修車。（原形動詞作受詞補語）

Tom's jokes **had** everyone laughing.
湯姆的笑話讓所有人大笑。（現在分詞作受詞補語）

Tina **had** her car washed.
提娜（請人）把車洗過了。（過去分詞作受詞補語）

4 get

 說明

get 之受詞為「人」時，get 有「說服」某人做某事之意。受詞為「事物」時，get 則有「讓」或「使」之意。

 句型

1 get + 受詞 + 不定詞片語（即 to + 原形動詞…）
2 get + 受詞 + 現在分詞
3 get + 受詞 + 過去分詞

 例句

Teddy finally **got** his friend to go exercise with him.
泰迪終於說服他朋友和他一起去運動。（不定詞片語作受詞補語）

I **got** the computer working again.
我重新讓電腦正常運作了。（現在分詞作受詞補語）

We must **get** this project done.
我們必須完成這項專案。（過去分詞作受詞補語）

CH 4

4-4

不完全及物動詞

(2) 知覺動詞

 例字

表 看 ：see、notice、watch、observe、look at
表 聽 ：hear、listen to
表 感覺 ：feel

1 表事實

 句型
知覺動詞＋受詞＋原形動詞

例句
I **saw** Polly <u>eat</u> a cookie.
我看到波莉吃一片餅乾。（原形動詞作受詞補語）

2 表進行中的動作

句型
知覺動詞＋受詞＋現在分詞

 例句
I **felt** the dog <u>licking</u> my leg.
我感覺到狗在舔我的腿。（現在分詞作受詞補語）

3 表被動狀態

句型
知覺動詞＋受詞＋過去分詞

 例句
Wayne **heard** his name <u>mentioned</u> several times.
韋恩聽到他的名字被數次提起。（過去分詞作受詞補語）

 **(3) 認定動詞**

例字
表 認為，看作 ：
regard、see、view、think、consider、deem

1 與 as 並用

 句型
regard / see / view A as B　　視 A 為 B
= think of A as B

例句
I **regard** Anna **as** my close friend.
我視安娜為我的好朋友。

2 與 to be 並用

句型
think / consider / deem A (to be) B　　視 A 為 B

例句
Many people **consider** Michael Jackson (to be) the greatest
pop singer ever.
許多人認為麥可‧傑克森是史上最偉大的流行歌手。

說明 此類動詞接受詞後常接介詞 into，再接名詞作受詞補語。

 例字 表 使……變成…… ：
change、transform、turn

 句型 change / transform / turn A into B　　將 A 改變為 B

 例句
The witch changed the donkey into a majestic horse.
女巫將驢子變成一匹駿馬。

Ross transformed his garage into an art studio.
羅斯將他的車庫改建成藝術工作室。

The heavy rain turned the ground into mud.
豪雨將土地變成爛泥巴。

＼ 即時演練 ／

單選題

① The teacher let the students ＿＿＿＿＿＿ the problem by themselves.
(A) to discuss　(B) discussed　(C) discussing　(D) discuss

② Going on vacation ＿＿＿＿＿＿ me happy.
(A) makes　(B) gets　(C) has　(D) lets

③ The angry mother finally got her son ＿＿＿＿＿＿ his room.
(A) clean　(B) to clean　(C) cleaning　(D) cleaned

④ As Amy was walking in the haunted house, she screamed because she felt her hand ＿＿＿＿＿＿ by someone.
(A) touch　(B) touches　(C) touching　(D) touched

⑤ I see this trip to London ＿＿＿＿＿＿ a great opportunity to practice English.
(A) for　(B) with　(C) as　(D) into

⑥ The police officer deemed John _____ for the incident.
(A) to being responsible   (B) to be responsible
(C) be responsible   (D) being responsible

⑦ The government transformed the quiet village _____ a busy tourist spot.
(A) over   (B) for   (C) into   (D) with

⑧ John had his friends _____ him to move into his new apartment.
(A) helped   (B) helping   (C) to help   (D) help

⑨ I consider my mother _____ a great role model.
(A) be   (B) to be   (C) being   (D) been

⑩ Technology made traveling to outer space _____.
(A) possibility   (B) possibly   (C) possible   (D) impossible

解 答				
① D	② A	③ B	④ D	⑤ C
⑥ B	⑦ C	⑧ D	⑨ B	⑩ C

Chapter 4 　動詞

4-5 　授與動詞

授與動詞為及物動詞的一種，意即動詞後應接受詞方能表達完整的語意，惟授與動詞之後須接兩個受詞：

授與動詞的受詞	用意
間接受詞（indirect object，常寫作 IO）	表授與的對象，通常為人
直接受詞（direct object，常寫作 DO）	表授與的東西，通常為物

I gave my mother flowers on Mother's Day.
母親節那天我送我媽媽花。

間接受詞

直接受詞

以下介紹授與動詞的用法：

1 主詞 + 授與動詞 + 間接受詞 + 直接受詞

My mother gave my elder sister a necklace.
　　　　　　　　間接受詞　　　直接受詞
我媽媽送我姊姊一條項鍊。

Johnny lent his friend some money.
　　　　　　間接受詞　　直接受詞
強尼借給他朋友一些錢。

2 主詞 + 授與動詞 + 直接受詞 + 介詞 (to / for) + 間接受詞

說明　若要將直接受詞放在間接受詞的前面，兩個受詞之間須加上介詞 to 或 for。

搭配介詞 **to**

| give (給) | sell (賣給) | hand (遞給) | send (寄給) |
| lend (借給) | show (展示給) | offer (提供) | tell (告訴) |

搭配介詞 **for**

| buy (買給) | make (做) | get (拿給) | order (點餐) |

例句

I **sent** Paula an email last night.
→ I **sent** an email **to** Paula last night.
　我昨晚寄了一封電子郵件給寶拉。

My grandmother made everyone scarfs to wear in winter.
→ My grandmother made scarfs for everyone to wear in winter.
　我奶奶為每個人做了圍巾好過冬。

\ 即時演練 /

句子重組

① for his birthday / her husband / Sarah / a gold watch / bought

_____.

② sold / his old bicycle / Joe / his friend

_____.

③ the old lady / for / Luke / a chair / got

_____.

④ to / My boss / someone else / offered / the job

_____.

⑤ the driver / The passenger / showed / his ticket

_____.

解　答

① Sarah bought her husband a gold watch for his birthday
② Joe sold his friend his old bicycle
③ Luke got a chair for the old lady
④ My boss offered the job to someone else
⑤ The passenger showed the driver his ticket

Chapter 4 　動詞

歸納先前章節內容可得知，動詞一般而言可分為五種：

動詞種類	是否有受詞	是否有補語
1 完全不及物動詞	✕	✕
2 不完全不及物動詞	✕	○（主詞補語）
3 完全及物動詞	○	✕
4 不完全及物動詞	○	○（受詞補語）
5 授與動詞	○（直接受詞、間接受詞）	✕

根據上述歸納，可形成英文的五大基本句型：

1 S + V（即：主詞 + 完全不及物動詞）

例句
The woman fainted.
　　　主詞　　　動詞
這名女子暈倒了。

2 S + V + SC（即：主詞 + 不完全不及物動詞 + 主詞補語）

例句
Everyone seems happy about the decision.
　主詞　　　動詞　　主詞補語
大家似乎都對這決策感到很滿意。

3 S + V + O（即：主詞 + 完全及物動詞 + 受詞）

例句
The writer finally finished his new book.
　　主詞　　　　　　動詞　　　　受詞
這名作家終於寫完他的新書。

4 S + V + O + OC（即：主詞 + 不完全及物動詞 + 受詞 + 受詞補語）

例句
Your mean words made the little girl very sad.
　　主詞　　　　　動詞　　　受詞　　　受詞補語
你的惡言使小女孩很難過。

5 S＋V＋IO＋DO（即：主詞＋授與動詞＋間接受詞＋直接受詞）

例句 The waiter handed Michelle a cup of coffee.
　　　主詞　　　動詞　　間接受詞　　直接受詞
服務生遞給蜜雪兒一杯咖啡。

＼ 即時演練 ／

請將下方句子與正確句型配對。

A S＋V	B S＋V＋SC	C S＋V＋O
D S＋V＋O＋OC	E S＋V＋IO＋DO	

① Mrs. Johnson teaches us English.

② Jasmine smiled happily.

③ I want to become a pilot.

④ John's oldest son became a lawyer.

⑤ A police officer saw Pete crossing the street.

⑥ The sun has set.

⑦ The speaker's story made everyone sad.

⑧ What you are eating smells good.

⑨ Abigail lent me some money.

⑩ I enjoy listening to jazz music.

解　　答				
①E	②A	③C	④B	⑤D
⑥A	⑦D	⑧B	⑨E	⑩C

Chapter 5

時態

Chapter 5 時態

5-1 簡單式

英文的動詞會用時態來表示時間關係。依照動作發生的時間，可分為 現在式 、 過去式 、 未來式 三種；依照動作進行的狀態可分為簡單式、進行式、完成式以及完成進行式四種。綜合而言，一共有十二種時態。本節介紹三種簡單式時態：

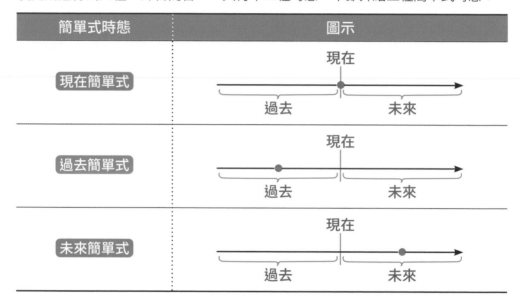

簡單式時態	圖示
現在簡單式	現在／過去／未來
過去簡單式	現在／過去／未來
未來簡單式	現在／過去／未來

以下分項介紹三種簡單式：

1 現在簡單式

現在簡單式的意義

1 表示現在的動作或狀態

例句

James looks tired.
詹姆士看起來很累。

I see a tall man standing there.
我看到一位高大的男子站在那裡。

My mom is a teacher.
我媽媽是老師。

2 表示現有的習慣性動作

 說明　表示習慣性的動作時，常與頻率副詞 every day（每天）、always（總是）、usually（通常）、never（從不）等並用。

例句　Sam **usually gets** up at eight o'clock.
山姆通常八點起床。

Bob **takes** the bus home **every day**.
鮑伯每天搭公車回家。

3 表示真理、事實、格言

 例句　The sun **rises** in the east.　太陽從東方升起。

Tokyo **is** the capital of Japan.　東京是日本的首都。

Knowledge **is** power.　知識就是力量。

4 表示未來

 說明　下列動詞與表示未來時間的副詞並用，可表示未來：

begin（開始）　　leave（離開）　　arrive（抵達）
start（開始）　　come（來）　　go（去）

 例句　The party **begins** at 6 p.m.
派對晚上六點開始。

We **leave** for France tomorrow.
我們明天出發去法國。

When Patrick **comes** next week, please show him around the city.
派翠克下週來訪時，請帶他在城裡到處看看。

2 過去簡單式

過去簡單式的意義

1 表示過去的動作或狀態

 例句　Mr. Wang **was** a professional athlete.
王先生曾經是職業運動員。

Emma **won** first place in the race.
艾瑪在比賽中榮獲第一。

2 表示過去的習慣或經驗

例句
I once **ran** 10 kilometers.
我有一次跑了十公里。

When Tom was in high school, he **went** to bed early every day.
湯姆讀高中時，他每天都早睡。

 深 度補充

「**used to + 原形動詞**」的用法

說明
片語「used to + 原形動詞」可用來表示過去的狀態或習慣。

例句
I **used to live** in Taichung.
我以前住在臺中。

Gina **used to go** to the gym regularly.
吉娜以前會定期去健身房。

3 未來簡單式

未來簡單式的意義

表示未來將發生的動作或狀態

說明
未來簡單式常用助動詞 will 搭配原形動詞的形式。

例句
It **will rain** tomorrow.
明天會下雨。

Anna **will go** on a trip next week.
安娜下週要去旅遊。

Dinner **will be** ready soon.
晚餐快要準備好了。

 深 度補充

其他亦可表示未來的句型

句型

❶ be going to + 原形動詞　　將要……

❷ be about to + 原形動詞　　即將要……

❸ be to + 原形動詞　　　　　預定要……

例句

I am going to visit my grandparents this weekend.
我這週末要去探望我祖父母。

The train is about to depart.
火車即將駛離。

We are to meet at the airport.
我們約好在機場見面。

＼ 即時演練 ／

請勾選下列句子的正確時態。

① Jerry will go to the movies with his friends tonight.
　　□ 現在簡單式　　　□ 過去簡單式　　　□ 未來簡單式

② Judy's parents live in the countryside by themselves.
　　□ 現在簡單式　　　□ 過去簡單式　　　□ 未來簡單式

③ None of us slept well last night.
　　□ 現在簡單式　　　□ 過去簡單式　　　□ 未來簡單式

④ My brother is a good swimmer.
　　□ 現在簡單式　　　□ 過去簡單式　　　□ 未來簡單式

⑤ We were really hungry before the party started.
　　□ 現在簡單式　　　□ 過去簡單式　　　□ 未來簡單式

解　答

① 未來簡單式　② 現在簡單式　③ 過去簡單式　④ 現在簡單式　⑤ 過去簡單式

Chapter 5 時態

5-2 進行式

進行式是用於強調 現在 、 過去 或 未來 的某一段時間內持續發生的動作或行為。本節介紹三種進行式時態：

進行式時態	句型	圖示
現在進行式	am / is / are + 現在分詞	現在（過去／未來）
過去進行式	was / were + 現在分詞	現在（過去／未來）
未來進行式	will be + 現在分詞	現在（過去／未來）

Ben **was working** during the day.
班白天在工作。

Ben **is having** a meal now.
班現在正在吃飯。

Ben **will be exercising** in the evening.
班晚上會去運動。

過去

現在

未來

以下分項介紹三種進行式：

 現在進行式

現在進行式的意義

1 表示現在正在繼續或進行中的動作

例句
Molly **is writing** a letter.
茉莉正在寫信。

Teddy **is tidying** up his bedroom.
泰迪在清理他的房間。

2 表示不久後會發生的動作或預定的計畫

說明
此類動詞多為 go、come、leave、arrive 等有「來去」意味的動詞。
做此意時，常與表未來的副詞並用。

例句
My friends **are coming** over this weekend.
我朋友週末要來我家。

I **am going** on a trip overseas next month.
我下個月要出國旅遊。

 過去進行式

過去進行式的意義

1 表示過去某時正在進行的動作

說明
過去進行式常與表示過去時間的副詞或 when、while 等連接詞引導的
副詞子句並用。

例句
I **was taking** a shower when you called last night.
你昨晚打電話來時我正在洗澡。

Jerry **was talking** to a girl when I walked in.
我進來時，傑瑞正在跟一名女生講話。

2 表過去某時的計畫或即將發生的事

例句
Steve called and said that he **was coming** soon.
史提夫來電說他很快就會來。

The old man **was dying**.
這名老人快死了。

③ 未來進行式

未來進行式的意義

表示未來某時將進行的動作

 說明　未來進行式常與表示未來時間的副詞並用。

 例句
We **will be waiting** for Wendy at the train station <u>tomorrow</u>.
我們明天會在火車站等溫蒂。

Tony **will be attending** a meeting <u>this afternoon</u>.
今天下午湯尼會參加一場會議。

④ 使用進行式應注意事項

1 「不」適用進行式的動詞

 說明　不適用進行式的動詞通常是描述某種狀態、情形，或是內心的意識，並無實質的動作舉止，故通常不用進行式呈現。

 例字

表狀態、存在

be（是，在）	appear（似乎）	stand（位於）
exist（存在）	seem（似乎）	lie（位於）

表所有

have（有）	possess（擁有）	belong to（屬於）
own（擁有）		

表知覺

hear（聽見）	taste（嚐起來）	see（看見）
sound（聽起來）	smell（聞起來）	feel（感覺）

表知識

know（知道）	understand（了解）	think（認為）
remember（記得）	believe（相信）	forget（忘記）

表情感

like（喜歡）	hope（希望）	hate（恨）
love（喜愛）	wish（希望）	want（想要）
dislike（不喜歡）		

例句

The man outside our house is seeming strange.（×）
→ The man outside our house seems strange.（○）
我們家外面的男子有點詭異。

Paula is having a large house.（×）
→ Paula has a large house.（○）
寶拉有一棟大房子。

I am seeing a little girl standing alone over there.（×）
→ I see a little girl standing alone over there.（○）
我看到那裡有個小女孩獨自一人站著。

No one is believing Keith's story.（×）
→ No one believes Keith's story.（○）
沒有人相信凱斯的故事。

Daisy is liking the color blue.（×）
→ Daisy likes the color blue.（○）
黛西喜歡藍色。

注意

上列動詞若作別的意思使用時，則可能可用進行式。以下以動詞 lie 為例說明：

Our grandfather's house lies on the top of the hill.
　　　　　　　　現在簡單式
我們爺爺的房子在山丘上。（此處 lie 表「位於」）

The little boy is lying.
　　　　　現在進行式
這名小男孩在說謊。（此處 lie 表「說謊」）

2 進行式表負面的意思

說明

在現在進行式與過去進行式中，be 動詞與現在分詞之間可置 always（總是）或 constantly（經常，不斷地）等副詞，此時多用來表示經常反覆發生且有負面意味的動作。

例句

My parents are always fighting.
我爸媽總是在吵架。

Rita is constantly changing her mind.
麗塔不斷在改變心意。

Gary **was** <u>always</u> playing video games instead of doing his homework.
蓋瑞總是在打電動而不是在寫作業。

Eddie **was** <u>constantly</u> complaining about his roommate.
艾迪不斷在抱怨他的室友。

＼ 即時演練 ／

請根據中文提示，在下列空格中填入正確的動詞時態。

① 現在正在下雨。

It ＿＿＿＿＿＿＿＿＿ (rain) right now.

② 安妮看電影時，有人打電話給她。

Someone called Annie when she ＿＿＿＿＿＿＿＿＿ (watch) a movie.

③ 明天這個時候，他們會在開車前往海灘的路上。

They ＿＿＿＿＿＿＿＿＿ (drive) to the beach at this time tomorrow.

④ 昨晚八點時莎莉正在看書。

Sally ＿＿＿＿＿＿＿＿＿ (read) a book at 8 o'clock last night.

⑤ 有人在敲門。請開門。

Someone ＿＿＿＿＿＿＿＿＿ (knock) on the door. Please open it.

⑥ 我們接下來的兩個月將會一起共事。

We ＿＿＿＿＿＿＿＿＿ (work) together for the next two months.

解　答		
① is raining	② was watching	③ will be driving
④ was reading	⑤ is knocking	⑥ will be working

Chapter 5　時態

5-3　完成式

本節介紹三種完成式時態：

完成式時態	句型	圖示
現在完成式	has / have + 過去分詞	現在 過去　未來
過去完成式	had + 過去分詞	現在 過去　未來
未來完成式	will have + 過去分詞	現在 過去　未來

I was hungry this morning. I had not eaten for 12 hours.
我今天早上很餓。我已經十二個小時沒吃東西了。

I have just eaten lunch.
我剛剛才吃完午餐。

I will have finished my diet plan by tomorrow.
到明天為止我就結束節食計畫了。

以下分項介紹三種完成式：

① 現在完成式

現在完成式的意義

1 表示到現在為止已完成的動作

例句
Oscar **has bought** a new car.
奧斯卡買了新車。

2 表示到現在為止的經驗

例句
I **have read** this book before.
我讀過這本書。

3 表示到現在仍在持續的動作或狀態

例句
George **has lived** in the countryside since he retired.
喬治退休後就一直住在鄉下。（可能還會繼續住著）

 深 度補充

「have been to + 某地」vs「have gone to + 某地」

說明
1 have been to + 某地　曾去過某地（現在已經不在某地）
2 have gone to + 某地　已經去某地
　　　　　　　　　　　　（現在在去某地的路上或現在在某地）

例句
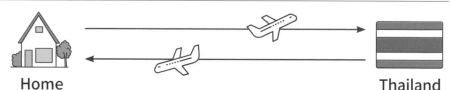
Home　　　　　　　　　　　　　　　　Thailand
Jason has been to Thailand before.
傑森去過泰國。

Home　　　　　　　　　　　　　　　　Thailand
Jason has gone to Thailand. He has not come back yet.
傑森已經去了泰國。他還沒回來。

❷ 過去完成式

過去完成式的意義

❶ 表示到過去某時為止已完成的動作

例句 By the time we woke up in the morning, Danny's plane had landed in London.
我們早上起床時，丹尼的飛機已經在倫敦降落了。

❷ 表示到過去某時為止的經驗

例句 I had never talked to a foreigner before I met Harry, an American colleague of mine.
在我遇見我的美國同事哈利之前，我從來沒跟外國人講過話。

❸ 表示持續到過去某時的動作或狀態

例句 Debbie had worked as a waitress for many years before she became a chef.
黛比成為廚師前做了多年的服務生。

 深 度補充

過去完成式通常不可單獨存在

說明 過去完成式使用時通常須與過去簡單式連用，以表示先後順序，即：
先發生的動作 → 用過去完成式
後發生的動作 → 用過去簡單式

例句 The bus had left when I arrived at the bus stop.
　　　　過去完成式　　　　過去簡單式
我到公車站時公車已經走了。

3 未來完成式

未來完成式的意義

1 表示到未來某時為止將完成的動作

例句　When Mom comes home, we **will have finished** cleaning the house.
媽媽回家的時候，我們就會打掃好家裡。

2 表示到未來某時為止的經驗

例句　If I watch this movie one more time, I **will have seen** it ten times.
如果我再看一次這部電影，我就會看了十次。

3 表示到未來某時為止將持續的動作或狀態

例句　By the end of this year, we **will have lived** here for five years.
到今年年底為止，我們將在這裡住滿五年。

4 使用完成式應注意事項

(1) 常與完成式搭配的副詞

1 just　剛剛

例句　George has **just** finished his homework.
喬治才剛寫完他的作業。

2 already　已經

說明　already 可用於表示動作已完成了，且常用於肯定句中，通常置於 have 與過去分詞之間，或置於句尾。

例句　I have **already** seen this movie.
→ I have seen this movie **already**.
我已經看過這部電影。

3 yet　還，尚

說明　yet 亦可用於表示動作已完成了，但常用於疑問句或否定句中，且通常置於句尾。

例句　Have you met Mr. Chen **yet**?　你與陳先生見過面了嗎？
Edward has not arrived **yet**.　愛德華還沒抵達。

(2)「不可」與現在完成式搭配的副詞

 說明 現在完成式不可與表過去明確時間的副詞並用，如 yesterday（昨天）、last week（上週）、in 2020（2020 年）、two days ago（兩天前）等。

注意

現在完成式可與含有「現在」意義的時間副詞並用，如 today（今天）、this morning（今天早上）、this week（這週）等。

 例句

Connie has bought some new clothes yesterday. (×)

→ Connie has bought some new clothes. (○)
康妮買了一些新衣服。

→ Connie bought some new clothes yesterday. (○)
康妮昨天買了一些新衣服。

No one has seen Michael in the office today.
今天沒有人在辦公室遇見麥可。

＼ 即時演練 ／

單選題

① Ned claimed that he ＿＿＿＿＿＿＿＿ the movie star in person before.
(A) had met   (B) is meeting
(C) meets   (D) will have met

② Henry ＿＿＿＿＿＿＿＿ this novel many times already.
(A) reads   (B) is reading
(C) will read   (D) has read

③ By the time you arrive, Tim ＿＿＿＿＿＿＿＿ for the airport already.
(A) will leave   (B) will have left
(C) is leaving   (D) has left

④ Sadie ＿＿＿＿＿＿＿＿ French for years before she moved to France.
(A) will have studied   (B) is studying
(C) had studied   (D) studies

⑤ The party _____ by the time you come.
(A) has ended   (B) will have ended
(C) ends   (D) ended

⑥ I _____ Eva for a long time.
(A) have known   (B) know
(C) will know   (D) had been knowing

解　答

① A　**理由** 空格前有過去簡單式的動詞 claimed（聲稱），且句尾為表過去時間的副詞 before（之前），故空格應置過去完成式之動詞。

② D　**理由** 副詞 already（已經）應與完成式並用。

③ B　**理由** By the time you arrive（等到你抵達時）表未來的時間，且句尾有副詞 already（已經），故空格應置未來完成式之動詞。

④ C　**理由** 空格後有過去簡單式的動詞 moved（搬家）以及 for years（有許多年），故空格應置過去完成式。

⑤ B　**理由** by the time you come（等到你來時）表未來的時間，故空格應置未來完成式。

⑥ A　**理由** for a long time（有好長一段時間）應與完成式並用，且根據語意，空格應置現在完成式。

Chapter 5 時態

5-4 完成進行式

本節介紹三種完成進行式時態：

完成進行式時態	句型	圖示
現在完成進行式	has / have been + 現在分詞	
過去完成進行式	had been + 現在分詞	
未來完成進行式	will have been + 現在分詞	

以下分項介紹三種完成進行式：

1 現在完成進行式

現在完成進行式的意義

表示過去某時開始的動作持續至今，仍在進行中或剛完成

例句

Karen **has been talking** on the phone for one hour.
凱倫已經講電話講一個小時了。

115

2 過去完成進行式

表示從過去較早的時間點開始之動作持續至過去較晚的時間點,而以當時來說,該動作仍在進行或剛完成

例句
The baby **had been sleeping** for a while before he started to cry.
小嬰兒已經睡了一陣子才開始哭。

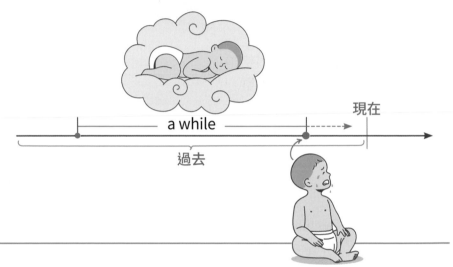

現在

a while

過去

 度補充

過去完成進行式通常不可單獨存在

說明
同過去完成式,過去完成進行式使用時通常須與過去簡單式連用,以表示先後順序,即:

先發生的動作 → 用過去完成進行式

後發生的動作 → 用過去簡單式

例句
Phil **had been waiting** for an hour before his girlfriend **arrived**.
　　　過去完成進行式　　　　　　　　　　　　　　過去簡單式
菲爾等了一個小時他的女友才抵達。

3 未來完成進行式

未來完成進行式的意義

表示過去某時開始的動作至今，仍在進行中並將延續至未來

例句 If the rain does not stop tomorrow, it will have been raining for an entire week.
如果明天雨沒停的話，就會下了一整個禮拜的雨。

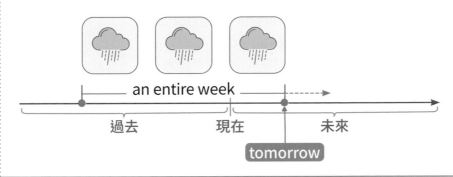

4 使用完成進行式應注意事項

(1)「不」適用完成進行式的動詞

 說明 同進行式，有些動詞通常不可用完成進行式來呈現。此類動詞通常是描述某種狀態、情形或是內心的意識，並無實質的動作舉止。此類動詞可見 6-2。

 例句 I have been owning my car since 2010. (×)
→ I have owned my car since 2010. (○)
我自從 2010 年就有這輛車了。

Liz has been forgetting what her mother had asked her to do. (×)
→ Liz forgot what her mother had asked her to do. (○)
麗茲忘記她媽媽請她做的事了。

(2) 完成式與完成進行式的差異

 說明 一般而言，完成式與完成進行式可表類似的意思，但完成式強調的是動作的執行或結果，完成進行式則是強調動作的持續性。

117

現在完成式 vs 現在完成進行式

I **have written** an email this morning.
我今天早上寫了一封電子郵件。

I **have been writing** an email this morning.
我今天早上都在寫電子郵件。

過去完成式 vs 過去完成進行式

We **had discussed** this problem for days
before the meeting started.
會議開始前我們已經討論這個問題好幾天了。

We **had been discussing** this problem
for days before the meeting started.
會議開始前有好幾天我們都在討論這個問題。

未來完成式 vs 未來完成進行式

Luke **will have lived** in this neighborhood for five years by the
end of this year.
今年年底路克就會在這個社區住滿五年。

Luke **will have been living** in this neighborhood for five years
by the end of this year.
今年年底路克就會在這個社區住滿五年。（未來可能還會住下去）

(3) since 及 for 與完成式或完成進行式的關係

❶ since　自從

since 可搭配完成式或完成進行式使用。since 可作介詞，之後接名詞（片語），例如表過去式的明確時間，如 last Monday（上週一）、two years ago（兩年前）等。since 亦可作從屬連接詞，引導副詞子句，**此副詞子句須採用過去式。**

完成式

$$主詞 + \begin{cases} has / have \\ had \\ will have \end{cases} + 過去分詞 + since...$$

完成進行式

主詞 + $\begin{cases} \text{has / have} \\ \text{had} \\ \text{will have} \end{cases}$ + been + 現在分詞 + since...

例句

Jim **has lived** here with his wife **since** last year.
　　　　　　　　　　　　　　表過去明確時間的名詞
吉姆自去年起就和太太住在這裡。（since 作介詞）

Jim **has lived** here with his wife **since** he quit his job.
　　　　　　　　　　　　　　　　　過去式的副詞子句
吉姆自從辭掉工作就和太太住在這裡。（since 作從屬連接詞）

Laura **has been learning** English **since** 2010.
　　　　　　　　　　　　　　　表過去明確時間的名詞
蘿拉自 2010 年起就在學英文。（since 作介詞）

Laura **has been learning** English **since** she started school.
　　　　　　　　　　　　　　　　　　過去式的副詞子句
蘿拉自開始上學起就在學英文。（since 作從屬連接詞）

2 for + 一段時間　已經持續……

說明

「for + 一段時間」可用於完成式或完成進行式，但不可與表瞬間動作的動詞並用，此類常見的動詞如下：

die（死亡）　　　　　go（去）　　　　　graduate（畢業）
come（來）　　　　　arrive（抵達）

句型

完成式

主詞 + $\begin{cases} \text{has / have} \\ \text{had} \\ \text{will have} \end{cases}$ + 過去分詞 + for + 一段時間

完成進行式

主詞 + $\begin{cases} \text{has / have} \\ \text{had} \\ \text{will have} \end{cases}$ + been + 現在分詞 + for + 一段時間

例句

Jim **has lived** here for five years.
吉姆已在這裡住了五年。

例句 Laura **has been learning** English **for more than ten years.**
蘿拉已經學英文超過十年了。

The old man has died for five years. (✕)

→ The old man has been **dead** for five years.
（○，改用形容詞 dead，表示狀態）

→ The old man **died five years ago.**
（○，改用過去簡單式，與明確的過去時間並用）

→ **It has been** five years **since** the old man died.
（○，改用「It has been + 一段時間 + since...」）
這位老人過世五年了。

\ 即時演練 /

單選題

① We _____ basketball for an hour when it began to rain.
(A) played　　　　　　　　(B) had been playing
(C) will play　　　　　　　(D) will have been playing

② When Paul graduates, he _____ law for four years.
(A) was studying　　　　　(B) studies
(C) will have been studying　(D) had been studying

③ Julie _____ ill for a few days. She should go see a doctor.
(A) feels　　　　　　　　(B) is feeling
(C) felt　　　　　　　　　(D) has been feeling

④ Ryan _____ at the company for five years before he was promoted.
(A) had been working　　　(B) will have been working
(C) works　　　　　　　　(D) is working

⑤ The students _____ this novel since the beginning of the semester.
(A) are reading　　　　　　　(B) will read
(C) will have been reading　　(D) have been reading

⑥ By the end of this year, Mr. Smith _____ English at our school for 20 years.
(A) will teach　　　　　　　(B) will have been teaching
(C) teaches　　　　　　　　(D) have been teaching

解　答

① B　理由　空格後有過去簡單式的動詞 began（開始）以及 for an hour（已經持續一小時），故空格應置過去完成進行式。

② C　理由　When Paul graduates（保羅畢業時）表未來的時間，且句尾有 for four years（持續四年），故空格應置未來完成進行式。

③ D　理由　空格後有 for a few days（持續幾天），故空格應置完成式或完成進行式。

④ A　理由　空格後有過去簡單式的動詞 was promoted（晉升）以及 for five years（持續五年），故空格應置過去完成進行式。

⑤ D　理由　空格後有 since the beginning of the semester（自學期開始），且根據語意，空格應置現在完成進行式。

⑥ B　理由　By the end of this year（到今年年底）表未來的時間，且句尾有 for 20 years（持續二十年），故空格應置未來完成進行式。

Notes

Chapter 6

助動詞

Chapter 6 助動詞

6-1 一般助動詞

助動詞顧名思義是幫助動詞的詞類，常放在動詞前，可分為兩大類：一般助動詞 及 情態助動詞 ；前者能使動詞表現出**時態**、**語態**、**否定**、**疑問**等變化，後者則是幫助動詞表達**義務**、**可能**、**需要**等情態。

分類	助動詞
一般助動詞	be 動詞 have do
情態助動詞	shall、should will、would can、could may、might must need、dare

以下分項介紹三個最常見的一般助動詞：

❶ be 動詞

be 動詞的形態				
原形	現在式	過去式	現在分詞	過去分詞
be	am is	was	being	been
	are	were		

be 動詞作助動詞的用法

1 形成進行式

 句型 be 動詞 + 現在分詞

 例句

I am	我在看電視。
You are	你 / 妳 / 你們在看電視。
He is	他在看電視。
She is	她在看電視。
We are	我們在看電視。
They are	他們 / 她們在看電視。

 watching TV.

It **is getting** dark. 天色漸暗了。

2 形成被動語態

 句型 be 動詞 + 過去分詞

 例句

Mr. Wilson **was elected** chairman of our company.
威爾森先生當選為本公司主席。

The book **was written** by my favorite author.
這本書是由我最喜歡的作家寫的。

3 表示「預定 / 會發生」、「命令」或「應該」

 句型 be 動詞 + to + 原形動詞

 例句

Kelly **is to see** the doctor this afternoon.
今天下午凱莉要去看醫生。

On that day, Ken met a person that
was to influence his whole life.
那天，肯遇到了會影響他一生的人。

No one **is to leave** this room without
the permission of the police.
沒有警察的允許，沒有人可以離開這房間。

You **are to fill** out this form and return it by the end of the class.
你要在課堂結束前填完並繳交這份表單。

注意

「be 動詞 + to + 原形動詞」之「to + 原形動詞」的語意若表示「目的」,則 be 動詞是作連綴動詞用,譯成「是」,而「to + 原形動詞」為不定詞片語作主詞補語。

The purpose of our meeting **is** to solve this problem.
　　　　　主詞　　　　　連綴動詞　　不定詞片語

本會議的目的是要解決這個問題。

❷ have

have 的形態				
原形	現在式	過去式	現在分詞	過去分詞
have	have has	had	having	had

have 作助動詞的用法

❶ 形成完成式

現在完成式

has / have + 過去分詞

過去完成式

had + 過去分詞

未來完成式

will have + 過去分詞

Linda **has saved** some money.
琳達存了一些錢。

My parents **had** already **eaten** dinner when I got home.
我回到家時我爸媽已經吃過晚餐了。

Students **will have learned** how to play guitar when they finish this class.
學生上完課就能學會如何彈吉他。

2 形成完成進行式

 句型

現在完成進行式

has / have been + 現在分詞

過去完成進行式

had been + 現在分詞

未來完成進行式

will have been + 現在分詞

 例句

Abby **has been practicing** yoga for three years.
艾比已經練瑜珈三年了。

Before Frank became a judge,
he **had been working** as a lawyer for ten years.
法蘭克成為法官前，當律師當了十年。

Gary and Irene **will have been dating** for six months by February.
到了二月，蓋瑞跟艾琳交往就滿六個月了。

3 do

do 的形態				
原形	現在式	過去式	現在分詞	過去分詞
do	do does	did	doing	done

do 作助動詞的用法

1 形成疑問句

 句型

1 Do / Does / Did ＋主詞＋原形動詞...?

2 疑問詞 (如 Who、What、Where、How 等) ＋ do / does / did ＋主詞＋原形動詞...?

 例句

Do you **like** singing?
你喜歡唱歌嗎？

例句

Did you pass the test?
你考試及格了嗎？

Where do you want to go on vacation?
放假時你想去哪裡？

2 形成否定句

句型

主詞 + do / does / did + not + 原形動詞...
= 主詞 + don't / doesn't / didn't + 原形動詞...

例句

Simon does not (= doesn't) know how to answer that question.
賽門不知道如何回答那個問題。

I tried to call Vince, but he did not (= didn't) pick up his phone.
我試圖要打電話給文斯，但他沒接。

3 強調語氣

說明

do、does、did 作助動詞並用於加強語氣時，可譯成「的確」或「真(的)」。

句型

主詞 + do / does / did + 原形動詞...

例句

Hank looks like his father.
漢克長得像他爸爸。

→ Hank does look like his father.
漢克長得真像他爸爸。（強調語氣）

4 代替動詞

說明

do、does、did 可用來代替句中已出現過的動詞及其之後的所有其他詞類 (簡稱述詞)，以避免重複。

例句

A: Do you know how to speak Japanese?
B: Yes, I do (= know how to speak Japanese).
　　　　　　　　　　　　述詞

A：你會說日文嗎？
B：會。

Betty can run as fast as Bill does (= runs).
貝蒂可以跑得跟比爾一樣快。

 度補充

be 動詞、do 以及 have 也可作主要動詞用

說明 上述 be 動詞、do 以及 have 除了可作助動詞之外，亦可作主要動詞用。

例句
My son **is** still a student.
我兒子仍是學生。（此處 is 為連綴動詞）

What are you **doing**?
你在做什麼？（此處 doing 為動詞，表「做」）

Mr. and Mrs. Green **have** two children.
格林夫婦有兩個小孩。（此處 have 為動詞，表「有」）

\ 即時演練 /

請根據中文提示，在下列空格中填入正確的一般助動詞，每格限填一字。

① 你知道現在幾點嗎？
_____ you know what time it is right now?

② 外面正在下大雨。
It _____ pouring outside right now.

③ 開始下雨了，但是麥克斯沒有帶雨傘。
It is starting to rain, but Max _____ have an umbrella
with him.

④ 自從肯去年搬到加拿大，就沒有人再見過他了。
Ken moved to Canada last year, and no one _____
seen him since.

⑤ 這棟建築物被建造的目的是提供遊民住所。
The building _____ built to provide homeless people
with a place to stay.

⑥ 詹姆士考試前確實有用功讀書。我好奇他為什麼考不及格。
James _____ study hard before the test. I wonder
why he didn't pass it.

⑦ 珍來到這座城市後一直都在下著雪，所以景色極美。

It _____ been snowing since Jane arrived in the city, so everything looked beautiful.

⑧ 蜜妮知道這個祕密，但瓊安不知道。

Minnie knows the secret, but Joanne _____.

⑨ 明天晚上父母親都要與孩子的老師會面。

Both parents _____ to meet with their child's teacher tomorrow evening.

⑩ 你昨晚晚餐吃什麼？

What _____ you have for dinner last night?

解　答				
① Do	② is	③ doesn't	④ has	⑤ was
⑥ did	⑦ had	⑧ doesn't	⑨ are	⑩ did

Chapter 6　助動詞

6-2　情態助動詞 shall 與 should

情態助動詞會置於**原形動詞**前，且具有功能性，用來表示許可、能力、可能性……等不同的語氣或態度。下列為常見的情態助動詞：

情態助動詞	否定形	縮寫形
shall should	shall not should not	shan't (少用) shouldn't
will would	will not would not	won't wouldn't
can could	can not (少用) / cannot could not	can't couldn't
may might	may not might not	mayn't (少用) mightn't (少用)
must	must not	mustn't
need	need not	needn't
dare	dare not	daren't (少用)

以下介紹情態助動詞 shall 與 should：

1 shall

shall 的用法

1 表未來

句型　第一人稱（如 I、We）+ shall + 原形動詞

注意

第一人稱以 shall 表未來為較正式或老派的用法。一般而言，使用 will 即可。

例句

I **shall** be old enough to learn how to drive next year.
= I **will** be old enough to learn how to drive next year.
我明年就年齡夠大可以學開車了。

2 徵求意願、提議或詢問

 句型

❶ Shall + 第一人稱 (如 I、We) + 原形動詞...?

❷ Let's + 原形動詞..., shall we?

❸ 疑問詞 + shall + 第一人稱 (如 I、We) + 原形動詞...?

例句

It's a bit hot today. **Shall I turn** on the fan?
今天有點熱。要不要我開電扇呢？

Shall we go out for dinner this evening?

= Let's go out for dinner this evening, **shall we**?
我們今天晚上要外出用餐嗎？

What **shall we do** today? 我們今天要做什麼?

3 表示保證或命令

 句型

$$\left.\begin{array}{l} \text{第二人稱 (如 You)} \\ \text{第三人稱 (如 He、She、It、They)} \end{array}\right\} + \text{shall} + \text{原形動詞}$$

 例句

You **shall do** as I say. 我說什麼你就做什麼。

They **shall** not **pass** the bridge.
他們不准過橋。

4 用於條文、法律、合約等，表示規範或命令

例句

The payment **shall** be transferred to the client's account.
費用將會匯入客戶的帳戶。

The fine **shall** not be more than NT$5,000.
罰款不得超過新臺幣五千元。

❷ should

should 的用法

1 表未來，為 shall 的過去式

 例句

Kevin asked me what time he **should** come over for the party.
凱文有問我他應該要幾點來參加派對。

2 表示義務 / 責任或建議，可譯為「應當」、「應該」

 You **should** exercise regularly.
= You **ought to** exercise regularly.
你應該要定期運動。

We **should** consult a lawyer before we sign the contract.
= We **ought to** consult a lawyer before we sign the contract.
我們簽約前應該要詢問律師。

注意

should 表示義務 / 責任或建議時，可以用 ought
to 取代。語氣上，ought to 較為正式。

3 用於疑問句中詢問意見

 Should I apply for this job?
我應該要應徵這份工作嗎？

What **should** we do about this problem?
針對這個問題我們該怎麼做？

4 用於假設，可譯為「萬一」

 If + 主詞 + should + 原形動詞, 主要子句
= Should + 主詞 + 原形動詞, 主要子句

 If anything **should happen** to me, please give this letter to
my parents.
= **Should** anything **happen** to me, please give this letter to my
parents.
萬一我發生什麼事，請把這封信給我父母。

5 表示可能性

 Our guest **should** be here by now. I'll go to meet him in the lobby.
我們的客人現在應該到了。我去大廳見他。

6 表錯愕、惋惜或驚喜之情緒，可譯為「竟然」、「居然」

 Funny you **should** mention that. I was
thinking the same.
真巧，你竟然提出那件事。我正有一樣的想法。

(1) should 用於 that 引導的名詞子句中

❶ It is + { necessary / essential / important / urgent } + that + 主詞 + should (可省略) + 原形動詞...

……應當……是有必要的 / 很重要的 / 很急迫的

例句
It is important that you (should) remember to send these emails by the end of the day.
你切記要在今天結束前寄出這些電子郵件。

❷ It is + { natural / surprising / amazing } + that + 主詞 + should (不可省略) + 原形動詞...

……會……是很正常的 / 令人驚訝的 / 很驚人的

例句
It is surprising that Jerry should be so considerate.
傑瑞會這麼體貼真令人意外。

❸ 主詞 + 意志動詞 + that + 主詞 + should (可省略) + 原形動詞...

說明
上方句型之意志動詞有下列幾類：
❶ 建議：suggest、recommend、advise、propose、urge (呼籲)
❷ 要求：ask、demand、require、request、insist (堅持)
❸ 命令：order、command

例句
The tour guide suggested that we (should) leave early for the airport.
導遊建議我們早點出發前往機場。

(2) should have + 過去分詞　　過去應該……(但未發生)

例句
I told you not to stay up so late.
You should have listened to me.
我告訴你不要熬夜熬到那麼晚。
你應該要聽我的。

| (3) shouldn't have + 過去分詞　　過去不應該……（但發生了） |

例句　Norman **shouldn't have been** so strict with the new employee.
諾曼不應該對新員工那麼嚴苛。

\ 即時演練 /

請根據中文提示，在下列空格中填入 shall、should 或 shouldn't。

① 吉娜身體不舒服的話應該要看醫生。
Gina _____ see a doctor if she is not feeling well.

② 我們要不要現在休息一下呢？
Let's take a break now, _____ we?

③ 開學第一天感到緊張是很自然的事。
It is natural that you _____ feel nervous on the first day of school.

④ 戴爾不應該做那麼危險的事。他受傷是自己活該。
Dale _____ have done such a dangerous thing. It's his own fault that he got hurt.

⑤ 大家對於總統發表那則聲明感到很驚訝。
Everyone was surprised that the president _____ make that statement.

| 解　答 |
| ① should　　② shall　　③ should　　④ shouldn't　　⑤ should |

Chapter 6 助動詞

6-3 情態助動詞 will 與 would

以下介紹情態助動詞 will 與 would：

1 will

will 的用法

1 表未來

例句
My friend **will** pick me up at the airport tomorrow.
我朋友明天會在機場接我。

2 表意願

例句
I **will** have a cup of coffee, thank you.
我想點一杯咖啡，謝謝。

3 表習慣、習性

例句
Kids **will** be kids.
小孩終究還是小孩。

4 用於疑問句中表示請求或詢問

例句
Will you join us for dinner?
你會跟我們共進晚餐嗎？

5 表命令

例句
You **will** report everything to me from now on.
從此刻起，你要將所有事情回報給我。

2 would

would 的用法

1 表過去的「將會」，為 will 的過去式

例句
Leah said she **would** come home before 10 p.m.
莉亞說她會在晚上十點之前回到家。

注意

請比較下列兩句：

1 Ron promised he **would** come to my wedding.
榮恩答應會參加我的婚禮。（暗示婚禮已結束）

過去　　　　　　　　　現在

2 Ron promised he **will** come to my wedding.
榮恩答應會參加我的婚禮。（暗示婚禮尚未發生）

過去　　　　現在　　　未來

由上可知，promise（答應）的動作發生於過去，而後續事件 come to my wedding（參加我的婚禮）若發生於過去時間，則使用 would。換言之，come to my wedding 若發生於未來（即現在尚未發生），則使用 will。

2 用於疑問句中客氣表示請求

| 說明 | 要請求他人做某事時，will 與 would 皆可使用，但 would 的語氣較為委婉、禮貌。 |

| 例句 | **Would** you give me a ride to the office?
你可以載我去辦公室嗎？ |

3 表過去的習慣

| 例句 | When Robin was a child, she **would** sometimes play tennis with her brother.
羅蘋小時候有時會跟她弟弟一起打網球。 |

4 用於假設，可譯為「就會」

| 句型 | If + 主詞 + 過去式動詞, 主詞 + would + 原形動詞 |

例句 If I had more money, I would travel abroad for a vacation.
如果我有更多錢，就會出國度假。

③ 常見的相關慣用語

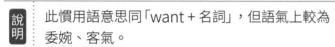
❶ would like to + 原形動詞　　想要……

 說明 此慣用語意思同 want to，但語氣上較為委婉、客氣。

 例句　　I want to go home now.（語氣較直接）
= I would like to go home now.（語氣較委婉）
我想要現在回家。

❷ would like + 名詞　　想要……

 說明 此慣用語意思同「want + 名詞」，但語氣上較為
委婉、客氣。

 例句　　I want a steak, please.（語氣較直接）
= I would like a steak, please.（語氣較委婉）
我想要一份牛排，麻煩你。

❸ would rather + 原形動詞 + than + 原形動詞　　寧願……也不願……

 例句 I would rather stay at home than go outside in this weather.
我寧願待在家也不要在這種天氣出門。

＼ 即時演練 ／

請根據中文提示，在下列空格中填入 will 或 would。

① 明天早上會是晴天，下午則會是多雲的天氣。
Tomorrow ＿＿＿＿＿＿＿＿ be sunny in the morning and
cloudy in the afternoon.

② 我寧願獨自一人也不要跟大衛約會。
I ＿＿＿＿＿＿＿＿ rather be alone than go on a date with David.

138

③ 奈德還在這裡工作時，他會去樓下的咖啡廳買咖啡。

When Ned still worked here, he _____ buy coffee from the café downstairs.

④ 凱特想要出國讀書，但她現在無法負擔。

Kate _____ like to study abroad, but she cannot afford it now.

⑤ 全體員工下週將開始居家辦公。

All employees _____ begin working from home next week.

解　　答				
① will	② would	③ would	④ would	⑤ will

6-4 情態助動詞 can 與 could

以下介紹情態助動詞 can 與 could：

1 can

can 的用法

1 表示能力，可譯為「能夠」、「會」

例句
Trevor **can** speak three languages.
= Trevor **is able to** speak three languages.
崔佛會說三種語言。

注意

can 表示能力時，可以用 be able to 取代，但用此取代時須注意下列事項：
1 主詞須為有行為能力之人或生物。
2 be able to 可搭配其他助動詞使用。

The CEO is very busy, so I'm not sure if he **will be able to** see you tomorrow.　執行長很忙，所以我不確定他明天是否可以見你。

2 表示許可，可譯為「可以」

例句
We **can** listen to music while working.
我們工作時可以聽音樂。

Can I go home now?　我現在可以回家嗎？

3 表示可能性，可譯為「有可能」

例句
It **can't** be true! I don't believe a word you say.
這不可能是真的！我不相信你所說的。

2 could

could 的用法

1 表過去有能力，為 can 的過去式

例句
My father **could** run marathons when he was young.
我父親年輕時能跑馬拉松。

2 表過去可以，為 can 的過去式

例句
The security guard told me I **could** park my car here.
警衛告訴我，我可以把車停在這裡。

3 用於疑問句中客氣表示請求

說明
與 would 類似，要請求他人做某事時，can 與 could 皆可使用，但 could 的語氣較為委婉、禮貌。

例句
Could you pass me the salt, please?
可以請你遞鹽給我嗎？

4 表猜測

例句
The doctor said recovery from this injury **could** take months.
醫生說這個傷的復原時間可能要數個月。

3 常見的相關慣用語

1 cannot / can't / couldn't help + 動名詞　　忍不住……
= cannot / can't / couldn't help but + 原形動詞

例句
When Sarah heard that joke, she **couldn't help laughing**.
= When Sarah heard that joke, she **couldn't help but laugh**.
莎拉聽到那笑話時，忍不住大笑。

2 can't be too + 形容詞　　再……也不為過

例句
We **can't be too careful** when driving.
我們開車時越小心越好。

3 can't have + 過去分詞　　不可能……（表示質疑或驚呼過去發生某事的可能性）

例句
Owen **can't have finished** this book already. It's nearly 500 pages long.　歐文不可能已經讀完這本書了。這本書將近五百頁。

4 could have + 過去分詞　　過去有可能……（但說話者真的不確定）；
過去本可以……（但未發生）

例句
The accident **could have been** caused by the young man, but the police are still investigating.
這起意外可能是這名年輕人造成的，但警察仍在調查中。

141

例句
You **could have done** your homework last night, but you didn't.
你昨晚原本可以寫完作業，但你沒有做到。

5 couldn't be + 比較級形容詞　　最為……

例句
Mobile payment **couldn't be more convenient**.
行動支付最方便不過了。

6 couldn't + 原形動詞 + more / less　　最 / 最不……

例句
Your idea is great. I **couldn't agree more**.
你的主意不錯。我完全同意。

To be honest with you, I **couldn't care less** about this issue.
老實告訴你，我對這件事一點都不在乎。

注意

couldn't care less 為英式英文，美式英文常用 could care less。

\ 即時演練 /

請根據中文提示，在下列空格中填入 can、can't、could 或 couldn't。

① 我不需要你的幫忙；我可以自己來。
I don't need help from you; I _____ do it by myself.

② 喬伊當時無法負擔那輛昂貴的車，所以她買了一輛較便宜的。
Joy _____ afford that expensive car at that time, so she bought a cheaper one.

③ 凱爾原本可以搭計程車回家，但他最後用走的。
Kyle _____ have taken a taxi home, but he walked instead.

④ 這不可能是對的路。我們應該迷路了。
This _____ be the right way. I think we're lost.

⑤ 很多年前，一條麵包只要新臺幣二十元就能買到，現在卻要超過六十元。
Many years ago, I _____ buy a loaf of bread for just NT$20, but now it costs more than NT$60.

解　答

① can　　② couldn't　　③ could　　④ can't　　⑤ could

Chapter 6 　助動詞

6-5 　情態助動詞 may 與 might

以下介紹情態助動詞 may 與 might：

❶ may

may 的用法

❶ 表示許可，可譯為「可以」

> **例句**
> You **may** choose whatever you want for your birthday.
> 你生日可以買任何你想要的東西。
>
> **May** I answer my phone now?　我現在可以接電話嗎？

❷ 表示推測，可譯為「可能」

> **例句**
> Kayla **may** be in a meeting right now.
> Don't call her.
> 凱拉現在可能在開會。不要打電話給她。

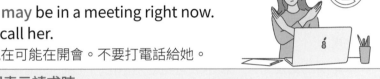

❸ 客氣詢問表示請求時

> **例句**
> **May** I borrow this book from you?
> 我可以跟你借這本書嗎？

❹ 禮貌性給予建議時

> **說明**
> 此常用於問句。

> **例句**
> **May** I suggest that you turn off your cell phone before you go
> to sleep?　我可以建議你在睡覺前關掉手機嗎？

❺ 常搭配 but（但是），暗意「雖然」

> **例句**
> The actor **may** be talented, but he has a terrible personality.
> 這名演員雖然很有才華，但他個性很糟。
>
> Walter **may** not be as fast as the others, but the quality of his
> work is the best.
> 華特雖然速度不及其他人，但他工作成果的品質是無人可比的。

6 表祈願，可譯為「但願」、「祝」

句型 May... + 原形動詞

例句 Sally's grandmother passed away yesterday.
May she rest in peace.　莎莉的奶奶昨天過世了。願她安息。

深 度補充

may 與 can 的差異

說明 一般而言，may 與 can 在某些情況下可交替使用，但 may 的語氣較為正式。兩者之差異如下：

	may	can / could
1 表許可	○	△（請見下方「注意」內容）
2 表能力	×	○
3 表可能性	○	○

注意

以嚴謹的文法而言，表示許可時應用 may，can 則是用來表示能力。但實際應用上，尤其是在日常對話中表示許可時，may 與 can 皆可使用，但 may 的語氣較為正式、有禮貌。

例句 **表許可**

　Can I go to the restroom? (劣)

→ May I go to the restroom? (佳)
　我可以去上廁所嗎？

表能力

　May you translate this sentence into Japanese? (×)

→ Can you translate this sentence into Japanese? (○)
　你可以把這句翻譯成日文嗎？

表可能性

　You shouldn't believe everything the thief says. He could / may be lying.
　你不應該相信小偷說的話。他可能在說謊。

❷ might

❶ 表過去的可能性，為 may 的過去式

例句
The news reporter said that the event might be postponed.
新聞記者說活動可能會延期。

❷ 表較低的可能性

說明
might 亦可用於表示現在或未來的可能性，但一般
認為 might 表示的可能性較 may 低。

例句
We might move to a bigger house when
our baby is born next year.
明年我們的嬰兒出生時，我們可能會搬到
更大的房子。

❸ 客氣詢問表示請求時

說明
might 可用於疑問句表示請求，此為正式用法，但此用法較少見。

例句
Might I ask you a question regarding this issue?（罕）
= May I ask you a question regarding this issue?（常見）
我可以針對這個議題問一個問題嗎？

❹ 禮貌性給予建議時

例句
It might be a good idea to hire a
personal trainer.
僱用一名私人教練或許是個好主意。

❸ 常見的相關慣用語

❶ may (very) well + 原形動詞　　很可能……

例句
What you're saying may (very) well be true.
你說的很有可能是真的。

❷ may / might as well + 原形動詞　　不妨……，要不就……

例句
We may as well start the meeting now. The others can join us
later.　　我們不妨現在開始開會吧。其他人可以晚點加入我們。

If all tourist destinations are crowded with people, we **might as well stay** at home.

如果所有觀光景點都擠滿人的話，我們乾脆待在家吧。

---

3 may / might have + 過去分詞　　過去可能……

 I can't find my wallet anywhere. I **may have left** it at the restaurant.

我到處都找不到我的錢包。我可能忘在餐廳了。

I **might have forgotten** to turn off the lights in my house before I went out.

我出門前好像忘記關家裡的燈了。

＼ 即時演練 ／

單選題

① Mom was worried that we ＿＿＿＿＿＿＿ be in danger when she couldn't reach us last night.
(A) might　　　(B) can　　　(C) shall　　　(D) has

② Owen is not here right now. He ＿＿＿＿＿＿＿ to our branch office.
(A) dare go　　　　　　　(B) is able to go
(C) had better go　　　　(D) might have gone

③ Roy ＿＿＿＿＿＿＿ not be talented, but he is hard-working.
(A) should　　　(B) would　　　(C) may　　　(D) could

④ The restaurant is only around the corner. We might as well ＿＿＿＿＿＿＿ there.
(A) to walk　　(B) walk　　(C) walked　　(D) walking

⑤ Congratulations! ＿＿＿＿＿＿＿ you and your bride have a long and happy marriage.
(A) Can　　　(B) Will　　　(C) Might　　　(D) May

解　答

① A	② D	③ C	④ B	⑤ D

Chapter 6　助動詞

6-6　情態助動詞 must、need 及 dare

以下介紹情態助動詞 must、need 及 dare：

❶ must

must 的用法
❶ 表示義務，可譯為「必須」
句型　must + 原形動詞
例句　All new employees **must report** to the reception desk first. 所有新進員工必須先到接待櫃檯報到。
❷ 表示禁止
句型　must not + 原形動詞
例句　You **must not leave** without my permission. 未經過我的允許你不准離開。
❸ 表示推測，可譯為「一定」、「肯定」
句型　**對現在的推測** ❶ must be + 形容詞 ❷ must be + 現在分詞 **對過去的推測** must have + 過去分詞
例句　Ross has been working nonstop all day. He **must be exhausted**.　羅斯不間斷地工作一整天。他肯定很累。 It **must be raining** outside. I see some people carrying umbrellas. 外面肯定在下雨。我看到有人拿著雨傘。 The ground is wet outside. It **must have rained** last night. 外頭地上是溼的。昨晚肯定下過雨了。

4 表極力勸說

例句
You **must** try this cake. It's the best cake in town!
你一定要吃吃看這個蛋糕。這是本地最好吃的蛋糕！

  **深** 度補充

must 與 have to 的差異

1 語氣上之差異

說明
一般情況下，表示「必須」時，must 與 have to 可互換使用。但兩者語意上仍有些微的差距：must 通常是因為他人命令或法律規範而形成義務上的強制；have to 則帶有勉強的意味，是由於某事很重要或必要，因此必須執行。

例句
Everyone, including the driver and all passengers, **must** wear a seat belt.
每個人，包含司機與所有乘客，都必須繫上安全帶。
(此處 must 強調法律規範上的強制性)

Everyone, including the driver and all passengers, **has to** wear a seat belt.
每個人，包含司機與所有乘客，都必須繫上安全帶。
(此處 has to 表示重要性或必要性)

2 表示的時間之差異

說明
一般而言，must 只用於表示現在或未來的狀況，have to 則可用於表示過去、現在及未來的情況。

例句

表過去

We must work yesterday. (×)

→ We **had to** work yesterday. (○)
我們昨天必須工作。

表現在

We **must** work today.

= We **have to** work today.
我們今天必須工作。

例句

表未來

We **must** work tomorrow.

= We **have to** work tomorrow.
我們明天必須工作。

3 用於否定

說明

must 之否定形態 must not 表示「不准」、「不可」，為禁止做某事，have to 之否定形態 don't have to 則表示「不必」，並非表示禁止或義務。

例句

You **must not** lend Billy any money.
你不准借給比利一毛錢。

You **don't have to** lend Billy any money.
你不必借給比利一毛錢。（但你可以）

4 口語上使用之差異

說明

非正式場合之口語會話中，較常使用 have to，而非 must。而 have to 也經常會改為 have got to 或 gotta [ˈɡɑtə]。

例句

I **have to** tell you a secret.

= I **have got to** tell you a secret.

= I **gotta** tell you a secret.
我必須跟你說個祕密。

❷ need

need 的用法

1 用於否定句中，表示「不必」、「不需要」

句型

need not / needn't + 原形動詞

例句

We needn't spend too much time on this topic. It will be handled by another team.
我們不需要花太多時間在這個議題上。它會由其他團隊來處理。

2 用於疑問句中，表示「需要……？」

句型

Need + 主詞 + 原形動詞... ?

例句

Need I **point** out your mistakes one by one?
需要我逐一說出你的過錯嗎？

A: Why do you like George?

B: He's handsome and rich. **Need** I **say** more?

A：妳為什麼喜歡喬治？

B：他又帥又有錢。我還需要多說什麼？

 深 度補充

need 也可作主要動詞用

說明 need 可作助動詞之外，亦可作主要動詞用。兩者用法之差異如下：

	助動詞 need	主要動詞 need
肯定句	need + 原形動詞 （常搭配有否定意義的字）	need to + 原形動詞 need + 名詞 / 動名詞
否定句	need not + 原形動詞	don't need to + 原形動詞
疑問句	Need + 主詞 + 原形動詞…?	Do + 主詞 + need to + 原形動詞…?

注意

❶ 助動詞 need 使用時，後接原形動詞且常用於否定句或疑問句，鮮少用於肯定句。一般而言，助動詞 need 用於肯定句為較正式的用法，常與含否定意義的字（如 no one、nobody、nothing 等）一起出現。

❷ 主要動詞 need 可接名詞（片語）或動名詞（片語）等作受詞，亦可接不定詞片語「to + 原形動詞」。用於否定句或疑問句時，則須搭配助動詞 do 或其變化形使用。

 例句 **肯定句**

No one **need know** where the proof came from. （need 為助動詞）
沒有人需要知道這證據是從哪裡來的。

I **need to water** my flowers when I go home.
（need 為主要動詞）
我回家時需要澆花。

例句

The injured woman **needs help**. (need 為主要動詞)
那名受傷的女士需要幫助。

My flowers **need watering**. (need 為主要動詞)
我的花需要澆水。

否定句

We **needn't spend** too much time on this topic. It will be handled by another team. (need 為助動詞)

= We **don't need to spend** too much time on this topic. It will be handled by another team. (need 為主要動詞)
我們不需要花太多時間在這個議題上。它會由其他團隊來處理。

疑問句

Need I point out your mistakes one by one? (Need 為助動詞)

= **Do I need to point** out your mistakes one by one? (need 為主要動詞)
需要我逐一說出你的過錯嗎？

3 **dare**

 dare 的用法

1 用於否定句中，表示「不敢」

 句型 dare not + 原形動詞

 例句 Amy **dare not / dared not talk** to that serious-looking man.
艾咪不敢跟那位長相嚴肅的男子說話。

注意

dare 與 not 並用時，dare 恆為助動詞，無 "Amy dares not talk to that serious-looking man." 的用法；dared not 中的 dared 則為過去式助動詞。

2 用於疑問句中，表示「某人敢……嗎？」

 句型 Dare + 人 + 原形動詞...?

 例句 **Dare** anyone **go** into that cave?
有人敢進去那個山洞嗎？

CH
6

6-6

情態助動詞 must、need 及 dare

151

dare 也可作主要動詞用

說明

dare 可作助動詞之外,亦可作主要動詞用。兩者用法之差異如下:

	助動詞 dare	主要動詞 dare
肯定句	×	dare (to) + 原形動詞
		dare + 人 + to + 原形動詞
否定句	dare not + 原形動詞	don't dare (to) + 原形動詞
疑問句	Dare + 人 + 原形動詞...?	Do + 人 + dare (to) + 原形動詞...?

注意

1 助動詞 dare 使用時,後接原形動詞且常用於否定句或疑問句,鮮少用於肯定句。

2 主要動詞 dare 用於否定句或疑問句時,則須搭配助動詞 do 或其變化形使用。

例句

肯定句

Only a few journalists **dare (to) report** that scandal.
(dare 為主要動詞)
只有少數幾位記者敢報導這起醜聞。

I **dared** Henry **to jump** in the pool.
(dare 為主要動詞,與 challenge 同義,表「挑戰」)
我諒亨利不敢跳進泳池。

否定句

Amy **dared not talk** to that serious-looking man.(dared 為助動詞)

= Amy **did not dare (to) talk** to that serious-looking man.
(dare 為主要動詞)
艾咪不敢跟那位長相嚴肅的男子說話。

疑問句

Dare anyone **go** into that cave?(Dare 為助動詞)

= **Does** anyone **dare (to) go** into that cave?(dare 為主要動詞)
有人敢進去那個山洞嗎?

❹ 常見的相關慣用語

❶ need only + 原形動詞　　只需……

例句
If you need anything else, you **need only ask**.
如果你還需要其他東西，只要開口問。

❷ needn't have + 過去分詞　　過去不必……（但已做了）

例句
You **needn't have arrived** so early. Everyone else was late.
你當時不必那麼早抵達。其他人都遲到了。

❸ I dare say + (that) + 子句　　我敢說……
＝ I daresay + (that) + 子句

例句
I dare say / daresay (that) everyone knows this secret already.
我敢說大家都知道這個祕密了。

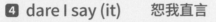

❹ dare I say (it)　　恕我直言

例句
The play was, **dare I say (it)**, quite boring.
恕我直言，這齣戲有點無聊。

❺ How dare...!　　……竟敢……！

例句
How dare you accuse me of stealing your money!
你竟敢指控我偷你的錢！

＼ 即時演練 ／

請根據中文提示，在下列空格中填入 must、need 或 dare。

① 艾拉的奶奶現在肯定將近九十歲了。
Ella's grandmother _____ be nearly 90 years old now.

② 你敢嚐嚐看這道異國料理嗎？
_____ you try this exotic dish?

③ 如果我們沒時間的話就不必參加研討會。
We _____ not go to the conference if we don't have time.

④ 你竟敢未經我的允許使用我的電腦！

How _____ you use my computer without my permission!

⑤ 傑瑞不敢跟他老闆說他犯的錯誤。

Jerry _____ not tell his boss about his mistake.

⑥ 我們需要把這課的重點寫下來嗎？

_____ we write the main points of the lesson down?

⑦ 我離開前必須要完成這個專案。

I _____ finish this project before leaving.

⑧ 顧客如果想要更多資訊，只需要打通電話給我們。

Customers _____ only give us a call if they want more information.

解　答				
① must	② Dare	③ need	④ dare	⑤ dare / dared
⑥ Need	⑦ must	⑧ need		

154

Chapter 7

形容詞 與 副詞

Chapter 7　形容詞　與　副詞

7-1　形容詞

形容詞是用來修飾名詞或代名詞，通常用來描述或修飾人事物，如大小、形狀、顏色、個性等屬性。此外，現在分詞、過去分詞、分詞片語、形容詞子句或複合形容詞等亦可被視為形容詞。一般而言，形容詞有下列兩種用法：

形容詞的用法		說明
限定用法	前位修飾	形容詞置於所修飾的名詞或代名詞前面或後面，直接修飾並限定此名詞或代名詞之範圍。
	後位修飾	
敘述用法		形容詞置於連綴動詞（如 be 動詞、seem、look 等）後面作主詞補語，或受詞後面作受詞補語，間接修飾並說明該名詞或代名詞之性質、狀態。

以下分項介紹形容詞的用法：

❶ 限定用法

> **前位修飾**

說明	形容詞置於所修飾的名詞或代名詞之前，稱為前位修飾。
句型	形容詞 + 名詞 / 代名詞
例句	The small garden is full of beautiful flowers. 這座小花園種滿了美麗的花。

 **度補充**

前位修飾時多個形容詞之排序

可以同時存在多個形容詞來修飾同一個名詞，但習慣上有固定的排序方式，順序大致如下：

順序	詞類	例字
1	限定詞（如冠詞、指示代名詞、所有格等）	a、the、this、my
2	數詞	first、one
3	描寫之形容詞	(★如下)
4	名詞（片語）	man（男子）、bag（袋子）

其中，描寫之形容詞的順序又可大致排列如下：

順序	意思	例字
1	意見、想法	lovely（可愛的）
2	大小	big（大的）
3	實際特徵	rough（粗糙的）
4	形狀	round（圓的）
5	年齡	young（年輕的）
6	顏色	red（紅的）
7	起源	Japanese（日本的）
8	材質	wooden（木製的）
9	目的	shopping（購物的）

注意

上述形容詞之順序為常見的排序方式，但並非硬性規定。基本原則為，**越接近名詞的形容詞，與名詞的關係越密切。**

例句

❶ ❻ ❾
Amy received a lovely red shopping bag for free.
　　　　　限定詞　**描寫之形容詞**　名詞
艾咪免費收到了一個可愛的紅色購物袋。

❶ ❼ ❽
Mike lent me his precious Japanese wooden plate.
　　　　　限定詞　　**描寫之形容詞**　名詞
麥克借給我他珍貴的日本木盤。

後位修飾

1 修飾某些代名詞時

 說明 形容詞置於所修飾的名詞或代名詞之後，稱為後位修飾。若被修飾之代名詞為 no-、any-、some- 或 every- 所形成的複合字或表示「……的人」的 those 時，則通常使用後位修飾。

 句型

$$\left\{ \begin{array}{l} \text{no-} \\ \text{any-} \\ \text{some-} \\ \text{every-} \\ \qquad \text{those} \end{array} \right. + \left[\begin{array}{l} \text{-one} \\ \text{-body} \\ \text{-thing} \end{array} \right] \left. \right\} + 形容詞$$

 例句

I want to eat something spicy for dinner today.

我今天晚餐想吃辣的東西。

Those responsible for the accident should be punished.

該為這起意外負責任的人應該要被懲罰。

2 固定搭配的「名詞 + 形容詞」組合

例字 heir apparent（法定繼承人）　　poet laureate（桂冠詩人）
a word unspoken（未說出口的話）

3 修飾有最高級形容詞或 all、every、only 等名詞片語時（為強調用）

 句型

$$\left\{ \begin{array}{l} \text{the + 最高級形容詞 + 名詞} \\ \text{all / every / only + 名詞} \end{array} \right\} + 形容詞$$

 例句

Taking the freeway is the fastest route possible.
（強調 possible）

= Taking the freeway is the fastest possible route.
（無強調 possible）
開高速公路是最快的可行路線。

This website offers courses in every subject imaginable.
（強調 imaginable）

= This website offers courses in every imaginable subject.
（無強調 imaginable）
所有想像得到的主題，這網站皆有開設課程。

158

4 以形容詞片語修飾時

 說明 形容詞片語除了由形容詞形成之片語之外,介詞片語、不定詞片語以及分詞片語亦可作為形容詞片語。

 句型 名詞 / 代名詞 + 形容詞片語

例句 Who is that boy with glasses?
　　　　　　　　　　　介詞片語作形容詞

戴著眼鏡的那名男孩是誰啊?

5 以形容詞子句修飾時

句型 名詞 / 代名詞 + 形容詞子句

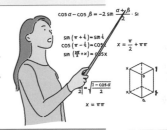

例句 I have an aunt who teaches math in high school.
　　　　　　　　　　　　形容詞子句

我有個阿姨在高中教數學。

❷ 敘述用法

 句型 **1** 主詞 + 連綴動詞 + 形容詞 (作主詞補語)

2 主詞 + 不完全及物動詞 + 受詞 + 形容詞 (作受詞補語)

 例字 大部分形容詞皆可用於限定用法與敘述用法。但有些形容詞較常用於敘述用法 (即做補語用,很少會置於名詞之前),如:

afraid (害怕的)	asleep (睡著的)	aware (知道的)
alike (相似的)	ashamed (羞愧的)	unable (不能的)
alive (活著的)	awake (醒的)	worth (值得的)
alone (單獨的)		

 例句 The alone boy looks unhappy. (×)
→ The lonely boy looks unhappy. (○)

這位孤單的男孩看起來很不開心。
(改用表「孤獨的」的 lonely 即可使用限定用法)

例句

→ The boy who looks unhappy is **alone**. (○)

看起來很不開心的男孩獨自一人。
（改為敘述用法，置於連綴動詞之後作主詞補語）

The bad weather made the situation **worse**.

糟糕的天氣使情況更糟了。

3 複合形容詞

複合形容詞的定義

 說明

複合形容詞是由兩個或兩個以上的單字合併的形容詞，通常是以連字符號 (-) 連接形成的。

複合形容詞的形成

1 與數字相關的複合形容詞

 例字

數字 + 名詞

a three-year plan（為期三年的計畫）

a two-story / two-storey apartment（兩層樓的公寓）

a one-hour meeting（耗時一個小時的會議）

數字 + 名詞 + 形容詞

a ten-year-old boy（十歲大的男孩）

2 名詞 / 形容詞 / 副詞 + 現在分詞

例字

名詞 + 現在分詞

record-breaking temperatures（打破紀錄的高溫 / 低溫）

a nail-biting game（令人緊張的比賽）

形容詞 + 現在分詞

a long-lasting friendship（持久的友誼） →

副詞 + 現在分詞

a never-ending task（沒完沒了的工作）

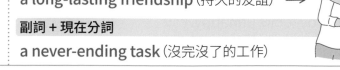

160

例字 **名詞 + 過去分詞**

a man-made lake (人造湖)

sun-dried tomatoes (曬乾的番茄)

形容詞 + 過去分詞

deep-fried chicken (炸雞)

an absent-minded student (心不在焉的學生)

old-fashioned clothes (過時的衣服)

副詞 + 過去分詞

an urgently needed fund (急需的資金)

a densely populated area (人口密集的區域)

(★ 以 -ly 結尾的副詞修飾其後的形容詞時，此副詞和形容詞之間通常不
加上連字符號 (-)。)

形容詞 + 名詞形成的過去分詞

a kind-hearted woman (好心的女子)

open-minded parents (心胸開闊的父母)

a warm-blooded animal (恆溫動物)

well / ill + 過去分詞

a well-known singer (著名的歌手)

an ill-tempered child (脾氣差的小孩)

4 其他形成組合

例字 **名詞 + 形容詞**

a world-famous celebrity (世界聞名的名人)

a duty-free shop (免稅店)

a smoke-free environment (禁菸的環境)

形容詞 + 名詞

a short-term goal (短期的目標)

a long-distance phone call (長途電話)

a high-pressure job (高壓的工作)

一、句子重組

① new / Lisa's / dress
I like _____ _____ _____.

② businessman / The / rich

_____ _____ _____
just bought another house.

③ wrong / something
There is _____ _____ with my cell
phone.

④ imaginable / the / vacation / best (★強調 imaginable)
We had _____ _____ _____
_____ in Hawaii.

⑤ asleep / girl / The / little / is

_____.

二、單選題

① This product's design is very _____. I believe it will
attract many customers.
(A) catching-eye　　　　(B) eye-catching
(C) caught-eye　　　　(D) eye-caught

② The writer made some _____ changes to his article
moments before it was published.
(A) lastly-minute　　　　(B) minute-lastly
(C) last-minute　　　　(D) minute-last

③ Ben is such a _____ child. He always does what he is
told.
(A) well-behaved　　　　(B) well-behaving
(C) well-behave　　　　(D) well-behavior

④ This is a _____ street. Vehicles can only drive in a single direction.
(A) ways-one (B) way-one
(C) one-ways (D) one-way

⑤ Jim and Ann are a _____ couple who just had their first grandchild.
(A) middle-aged (B) middle-aging
(C) middle-age (D) middle-ages

解　答

一、① Lisa's new dress
② The rich businessman
③ something wrong
④ the best vacation imaginable
⑤ The little girl is asleep

二、① B　理由 eye-catching [ˈaɪ ˌkætʃɪŋ] *a.* 引人注目的
② C　理由 last-minute [ˌlæst ˈmɪnɪt] *a.* 最後一刻的
③ A　理由 well-behaved [ˌwɛl bɪˈhevd] *a.* 行為端正的，規規矩矩的
④ D　理由 one-way [ˌwʌn ˈwe] *a.* 單行的，單程的
⑤ A　理由 middle-aged [ˌmɪdl̩ ˈedʒd] *a.* 中年的

7-2　副詞

副詞是用來修飾動詞、形容詞、其他副詞或全句的詞類。一般而言，副詞可分為三種：**一般副詞**、**疑問副詞**（如 when、where、why、how）以及**關係副詞**（如 when、where、why）。本節將針對一般副詞進行介紹。

① 一般副詞的種類

1 狀態副詞

| 說明 | 狀態副詞又稱情態副詞或情狀副詞，是用來說明某動作發生的情形或狀態。（狀態副詞可以放在動詞前或後，亦或句子前或後。） |

| 例字 | angrily（生氣地）　comfortably（舒適地）　quickly（很快地）
carefully（小心地）　politely（禮貌地）　suddenly（突然地） |

| 例句 | Ken suddenly cried.
= Ken cried suddenly.
= Suddenly, Ken cried.
肯突然哭了。

Please read the contract carefully before you sign it.
= Please carefully read the contract before you sign it.
簽合約之前請詳細閱讀。 |

2 時間副詞

| 說明 | 時間副詞是用來表示某動作發生的時間點或持續的時間長度。 |

| 例字 | now（現在）　early（早）　recently（近期）
today（今天）　then（那時）　soon（不久） |

| 例句 | Kate is meeting a client today.　凱特今天要跟客戶見面。
The singer recently released a new song.
這名歌手近期發布了新歌。
See you soon!　再見！/ 待會兒見！ |

3 頻率副詞

 說明　頻率副詞是用來表示某動作或情形發生的頻率。

 例字

100% always（總是）	90% usually（通常）	75% frequently（頻繁地）
63% often（經常）	50% sometimes（有時）	38% occasionally（偶爾）
10% rarely / seldom（很少）	5% hardly ever（幾乎沒有）	0% never（從不）

 例句

I've **always** wanted to travel to Europe.
我一直都很想去歐洲旅遊。

Mary is **sometimes** late for school.
瑪莉有時候會上學遲到。

Holly has **never** cheated on a test before.
荷莉從來沒有考試作弊過。

4 地方副詞

 說明　地方副詞是用來表示位置或方位的副詞，通常指動作發生之處或發展之方向。

 例字

here（這裡） 　　　there（那裡）

CH
7

7-2

副詞

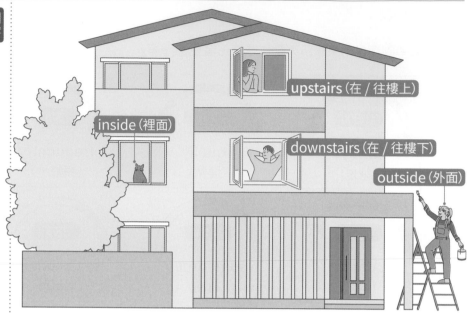

upstairs（在／往樓上）

inside（裡面）

downstairs（在／往樓下）

outside（外面）

例句

Let's sit here. 我們坐這裡吧。

There are children playing outside. 外面有小孩在玩。

Henry came downstairs to make breakfast in the kitchen.
亨利下樓到廚房做早餐。

5 程度副詞

說明

程度副詞是用來表示某件事或某情形的程度。

例字

almost（差點，幾乎）	too（太）	quite（很；頗）
completely（完全地）	really（實在，的確）	very（很）

例句

I'm almost done with my homework. 我快要寫完功課了。

The food in this restaurant is quite good.
這間餐廳的食物蠻好吃的。

It will be very cold tomorrow. 明天會非常冷。

6 評論性副詞與觀點副詞

說明

評論性副詞是用來表示說話者的想法、意見或態度等，而觀點副詞則是用來表達觀點或討論的面向。許多評論性副詞也可作觀點副詞，會視句子的脈絡而定。

例字 | apparently（據／聽說；看來）　normally（正常地）
fortunately（幸運地）　obviously（顯然地）
hopefully（但願）　personally（就個人而言）

例句 | Apparently, the party this weekend is canceled because of the typhoon.　據說這週末的派對因為颱風而取消了。

Fortunately, no one was hurt in the accident.
很幸運地，沒有人在意外中受傷。

Personally, I don't think that's a good idea.
我個人認為這不是好主意。

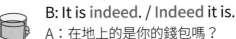

7 肯定／否定副詞

說明 | 此類副詞為用來表示肯定或否定。

例字 | yes（是）　exactly（確實）　of course（當然）
certainly（當然）　no（不）　indeed（的確）

例句 | A: May I have a glass of water?
B: Certainly.
A：我可以要一杯水嗎？
B：當然。

A: Is this your wallet on the floor?
B: It is indeed. / Indeed it is.
A：在地上的是你的錢包嗎？
B：是的。

8 焦點副詞

說明 | 焦點副詞為用來強調句子的某個部分。

例字 | only（僅，只）　especially（尤其）
even（甚至）　particularly（尤其）

例句 | This math question is so easy. Even my niece knows the answer.
這道數學題太簡單了。連我姪女都知道答案。

❷ 形容詞如何形成副詞

規則的變化

1 一般形容詞

說明 | 字尾加 ly 即可形成副詞。

例字	loud ▸ loudly (大聲地)　　clear ▸ clearly (清楚地) quick ▸ quickly (快地)　　fortunate ▸ fortunately (幸運地) usual ▸ usually (通常)　　sudden ▸ suddenly (突然)

注意

有些形容詞本身字尾即為 ly，但它們並非副詞，而是形容詞，如：

friendly (友善的)　　lovely (快樂的；漂亮的)　　timely (適時的)

lively (生氣勃勃的)　　lonely (寂寞的)　　costly (昂貴的)

2 字尾為 le

說明	此時 le 改為 ly 即可形成副詞。

例字	simple ▸ simply (簡單地)　　possible ▸ possibly (可能地) comfortable ▸ comfortably (舒適地)

例外

whole ▸ wholly (完全地)

3 字尾為 ll

說明	此時 ll 改為 lly 即可形成副詞。

例字	full ▸ fully (全部地) dull ▸ dully (沉悶地)

4 字尾為子音 + y

說明	此時去 y 改為 ily 即可形成副詞。

例字	easy ▸ easily (容易地)　　angry ▸ angrily (生氣地) happy ▸ happily (快樂地)　　necessary ▸ necessarily (必要地) lucky ▸ luckily (幸運地)　　heavy ▸ heavily (沉重地)

5 字尾為 ue

說明	此時去 e 改為 uly 即可形成副詞。

例字	true ▸ truly (真正地)

6 字尾為 ic

 說明 此時 ic 後加 ally 即可形成副詞。

例字
basic ▸ basically（基本上）　　　tragic ▸ tragically（悲情地）
economic ▸ economically（在經濟上，就經濟而言）

例外

public ▸ publicly（公開地）

不規則的變化

 1 形容詞與副詞同形

例字
early（早的）▸ early（早）　　　long（長久的）▸ long（長久地）
hard（辛苦的）▸ hard（費勁地）　fast（快速的）▸ fast（快速地）
late（晚的）▸ late（晚）　　　　slow（慢的）▸ slow / slowly（慢地）
next（下一個的）▸ next（下次；然後）

 2 其他不規則變化

例字
good（好的）▸ well（很好地）

 3 副詞的功能

 1 修飾動詞

說明
修飾動詞時，副詞可置於句子的下列三個位置：

1 句首，即主詞之前。

2 句中，即主詞與動詞之間；若有助動詞，則須置該助動詞之後。

3 句尾，即動詞之後；若有受詞，則須置該受詞之後。

句型
　　↑ 主詞（＋助動詞）↑ ＋動詞（＋受詞）↑

1 副詞　　　　　**2** 副詞　　　　　**3** 副詞

 例句
Jenna finished her job quickly.
= Jenna quickly finished her job.
珍娜很快就完成工作。

例句
Sometimes I hear the old man talking to himself.
= I sometimes hear the old man talking to himself.
= I hear the old man sometimes talking to himself.
= I hear the old man talking to himself sometimes.
我有時候會聽到那名老人自言自語。

2 修飾形容詞或其他副詞

說明
修飾形容詞或其他副詞時，副詞通常置於該詞的前方。此類副詞通常為頻率副詞（如 often、never）或程度副詞（如 really、quite）。

句型
副詞 + 形容詞 / 副詞

例句
Walter is often sick.　華特很常生病。
Carmen sings quite well.　卡門唱歌蠻好聽的。

3 修飾全句

說明
修飾全句時，副詞通常置於句首，之後置逗點；有時也可置句中或句尾。此類副詞通常為時間副詞（如 now、today）或評論性副詞與觀點副詞（如 hopefully、unfortunately）。

例句
Today, our school is going on a field trip to the museum.
= Our school is going on a field trip to the museum today.
我們學校今天要去博物館校外教學。

Unfortunately, I can't go to work today because I caught the flu.
= I can't go to work today, unfortunately, because I caught the flu.
= I can't go to work today because I caught the flu, unfortunately.
不幸地，我今天沒辦法上班因為我得流感了。
（前兩句 unfortunately 置句首與句中較為強調「不幸沒辦法上班」之事，第三句中 unfortunately 置句尾較為強調「不幸得流感」之事）

4 修飾名詞或代名詞

說明
少數副詞可用於修飾名詞或代名詞。地方副詞（如 here、upstairs）與時間副詞（如 today、tonight）修飾名詞時可置名詞後方，而其他副詞如 only、even 等則通常置名詞前方。

例句
The bedroom upstairs is very pretty.　樓上的臥室很漂亮。
The party tonight will start at seven.　今晚的派對會在七點開始。

Only you can solve this problem.　只有你能解決這個問題。

一、單選題

① The protesters shouted _____ at the police.
(A) anger   (B) angry   (C) angrily   (D) angrier

② Since none of us had an umbrella, we all ran _____ when it started to rain.
(A) inside   (B) early   (C) later   (D) even

③ Please do not talk _____ in the library because you may distract others from reading or studying.
(A) closely   (B) loudly   (C) easily   (D) silently

④ Except for the beginning part, these two songs sound _____ exactly the same.
(A) enough   (B) never   (C) only   (D) almost

⑤ When the earthquake occurred, we were worried about the exhibition in the museum. _____, nothing was damaged.
(A) Honestly   (B) Sadly
(C) Luckily   (D) Unfortunately

二、請寫出下列形容詞形成的正確副詞。

形容詞	副詞
① sad	_____
② early	_____
③ probable	_____
④ steady	_____
⑤ automatic	_____

CH
7

7-2

副詞

解　答

一、① C   ② A   ③ B   ④ D   ⑤ C
二、① sadly   ② early   ③ probably   ④ steadily   ⑤ automatically

Chapter 7 形容詞 與 副詞

7-3 特殊副詞的用法

❶ very 與 much

❶ very 很，非常

說明

very 置一般形容詞或副詞前，用以強調。

> **注意**
>
> 有些本身已帶有強調意味的形容詞不宜與 very 搭配使用，而是應使用 really、totally、absolutely 等副詞修飾。此類常見的形容詞如下：
>
> amazing（驚人的）　　fantastic（極好的）　　terrible（糟糕的）
> awful（糟糕的）　　　horrible（可怕的）　　wonderful（美好的）
> excellent（極好的）　　perfect（完美的）

例句

It turned very cold today.　今天變得很冷。
Tony drives very fast.　湯尼開車開得很快。
The movie was very amazing. (×)
→ The movie was absolutely amazing. (○)
　這部電影令人非常驚豔。

❷ much 很，非常

說明

much 可修飾的內容如下：
❶ 動詞，此時 much 多改為 very much。
❷ 比較級的形容詞或副詞。
❸ 有 too（太）修飾的形容詞或副詞。
❹ 作形容詞用的過去分詞，此時 much 也可寫作 very much。

> **注意**
>
> 有些經常作形容詞的過去分詞，如 tired（疲倦的）、pleased（滿意的）、surprised（驚訝的）等等，亦可使用 very 來修飾，而與 (very) much 相比之下，very 較常被使用。

例句	Zoe likes the color purple very much.　柔伊非常喜歡紫色。

Tanya looks much younger than her age.
坦雅長得比她實際年齡還要年輕許多。

This couch is much too big to put in our living room.
這個沙發太大了，沒辦法放在我們的客廳。

The boss was much / very / very much pleased
with our presentation.
老闆對於我們的報告內容感到很滿意。

❷ little 與 a little

❶ little　（幅度）很少，幾乎沒有

說明 little 除了可作形容詞表示「小的」之外，亦可作副詞使用。作副詞時，
表示「（幅度）很少，幾乎沒有」。

例句 My hometown has changed little throughout the years.
多年過去，我的家鄉幾乎沒怎麼變。

❷ a little　一點，稍微

說明 a little 作副詞時，表示「一點，稍微」，也可寫作 a little bit。

例句 Taylor fell sick yesterday, but he is feeling a little (bit) better
today.
泰勒昨天生病了，但他今天好轉了些。

❸ already 與 yet

❶ already　已經

說明 already 通常用於肯定句中，且句子多採現在完成式、過去完成式或過
去簡單式。另外用於肯定句或疑問句時，也有表示對於某件事竟然已經
發生而感到驚訝之意。

例句 I've already had breakfast.　我已經吃過早餐了。

It's too late to call Kent. His plane took off already.
現在打電話給肯特太遲了。他的飛機已經起飛了。

Is it midnight already?　竟然已經午夜了？

2 yet 還 / 尚（未）

說明 yet 為表示強調的副詞，通常用於否定句或疑問句，且句子多採現在完成式或過去完成式。

例句 Roger has not found a job yet.
羅傑還沒找到工作。

4 ⬤ sometimes、sometime 與 some time

1 sometimes 有時候

說明 sometimes 為頻率副詞，表示「有時候」。
使用時，sometimes 可置句首、句中或句尾。

例句 　　Sometimes I go jogging in the gym.
= I sometimes go jogging in the gym.
= I go jogging in the gym sometimes.
有時候我會去健身房慢跑。

2 sometime 某時

說明 sometime 為副詞，表示「（未來或過去的）某時」，通常可與另一個表示明確或大略時間點的副詞或副詞片語並用。

例句 We should get together sometime.
我們應該找個時間聚一聚。

Nicole plans to take a vacation sometime in July.
妮可計劃七月某個時候去度假。

Vincent quit his job sometime last year.
文森去年某個時候辭職了。

3 some time 一段時間

說明 some time 為名詞片語，可搭配 for 使用，表示「持續一段時間」。

例句 It will take some time for Sarah to prepare the meal.
莎拉備餐需要花一點時間。

Josh had waited for some time before his friends arrived.
喬許等了一陣子他的朋友才抵達。

⑤ someday、one day、the other day 以及 some other day

① someday 將來有一天，有朝一日

說明 someday 為副詞，表「未來不確定的某一天」。

例句 Gordon hopes to start his own business someday.
戈登希望有朝一日可以自己創業。

② one day 某日

說明 one day 為副詞片語，可用於表示「過去的某日」或「將來的某一天」。表前者時，意近於 the other day；表後者時，意近於 someday。

例句 One day, Jake moved out of his house after having a terrible argument with his parents.
傑克某天跟他爸媽大吵一架後就搬出去了。

I'd love to travel to Europe one day. 有朝一日我想去歐洲旅遊。

③ the other day 前幾天

說明 the other day 為副詞片語，表「過去幾天前」。the other 亦可搭配其他時間使用，如 the other morning (前幾天早上)、the other week (前幾週) 等。

例句 I bumped into Eve the other day.
我前幾天巧遇伊芙。

④ some other day 改天

說明 some other day 可作副詞片語，表「改天」，指未來的某一天。

例句 I'm sorry. Ms. Lee can't meet you today due to an emergency. Could you come back some other day?
很抱歉。由於突發狀況，李小姐今天無法與您會面。您可否改天再來呢？

⑥ ago 與 before

① ago 以前

說明 ago 表從「現在」的時間點為準，往過去算若干時間的「以前」。ago 須置表示一段時間的名詞 (片語) 之後，且句子須採過去簡單式。

| 例句 | Ted started his new job two weeks ago. 泰德兩週前開始新的工作。 |

過去　　　　　　　　　　　現在

two weeks

2 before　以前

| 說明 | before 作副詞時，有下列兩種用法：
1 可置表示一段時間的名詞 (片語) 之後，但此時通常是表示從「過去」的某個時間點為準，往過去算若干時間的「以前」，且句子通常採過去完成式。
2 before 亦可單獨使用作副詞，泛指「以前，過去」，可與過去簡單式、現在完成式或過去完成式並用。 |

| 例句 | Wayne left for the US last Saturday. He (had) planned his trip only a few days before.
韋恩上週六出發去美國了。他出發的幾天前才規劃行程。 |

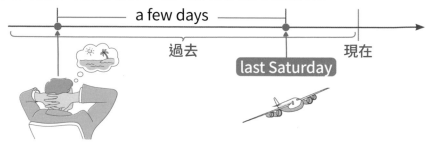

a few days

過去　　　　　　　　　　　現在

last Saturday

I think I have heard this song before.　我以前好像聽過這首歌。

7 enough

enough 的用法

| 說明 | enough 可作形容詞，表「充分的」，置於名詞前；enough 亦可作副詞，表「充分地，很」，使用時應置動詞、形容詞或副詞之後。 |

| 例句 | **作形容詞**

We don't have enough time to do all these things.
我們時間不夠，無法做全部的事。 |

176

作副詞

Make sure you <u>drink</u> enough while hiking.
健行時你務必要喝足夠量的水。

Gina's room is not <u>big</u> enough for her.　吉娜的房間對她來說不夠大。

Kyle has been working in the bank <u>long</u> enough to know the ins and outs of finance.　凱爾在銀行工作夠久，已充分理解理財的大小事。

＼ 即時演練 ／

請圈選出正確的副詞。

① The little boy is (much / very) too short to go on the rollercoaster.

② Nancy ran as fast as she could, but the bus had (yet / already) left when she reached the bus stop.

③ Mark is not in his office right now. He just left an hour (ago / before).

④ According to the police, the thief broke into the house (sometime / some time) during the night.

⑤ The couple wishes to buy a house of their own (the other day / someday).

⑥ The poor family's situation has improved very (little / a little) throughout the years; they still have trouble making ends meet.

⑦ Pam bought a new novel last week, but she has not started reading it (already / yet).

⑧ Emily's friend introduced her to Henry last night, but Emily felt like she had seen him (ago / before).

⑨ Unfortunately, May's grades are not good (already / enough) to enter the country's top university.

⑩ Support and encouragement from parents are (very / much) important to children.

解　答				
① much	② already	③ ago	④ sometime	⑤ someday
⑥ little	⑦ yet	⑧ before	⑨ enough	⑩ very

Notes

178

Chapter 8

介詞

Chapter 8 介詞

8-1 有關時間的介詞

介詞又稱前置詞，其後接受詞，以表示此受詞與句中其他字之間的**時間**、**地方**、或因果等關係。介詞片語則為「介詞 + 受詞」，可作形容詞、副詞或名詞用。

以下先介紹有關時間的介詞：

① 有關時間的常見介詞

at	on	in
一特定時間點 / 短暫的時間	某一日子 / 日期等	較長的時間

❶ at + { 一特定時間點 / 短暫的時間 } 在……

說明	常用於時刻、正午 / 半夜、早 / 午 / 晚餐、年齡、日出 / 落等。

例句	at nine（在九點） at 3:20（在三點二十分） at noon / midnight（在中午 / 半夜）	at breakfast / lunch / dinner（在早 / 午 / 晚餐時） at the age of eight（八歲時） at sunrise / dawn（日出時） at sunset / dusk（日落時）

註	at night（在晚上）為例外，雖然 night 為較長的時間，但其介詞須用 at。

例句	Roger enjoys listening to music **at night**. 羅傑晚上喜歡聽音樂。

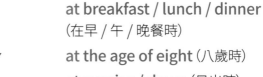

2 **on + 某一日子 / 日期   在……**

 說明　常用於星期幾、節日、某月某日、某日的早上 / 下午 / 晚上等。

 例句

on Friday（在週五）
on Christmas
（在聖誕節）
on September 10th
（在九月十日）
on Wednesday afternoon
（在週三下午）

on the morning of the
meeting / March 20th, 2010
（在會議當天上午 / 在 2010 年三月
二十日的早上）

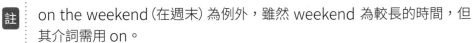 註　on the weekend（在週末）為例外，雖然 weekend 為較長的時間，但其介詞需用 on。

 例句

Stan likes to watch television on the weekend.
史坦週末時喜歡看電視。

3 **in + 較長的時間   在……期間**

 說明　常用於月分、季節、年分、世紀、上下午及傍晚、年齡等。

 例句

in November（在十一月）
in summer（在夏天）
in 2023（在 2023 年）
in the 21st century
（在二十一世紀）

in the morning / afternoon /
evening（在早上 / 下午 / 晚上）
in his twenties / forties
（在他二十幾歲 / 四十幾歲時）

 註

in 其他常見的用法為：

in + 一段時間　　在……時間之內（= within + 一段時間）；在……時間之後

★ 當 in 表後者之意時，時態常用未來式。

 例句

We can finish this project in / within two months.
我們可以在兩個月內完成此專案。

Honey, I'll call you back in ten minutes.
親愛的，我十分鐘後回電話給你。

2 其他有關時間的介詞

---

1 within + 一段時間　　在……時間內 (= in)

例句　The store said it could deliver pizza to anywhere in this city **within** 40 minutes.

= The store said it could deliver pizza to anywhere in this city **in** 40 minutes.
這家店說其可在四十分鐘內將披薩送到此城市任一處。

---

2 after + 時間點 / 一段時間　　在……之後

例句　**After** nearly one year at sea, the sailor finally came back home.
這船員在海上待了快一年後,終於回到了家。

---

3 before + 時間點 / 一段時間　　在……之前

例句　Lucy had jet lag, so she went to bed **before** noon.
露西有時差,所以她中午前就去睡覺了。

---

4 by + 時間點　　到……之前,不遲於……

註　by 和 before 意思相近,但其實有所不同:
by + 時間點　　★ 有包含該時間點
before + 時間點　　★ 沒有包含該時間點

例句　We should hand in the report **by** Friday.
我們應該在週五前交報告。
★ 報告最遲可週五交。

We should hand in the report **before** Friday.
我們應該在週五前交報告。
★ 報告最遲僅可週四交,週五交算遲交。

---

5 from... to...　　從……(時間) 到……(時間)

例句　Ben usually works **from** 9 a.m. **to** 7 p.m.
班通常從早上九點工作到晚上七點。

---

6 until / till + 時間點　　直到……

例句　My brother stayed up **until** 1:30.
我弟弟熬夜到一點半。

7 since + 時間點　自……以後

 常搭配完成式或完成進行式。

 Cindy and Tom haven't seen each other since last year.
辛蒂和湯姆從去年起就沒見過面了。

8 for + 一段時間　達 / 計……

 常搭配完成式或完成進行式。

 Nora has been studying English for three years.
諾拉已學英文三年了。

9 over / during + 一段時間　在……期間

 Marge decided to spend some time learning Spanish over / during the summer vacation.
瑪芝決定暑假時花些時間學西班牙語。

 以下相關用法常搭配現在完成式：
over the past / last + 一段時間

 Over the past / last few days, I've heard my neighbors fighting more often.
在過去的幾天裡，我經常聽到鄰居在吵架。

10 through / throughout + 一段時間　從頭至尾，整個……

 All through / throughout his life, Ralph devoted his attention to protecting the ocean.
雷夫終其一生都在致力於保護海洋。

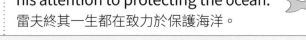

11 between... and...　在……（時間）和……（時間）之間

 We'd better leave between 4 and 5 o'clock.
我們最好在四點到五點之間離開。

12 about / around + 時間點 / 一段時間　大約……

 I went to bed at about 11 p.m. yesterday.
我昨天大約十一點上床睡覺。

13 toward(s) + 時間點　　接近……時間點

例句 It was **toward** the afternoon when the child finally felt tired and fell asleep.　接近下午時，那孩子終於覺得累就睡著了。

＼ 即時演練 ／

一、請在下列空格中填入 at、on 或 in。

① The manager arrived in New York ＿＿＿＿＿＿＿＿＿ Friday.
② Lauren usually gets up ＿＿＿＿＿＿＿＿＿ seven.
③ My grandmother likes to read some books ＿＿＿＿＿＿＿＿＿ the afternoon.
④ The fundraising event will be held ＿＿＿＿＿＿＿＿＿ November 5th.
⑤ The parade will start ＿＿＿＿＿＿＿＿＿ noon this Sunday.

二、單選題

① ＿＿＿＿＿＿＿＿＿ 2016, Kelly was the sales manager in this company. Now she is a baker, which is her dream job.
(A) At　　　　(B) On　　　　(C) Until　　　(D) About

② Ryan was so tired that he kept nodding off ＿＿＿＿＿＿＿＿＿ the performance. That's why he didn't know what it was about.
(A) on　　　　(B) during　　　(C) after　　　(D) under

③ The bank is open ＿＿＿＿＿＿＿＿＿ Monday to Friday.
(A) from　　　(B) in　　　　(C) between　　(D) over

④ Louis seldom answers his phone ＿＿＿＿＿＿＿＿＿ 10 p.m. because he usually goes to bed early.
(A) before　　(B) after　　　(C) for　　　　(D) in

⑤ Roy has lived in this village ＿＿＿＿＿＿＿＿＿ 30 years.
(A) since　　　(B) by　　　　(C) till　　　　(D) for

解　答

一、	① on	② at	③ in	④ on	⑤ at
二、	① C	② B	③ A	④ B	⑤ D

Chapter 8　介詞

介詞除了可以用以表示與時間相關的意思之外，也可用來表示位置或方向等。
此類有關地方的介詞如下：

❶ 有關地方的常見介詞

at	on	in
在某定點或 某建築物附近	在某平／表面上	在某個空間裡或 較大的地方

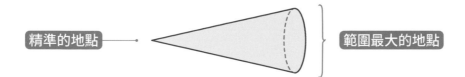

精準的地點 ──── 範圍最大的地點

❶ at + { 某定點
某建築物附近 }　在……地方

說明	**常用於** ❶ 住址、公車站、特定活動地點　　❷ 得到服務或治療的店
例句	**at** 27 Union St., San Francisco, California （位於加州舊金山聯合街二十七號） **at** the bus stop（在公車站） **at** the wedding / concert（在婚禮／音樂會上） **at** a hairdresser's / dentist / dentist's（在髮廊／牙醫診所）

185

| 註 | sit **at** a desk（坐在書桌前），介詞須用 at，而非用 in front of（在……之前）。 |

| 例句 | You should stretch after **sitting at the desk** all day.
坐在桌前一整天後，你該伸展一下身體。 |

2 on + 某平 / 表面上　　在……上面

| 說明 | **常用於**
1 桌 / 牆 / 樓層等平面上　　**3** 河 / 海 / 湖岸上
2 島上　　**4** 交通工具（乘客可在其中站立）等 |

| 例句 | on **a table / a wall / the third floor**（在桌上 / 牆上 / 三樓）
on **an island**（在島上）
on **the east coast of the country**（在該國東海岸）
on **a bus / train / plane**（在公車 / 火車 / 飛機上） |

| 註 | on **a ceiling**（在天花板上），介詞須用 on，而非用 under 等其他介詞。 |

| 例句 | One of the fans **on the ceiling** doesn't work properly.
天花板上的一個風扇壞了。 |

3 in + { 在某個空間裡 / 較大的地方 }　　在……裡面

| 說明 | **常用於**
1 建築物內、海洋、世界　　**3** 交通工具（尤指乘客不可站立，僅能坐著的交通工具，如小汽車、戰鬥機等）
2 地區 / 城市 / 州 / 國家 / 大洲 |

| 例句 | in **the living room**（在客廳）
in **the ocean / world**（在海洋中 / 在世界上）
in **Paris**（在巴黎）
in **Arizona**（在亞利桑那州）
in **Germany**（在德國）
in **a car / taxi**（在車上 / 在計程車上） |

| 註 | on **a farm**（在農場），介詞須用 on，而非用 in。 |

| 例句 | Roger worked **on a farm** during the summer vacation.
羅傑暑假在農場工作。 |

 說明

at + 商店 / 公共場所等
★ 視為會面處或一定點。

in + 商店 / 公共場所等
★ 強調在此場域裡面。

 例句

I'll meet you **at the airport** at 10 a.m.
早上十點在機場見。
★ 說話者視機場為一會面處或一定點。

In the early morning, only a few passengers could be seen **in the airport**.
一大早，機場只見幾名旅客。
★ 強調在機場裡面所看到的情形。

---

❷ 其他有關地方的介詞

❶ before 在……前面 = in front of	❷ behind 在……後面 = in back of（美式） = at the back of（英式）
圖示 	
例句 We stood before the palace and took photos. 我們站在宮殿前拍照。	There is a yard behind Judy's house. 茱蒂家後面有個院子。

❸ over 在……的上方 / 空	❹ under 在……下方
圖示 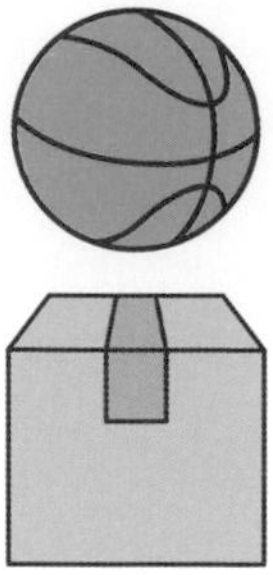 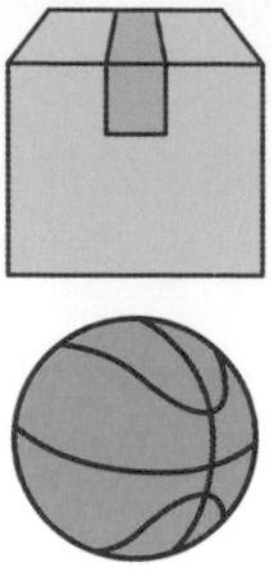	
註 ❶ 近義於 above。 ❷ 不碰到接觸面（在此如箱子）。	近義於 below。
例句 There is a clock over the whiteboard. 白板上方有個時鐘。	The baseball is under the car; I couldn't reach it. 棒球在車底下；我拿不到。

❺ above 在……上方	❻ below 在……下方
圖示 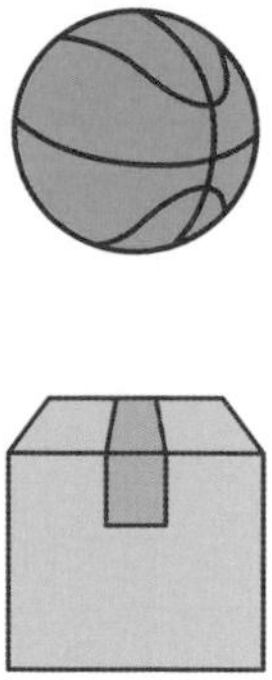 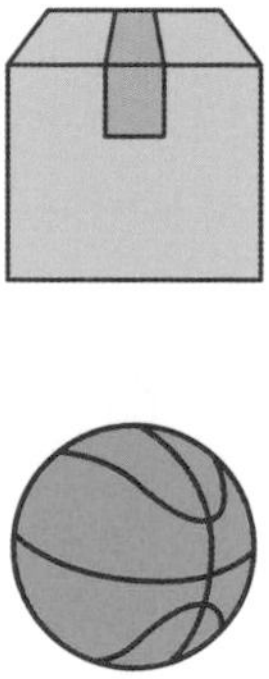	
註 ❶ 近義於 over。 ❷ 兩物相距較遠時用 above，而非 over。	❶ 近義於 under。 ❷ 兩物相距較遠時用 below，而非 under。
例句 I'd like to hang a painting above the sofa. 我想在沙發上掛幅畫。	My sister prefers wearing skirts below the knee. 我姊比較喜歡穿長度過膝的裙子。

7 beneath 在……下方	8 by 在……旁邊;接近
圖示	圖示 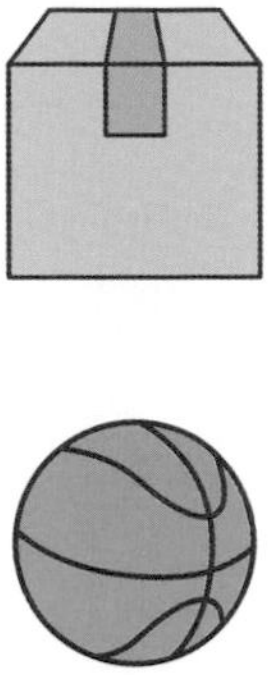 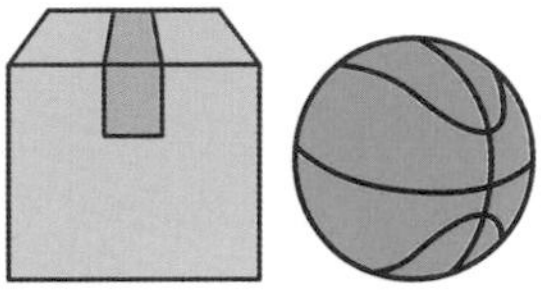
註 較常見於正式寫作。（口語較常用 under / below）。	by 表「在……旁邊」時，其義同 beside、alongside 以及 next to。
例句 My family like to chat in the yard **beneath** the stars. 我家人喜歡在夜晚的星空下在院子裡聊天。	例句 My brother was playing with his toys **by** the TV. 我弟弟在電視機旁玩玩具。

9 between... and... 在……和……之間	10 among / amid 在……其中
圖示	圖示 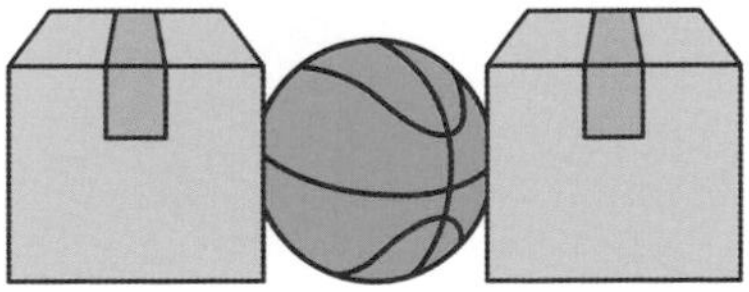 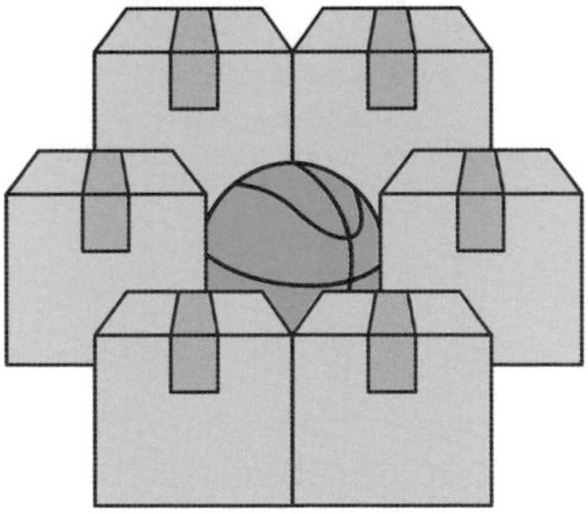
註 常用於兩者。	常用於三者以上。
例句 Ross stood **between** his grandfather **and** mother. 羅斯站在他的爺爺和母親之間。	例句 The new teacher is sitting **among** the kids. 新老師坐在孩子們之間。

CH 8

8-2

有關地方的介詞

189

⑪ around 圍繞	**⑫ across** 橫跨
圖示 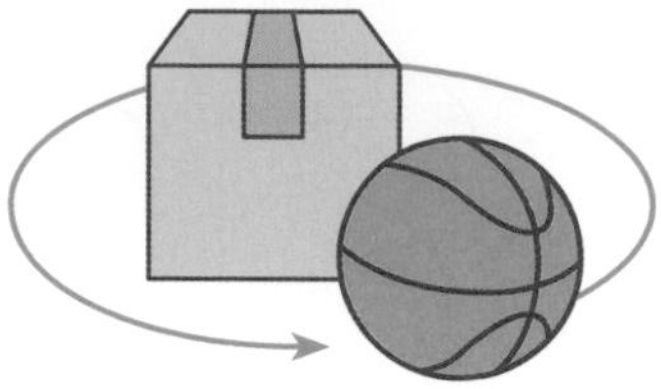 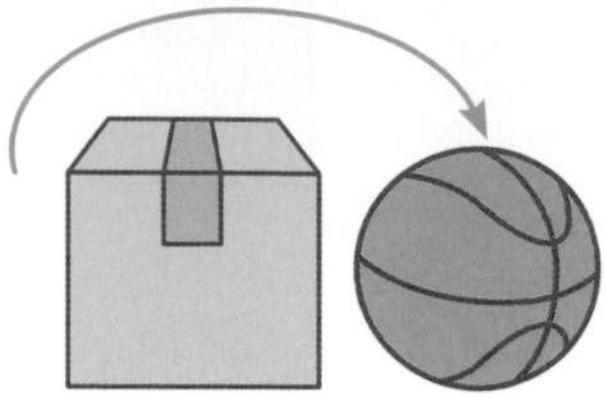	

We all sat around the dinner table and enjoyed a hearty Thanksgiving dinner. 我們全圍著餐桌坐，享受了一頓感恩節大餐。	Mike walked across the street to buy a coffee. 麥克過馬路去買杯咖啡。
例句	

⑬ up 往上	**⑭ down** 往下
圖示 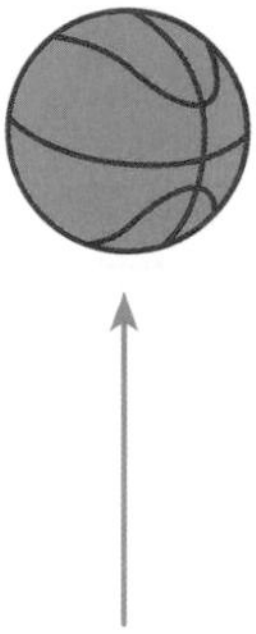 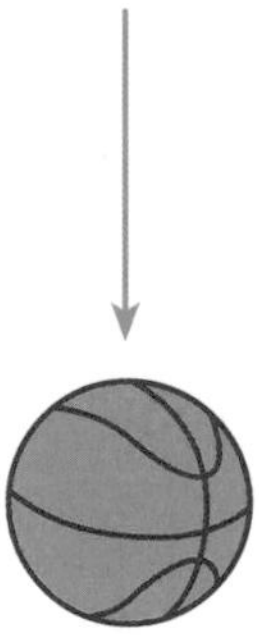	

Sean climbed up the tree to see the bird's nest. 尚恩爬上樹去看鳥巢。	Mandy ran down the stairs to answer the door. 曼蒂跑下樓去開門。
例句	

15 along 沿著	16 to / toward(s) 向／朝
圖示 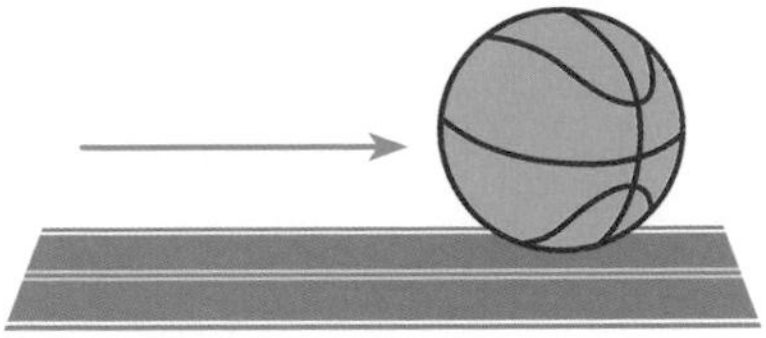 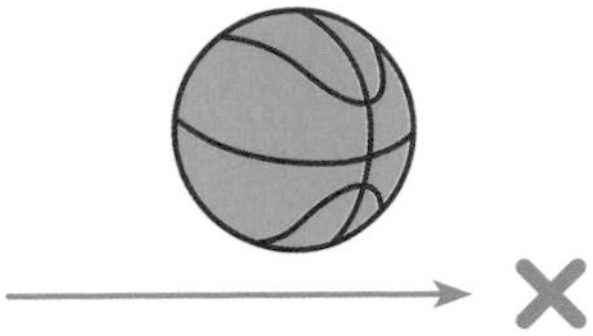	
例句 Stan walked along the river. 史坦沿著河邊走。	We were heading to / toward(s) my uncle's house. 我們正前往我舅舅家。

17 from... to... 從……到……	18 opposite 在……的對面
圖示 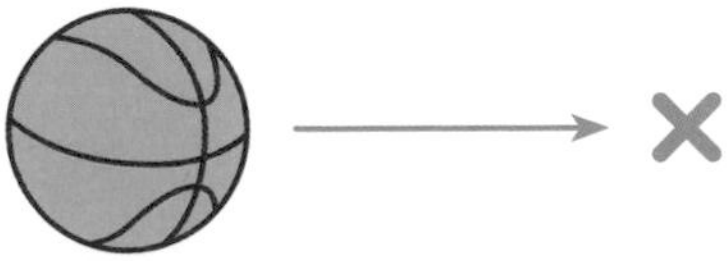 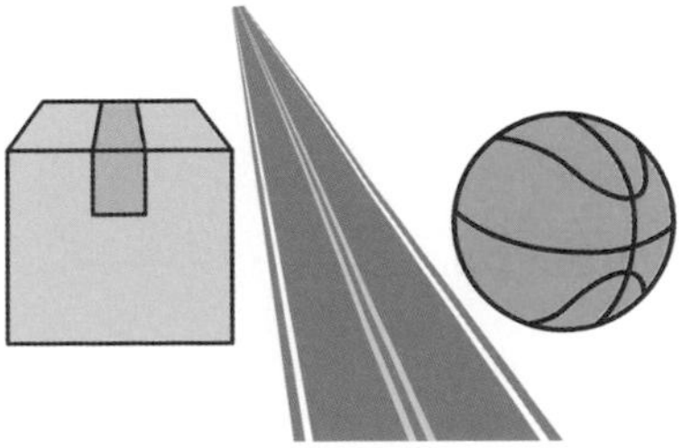	
例句 It's a 5-minute walk from my home to my school. 從我家到學校走路五分鐘。	Taylor's house is opposite a school. 泰勒家在一間學校的對面。

	⑲ into 進入……	**⑳ onto** 到……之上
圖示	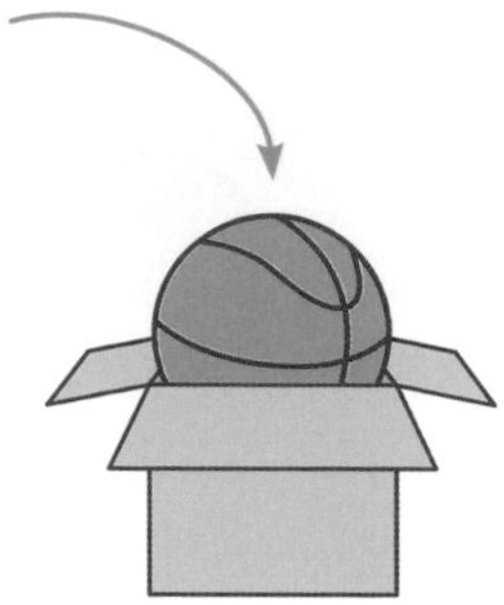	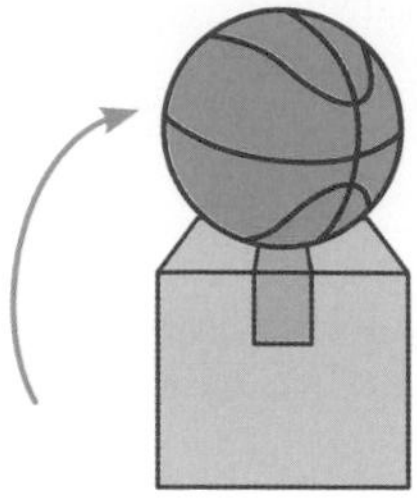
例句	The secretary came into the meeting room with snacks. 祕書拿著點心走進了會議室。	Nora walked onto the stage and started to dance. 諾拉走上舞臺便開始跳起舞來。
	㉑ inside 在……裡面	**㉒ outside** 在……外面
圖示	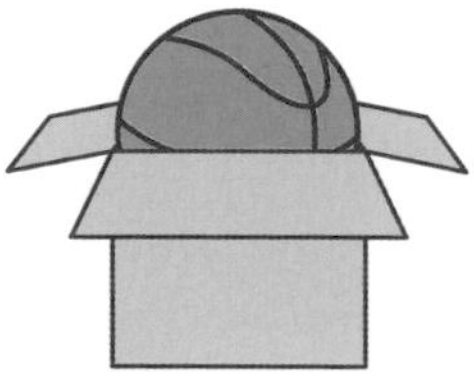	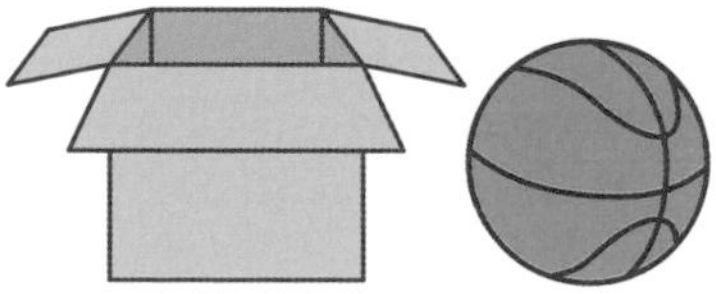
例句	There is a lot of money inside the safe. 保險箱裡有很多錢。	I'll meet Vince outside the department store. 我會在百貨公司外頭和文斯碰面。

23 through 穿 / 通過	24 against 緊靠
圖示	
例句 The boy wormed **through** the crowd to the stage. 那小男孩擠過人群，到了舞臺前。	Will was tired and leaned **against** the electricity pole. 威爾很累，就靠在電線桿上。
25 past 經過	26 beyond 在……另一邊的遠處
圖示	
例句 The library is around the corner, just **past** the bank. 圖書館就在附近，經過銀行就到了。	I could see a vast field of sunflowers **beyond** the hill. 我可以看到山丘遠處有一大片向日葵。

\ 即時演練 /

一、請在下列空格中填入 at、on 或 in。

① Honey, I'm _____ the dentist's; I won't be home until noon.

② The coffee shop is _____ the fifth floor.

有關地方的介詞

③ We have to reduce plastic waste _____ the ocean.

④ My brother lives _____ 76 Water Street, Brooklyn, New York City.

⑤ Conductor, a man just passed out _____ the train.

二、單選題

① Don't use your cell phone when you walk _____ a street. That's really dangerous since there are so many cars.
(A) after   (B) against   (C) between   (D) across

② Kyle came _____ the dining room and started to set the table.
(A) into   (B) outside   (C) beyond   (D) onto

③ Look at this picture: My father is sitting _____ Uncle Joe and Auntie Lauren. They were so young then.
(A) among   (B) through   (C) toward   (D) between

④ Just go _____ this street and turn right at the second crossroads. Then you can see the train station on your left.
(A) against   (B) between   (C) along   (D) before

⑤ The cat was so afraid of the big dog that it hid _____ the car.
(A) among   (B) under   (C) past   (D) across

⑥ How long will it take to drive _____ London to Dover?
(A) from   (B) beneath   (C) above   (D) opposite

⑦ Since the elevator was out of order, I had no choice but to walk _____ the stairs to the 6th floor.
(A) against   (B) below   (C) up   (D) behind

解 答				
一、① at	② on	③ in	④ at	⑤ on
二、① D	② A	③ D	④ C	⑤ B
⑥ A	⑦ C			

Chapter 8 介詞

8-3 與因果相關的介詞

此類介詞包括有關 原因 、 結果 及 目的 的介詞，茲分述如下：

1 有關「原因」的介詞

1 for

 說明　常出現於下列片語

1 be famous / noted for...　以……而著稱

2 be remembered for...　因……為大家所熟知

3 apologize for...　因……而道歉

4 punish sb for + N/V-ing　因……處罰某人

 例句　This bakery **is famous / noted for** its strawberry pies.
這家麵包店的草莓派很有名。

Nathan **is** best **remembered for** his generosity.
納森因他的慷慨大方而被人們銘記在心。

We **apologize for** the delay in the delivery of the products.
因延遲寄送產品，我們深表歉意。

Daddy **punished** Oscar **for** talking back.
因奧斯卡頂嘴，爸爸就懲罰了他。

2 out of

 說明　常出現於下列片語

1 out of respect　出於尊重

2 out of pity　出於同情 / 憐憫

3 out of interest　因感興趣 / 感到好奇

4 out of curiosity　出於好奇

 例句　**Out of respect**, Randy took off his hat and bowed to the statue.
出於尊重，藍迪脫帽向雕像鞠躬。

CH
8

8-3

與因果相關的介詞

195

例句 **Out of pity**, my mother cooked food for some of the flood victims.
出於同情，我媽媽做飯給一些洪水的災民吃。

Out of interest, I asked Ned why he wanted to learn Spanish.
因感到好奇，我問奈德為何要學西班牙文。

Out of curiosity, I asked Owen how he could make so much money.
出於好奇，我問歐文他怎麼能賺那麼多錢。

③ in

說明 其後常加動名詞。

例句 **In** trying to make his girlfriend happy, Rick spent lots of money buying gifts for her.　瑞克為了讓女友開心，花了很多錢買禮物給她。

④ from

說明 **常出現於下列片語**

❶ suffer from...　罹患……（疾病）

❷ tell + that 子句 + from sth　因某事物知道……
= **tell from sth + that 子句**

❸ be weak from hunger　因飢餓而變得虛弱
= **be weak with hunger**

❹ conclude from sth + that 子句　因某事物而做出……的結論

例句 Leo has been **suffering from** depression since his son passed away.　自從李歐的兒子過世後，他便飽受憂鬱症的折磨。

I could **tell that** the man was from the UK **from** his accent.
= I could **tell from** the man's accent **that** he was from the UK.
我可以從這男子的口音知道他是英國人。

The refugees **were weak from hunger**.
這些難民因飢餓而變得很虛弱。

Luke **concluded from** the articles **that** healthy diets can help prevent many diseases.
路克從這些文章得出結論：健康的飲食有助於預防很多疾病。

5 of

 常出現於下列片語

1 die of... 死於（事故或疾病等）
= die from...

2 be proud of... 因……而感到自豪／驕傲

3 be fond of... 很喜歡……

4 as a result of... 因為……

 The poor woman **died of / from** breast cancer.
這可憐的女子死於乳癌。

I'm **proud of** my dad because he takes good care of our family.
因為我爸很照顧家人，我以他為榮。

Iris **is** very **fond of** cheesecake. 艾麗絲真的很喜歡起司蛋糕。

More than three people died **as a result of** the car accident.
此車禍造成三人以上死亡。

6 with

 常出現於下列片語

1 be sick with the flu 得了流感

2 shake with anger / rage 氣得發抖 →
= tremble with anger / rage

3 shiver with cold 冷得發抖

4 weep with joy / relief 喜極而泣／如釋重負激動落下淚水

 Poor Katrina—she's **sick with the flu** and can't cook for herself.
可憐的卡翠娜，她得了流感沒辦法自己煮飯來吃。

Robbie was **shaking with anger** after learning that his daughter had run away with his employee Ken.
羅比得知他女兒和他的員工肯私奔後，氣得全身發抖。

Lena was **shivering with cold**; she didn't know the summer temperatures on this mountain could be so low.
莉娜冷得瑟瑟發抖；她不知道夏天這山上的溫度會這麼低。

After hearing her son was safe and sound, the mother **wept with relief**. 得知兒子平安無事後，那位母親如釋重負，激動落下淚水。

CH 8

8-3

與因果相關的介詞

197

❷ 有關「結果」的介詞

to

說明 **常出現於下列片語**

❶ tear... to pieces　把……撕成碎片

❷ break... to bits　把……打成碎片

❸ increase / raise A to B　將 A 增加到 B

❹ be sentenced to death　被判死刑

例句 When he read the false report, the actor was so angry that he tore the newspaper to pieces.
這個演員看到這篇假新聞時，氣得把報紙撕碎。

Eugene broke the vase to bits in a fit of anger.
尤金一怒之下把花瓶打破了。

The company's new manager increased / raised Jacob's monthly salary to NT$80,000.
公司的新經理將雅各的月薪提高到新臺幣八萬元。

The killer was sentenced to death.　那凶手被判死刑。

into

說明 **常出現於下列片語**

❶ turn / change / transform A into B　把 A 變成 B

❷ grow into...　成長 / 發展為……

❸ translate... into + 語言　把……翻譯成某語言

❹ fall into a deep / long sleep　進入深度睡眠 / 長時的睡眠

例句 The witch turned the mouse into a bird.　女巫把老鼠變成一隻鳥。

With the passage of time, Donna has grown into a beautiful lady.
隨著時間的消逝，唐娜已長大，變成漂亮的小姐了。

Harold translated the article into German.
哈洛德把這文章翻譯成德文。

After she got on the bus, Edna soon fell into a deep sleep because she was so tired.
上公車後，伊德娜因為太累了，很快就熟睡了。

❸ 有關「目的」的介詞

❶ for

 說明

常出現於下列片語

❶ be used for... 用來……

❷ prepare for... 準備……

❸ invite sb for sth 邀請某人來參加……

❹ for pleasure 消遣娛樂用

 例句

These colorful balloons will **be used for** decoration.
這些五顏六色的氣球將用來做裝飾。

Rex is **preparing for** the final exam next week.
雷克斯在準備下週的期末考。

Duke **invited** Blanche **for** a drink at the coffee shop.
杜克邀請白蘭琪到咖啡店去喝杯飲料。

Cheryl went to London **for pleasure**, not for business.
雪瑞兒是去倫敦玩，不是去出差。

❷ after

 說明

常出現於下列片語

❶ be after... 試著要抓 / 找……

❷ go / chase / run after... 追……

❸ drive after... 開車追……

 例句

No, Chuck can't stay here. Don't you know the police **are after** him?
不行，查克不能待在這裡。你難道不知道警察在追捕他嗎？

The boy **chased after** the robber, but the robber got into a car and drove away.
那男孩追趕搶匪，但搶匪上了車，揚長而去。

A police car **drove after** a scooter rider on the busy street.
一輛警車在繁忙的街道上追著一名機車騎士。

CH 8

8-3

與因果相關的介詞

句子重組

① disease / suffers / liver / My uncle / from

_____.

② ankle bones / to bits / Fred's / were / broken

_____.

③ my brother / telling / My mother / for / a big lie / punished

_____.

④ into / the novel / will / translate / Chinese / Dolly

_____.

⑤ fond / Evelyn / of / very / jazz music / is

_____.

⑥ of / some food / out / I gave / pity / the beggar

_____.

⑦ dinner / My sister / some of her friends / for / invited

_____.

⑧ with / the news, / anger / Jim / was shaking / Because of

_____.

解 答

① My uncle suffers from liver disease
② Fred's ankle bones were broken to bits
③ My mother punished my brother for telling a big lie
④ Dolly will translate the novel into Chinese
⑤ Evelyn is very fond of jazz music
⑥ I gave the beggar some food out of pity
⑦ My sister invited some of her friends for dinner
⑧ Because of the news, Jim was shaking with anger

Chapter 8 介詞

8-4 與論述相關的介詞

此類介詞包括有關 贊成 、 反對 、 比較 、 相似 及 雖然 的介詞，茲分述如下：

❶ 有關「贊成」的介詞

1 for

說明

常出現於下列片語

❶ be for... 支持……

❷ vote for... 投票給 / 贊成……

❸ argue for... 提出支持……

❹ evidence for... 支持……的證據

例句

It seems that many people are for this candidate.
似乎很多人支持這位候選人。

Please vote for this plan. 請投票支持本計畫。

Many employees in the factory argued for a better working environment.
工廠許多員工都支持要有更好的工作環境。

This is the powerful evidence for global warming.
這是全球暖化的有力證據。

2 with

說明

常出現於下列片語

❶ be with... 支持……

❷ go along with... 支持……

例句

Go to ask Gary whether he is with us or against us.
去問蓋瑞他是支持還是反對我們。

I would go along with the project that Daphne mentioned.
我會支持達芙妮提到的方案。

2 有關「反對」的介詞

against

說明 **常出現於下列片語**

❶ be against... 反對……

❷ vote against... 投票反對……

❸ argue against... 提出反對……

❹ evidence against... 不利於……的證據

例句 Gina was against this financial policy.
吉娜反對這項財政政策。

All the people in this village voted against the construction of a landfill site.
所有村民一致投票反對興建垃圾掩埋場。

Several politicians argued against the proposal.
有些政治人物反對該提案。

We have found a lot of evidence against Herbert.
我們發現很多不利於赫伯特的證據。

 3 有關「比較」的介詞

❶ with

說明 **常出現於下列片語**

❶ compare A with / to B 比較 A 與 B

❷ in comparison with / to... 與……相比之下
= by comparison with...

❸ contrast A with B 將 A 與 B 做對照

❹ in sharp contrast with / to... 與……形成強烈的對比

例句 It's interesting to compare American customs with French ones.
比較美國與法國的習俗相當有趣。

In comparison with the test last week, this one was very difficult.
與上週的考試比起來，這次的考試很難。

例句 Contrast this year's profit with last year's, and you'll know why the manager is not happy.
對比今年與去年的利潤，你就知道為什麼經理很不高興了。

Denise's kindness was in sharp contrast with her husband's impoliteness.　丹妮絲的親切友好與她丈夫的無禮形成強烈對比。

2 to

 說明 **常出現於下列片語**

1 prefer A to B　喜歡 A 甚於 B

2 A be superior to B　A 比 B 優秀

3 A be inferior to B　A 比 B 差

4 數字 + to + 數字　……比……

 例句 Britney prefers jazz to classical music.
布蘭妮喜歡爵士樂甚於古典樂。

This van is far superior to that one in terms of comfort.
就舒適性而言，這輛廂型車要比那一輛棒多了。

The clothes in this store are greatly inferior to the ones I bought online.
這家店的衣服遠不如我在網路上買的衣服好。

The score was six to four. The blue team won!
比分是六比四。藍隊贏了！

3 by

 說明 **常出現於下列片語或句型**

1 increase by + 數字　增加了……
　= go up by + 數字

2 decrease / fall by + 數字　減少了……

3 A + be 動詞 + 形容詞比較級 + than + B + by + 數字
　A 比 B 更……（若干單位）

4 A + 動詞 + 副詞比較級 + than + B + by + 數字
　A 比 B 更……（若干單位）

例句 The average price of the mooncakes increased by 10 percent this year.

= The average price of the mooncakes went up by 10 percent this year.
今年月餅的價格平均上漲了 10%。

Because of the economic depression, the house prices decreased / fell by about 12%.
由於經濟蕭條，房價下跌了約 12%。

Herman's younger brother is taller than he is by about 10 centimeters.　赫曼的弟弟比他高約十公分。

My brother earns more than I do by about NT$10,000.
我哥的收入比我多新臺幣一萬元左右。

4 有關「相似」的介詞

1 with

說明 **常出現於下列片語**

1 have much / a lot in common (with sb)
（與某人）有很多共同點

2 have little / nothing in common (with sb)
（與某人）有很少 / 沒有共同點

例句 Elva has a lot in common with her grandmother. For example, both of them like noodles better than rice.
艾娃和她祖母有很多共同點。例如，她們倆都比較喜歡吃麵，而不是吃飯。

Even though Craig and Jamie are twins, they have very little in common with each other.
雖然克雷格和傑米是雙胞胎，他們彼此的共同點卻很少。

2 to

說明 **常出現於下列片語或句型**

1 compare A to B　認為 A 和 B 很相似，把 A 比作 B

2 A be similar to B　A 與 B 很相似

例句 What would you compare life to—a long journey, a movie, or a box of chocolates?
你會把人生比喻成什麼？一段漫長的旅程、一部電影，還是一盒巧克力？

Eleanor's taste in clothes is similar to mine.
伊琳諾的穿著品味和我很相似。

3 as

 說明 **常出現於下列片語或句型**

1 as soon as possible　盡快

2 A + be 動詞 + as + 形容詞 + as + B　A 和 B 一樣……

3 A + 動詞 + as + 副詞 + as + B　A 和 B 一樣……

 例句 We need to get someone to fix the bathroom as soon as possible.
我們得盡快找人來修理洗手間。

Isaac is as smart as his father.
艾薩克像他爸爸一樣聰明。

Emma was so tired that she walked as slowly as a turtle.
艾瑪累到走路走得像烏龜一樣慢。

4 like

 說明 **常出現於下列片語**

1 be like...　像……

2 look / taste / sound / smell / feel like...
長得像 / 嚐起來 / 聽起來 / 聞起來 / 感覺像

3 seem like...　看起來像……

 例句 Jeff thinks his coworkers are like his family members as everyone is so kind to each other.
傑夫認為他的同事就像家人一樣，因為每個人都對彼此很好。

Erin looks like her father.
艾琳長得像她爸爸。

The man seems like a nice guy.
那男子看起來是個好人。

CH
8

8-4

與論述相關的介詞

5 有關「雖然」的介詞

with (= for all)

 說明 此義同於 in spite of 及 despite，而 with 之後常加 all，且主要句子常會使用副詞 still (仍然)。

 例句 With all his hard work, Ricky still didn't pass the exam.
= For all his hard work, Ricky still didn't pass the exam.
儘管瑞奇很努力，他仍然沒有通過考試。

＼ 即時演練 ／

句子重組

① to / she was / Judith / her sister / inferior / thought

_____.

② as / her mother / is / as / Lynn / beautiful

_____.

③ the ban on / argued / fishing in this area / Some people / against

_____.

④ lover / sunshine / The writer / to / compared his

_____.

⑤ thinks / like / Owen / taste / ice cream / sweet potatoes

_____.

⑥ with his brother, / Max / comparison / quiet / By / is

_____.

⑦ this year / 20% / The sales / by / increased

_____.

⑧ nothing / Kelly / common / in / with her sister / has

_____.

① Judith thought she was inferior to her sister

② Lynn is as beautiful as her mother

③ Some people argued against the ban on fishing in this area

④ The writer compared his lover to sunshine

⑤ Owen thinks sweet potatoes taste like ice cream

⑥ By comparison with his brother, Max is quiet

⑦ The sales this year increased by 20%

= The sales increased by 20% this year

⑧ Kelly has nothing in common with her sister

CH
8

8-4

與論述相關的介詞

Chapter 8　介詞

8-5　與媒介相關的介詞

此類介詞有兩類：有關 **方式 / 執行動作者** 的介詞，及有關 **書寫 / 表達** 的介詞，茲分述如下：

❶ 有關「方式 / 執行動作者」的介詞

❶ by + { 表方式的名詞 動名詞 }

 說明
「**by + 方式**」常出現於下列片語

❶ by credit card / check　用信用卡 / 支票（付款）

❷ by hand　用手，手工製作；親自

❸ by machine　用機器製作

❹ by phone / email / mail / letter
以打電話 / 電子郵件 / 信件的方式聯絡

 例句
I'd like to pay by credit card, thanks.
我想用信用卡付款，謝謝。

This straw hat was made by hand.
這頂草帽是手工做的。

Nowadays, most rice is harvested by machine.
現在大部分稻米收割都是用機器。

I usually contact my customers by email, not through messaging apps.
我通常用電子郵件聯繫我的客戶，而不是用通訊軟體。

The old lady makes her living by selling homemade steamed buns.　這位老太太靠賣手工饅頭來謀生。

註　「使用現金」為 in cash，介詞為 in，而非 by。

 例句
My father prefers to pay in cash.
我爸爸喜歡付現。

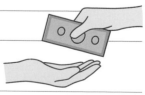

2 by + { 交通工具 / 交通工具行走 / 飛行 / 航行之處 }

說明 常出現於下列片語

1 by bus / car / taxi / train / plane / boat
搭公車 / 汽車 / 計程車 / 火車 / 飛機 / 船

2 by road / rail / air / sea 以陸路 / 鐵路運輸 / 空運 / 海運方式

例句 Lindsay goes to school **by bus** every day.
琳賽每天搭公車上學。

We'll deliver the products **by air** tomorrow.
我們明天會空運這些產品。

3 by + 執行動作者

說明 常使用於被動語態 (即 be 動詞 + 過去分詞 + by...)。

例句 This organization **was established by Hazel Johnson** in 1962.
此組織由海柔‧強生於 1962 年成立。

4 with + 工具

說明 常出現於下列片語

1 wipe A with B 用 B 擦拭 A

2 fasten A with B 用 B 固定好 / 繫牢 A

3 stir A with B 用 B 攪拌 A

4 decorate A with B 用 B 布置 A

例句 My sister **wiped** the tiles **with** a cloth.
我姊姊用抹布擦磁磚。

You should **fasten** the documents together **with** a paper clip.
你應該用迴紋針將這些文件固定在一起。

Heather **stirred** the coffee **with** a spoon while she waited for her cake to arrive.
海瑟在等蛋糕來時，用湯匙攪拌著咖啡。

Laura **decorated** her bedroom **with** her favorite singer's posters.
蘿拉用她最喜歡的歌手海報來布置她的房間。

2 有關「書寫 / 表達」的介詞

1 in + 工具

說明 **常出現於下列片語**

1 in pencil / pen　用鉛筆 / 筆寫

2 in capital / small letters　用大 / 小寫字母

3 in oils / watercolor　用油畫 / 水彩顏料

4 in silence / whispers / a whisper　靜靜地 (做某事) / 小聲地說

例句 Isn't the passage written in pencil? Just erase any word you don't like.

這段文字不是用鉛筆寫的嗎？就擦掉任何你不喜歡的字就好。

You could write the phrase in capital letters if you want to emphasize it.

如果你想強調這片語，可以用大寫字母寫。

Many famous artists paint in oils.

很多知名藝術家都畫油畫。

To my surprise, Randy didn't turn on the TV and just ate dinner in silence.

令我很驚訝的是藍迪沒開電視，就只是靜靜地吃晚飯。

2 in + 語言

例句 Irene's father always speaks to her in English, while her mother likes to talk to her in Chinese.

艾琳的父親總是和她說英文，而她母親則喜歡用中文和她說話。

單選題

① If you pay _____ cash, I can offer you a 5% discount.
   (A) down   (B) in   (C) over   (D) on

② We're going to the island _____ boat this Saturday.
   (A) with   (B) on   (C) in   (D) by

③ Before they got married, my father and mother usually contacted each other _____ mail.
   (A) in   (B) by   (C) from   (D) with

④ After the meal, Kimberly wiped her mouth _____ a tissue.
   (A) with   (B) off   (C) about   (D) for

⑤ The two girls are talking _____ a whisper. They're not speaking ill of me, are they?
   (A) at   (B) up   (C) in   (D) as

CH
8

8-5

與媒介相關的介詞

解　答				
① B	② D	③ B	④ A	⑤ C

Chapter 8　介詞

8-6　與連結性相關的介詞

此類介詞包括有關 關於 、 對於 、 連結 / 繫住 及 分開 的介詞，茲分述如下：

1 有關「關於」的介詞

❶ about

 說明 **常出現於下列片語**

❶ talk about...　談論有關……

❷ write about...　寫有關……

❸ ask (sb) about...　詢問 (某人) 有關……

❹ tell sb about...　告訴 (某人) 有關……

 例句 Ralph and his friends spent the evening talking about art.
雷夫和他朋友花了一個晚上在談論藝術。

The teacher asked the students to write about their favorite movies.
老師請學生寫他們最喜歡的電影。

The professor asked Nathan about his progress in the research.
教授詢問納森他的研究進度。

Owen told his daughter about her grandfather.
歐文告訴他女兒有關她爺爺的事。

❷ on

 說明 **常出現於下列片語**

❶ a book on / about...　有關……的書

❷ a report on / about / of...　有關……的報導 / 報告

❸ news on / about / of...　有關……的新聞

❹ an article / essay on / about...　有關……的文章 / 散文

My brother was reading **a book on** the Middle Ages.
我哥哥正在讀一本有關於中世紀的書。

Greta wrote **a report on** the fashion industry's effects on the earth.
葛瑞塔寫了一篇有關時尚產業對地球影響的報告。

Is there any **news on** the plane crash?
有關於那場飛機失事的消息嗎？

There is another **article on** climate change in the newspaper today. 今天報上又有關於氣候變遷的文章了。

❸ of

說明

常出現於下列片語

❶ speak of / about... 談 / 說起……

❷ think of... 想到……

❸ dream of / about... 夢想……

❹ approve of... 贊同……

例句

My grandfather has never **spoken of** the accident. That's (the reason) why we didn't know he was involved in it.
我爺爺從來沒提過那次意外事故。那就是為什麼我們都不知道他曾牽涉其中的原因。

I met Justin's female friend at a party the other day, but I couldn't **think of** her name.
前幾天我在派對上遇到賈斯汀的女性友人，但我想不起她叫什麼名字。

Honey, this is the house we've always **dreamed of**, isn't it?
親愛的，這就是我們一直夢寐以求的房子，不是嗎？

Norman felt upset when nobody **approved of** his idea at the meeting. 會議上沒有人贊同諾曼的點子，他感到很難過。

❹ with

說明

常出現於下列片語

❶ be careful / careless with... 在……方面很小心 / 粗心大意

❷ be pleased with... 很滿意 / 讚賞……

❸ have a problem with... 不同意……，反對……

❹ There is something wrong with... ……出問題 / 故障

例句 Be careful with the vase. It may break.
小心這個花瓶。很容易破的。

My grandparents **were** very **pleased with** the new house.
我爺爺奶奶很滿意這棟新房子。

The boss said he **had a problem with** your plan.
老闆說他不同意你的計畫。

There's something **wrong with** Janice's phone.
珍妮絲的電話出了點問題。

❷ 有關「對於」的介詞

❶ for

說明 **常出現於下列片語**

❶ be difficult for sb　對某人來說……是很困難的

❷ It is time for sb to + 原形動詞　該是某人做……的時候了

❸ feel for sb　同情 / 憐憫某人

❹ have / feel admiration for...　欽佩 / 讚賞……

例句 Talking to strangers **is difficult for** Marcia since she is so shy.
與陌生人交談對瑪西亞來說很困難,因為她很害羞。

It's time for me **to** let go of the past.　是時候我該放下過去了。

Seth **felt for** the refugees because he was also forced to leave his country when he was young.
塞斯很同情這些難民,因為他小時候也被迫離開他的國家。

I **felt** deep **admiration for** Sam's generosity.
我對山姆的慷慨大方深表欽佩。

❷ to

說明 **常出現於下列片語**

❶ It seems to sb + that 子句　對某人來說……似乎……

❷ It is clear to sb + that 子句
　對某人來說……顯而易見,某人清楚知道……

❸ be strange to sb　對某人來說很陌生

❹ A be nothing to B　A 對 B 來說一點都不重要了

例句 It seems to me that your mother has done her best to support you. 在我看來，你媽媽似乎已盡力支援你了。

It was clear to me that your boyfriend didn't love you anymore. 我很清楚，妳男友已不再愛妳了。

These spices are strange to me; I've never used them in my life. 這些香料對我來說很陌生；我一生中從未用過這些香料。

Don't worry. Robert is nothing to me now. On reflection, he was never my Mr. Right. 別擔心。羅伯特現在對我來說一點都不重要了。 仔細想想，他從來都不是我的真命天子。

❸ 有關「連結 / 繫住」的介詞

❶ of

說明 **常出現於下列片語**

A of B　B 的 A

例句 The result of the game was very disappointing. 這場比賽的結果令人很失望。

❷ to

說明 **常出現於下列片語**

❶ attach A to B　將 A 附著 / 固定於 B 上

❷ tie A to B　（用線 / 繩子等）把 A 固定在 B 上

❸ connect A to / with B　連接 A 和 B

❹ stick to...　黏住……；堅守……

例句 I've attached three files to the email.　我在電子郵件已附上三個檔案。

Patty tied the dog to the bench and fed it some food. 派蒂把狗綁在長凳上，餵牠吃了一些食物。

You didn't connect the keyboard to the computer. That's why you can't type anything. 你沒有把鍵盤連到電腦。那就是為何你不能輸入任何字的原因。

The peanut butter stuck to the roof of Shane's mouth. 花生醬黏在夏恩的上顎上。

4 有關「分開」的介詞

1 from

 說明 **常出現於下列片語**

1 be different from...　與……不同
= differ from...
2 tell A from B　區別 A 與 B
3 prevent... from + 動名詞　阻止……做……；使……無法……
4 protect A from B　保護 A 免受 B 的傷害

例句 Walter is very **different from** his brother in personality.
= Walter **differs** greatly **from** his brother in personality.
華特和他弟弟個性方面很不一樣。

Can you **tell** the fake painting **from** the real one?
你能分辨出這幅假畫和真畫嗎？

Phil's injured ankle **prevented** him **from** joining the marathon.
菲爾腳踝受傷而無法參加馬拉松比賽。

Eating less processed food can **protect** you **from** a lot of diseases.
少吃加工食品可避免得到很多疾病。

2 off

 說明 **常出現於下列片語**

1 take... off / take off...　脫掉 (衣物 / 鞋 / 帽等)
2 keep (A) off B　(使 A) 不接近 B
3 tear... off / tear off...　撕下……，把……撕開 / 掉
4 A fall off (B)　A (從 B) 掉下來

 例句 Please **take off** your hat when you enter the building.
進入室內請脫帽。

Didn't you see the sign that says "**Keep off** the grass"?
你沒看到「請勿踐踏草地」的標誌嗎？

Matt **tore off** the wrapping paper and opened his gift.
麥特撕下包裝紙，打開他的禮物。

Marge keeps **falling off** the bike because she hasn't learned how to ride it properly.
瑪芝總是從腳踏車上摔下來，因為她還沒學會如何正確地騎車。

③ of

說明

常出現於下列片語

❶ rob A of B　搶奪 A 身上的 B

❷ clear A of B　洗脫 A 有關 B 的嫌疑

❸ rid A of B　讓 A 擺脫 / 清除掉 B

❹ strip A of B　剝奪 A 的 B 以作為懲罰

★ 以上片語中的 of 相當於 from，有「脫離」的意思。

例句

A man wearing a raincoat **robbed** Stan **of** all the money he had.
一名穿雨衣的男子搶了史坦身上所有的錢。

The jury **cleared** Martin **of** all the charges.
陪審團洗脫了所有對馬丁的指控。

The mayor promised he would do whatever he could to **rid** the city **of** crime.
市長承諾將竭盡所能讓此城市的犯罪消失。

Kenny was **stripped of** his scholarship after he was caught cheating on the exam.
肯尼考試作弊被發現後，他的獎學金就被取消以示懲戒。

＼ 即時演練 ／

單選題

① Would you please help me connect the speakers ＿＿＿＿＿＿ the computer?
(A) of　　　　(B) to　　　　(C) till　　　　(D) as

② The manager said he was very pleased ＿＿＿＿＿＿ the results.
(A) with　　　(B) in　　　　(C) as　　　　(D) up

③ Jimmy was stripped _____ his driver's license because of his repeated drunk driving.
(A) over   (B) with   (C) about   (D) of

④ The news _____ the state of the economy shocked many people.
(A) against   (B) on   (C) off   (D) to

⑤ The heavy rain prevented us _____ going on a picnic today.
(A) into   (B) upon   (C) from   (D) through

⑥ I really don't approve _____ the way Rick treats his employees.
(A) on   (B) about   (C) with   (D) of

⑦ I have great admiration _____ Roger, who has devoted his time to helping the orphans.
(A) for   (B) to   (C) at   (D) by

⑧ Mom, I'd like to eat this snack, but I can't tear _____ the top of the packet.
(A) up   (B) off   (C) on   (D) at

解 答				
① B	② A	③ D	④ B	⑤ C
⑥ D	⑦ A	⑧ B		

Chapter 8 　介詞

此類介詞包括有關 穿著／顏色 、(擁)有 、 程度／數量 及 情況 的介詞，茲分述如下：

❶ 有關「穿著／顏色」的介詞

❶ in + 服裝

說明	表「穿……(服裝)」。in 和「服裝」之間可加定冠詞 the 或不定冠詞 a(n)，但下列片語除外：**in uniform** 穿著制服
例句	Who is the girl **in** the green coat? 那個穿綠色外套的女孩是誰？ Who is that boy **in uniform**? 那個穿制服的男孩是誰？

❷ in + 顏色

說明	表「穿……顏色(的服裝)；(服裝)為……顏色」。in 和「顏色」之間不加定冠詞 the。
例句	You look great **in** purple. 你穿紫色的衣服很好看。 May I ask if you have this kind of dress **in** gray? 請問你們有這一款灰色的洋裝嗎？

❷ 有關「(擁)有」的介詞

with

說明	此介詞後常接 hair (頭髮)、eyes (眼睛)、beard (下巴及兩耳下方的鬍鬚)、sunglasses (太陽眼鏡)、accent (口音) 等名詞。
例句	The boy **with** brown hair is my brother. 有一頭棕色頭髮的男孩是我哥哥。 It seems that the woman **with** a foreign accent comes from South America. 那個帶有外國口音的女子似乎來自南美洲。

219

3 有關「程度 / 數量」的介詞

1 at

說明 常出現於下列片語或句型
1 sell at / for + 價格 + each　每個賣……錢
2 at + 數字 + degrees　（溫度）在……度
3 drive at + 數字 + kilometers / miles per hour
　以……公里 / 英里的時速行駛
4 at high / low speed　以高 / 低速行駛

例句 The dolls **sell at** NT$150 **each**.
這些玩偶每個賣新臺幣一百五十元。

Don't you know water freezes **at** zero **degrees**?
你不知道水在零度時會結冰嗎？

The drunk man **drove at** 210 **kilometers per hour**.
那醉漢以每小時兩百一十公里的時速行駛。

Our car was traveling **at high speed** on the freeway.
我們的車子在高速公路上高速行駛。

2 for

說明 此介詞後常接一段距離 / 時間。接「一段時間」時，常使用現在完成式
（即 have / has + 過去分詞）、現在完成進行式（即 have / has been + 現
在分詞）或過去完成進行式（即 had been + 現在分詞）。此介詞亦常出現
於下列片語：
1 for a while　有一段時間
2 for a long time　很長一段時間

例句 The man walked **for** miles in the desert and couldn't
see any villages.
那男子在沙漠裡走了好幾英里路，並沒有看到任何村莊。

The principal **has been waiting for** you **for a while**.
校長等你有一段時間了。

Nathan **has lived** in the UK **for a long time**, but he still
speaks with an American accent.
納森在英國住了很久，但他說話仍帶有美國口音。

3 by

 說明

常出現於下列片語

1 by degrees　逐漸

2 measure + 數字 + (單位) + by + 數字 + (單位)
　 為長……寬……，面積為……乘……

3 be paid by the hour / day / week　按小時 / 天數 / 週數領錢

4 be sold by the kilogram / pound　以公斤 / 磅來販售

 例句

Under Mr. Brown's guidance, my English is getting better by degrees.　在布朗老師的指導下，我的英文正逐漸進步。

My bedroom measures 4 meters by 3 meters.
我的臥室長四公尺，寬三公尺。

The part-time workers at the coffee shop are paid by the hour.
這家咖啡店的兼職員工是按小時計酬。

The fruit and vegetables in this country are sold by the kilogram, not by the pound.
這國家的蔬果是以公斤來販售，而不是以磅來販售。

4 有關「情況」的介詞

1 in

 說明

常出現於下列片語

1 in good / bad condition　情況很好 / 不佳

2 be in danger　有危險

3 be in trouble　有麻煩

4 in public / private　公開地 / 私下地

 例句

The second-hand van is still in good condition.
這輛二手廂型車的車況仍很不錯。

Mr. President, you have to leave right now. You're in great danger.
總統先生，您現在必須離開。您現在非常危險。

We all came to help Norman when we found out that he was in trouble.　我們得知諾曼有難時都來幫他一把。

CH
8

8-7

與特點、性質相關的介詞

例句 Let's not talk about this in public; we can discuss it in private later.
我們不要在公開場合討論這件事；我們可以稍後私底下討論。

❷ under

 說明 常出現於下列片語

❶ under... conditions / circumstances　在⋯⋯情況下

❷ be under arrest　被逮捕

❸ be under discussion　在討論中

❹ be under construction　在興建中

 例句 The general was pleased that you all performed very well under such stressful conditions.
將軍很高興你們在如此有壓力的情況下都表現得很好。

"Freeze! You're under arrest!" shouted the plain-clothes policeman.　便衣警察喊道：「不許動，你被捕了！」

The project is still under discussion.　這專案仍在討論中。

There are two new houses under construction.
有兩棟新房子正在興建中。

❸ at

說明 常出現於下列片語

❶ at war / peace　在戰爭中的 / 和平的

❷ at rest　長眠（意指過世）；不動

❸ at ease　感到自在

❹ at risk　有風險的，處境危險

 例句 The images of people at war made Hank feel uncomfortable.
那些在戰爭中的人們的畫面讓漢克感到很不舒服。

After battling the illness for several years, Uncle George is finally at rest.
與病魔纏鬥了幾年後，喬治叔叔終於可以安息了。

I don't want Phil to be my partner. I never feel at ease with him.
我不想讓菲爾成為我的搭檔。和他在一起我從不曾感到自在過。

例句 The serious disease was spreading rapidly, and the elderly and children were more **at risk** than others.

這個嚴重的疾病迅速地蔓延，且老人及孩童面臨的風險比其他人更大。

＼ 即時演練 ／

單選題

① The double bedroom measures 12 feet _____ 10 feet.
(A) at   (B) with   (C) in   (D) by

② At sea level, water boils _____ 100 degrees Celsius.
(A) at   (B) in   (C) as   (D) with

③ Don't worry. The doctor said our son is _____ good condition.
(A) from   (B) of   (C) in   (D) up

④ You'll look pretty cool _____ that sports jacket.
(A) on   (B) by   (C) as   (D) in

⑤ A shopping mall is _____ construction near the park.
(A) behind   (B) under   (C) over   (D) below

⑥ Kenny hopes that his country will be _____ peace one day.
(A) at   (B) on   (C) into   (D) by

⑦ The woman _____ the sunglasses is Matthew's mother.
(A) on   (B) with   (C) by   (D) at

CH 8

8-7

與特點、性質相關的介詞

解　　答				
① D	② A	③ C	④ D	⑤ B
⑥ A	⑦ B			

Chapter 8 介詞

8-8 其他具常見意義的介詞

包括有關 來源 / 材料 、 給予 、 除外 、 當作 / 作為 等的介詞，茲分述如下：

❶ 有關「來源 / 材料」的介詞

1 from

說明　**常出現於下列片語**

　　1 come from...　來自……

　　2 buy A from B　從 B 買 A

　　3 choose (A) from B　從 B 選 (A)

　　4 be made from...　由……所製成 (製成品的原料已變)

例句

Denise comes from a small town in the south of France.
丹妮絲來自南法的一個小鎮。

I bought this winter hat from my sister's friend for just NT$150.
我從我姊姊朋友那裡買了這頂冬天的帽子，只花了新臺幣一百五十元。

There are plenty of shoes you can choose from in our store.
我們店裡有很多鞋子可供選擇。

This sauce is made from peanut butter, soy sauce, garlic, sugar, and lemon juice.
這醬汁是花生醬、醬油、大蒜、糖和檸檬汁做的。

2 of

說明　**常出現於下列片語**

be made of...　由……所製成 (製成品的原料不變)

例句

This desk is made of wood.
這張書桌是木頭做的。

❷ 有關「給予」的介詞

❶ for

說明

常出現於下列片語

❶ be for... 給……

❷ a message for... 給……的訊息

❸ buy sth for sb 買某物給某人

　= buy sb sth

❹ provide sth for sb 提供某物給某人

例句

This Christmas gift **is for** you. 這聖誕禮物是給你的。

Herbert, here's **a message for** you from one of your customers.
赫伯特，這裡有你一位客戶給你的訊息。

Debbie **bought** an expensive watch **for** her mother.

= Debbie **bought** her mother an expensive watch.
黛比買了一個很貴的手錶給她媽媽。

This organization **provides** scholarships **for** international
students. 此組織為國際學生提供獎學金。

❷ to

說明

常出現於下列片語

❶ give sth to sb 把某物給某人

❷ show sth to sb 把某物展現給某人

❸ send sth to sb 寄某物給某人

❹ tell sth to sb 把某事告訴某人

例句

Please **give** that dictionary **to** me. 請把那本字典拿給我。

Eddy **showed** his childhood photos **to** me. He was really chubby
then. 艾迪給我看了他小時候的照片。那時他真的是胖嘟嘟的。

Bruce **sent** a bunch of roses **to** his girlfriend.
布魯斯寄給他女友一束玫瑰花。

Don't you know Bonnie is a big mouth? She'll **tell** your secret **to**
everybody.
你難道不知道邦妮是個大嘴巴嗎？她會把你的祕密告訴所有人。

CH 8

8-8

其他具常見意義的介詞

❸ 有關「除外」的介詞

❶ except (for)

註 | except、except for 皆可作為介詞使用,意義相同;except 另可當連接詞使用,但不可置句首。

例句 | No one can deal with this problem **except (for)** Dale.
除了戴爾以外,沒人能處理這個問題。

❷ but

說明 | 義同於 except。常出現於下列片語
❶ nothing but...　只會 / 有 / 是……
❷ anything but...　一點也不……,根本不……
❸ but for...　除了……之外

例句 | The meeting could be held any day **but** / **except** Tuesday.
會議可以在任何一天開,除了週二以外。

For days, Cindy ate **nothing but** / **except** vegetables because she was on a diet.
好幾天以來,辛蒂只吃蔬菜,因為她在節食。

Kent is **anything but** handsome, but he is truly a sweet boy.
= Kent is **far from** handsome, but he is truly a sweet boy.
= Kent is **not** handsome **at all**, but he is truly a sweet boy.
肯特一點也不帥,但他確實是個很討人喜歡的男孩。

The park was empty **but for** a few dogs.
= The park was empty **except for** a few dogs.
公園很空蕩,只有幾隻狗。

❸ beyond

說明 | 義同於 except。常用於否定句。

例句 | Kate knew nothing about cooking **beyond** / **except** how to make instant noodles.
除了會泡泡麵之外,凱特對烹飪一無所知。

4 有關「當作 / 作為」的介詞

1 as

常出現於下列片語

1 use A as B　用 A 作為 B

2 choose A as B　選 A 為 B

3 regard A as B　把 A 視為 B
= look on / upon A as B
= think of A as B
= see / view A as B

4 disguise oneself as...　喬裝成⋯⋯
= sb be disguised as...

Candice **uses** her garage **as** an office.
坎蒂絲把她的車庫當作辦公室來使用。

We **chose** Andrew **as** our class leader.
我們選了安德魯當我們的班長。

We all **regard** Calvin **as** a hero.
我們都把卡爾文視為英雄。

The police officer **disguised himself** as a beggar so he wouldn't be noticed.
那警察喬裝成乞丐，這樣就沒人會注意到他。

2 in

常出現於下列片語

1 in reply to...　回答 / 覆⋯⋯

2 in response to...　對⋯⋯做出回應

3 in return for...　以回報⋯⋯

4 in exchange for...　交換⋯⋯

Ariel wrote a brief message **in reply to** her customer's email.
艾莉兒寫了一封簡訊來回覆她客戶的電子郵件。

The mayor soon quit **in response to** public anger.
市長很快就因眾怒而辭職。

其他具常見意義的介詞

227

I treated Dominic to dinner **in return for** his help.
我請多明尼克吃晚餐以回報他的幫忙。

I gave Herman a pen **in exchange for** his eraser.
我用一支筆和赫曼換一個橡皮擦。

＼ 即時演練 ／

單選題

① When could you send the samples ＿＿＿＿＿＿＿ us?
　(A) from　　　(B) to　　　(C) but　　　(D) in

② Many people view Haley ＿＿＿＿＿＿＿ an actress, but actually she usually directs movies.
　(A) for　　　(B) with　　　(C) of　　　(D) as

③ Cheese is made ＿＿＿＿＿＿＿ milk.
　(A) of　　　(B) beyond　　　(C) from　　　(D) in

④ Mom, I'd like to give Karen some home-made cookies ＿＿＿＿＿＿＿ return for her help.
　(A) in　　　(B) on　　　(C) for　　　(D) of

⑤ The charity provides free meals ＿＿＿＿＿＿＿ the homeless every day.
　(A) except　　　(B) for　　　(C) as　　　(D) in

⑥ Greta tried every kind of sport ＿＿＿＿＿＿＿ water sports because she has a fear of water.
　(A) for　　　(B) as　　　(C) in　　　(D) but

解　答

①B　　②D　　③C　　④A　　⑤B

⑥D

Chapter 9

連接詞

Chapter 9　連接詞

9-1　對等連接詞

連接詞是用來連接句子中的單字、片語或子句，主要可分為**對等連接詞**、**相關連接詞**以及**從屬連接詞**三種：

連接詞分類	作用	例字
對等連接詞	連接對等的單字、片語或子句	and、but、or、nor、for、so、yet
相關連接詞	以成對使用的連接詞連接詞性相同的單字、片語或子句	both... and...、either... or...、neither... nor...
從屬連接詞	引導從屬子句，修飾主要子句	although、because、if、since、while 等

以下分項介紹各個對等連接詞：

1 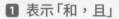 and

and 的用法
1 表示「和，且」
例句：Mom bought some fruit **and** vegetables from the supermarket.　媽媽從超市買了一些蔬菜水果。
2 表示先後發生的動作
例句：Sally walked in the house **and** took her shoes off by the door. 莎莉走進屋內後將鞋子脫下放在門旁。
3 表示同時進行的動作
例句：Please don't text **and** drive. It is a dangerous thing to do. 請不要邊開車邊傳訊息。這是很危險的行為。
4 表示「就會」
說明：and 表此意時，常接在祈使句或命令句之後，表示對方若做某事就會有某成果，通常此成果為正面的。

230

句型：祈使句, and + 主詞 + 助動詞（通常為 will、can）+ 原形動詞

 例句：Work hard, **and** there will be a chance of promotion for you.
你努力工作就會有機會升遷。

❷ but

but 的用法

1 表示對比或語氣轉折，可譯為「但」

 例句：My grandparents are old, **but** they're still very fit and healthy.
我的爺爺奶奶很老，但他們仍身強體壯。

2 表示「除了」，意同 except

 例句：Because of the heavy rain, we can't do anything **but** sit and wait.
由於下著大雨，我們什麼事都做不了只能坐著等待。

Charlie has no choice **but** to work overtime today.
查理逼不得已只好今天加班。

❸ or

or 的用法

1 表示「或」

 例句：For the long weekend, should we stay at home **or** go on a trip?
這次的長假我們要待在家還是出去玩？

2 表示「否則」（用於警告用）

 例句：Bring an umbrella with you, **or** you'll get wet.
帶把雨傘出門，否則你會淋溼。

3 表示「不然」（用於證明之前的陳述為真）

 例句：Someone must be at home, **or** the lights wouldn't be on.
肯定有人在家，不然燈不會是開著的。

4 表示「即，又稱」

| 例句 | This book is a biography, **or** the story of someone's life written by another person.
這本書是傳記，也就是由另一人撰寫某人一生的故事。 |

5 於否定句中時表示「和」

| 例句 | Karen's purse has just been stolen. She has <u>no</u> cash **or** credit cards.
凱倫的錢包剛被偷了。她沒有現金和信用卡了。 |

❹ nor

nor 的用法

表示「也不」

| 說明 | nor 可置否定句後表示「也不」，而 nor 引導的子句須用倒裝句，即主詞與助動詞交換位置。 |

| 句型 | 否定句, nor + 助動詞 + 主詞 |

| 例句 | This new movie is not the director's best work, **nor** is it his worst.

這部新的電影不是導演的最佳作品，也不是他最糟的作品。 |

❺ for

for 的用法

表示「因為」

| 說明 | 在正式的英文書寫中，連接詞 for 可用以表示「因為」，意同 because。此時通常置於主要子句之後，作為補充說明。 |

| 例句 | Tom must be very tired, **for** he has not slept for nearly 24 hours.
湯姆肯定很累，因為他將近二十四小時沒睡了。 |

6 so

so 的用法

1 表示結果，可譯為「所以」

例句
Debbie was not feeling well, **so** she went to see the doctor.
黛比不太舒服，所以去看了醫生。

2 表示目的或理由

說明
連接詞 so 表示目的或理由時，亦可寫作 so that。

例句
Please be quiet **so (that)** I can hear what the professor is saying.
請安靜，這樣我才可以聽到教授在說什麼。

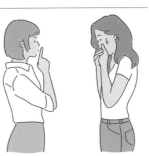

 7 yet

yet 的用法

表示「但是，然而」

說明
連接詞 yet 可用以表示「但是，然而」，意同 but，但語氣更為強烈，且 yet 可與 and 搭配使用。

例句
Ethan came up with a simple **yet** effective solution to the problem.
伊森想到一個簡單但有效的解決方式。

Wendy has a high-paying job, **and yet** she seems to be always out of money.
溫蒂有個很高薪的工作，但她似乎總是缺錢。

請圈選出正確的連接詞。

① You should exercise more, (or / and) you'll gain weight.

② Toby was hungry in the afternoon, (so / or) he bought some snacks at the convenience store.

③ The student quietly walked into the classroom (but / and) sat in the seat in the corner.

④ I don't like the color yellow, (nor / or) do I like the color pink.

⑤ The team did their best in the game, (yet / so) they could not beat their opponent.

⑥ Ted disagreed with his colleague, (and / but) he did not want to argue with her.

⑦ Customers can pay in cash (nor / or) by credit card.

⑧ Winnie remained quiet for the entire day, (yet / for) she was feeling under the weather.

⑨ We left early for the airport (but / so) we wouldn't miss our flight.

⑩ Water these plants daily (and / or) they'll grow well.

解 答				
① or	② so	③ and	④ nor	⑤ yet
⑥ but	⑦ or	⑧ for	⑨ so	⑩ and

9-2　相關連接詞

相關連接詞為成對使用的連接詞，若將其拆散個別單獨使用，則會改變其意義。相關連接詞的功能與對等連接詞類似，是用於連接兩個詞性相同的**單字、片語**或**結構類似的子句**。

以下介紹常見的相關連接詞：

❶ both... and...　……以及……；既……又……

 說明 ｜ both... and... 若是用於連接主詞，其後須接複數動詞。

例句 ｜ **Both** Eric **and** his wife enjoy cooking.
艾瑞克以及他老婆都喜歡烹飪。

This machine can **both** sweep **and** mop the floor.
這臺機器既可以掃地也可以拖地。

❷ as well as...　以及……；不但……而且……

說明 ｜ as well as 若是用於連接主詞，其後的動詞須依據第一個主詞做單複數變化。as well as... 前後也可加逗點。

例句 ｜ Jeff(,) **as well as** some of his friends(,) wants to learn Spanish.

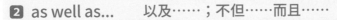

傑夫與他的一些朋友想要學西班牙文。
(第一個主詞 Jeff 為單數，故用單數動詞 wants)

This company sells household goods(,) **as well as** portable electronic devices.
這間公司不僅賣家用電器，也賣可攜式電子裝置。

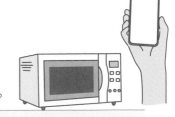

❸ rather than...　而非……

說明 ｜ 同 as well as，rather than 若是用於連接主詞，其後的動詞使用單數或複數須視第一個主詞而定。

例句

The teacher rather than the students is wrong.

錯的是老師而非學生們。

（第一個主詞 The teacher 為單數，故用單數動詞 is）

Gary likes to chat in person rather than send messages.
蓋瑞喜歡當面聊天而非傳訊息。

4 not... but...　　不是……而是……

 說明

not... but... 連接兩個名詞或代名詞作主詞時，其後的動詞使用單數或複數須視最接近動詞之主詞而定。

 例句

Not my parents but my grandfather comes from Taichung.

不是我爸媽而是我爺爺來自臺中。

（最接近動詞之名詞 my grandfather 為單數，
故用單數動詞 comes）

niece　uncle

This little girl is not my daughter but my niece.
這小女孩不是我的女兒而是我的姪女。

5 not only... but also...　　不但……而且……
= not only... but... as well

 說明

使用 not only... but also... 時須注意下列三點：

❶ 若是用於連接主詞，動詞須依照最近的主詞作變化。

❷ 連接主要子句時，則須將 also 置於句中。然而，also 也可予以省略。

❸ 若是連接主要子句，not only 後的主要子句須採倒裝句構，即主詞與 be 動詞或助動詞的位置調換，若遇一般動詞則須在主詞前依人稱與時態置 do、does 或 did。

 例句

Not only Max but also his brothers are on the basketball team.

= Not only Max but his brothers are on the basketball team as well.
不僅是麥克斯在籃球隊上，他的兄弟們也在隊上。

（最接近動詞之名詞 his brothers 為複數，故用複數動詞 are）

Andrew not only starred in this movie but also directed it.
= Andrew not only starred in this movie but directed it as well.
安德魯不僅主演了這部電影，他也是這部電影的導演。

236

例句

Not only can Lily sing, but she can **also** dance.

= Not only can Lily sing, but she can dance **as well**.

莉莉不僅會唱歌也會跳舞。

6 whether... or...　……或者……；不論……或……

 例句

When the earthquake occurred last night, Becky was not sure **whether** to stay indoors **or** go outside.

昨晚地震發生時，貝琪不確定要待在室內還是到室外。

We're likely to be late **whether** we take a taxi **or** the bus.

不論是搭計程車還是公車，我們都很可能會遲到。

7 either... or...　不是……就是……

 說明

either... or... 連接兩個名詞或代名詞作主詞時，其後動詞使用單複數之規則如下：

主詞	動詞
單數 / 不可數 + 單數 / 不可數	單數
複數 + 複數	複數
單數 / 不可數 + 複數	依據最近的主詞

 例句

Either tea **or** coffee goes well with this dessert.
　　　　不可數　　不可數

這份甜點跟茶或咖啡都很搭。

（連接兩個不可數名詞，故用單數動詞 goes）

Either the chairs **or** the tables have to be moved.
　　　　　複數　　　　　複數

不是移走椅子就是要移走桌子。

（連接兩個複數名詞，故用複數動詞 have）

Either my mom **or** my aunts are making dinner tonight.
　　　　單數　　　　複數

我媽媽或我阿姨們要做今晚的晚餐。

（最接近動詞之名詞 my aunts 為複數，故用複數動詞 are）

John is not coming to the party. He **either** doesn't want to attend **or** is too busy.

約翰沒有要參加派對。他不是不想參加就是太忙了。

CH 9

9-2

相關連接詞

8 neither... nor...   既不……也不……

說明	neither... nor... 連接兩個名詞或代名詞作主詞時，其後動詞使用單複數之規則同 either... or...。

| 例句 | Neither the scarf nor the gloves are for sale. |

<u>Neither</u> the scarf <u>nor</u> <u>the gloves</u> <u>are</u> for sale.
　　　　　 單數　　　　　　 複數

這條圍巾跟手套都是非賣品。
（最接近動詞之名詞 the gloves 為複數，故用複數動詞 are）

To our surprise, Erica was **neither** shocked **nor** angry when she heard the bad news.
令我們驚訝的是，艾瑞卡聽到這則壞消息時既不震驚也不生氣。

＼ 即時演練 ／

單選題

① Liz is not a chef _____ a waitress. Her job is to serve customers and take their orders.
(A) but   (B) or   (C) nor   (D) and

② Louis played _____ soccer and baseball when he was in college.
(A) either   (B) neither   (C) whether   (D) both

③ Salt rather than sugar _____ added to this dish.
(A) are   (B) were   (C) was   (D) being

④ Not only _____ the story, but she also drew the pictures.
(A) Nora did write   (B) did Nora write
(C) Nora wrote   (D) wrote Nora

⑤ Paul is traveling to Boston next month. He will either stay at a relative's house _____ stay in a hotel.
(A) or   (B) nor   (C) but   (D) and

⑥ The skirt as well as the pants _____ made by Mandy.
(A) will   (B) is   (C) were   (D) was

⑦ The customer is not sure whether to order the beef
_____ the chicken.
(A) and   (B) or   (C) nor   (D) but

⑧ Neither Roger nor his girlfriend _____ a big wedding
ceremony when they get married.
(A) want   (B) wants   (C) wanting   (D) to want

解　答				
① A	② D	③ C	④ B	⑤ A
⑥ D	⑦ B	⑧ B		

Chapter 9 　連接詞

9-3　從屬連接詞

從屬連接詞是用來引導**從屬子句**（包含**名詞子句**、**形容詞子句**以及**副詞子句**），進而修飾主要子句。從屬子句本身句意不完整，故無法獨立存在，必須與另一主要子句並用才可形成完整的句子：

例句分析	
When you called me,	I was taking an afternoon nap.
你打電話給我時，	我正在睡午覺。
從屬子句（之副詞子句）	主要子句

從屬連接詞本身即可表示時間、因果、對比、條件等意思，如上方例句中的 when 即表示「……的時候」之時間關係。從屬連接詞的數量眾多，以下依照從屬連接詞之意思列舉一些較常見的從屬連接詞：

❶ 常見的從屬連接詞

❶ 表時間的從屬連接詞

例字
when（當……的時候）	since（自從……）
while（當……的時候）	until / till（直到……）
as（當……的時候，隨著）	once（一旦）
before（在……之前）	as soon as（一……就……）
after（在……之後）	every time / whenever（每當）

例句

When Nina first met Joe, she thought he was younger than her.
妮娜初次見到喬時以為他比她年輕。

While the Smiths were on vacation, someone broke into their house.
史密斯一家在度假時，有人闖進他們家。

As time went by, our company grew bigger and bigger.
隨著時間過去，本公司規模越來越大。

240

Cindy is writing down the main points of the lesson **before** she forgets.
辛蒂趁還沒忘記前把課程重點寫下來。

Josh started a new job soon after he graduated from college.
喬許大學畢業後不久就開始新工作了。

I haven't seen Ian, a friend from college, since we graduated.
自從我們畢業之後我就沒見過我的大學朋友伊恩了。

The children played on the playground until / till it got dark.
孩子們在兒童遊戲場玩到天黑為止。

Jane plans to hold a party once she settles into her new house.
小珍打算新家整頓好後就辦個派對。

As soon as the teacher left the classroom, the students started chatting.　老師一離開教室，學生們就開始聊天。

Eric's right knee hurts every time / whenever he runs.
每當艾瑞克跑步時，他的右膝就會痛。

深 度補充

when 與 while 之差異

說明　when 與 while 皆可用於表示「當……的時候」，然而兩者用法仍有些許不同。兩者之區別大致如下：

引導之事件	使用 when 或 while
瞬間事件 + 延續性事件	when / while
延續性事件 + 延續性事件	while
瞬間事件 + 瞬間事件	when
有先後順序的兩件事	when
表示年紀	when

注意

1 根據上述，兩事件若為「瞬間事件 + 延續性事件」，即可用 when 或 while 引導該延續性事件。然而，若是要引導該瞬間事件，則只能用 when，不可用 while。

2 除了上述之區別外，while 引導的副詞子句較常使用進行式以表示持續一段時間的動作，而 when 則視情況使用簡單式或進行式。

I was taking a shower **while** the phone rang. (×)
　　延續性事件　　　　　　　瞬間事件

→ I was taking a shower **when** the phone rang. (○)

→ The phone rang **when** / **while** I was taking a shower. (○)
我洗澡的時候電話響了。

While Tina was cleaning the house, her husband was sleeping.
　　　延續性事件　　　　　　　　延續性事件
提娜打掃屋子的時候她的老公在睡覺。

The little girl screamed **when** she saw a spider.
　　瞬間事件　　　　　　　瞬間事件
這名小女孩看到蜘蛛時尖叫了。

The suspicious man ran away **when** he saw the police.
　　後發生之事件　　　　　　　先發生之事件
這名可疑的男子看到警察就跑走了。

When my grandfather was 18, he joined the army.
　　　表示年紀
我爺爺十八歲便從軍了。

---

2 表原因的從屬連接詞

because（因為）　　**as**（因為）　　since（因為）

We decided to go home **because** it was too hot outside.
我們決定回家，因為外面太熱了。

The new employee may need some help **as** he
is unfamiliar with our procedure.
這名新員工可能需要幫忙，因為他對我們的流程不熟悉。

Since Amy had put on some weight, she decided to go on a diet.
由於艾咪體重增加了一些，她決定要節食減肥。

3 表目的的從屬連接詞

so (that)...（為了……；以便……）
in order that...（為了……）
for fear (that)...（以免……）

242

注意

so that 與 in order that 的意思相似，但 so that 較常使用，而 in order that 為較正式的用法。

 例句

We bought the movie tickets online **so (that)** we could choose our own seats.
我們在網路上買了電影票以便可以自己選擇位子。

Please print out this form **in order that** you can sign it.
請印出這份表格以便您簽名。

Erin agreed to the new company policy **for fear (that)** she might lose her job.
艾琳同意新的公司政策以免失去工作。

4 表條件的從屬連接詞

 例字

if（如果）	on condition that...（只要／條件是……）
in case（以防萬一）	provided / providing that...（只要／假如……）
unless（除非）	suppose / supposing that...（假如……）
as long as / so long as（只要）	

例句

If you don't study hard, you will likely fail the test.
如果你不用功讀書，很有可能會考試不及格。

Andy wore his jacket **in case** it got cold at night.
安迪穿了外套以防晚上變冷。

The security guard can't let strangers in **unless** they have an invitation.
除非有邀請函，不然警衛不能讓陌生人入內。

Bill lets his daughter go out after school **as long as / so long as** she comes home before 9 p.m.
比爾准許他的女兒放學出去玩，只要她在晚上九點前回到家。

Alan told me his secret **on condition that** I never tell anyone else.
艾倫告訴我他的祕密，條件是我永遠不告訴其他人。

You can bring your pets on the train, **provided / providing that** they are put in a cage.
你可以帶寵物上火車，只要牠們有安置在籠內。

例句 Suppose / Supposing that the typhoon comes tomorrow, should we cancel our trip? 假如明天有颱風的話，我們要取消行程嗎？

5 表對比的從屬連接詞

 例字 while（然而；雖然）　　　　　whereas（然而）

> **注意**
> 表示「然而」之對比意思時，while 與 whereas 同義，可互相替換，此時 while 視為對等連接詞。但 while 若表「雖然」，則兩者不可互換，此時 while 等同於 although。

 例句 While Tom is willing to help, there is not much that he can do.
雖然湯姆想幫忙，但沒有什麼事可以給他做。

Amber has red hair while / whereas her sister Carol has blonde hair.
安柏的頭髮是紅色的，而她姊姊卡蘿是一頭金髮。

Amber　　Carol

6 表轉折的從屬連接詞

 例字 although / though（雖然）　　　even if（即使）
even though（儘管）

 例句 Although / Though Julie is not very wealthy, she is happy with her life. 雖然茱莉並不富裕，她對她的生活感到很滿意。

Even though Seth had a big lunch, he still felt hungry in the afternoon. 儘管塞斯午餐吃得很豐盛，他下午還是很餓。

Even if it rains, we will still go to the event.
即使下雨，我們還是會參加活動。

 度補充

although 與 though 之差異

 說明 although 與 though 的差異主要有下列兩點：
1 作連接詞時，although 與 though 兩者都可用來表示「雖然」。然而，though 較常用於日常口語會話中，正式對話或書寫則較常使用 although。
2 though 可作副詞，表示「但是」，此時與 however、nevertheless 同義，且不可與 although 互換使用。

例句

<u>**Although / Though**</u> Melvin's dog is small, it barks very loudly.
　　　　連接詞

雖然馬文的狗很小隻，牠叫聲非常響亮。

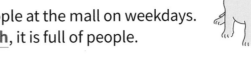

There aren't a lot of people at the mall on weekdays.
On the weekend, **though**, it is full of people.
　　　　　　　　副詞

平日購物中心裡的人不多，但到了週末就人山人海。

❷ 使用從屬連接詞應注意事項

❶ 句中逗點的位置

 說明

從屬連接詞所引導的副詞子句若置於句首，該副詞子句與主要子句之間一般須置逗點；若副詞子句置於主要子句之後，則通常不須置逗點。

 例句

<u>Because Ted's friends forgot his birthday</u>, <u>he is angry</u>.
　　because 引導的副詞子句　　　　　　主要子句

= <u>Ted is angry</u> <u>because his friends forgot his birthday</u>.
　　主要子句　　　　　because 引導的副詞子句

因為泰德的朋友忘記他的生日，所以他很生氣。

❷ 應避免雙重連接

 說明

一般而言，句子中可以出現多個連接詞，但有些連接詞不可在同一句子中一起出現。以下是關於此狀況常犯下的錯誤，應避免：

❶ because... so... (×)

❷ although / though... but / yet... (×)

 例句

Because my cell phone ran out of battery,
so I could not call you. (×)

→ **Because** my cell phone ran out of battery,
I could not call you. (○)

→ My cell phone ran out of battery, **so** I could
not call you. (○)

我的手機沒電，所以無法打電話給你。

CH
9

9-3

從屬連接詞

245

Although Sandy went to bed early last night, **but / yet** she still felt tired in the morning. (×)

→ **Although** Sandy went to bed early last night, she still felt tired in the morning. (○)

→ Sandy went to bed early last night, **but / yet** she still felt tired in the morning. (○)

雖然珊蒂昨晚提早就寢，她早上仍感到很疲倦。

3 連接性副詞

連接性副詞又稱轉折語，本身是副詞，與從屬連接詞不同，不可用於連接兩個句子。連接性副詞主要的功能是用於轉折或承接，可依其意思大致分項列舉如下：

連接性副詞之意思	例字
表示附加	also、in addition、moreover、furthermore、additionally、besides
表示對比	however、nevertheless、instead、in contrast、on the contrary
表示因果	therefore、thus、consequently、as a result
表示舉例	for example、for instance
表示強調	actually、in fact、as a matter of fact
表示總結	in short、in conclusion、all in all

I know Rick, **however** I am not friends with him.
(×，however 為副詞，不可直接用於連接兩句)

→ I know Rick. **However,** I am not friends with him.
(○，副詞 however 可置句首用於修飾全句)

→ I know Rick**; however,** I am not friends with him.
(○，however 為副詞，前可置分號連接兩句)

→ I know Rick**, but** I am not friends with him.
(○，but 為連接詞，可直接連接兩句)
我知道瑞克，但我跟他不是朋友。

Liz is very responsible, therefore I like working with her.
（✗，therefore 為副詞，不可直接用於連接兩句）

→ Liz is very responsible. Therefore, I like working with her.
（○，副詞 therefore 可置句首用於修飾全句）

→ Liz is very responsible; therefore, I like working with her.
（○，therefore 為副詞，前可置分號連接兩句）

→ Liz is very responsible, so I like working with her.
（○，so 為連接詞，可直接連接兩句）
麗茲很有責任感，所以我喜歡跟她共事。

＼ 即時演練 ／

一、單選題

① Paula has been afraid of rats _____ she was a little girl.
(A) while　　　(B) since　　　(C) until　　　(D) once

② Jane won't be in the office tomorrow _____ she is taking the day off.
(A) because　　(B) before　　(C) unless　　(D) while

③ The little girl didn't want to play the game _____ she might lose and cry.
(A) so that　　　　　　　(B) on condition that
(C) provided that　　　　(D) for fear that

④ _____ you work hard, you are likely to receive a raise.
(A) In case　　　　　　(B) Even though
(C) As long as　　　　(D) In order that

⑤ _____ Stuart can't pay me back, I'll still lend him the money.
(A) Even if　　(B) So long as　(C) Every time　(D) So that

二、請圈選出正確的連接詞或副詞。

① (While / When) Evan was ten, he broke his arm in an accident.

② (Until / While) Claire's idea was creative, her manager thought it would cost too much money.

③ Ivan forgot to close the front door (when / while) he came into the house.

④ Denise is a terrible dancer; she sings well, (although / though).

⑤ The data was not useful at all, (moreover / and) many details were wrong.

解　答				
一、① B	② A	③ D	④ C	⑤ A
二、① When	② While	③ when	④ though	⑤ and

248

Chapter 10

分詞

Chapter 10   分詞

10-1   現在分詞與過去分詞

分詞是由動詞演變而來的，可分為現在分詞與過去分詞，區別如下：

分詞種類	現在分詞	過去分詞
形式	動詞 + ing	動詞 + ed
表示的語態	主動	被動
表示的動作	正在進行	已完成

❶ 分詞的功用

(1) 與助動詞並用以形成各種時態或被動語態：

❶ 進行式（即：be 動詞 + V-ing）

例句 My brother **is washing** the dishes.
我哥哥正在洗碗。

❷ 完成式（即：have / has / had + 過去分詞）

例句 Carrie **has finished** her homework.
凱莉已經寫好功課了。

❸ 被動語態（即：be 動詞 + 過去分詞）

例句 The flight **was canceled**.
該班機被取消了。

(2) 作形容詞：修飾之後或之前的名詞

❶ 修飾之後的名詞

例句 The **crying boy** is my neighbor's son.
那個在哭的男孩是我鄰居的兒子。

The **injured soldier** insisted that he could still fight.
那名受傷的士兵堅持認為他還能打仗。

2 修飾之前的名詞

例句
Do you know the girl singing on stage?
你認識在舞臺上唱歌的女孩嗎？

The man arrested by the police on the street was a thief.
在街上被員警逮捕的那個人是個小偷。

(3) 作副詞：修飾之後的形容詞

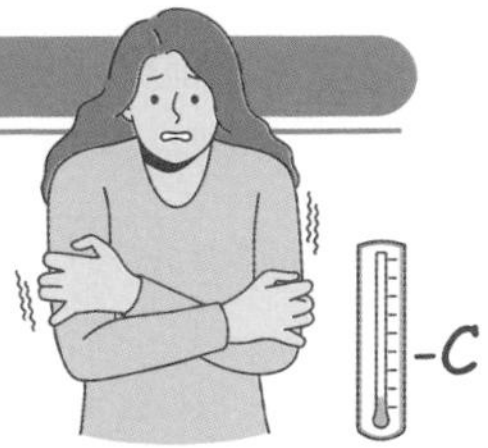

圖示
副詞 + 形容詞

例句
Gosh, it's freezing cold today.　天哪，今天好冷。
I won't stay in the boiling hot car.　我才不會待在這熱如燒鍋的車上。

(4) 作主詞補語：對主詞做補充說明

圖示
主詞 + 動詞 + 主詞補語

例句
The movie sounds exciting.　這部電影聽起來很刺激。
Tom looked confused.　湯姆看起來很困惑。

(5) 作受詞補語：對受詞做補充說明

圖示
主詞 + 動詞 + 受詞 + 受詞補語

例句
I saw Hank jogging in the park on my way home.
我在回家的路上看到漢克在公園慢跑。
Susan got her computer fixed.
蘇珊的電腦修好了。

2 動詞變成現在分詞的規則

1 一般動詞

說明
直接在字尾加 ing 即可

例字	look ▸ looking（看）	work ▸ working（工作）
	borrow ▸ borrowing（借）	attend ▸ attending（參加）

❷ 字尾為不發音的 e

說明	此時去掉 e，再加 ing

例字	bake ▸ baking（烘烤）	smile ▸ smiling（微笑）
	dance ▸ dancing（跳舞）	arrive ▸ arriving（到達）

註	字尾為 oe 或 ye 時，e 不去掉，直接加 ing

例字	tiptoe ▸ tiptoeing（踮起腳走）	shoe ▸ shoeing（給（馬）釘蹄鐵）
	canoe ▸ canoeing（划獨木舟）	dye ▸ dyeing（給……染色）

❸ 字尾為 c（發音為 [k]）

說明	此時加 k，再加 ing

例字	picnic ▸ picnicking（野餐）	traffic ▸ trafficking（非法買賣）
	panic ▸ panicking（恐慌）	mimic ▸ mimicking（模仿）

❹ 字尾為 ie

說明	此時去掉 ie 加 y，再加 ing

例字	lie ▸ lying（說謊）	die ▸ dying（死亡）
	tie ▸ tying（捆）	

❺ 單音節動詞的字尾為「單一短母音＋單子音」

說明	此類動詞要重複字尾，再加 ing

例字	shop ▸ shopping（購物）	plan ▸ planning（計劃）
	stop ▸ stopping（停止）	jog ▸ jogging（慢跑）

註	請注意在此字尾指的單一短母音和單子音皆是指**字母**，而非音標。故如 wear [wɛr]（穿；戴）的後半部是單一短母音 [ɛ]＋單子音 [r]，但其母音的字母為 ea（即兩個母音的字母），因此其加 ing 並不用重複最後一個子音的字母，即其 ing 的形式為 wearing。

6 兩個音節以上的動詞，重音在最後一個音節，其字尾為「單子音 + 單一短母音 + 單子音」，或其字尾的發音為 [ɝ]

| 說明 | 此類動詞要重複字尾，再加 ing |

| 例字 | permit ▸ permitting（允許）　prefer ▸ preferring（偏好）
omit ▸ omitting（省略）　occur ▸ occurring（發生） |

3 動詞變成過去分詞的規則

規則變化

1 一般動詞

| 說明 | 直接在字尾加 ed 即可 |

| 例字 | look ▸ looked（看）　work ▸ worked（工作）
borrow ▸ borrowed（借）　attend ▸ attended（參加） |

2 字尾為 e（不論發音與否）

| 說明 | 此時直接加 d |

| 例字 | bake ▸ baked（烘烤）　smile ▸ smiled（微笑）
agree ▸ agreed（同意）　free ▸ freed（釋放） |

3 字尾為 c（發音為 [k]）

| 說明 | 此時加 k，再加 ed |

| 例字 | picnic ▸ picnicked（野餐）　traffic ▸ trafficked（非法買賣）
panic ▸ panicked（恐慌）　mimic ▸ mimicked（模仿） |

4 字尾為「子音 + y」

| 說明 | 此時去掉 y，再加 ied |

| 例字 | try ▸ tried（嘗試）　study ▸ studied（學習）
carry ▸ carried（攜帶）　marry ▸ married（結婚） |

5	單音節動詞的字尾為「單一短母音 (的字母) + 單子音 (的字母)」
說明	此類動詞要重複字尾，再加 ed
例字	shop ▸ shopped (購物)　　plan ▸ planned (計劃) stop ▸ stopped (停止)　　jog ▸ jogged (慢跑)

6	兩個音節以上的動詞，重音在最後一個音節，其字尾為「單子音 + 單一短母音 + 單子音」，或其字尾的發音為 [ɝ]
說明	此類動詞要重複字尾，再加 ed
例字	permit ▸ permitted (允許)　　prefer ▸ preferred (偏好) omit ▸ omitted (省略)　　occur ▸ occurred (發生)

不規則變化

詳細列表請參考附錄一：不規則動詞變化表的過去分詞部分。

❹ 情緒動詞

情緒動詞	
定義	為表達情緒或心理感受的動詞
例字	interest (使感興趣)　　worry (擔心)　　annoy (使生氣) satisfy (使滿意)　　excite (使興奮)　　frighten (使害怕)

情緒動詞的現在分詞與過去分詞作形容詞

	情緒動詞的現在分詞	情緒動詞的過去分詞
形式	動詞 + ing	動詞 + ed
意思	令人……的	感到……的

254

常修飾	事物	人
常見用法	❶ 現在分詞 + 名詞 ❷ 事物 + be 動詞 / 連綴動詞 + 　現在分詞	❶ 過去分詞 + 名詞 ❷ 人 + be 動詞 / 連綴動詞 + 　過去分詞
例字及其搭配詞	interesting (令人覺得有趣的) satisfying (令人有滿足感的) exciting (令人興奮的) worrying (令人擔心的) annoying (令人生氣的) frightening (令人害怕的) 	interested in... (對……感興趣的) satisfied with... (對……感到滿意的) excited about / at / by... (對……很興奮的) worried about... (擔心……的) annoyed at / about... (對……感到生氣的) frightened about / of... (對……感到害怕的) scared of... (對……感到害怕的)
註	❶ scared 表「感到很害怕的」，而表「令人害怕的」並非 scaring，而是既有的形容詞 scary。 ❷ 關於此類用字為數眾多無法一一列舉，建議讀者遇到此類字詞可以查詢字典然後熟記。	
例句	I won't see that frightening movie again. 我不會再看那部很恐怖的電影了。 The cartoon was exciting for the children. 這卡通讓孩子們興奮不已。	The annoyed man banged on the door. 那個惱怒的男子砰砰地敲門。 Bob was worried about his daughter's health. 鮑伯很擔心他女兒的健康。

一、請寫出下列單字正確的現在分詞 (V-ing)。

原形動詞 VS 現在分詞 (V-ing)		原形動詞 VS 現在分詞 (V-ing)	
① move	_____	⑤ panic	_____
② tie	_____	⑥ commit	_____
③ walk	_____	⑦ dye	_____
④ set	_____	⑧ run	_____

二、請寫出下列單字正確的過去分詞 (p.p.)。

原形動詞 VS 過去分詞 (p.p.)		原形動詞 VS 過去分詞 (p.p.)	
① help	_____	⑤ hurry	_____
② tidy	_____	⑥ picnic	_____
③ wave	_____	⑦ need	_____
④ stop	_____	⑧ refer	_____

三、請圈選出正確的形容詞。

① All of the workers were (shocking / shocked) at the bad news.

② What you just said is quite (interesting / interested).

③ David has been (fascinating / fascinated) by stars since he was a boy.

④ Winnie was really (tiring / tired) from the hiking.

⑤ This is a very (touching / touched) story.

解　答

一、① moving　② tying　③ walking　④ setting　⑤ panicking
　　⑥ committing　⑦ dyeing　⑧ running

二、① helped　② tidied　③ waved　④ stopped　⑤ hurried
　　⑥ picnicked　⑦ needed　⑧ referred

三、① shocked　② interesting　③ fascinated　④ tired　⑤ touching

Chapter 10　分詞

10-2　用分詞作補語的常見動詞

依不同動詞的使用方式，分詞在句子中可作主詞補語或受詞補語。以下依分詞作**主詞補語**或**受詞補語**分項闡述：

❶ 用分詞作主詞補語的常見動詞

除了上節提到連綴動詞的用法之一「主詞 + 連綴動詞 + 情緒動詞的現在分詞 / 過去分詞」為分詞作主詞補語的句型之外，以下茲列舉一些也是用分詞作主詞補語的動詞：

(1) come　來

句型	主詞 + come + { 現在分詞　★表主詞「主動」 過去分詞　★表主詞「被動」

例句

As soon as he saw his grandmother, the little boy **came running** to hug her.　小男孩一看到他的奶奶，就跑過來抱她。

The secretary **came unnoticed** into the meeting room since everyone was focusing on Lisa's presentation.
由於每個人都在專心聽麗莎報告，沒人注意到祕書進到會議室來。

(2) sit　坐；位於

句型一	主詞 + sit + 現在分詞　★表主詞「主動」 　　　（坐）

例句

The guests **sat chatting** and **laughing** in the yard as Judy and her husband prepared dinner.
茱蒂和她老公準備晚餐時，客人們都坐在院子裡談笑風生。

句型二	主詞 + sit + 過去分詞　★表主詞「被動」 　　　（位於）

例句

Due to the lockdown to control the disease, the rides in amusement parks have been **sitting unused** for a while.
因為要控制該疾病而封城，遊樂園的遊樂設施已閒置一陣子了。

(3) lie　躺；處於……狀態

句型一	主詞 + lie + 現在分詞　★表主詞「主動」 （躺）
例句	As Ella and her friends lay laughing in the grass, they wished the moment would last forever. 艾拉和她朋友躺在草地上大笑時，他們希望這一刻能永遠持續下去。
句型二	主詞 + lie + 過去分詞　★表主詞「被動」 （處於）
例句	One of the paintings by this famous artist lay hidden in the castle for over a century. 這位知名藝術家的其中一幅畫隱身藏在這座城堡裡超過一百年。

❷ 用分詞作受詞補語的常見動詞

(1) 知覺動詞（尤指 see、hear、listen to、feel等）

句型	主詞 + 知覺動詞 + 受詞 + ⎰ 原形動詞 / 現在分詞　★表受詞「主動」 ⎱ 過去分詞（較少見）　★表受詞「被動」
例句	My mom heard her cell phone ringing, but she didn't know where exactly the sound was coming from. 我媽聽到她手機響，但不知道聲音究竟是從哪裡來。 Jill never saw her father depressed. He always looked on the bright side.　吉兒從沒看過她父親沮喪過。他總是很樂觀。

(2) 使役動詞 make / have / let / get　使 / 讓

句型一	主詞 + make / have + 受詞 + ⎰ 原形動詞　★表受詞「主動」 ⎱ 過去分詞　★表受詞「被動」
例句	Eating highly processed food will make you want to eat more. 吃高度加工的食物會讓你想吃更多。 I'm going to have my hair cut tomorrow. 我明天要去剪頭髮。

| 句型二 | 主詞 + get + 受詞 + { to + 原形動詞　★ 表受詞「主動」 / 過去分詞　★ 表受詞「被動」 |

例句

How did you get the children to become so quiet?
你是怎麼讓這些孩子變這麼安靜的？

Have you gotten your car fixed?
你的車修好了嗎？

| 句型三 | 主詞 + let + 受詞 + { 原形動詞　★ 表受詞「主動」 / be + 過去分詞　★ 表受詞「被動」 |

例句

Don't let Mom know I was late for school again.
別讓媽知道我上學又遲到了。

Please fill in this form and let your opinions be heard.
請填寫此表格好讓我們知道您的意見為何。

CH
10

10-2

用分詞作補語的常見動詞

(3) find、leave / keep、catch 等

| 句型 | 主詞 + { find (發現) / leave / keep (使保持) / catch (發現 / 撞見) } + 受詞 + { 現在分詞　★ 表受詞「主動」 / 過去分詞　★ 表受詞「被動」 } |

例句

I often found my grandmother sitting quietly on the sofa and looking at old photos.
我經常發現我奶奶靜坐在沙發上看著舊照片。

The volunteer work keeps my grandfather occupied, so he seldom feels bored.
當志工讓我爺爺很忙，所以他幾乎都不覺得無聊。

(4) want　想要 / 希望

| 句型 | 主詞 + want + 受詞 + { to + 原形動詞　★ 表受詞「主動」 / 過去分詞　★ 表受詞「被動」 } |

例句

Do you want me to give you a ride?
要我載你一程嗎？

The manager wants the products sent today.
經理想今天就把這些產品寄出去。

① Although the superstar got a lot of birthday presents, many of them still lay _____ one month after her birthday.
(A) open   (B) opened   (C) unopened   (D) opening

② Mark came _____ into the room and told me he got promoted.
(A) rush   (B) rushing   (C) rushed   (D) to rush

③ The little boy sat _____ as he waited to see the dentist in the clinic.
(A) tremble   (B) trembled   (C) to tremble   (D) trembling

④ Steve's mother worried about him because he hadn't eaten anything for a day. The food sat _____ on his desk.
(A) touch   (B) touching   (C) untouched (D) untouchable

⑤ Could you get the stove _____ tomorrow?
(A) fixing   (B) fix   (C) to fix   (D) fixed

⑥ When are you going to have your new house _____?
(A) painted   (B) painting   (C) paint   (D) to paint

⑦ I caught my brother _____ my mom's money.
(A) stolen   (B) stole   (C) stealing   (D) steal

⑧ Don't let yourself _____ by the salesman.
(A) fooled   (B) fool   (C) fooling   (D) be fooled

⑨ We heard the boss _____ loudly in his office.
(A) shouting   (B) to shout
(C) shouted   (D) to have shouted

⑩ I caught Larry _____ with terror in front of a spider.
(A) to freeze   (B) frozen   (C) froze   (D) freezing

① C 　理由　主詞 many of them 是指「很多禮物」，因此空格應為過去分詞以
表被動；又根據上下文得知句意應為：很多禮物還「沒拆開」來。

② B 　理由　主詞 Mark（馬克）為「人」，且根據上下文得知前半句句意應為：
馬克「衝進」房間，故空格應為現在分詞以表主動。

③ D 　理由　主詞 The little boy（小男孩）為「人」，且根據上下文得知男孩應
是坐著「發抖」，故空格應為現在分詞以表主動。

④ C 　理由　空格本句之主詞 The food（食物）為「物」，且根據上下文得知第
二句句意應為：放在他桌上的食物沒「被動過」，因此空格應為過
去分詞以表被動。

⑤ D 　理由　受詞 the stove（火爐）為「物」，且根據上下文得知火爐應是「被
修理」，故空格應為過去分詞以表被動。

⑥ A 　理由　受詞 your new house（你的新房子）為「物」，且根據上下文得知
新家應是「被粉刷」，故空格應為過去分詞以表被動。

⑦ C 　理由　受詞 my brother（我弟弟）為「人」，且根據上下文得知句意應
為：我逮到弟弟「偷」媽媽的錢，故空格應為現在分詞以表主動。

⑧ D 　理由　本句句意為：別讓自己「被」推銷員「騙」了，因此空格應為過去
分詞以表被動；又 let（讓）的用法之一為「let + 受詞 + be + 過去
分詞」，其中 be 不可省略。

⑨ A 　理由　受詞 the boss（老闆）為「人」，且根據上下文得知句意應為：我
們聽到老闆大聲「吼叫」，故空格應為現在分詞以表主動。

⑩ B 　理由　sb be frozen with terror 表「某人嚇呆 / 傻了」，故空格應為過
去分詞以表被動。

CH
10

10-2

用分詞作補語的常見動詞

Chapter 10　分詞

10-3　有關分詞的句型簡化

此類句型大致上有兩種：分詞構句 和 分詞片語，以下將分別闡述：

1 分詞構句

以下兩種子句可利用分詞構句使句子更加精簡：

1 副詞子句　　**2** 對等子句

分詞構句常用於表達下列意思：

原因	because / since / as 等
前後時間順序	after、as soon as / on / upon、before、as、and 等
行為同時發生	when / while、and 等
條件	if 等
讓步	although / (even) though 等
額外資訊或結果	and

(1) 簡化副詞子句成分詞構句

1 副詞子句和主要子句的主詞相同時，刪除副詞子句的主詞。

2 副詞子句的動詞：

　①一般動詞 → 改成現在分詞

　② be 動詞 → 改成現在分詞 being 後可予以省略

3 刪除引導副詞子句的從屬連接詞如 because 等。

（若刪除後句意不明，則須保留。）

~~Because~~ ~~she~~ ~~felt~~ really tired, Dora went to bed early.
　　　Feeling

= Feeling really tired, Dora went to bed early.

因為實在是太累了，朵拉很早就去睡覺了。

~~As he was~~ touched by the movie, Gary cried a lot.
     (Being)

= (Being) Touched by the movie, Gary cried a lot.
因為被這部電影所感動，蓋瑞嚎啕大哭了起來。

 註 1
副詞子句若為否定句，not 須置於分詞之前。若有助動詞 do / does / did，則須刪除。

 例句
Since he didn't know what to do, Jeff just took out his cell phone again and read some news stories.

= Not knowing what to do, Jeff just took out his cell phone again and read some news stories.
由於傑夫不知道要做什麼，他就再拿出手機看了一些新聞報導。

 註 2
副詞子句若為現在 / 過去完成 (進行) 式，動詞須改成如下：

1 完成式：
「have / has + 過去分詞」或「had + 過去分詞」
→ 改成「having + 過去分詞」

2 完成進行式：
「have / has been + 現在分詞」或「had been + 現在分詞」
→ 改成「having been + 現在分詞」

3 完成式的被動語態：
「have / has been + 過去分詞」或「had been + 過去分詞」
→ (having been) + 過去分詞

 例句
Because she has lived here for about 10 years, Linda knows which local restaurant is the best.

= Having lived here for about 10 years, Linda knows which local restaurant is the best.
因為琳達在這裡住了大約十年，她知道本地哪家餐廳最好。

As he had been waiting for his meal for one hour, Kenny asked the waiter what was wrong.

= Having been waiting for his meal for one hour, Kenny asked the waiter what was wrong.
肯尼等餐等了一個小時，於是問服務生怎麼一回事。

例句

After he had been told that he passed the exam, Hank jumped up and down.

= **(Having been) Told** that he passed the exam, Hank jumped up and down.

有人告訴漢克他通過了考試後,他雀躍不已。

(2) 簡化對等子句成分詞構句

 步驟

1. 由對等連接詞 and 連接的兩個對等子句的主詞相同時,視語意刪除其中一個子句的主詞。

(若兩個子句的主詞一個是用名詞表示,另一個是用代名詞表示,而刪除的主詞為名詞時,剩餘的代名詞應改成該名詞)

2. 主詞已刪除的子句:

  ① 一般動詞 → 改成現在分詞

  ② be 動詞 → 改成現在分詞 being 後可予以省略

3. 刪除 and。(若原本 and 之前無逗點,則刪除 and 後須加上逗點。)

 例句

Calvin leaned on the wall, ~~and he~~ ~~replied~~ to some messages. **replying**

= Calvin leaned on the wall, **replying** to some messages.

卡爾文靠在牆上,回覆一些訊息。

Terry ~~was~~ scolded for hurting his sister, ~~and he~~ admitted
  (Being)   **Terry**
he was guilty.

= **(Being) Scolded** for hurting his sister, **Terry** admitted he was guilty.

泰瑞傷了妹妹被罵,便承認自己有錯。

Nancy ~~was~~ dancing slowly alone, ~~and she~~ was drinking some champagne.   **Nancy**

= **Dancing** slowly alone, **Nancy** was drinking some champagne.

或 Nancy was dancing slowly alone, ~~and she was~~ drinking some champagne.

= Nancy was dancing slowly alone, **drinking** some champagne.

南希獨自慢舞,喝著香檳。

註 1 已刪除的子句若為否定句，not 置於分詞之前。
（若有助動詞 do / does / did 也刪除。）

 例句

Erin drew the picture again and again, **and she still didn't feel** satisfied with it.

= Erin drew the picture again and again, **still not feeling** satisfied with it.
艾琳這張圖畫了一遍又一遍，還是感到不滿意。

 註 2 已刪除的子句若為現在 / 過去完成（進行）式，動詞須改成如下：

1 完成式：
「have / has + 過去分詞」或「had + 過去分詞」
→ 改成「having + 過去分詞」

2 完成進行式：
「have / has been + 現在分詞」或「had been + 現在分詞」
→ 改成「having been + 現在分詞」

3 完成式的被動語態：
「have / has been + 過去分詞」或「had been + 過去分詞」
→ (having been) + 過去分詞

 例句

The little boy **had eaten** a big meal, **and he** couldn't eat anything more.

= **Having eaten** a big meal, **the little boy** couldn't eat anything more.
小男孩已吃了一頓大餐，再也吃不下任何東西了。

Eric **has been playing** basketball for three hours, **and he** still wants to continue.

= **Having been playing** basketball for three hours, **Eric** still wants to continue.
艾瑞克已經打籃球三個小時了，他還想繼續打。

Rita **had been trained** very well, **and she** deserved first prize.

= **(Having been) Trained** very well, **Rita** deserved first prize.
麗塔受過很好的訓練，她得到第一名實至名歸。

獨立分詞構句

 定義 副詞子句和主要子句的主詞不同時，或是 and 連接的兩個對等子句的主詞不同時，為精簡句子可使用獨立分詞構句。

 步驟 同分詞構句的步驟，只是不刪除任一個子句的主詞（即沒有步驟一）。

 例句

~~Because~~ the prime minister ~~was~~ seriously ill, the meeting
        being
was canceled.

= The prime minister being seriously ill,
  the meeting was canceled.
  由於首相病重，會議取消了。

~~Since~~ the convincing proof ~~had~~ been destroyed, Dan failed
        having
to prove his innocence.

= The convincing proof having been destroyed, Dan failed to
  prove his innocence.
  由於有力的證據已被破壞，丹未能證明自己的清白。

~~Sally's~~ hair ~~was~~ blowing in the wind, ~~and she~~ looked just
Her   Sally
like a movie star.

= Her hair blowing in the wind, Sally looked
  just like a movie star.
  莎莉的頭髮隨風飄揚，看起來就像個電影明星。

❷ 分詞片語（形容詞子句化簡法）

 說明 一個句子含有限定用法的形容詞子句（即關係代名詞之前無逗點的形容詞子句）時，為精簡句子可將該子句簡化成分詞片語，而此形容詞子句化簡法僅適用於關係代名詞為形容詞子句中的主詞時。

步驟
1 刪除關係代名詞 who、which 或 that。
2 形容詞子句的動詞改為分詞：
   ① 一般動詞 → 改成現在分詞
   ② be 動詞 → 改成現在分詞 being 後可予以省略

 例句

According to the study, students who / that live in poverty tend to sleep less.

= According to the study, students living in poverty tend to sleep less.

根據研究，貧困的學生往往睡得更少。

The man who / that is talking with my father is my uncle.

= The man talking with my father is my uncle.

和我父親說話的人是我舅舅。

The cakes from the bakery are not as delicious as the ones which / that are made by my mom.

= The cakes from the bakery are not as delicious as the ones made by my mom.

這家麵包店的蛋糕沒有我媽媽做的蛋糕好吃。

\ 即時演練 /

單選題

① _____ in the company for more than 10 years, Kevin is an experienced salesman.
(A) Has worked   (B) Having worked
(C) Worked   (D) Work

② Who is the girl _____ badminton with Jeff in the yard?
(A) play   (B) played   (C) playing   (D) plays

③ Many villagers went to the mountains with their dogs, _____ for the missing boy.
(A) search   (B) searched   (C) to search   (D) searching

④ _____ in Spain for a decade, Steve could probably answer any question about the country.
(A) Having been living   (B) Has been living
(C) Has Lived   (D) Lived

⑤ Emily stood at the door, _____ goodbye to her grandparents.
(A) said   (B) saying   (C) say   (D) says

⑥ I think the dish _____ by Jamie is the best.
(A) cook   (B) cooking   (C) cooks   (D) cooked

⑦ _____ enough money, Rex decided to walk home.
(A) Didn't have   (B) Doesn't have
(C) Not having   (D) Not had

⑧ Although _____, the mother still gave the food to her children first.
(A) was very hungry   (B) very hungry
(C) be very hungry   (D) to be very hungry

⑨ Here is another building _____ by this famous architect.
(A) designing   (B) design   (C) designed   (D) designs

⑩ John _____, we had no choice but to look for his replacement.
(A) having been fired   (B) being firing
(C) had been fired   (D) was fired

268

① B　理由　此為化簡副詞子句成分詞構句，原句為：
Because he has worked in the company for more than 10 years, Kevin is an experienced salesman.

② C　理由　此為化簡形容詞子句成分詞片語，原句為：
Who is the girl who / that is playing badminton with Jeff in the yard?

③ D　理由　此為化簡對等子句成分詞構句，原句為：
Many villagers went to the mountains with their dogs, and they searched for the missing boy.

④ A　理由　此為化簡副詞子句成分詞構句，原句為：
Because he has been living in Spain for a decade, Steve could probably answer any question about the country.

⑤ B　理由　此為化簡對等子句成分詞構句，原句為：
Emily stood at the door, and she said goodbye to her grandparents.

⑥ D　理由　此為化簡形容詞子句成分詞片語，原句為：
I think the dish which / that was cooked by Jamie is the best.

⑦ C　理由　此為化簡副詞子句成分詞構句，原句為：
Because he didn't have enough money, Rex decided to walk home.

⑧ B　理由　此為化簡副詞子句成分詞構句，原句為：
Although she was very hungry, the mother still gave the food to her children first. (此處的 Although 不能省略，因會造成句意上的落差。)

⑨ C　理由　此為化簡形容詞子句成分詞片語，原句為：
Here is another building which / that was designed by this famous architect.

⑩ A　理由　此為化簡副詞子句成獨立分詞構句，原句為：
After John had been fired, we had no choice but to look for his replacement.

CH
10

10-3

有關分詞的句型簡化

269

10-4　常見分詞慣用語

有些現在分詞或過去分詞常會搭配其他字詞形成慣用語，且具有固定的形式以及固定的用法。以下依用法分項闡述：

❶ 當副詞片語用

❶ generally / broadly / roughly speaking
一般來說 / 大體上來說

> 例句　Generally speaking, gaining too much weight is not good for your health.　一般來說，體重增加太多有害健康。

❷ strictly speaking　嚴格來說

> 例句　Strictly speaking, your mother can only have five teaspoons of oil a day.　嚴格來說，你母親一天只能攝取五茶匙的油。

❸ honestly / frankly speaking　老實說 / 坦白說

> 例句　Honestly speaking, I never thought Bruce would win the gold medal.　老實說，我從沒想過布魯斯會拿金牌。

❷ 當介詞片語用

❶ speaking / talking of...　說到 / 起……

> 例句　Speaking of Derek, I heard that he broke up with his girlfriend.　說到德瑞克，我聽說他和他女友分手了。

❷ judging from / by...　根據……判斷 / 來看

> 例句　Judging from his appearance, the man seems to be the leader of this tribe.　從這男子的外表來看，他似乎是這部落的首領。

❸ concerning / regarding...　關於……（= about...）

> 例句　The professor conducted a study regarding the native people on this island.　教授對此島上的原住民進行了研究。

4 according to...　　根據……

例句　According to those living near the house, the fire broke out at about 2:00 a.m.　根據住在這房子附近的人說，火災發生在凌晨兩點左右。

5 considering / given...　　考慮到……
= considering how... / who...　　考慮到……多麼／誰……

例句　Considering the money and time our company has spent on it, this product is not so satisfying.　考慮到我們公司在這產品上所花費的金錢和時間，這產品並不是那麼令人滿意。

6 including...　　包括……（= ... included）

例句　We should all take part in the singing contest, including Ada.
= We should all take part in the singing contest, Ada included.
我們應該要參加歌唱比賽，包括艾達在內。

7 excluding...　　除……之外，不包括……（= ... excluded）

例句　All clothes here are 40% off, excluding new arrivals.
= All clothes here are 40% off, new arrivals excluded.
除了新品外，這裡所有衣服都打六折。

8 following...　　在……之後（= after...）

例句　Following the fashion show, there will be an after-party.
時裝秀結束後，會有一場小型的派對。

3 當連接詞用

1 providing / provided + (that) 子句　　如果……（= if）
= supposing / suppose + (that) 子句

註　此處 suppose 當連接詞用法，不是動詞，故無動詞變化形。

例句　Providing that you have a balanced diet and exercise regularly, you can keep in shape easily.
如果飲食均衡並規律運動，就可保持健康體態。

2 seeing that / as + 主詞 + 動詞　　既然／因為……

例句　Seeing that you're busy, I'll talk to you later.
因看你在忙，我晚一點再跟你聊。

3 considering + (that) 子句　　考慮到……

= given (the fact) + that 子句

例句
Considering that she has never played tennis before, Gail is pretty good.
考慮到蓋兒以前從沒打過網球,她表現得還算不錯。

\ 即時演練 /

單選題

① _____ his voice, he must have just woken up.
(A) Judged from　　　　　　(B) Judging from
(C) Being judged by　　　　(D) To judge by

② _____ that you pass the exam, we can travel abroad during the summer vacation.
(A) Provided　　　　　　　(B) To provide
(C) Being provided　　　　(D) Being providing

③ _____, the writer is British, not Japanese, since he has British nationality.
(A) Over and over　　　　　(B) Some day
(C) Now and then　　　　　(D) Strictly speaking

④ _____ the news, there was a serious car accident on the freeway.
(A) Instead of　　　　　　(B) According to
(C) Rather than　　　　　(D) Due to

⑤ _____ how little he is, it is quite amazing that this boy finished the race.
(A) Considered　　　　　　(B) To consider
(C) Considering　　　　　(D) Consider

解　答

① B	② A	③ D	④ B	⑤ C

Chapter 11

動名詞

273

Chapter 11 動名詞

11-1 動名詞的功能：作主詞、受詞、主詞補語或同位語

動名詞即由動詞演變而來的名詞，是原形動詞再加 ing，形式和現在分詞一樣，但兩者的用法卻不同：

❶ 動名詞與現在分詞之比較

	動名詞	現在分詞
形式	原形動詞 + ing	
用法	當「名詞」使用；表用途等	當「形容詞」使用；表動作等
例句	Dale enjoys cooking. 戴爾很喜歡烹飪。 ★ 及物動詞 enjoys 後面接受詞，cooking 在此為動名詞，扮演名詞的角色。 Where did you buy these dancing shoes? 你在哪裡買這些舞鞋的？ ★ dancing shoes 表「舞鞋」，dancing 在此表用途，故為動名詞。	Eddy is cooking. 艾迪在煮飯。 ★ 此句為現在進行式「be 動詞 + 現在分詞」，cooking 在此為現在分詞用來形成時態。 A dancing kid suddenly became popular on the internet. 網路上一個在跳舞的小孩突然走紅。 ★ A dancing kid 表「一個在跳舞的小孩」，dancing 在此表動作，故為現在分詞。

❷ 動名詞的功能

動名詞（片語）擔任名詞的角色，其功能可作主詞、受詞、主詞補語或同位語，以下茲分別闡述：

(1) 作主詞

 例句
Painting is my grandfather's hobby.
畫畫是我爺爺的嗜好。

註 動名詞（片語）作主詞時，其視為單數，因此其後的動詞須為第三人稱單數形。

(2) 作受詞

1 在介詞後作受詞

 例句
Gary was worried about failing the test again.
蓋瑞擔心考試再次不及格。

2 在及物動詞後作受詞

 例句
My sister likes reading.
我姊姊喜歡閱讀。

(3) 作主詞補語：對主詞做補充說明

 例句
Dana's favorite sport is swimming.
黛娜最喜歡的運動是游泳。

(4) 作同位語：對之前的名詞等做補充說明

 例句
One of Gina's hobbies, skiing, costs a lot of money.
吉娜的嗜好之一是滑雪，而那所費不貲。

3 動名詞的否定形式

 句型
not + 動名詞

 例句
Not taking the medicine regularly will put you at risk.
不定期服藥會帶來風險。

Karen felt bad about not being able to help the poor animal.
凱倫對於無法幫助那隻可憐的動物感到很難過。

CH
11

11-1

動名詞的功能：作主詞、受詞、主詞補語或同位語

❹ 下列動詞後可接動名詞，以作受詞用

 句型 動詞 + 動名詞（片語）

例字

enjoy（喜愛）	suggest / recommend / advise（建議）	imagine（想像）
finish（結束）		involve（包含）
mind（介意）	consider（考慮）	appreciate（感激）
quit（停止）	avoid（避免）	anticipate（預期）
miss（錯過；想念）	dislike（不喜歡）	report（報告，匯報）
keep（繼續）	delay / postpone（使延遲）	recall（回想起）
practice（練習）	admit（承認）	resist（克制）
deny（否認）	risk（冒險）	escape（逃脫）

 例句

It's so hot today, so I suggest staying home and listening to music.
今天太熱了，所以我建議待在家裡聽音樂。

Have you considered moving to the city?
你有考慮過要搬到都市嗎？

You should avoid mentioning the sensitive topic at the meeting.
你應該避免在會議上提及這敏感話題。

 ❺ 下列動詞後可接動名詞，以表「被動」

 句型
動詞 + 動名詞
= 動詞 + be 動詞 + 過去分詞

 例字
need（需要）
deserve（應 / 值得）

例句

This old car needs fixing.
= This old car needs to be fixed.
這輛老車需要修理一下。

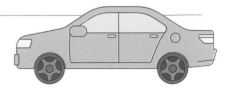

What Eliot said yesterday deserves mentioning.
= What Eliot said yesterday deserves to be mentioned.
艾略特昨天說的話應該提一下。

276

6 下列動詞後可接動名詞或不定詞片語（即 to + 原形動詞），意思相同

句型

動詞 + 動名詞
= 動詞 + to + 原形動詞

例字

begin / start（開始）	hate（厭惡）	cease（停止）
love（愛）	prefer（偏好）	stand / bear（忍受）
like（喜歡）	continue（繼續）	propose（打算，計劃）

例句

It **started** raining, so Haley closed all the windows.
= It **started** to rain, so Haley closed all the windows.
開始下雨了，所以海莉把窗戶都關起來。

Keith **prefers** eating a whole foods diet.
= Keith **prefers** to eat a whole foods diet.
凱斯偏好吃原型食物。

7 下列動詞後可接動名詞或不定詞片語（即 to + 原形動詞），但意思不同

1 stop +
動名詞　　　　停止做……
to + 原形動詞　停下手邊之事去做……

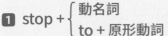

例句

Stop watching TV. Come to help me.　別看電視了。來幫幫我。
Being thirsty, Luke **stopped** to buy a coffee.
因路克口渴了，他便停下來買了杯咖啡。

2 remember +
動名詞　　　　記得已做過……
to + 原形動詞　記得要去做……

例句

Julie **remembered** visiting this place before.
茱莉記得曾來過此處。

Remember to turn off the lights when you leave.
你走時記得要把燈關掉。

3 forget +
動名詞　　　　忘記已做過……
to + 原形動詞　忘記要去做……

例句

I'll never **forget** seeing the beautiful sunrise on the beach for the first time.　我永遠不會忘記第一次在海灘看到美麗日出的情景。
I **forgot** to wake up my brother this morning.
我今早忘記叫我弟起床了。

CH 11

11-1

動名詞的功能：作主詞、受詞、主詞補語或同位語

4 try +
- 動名詞 — 嘗試做…… ★ 不一定盡全力去做
- to + 原形動詞 — 設法要做…… ★ 盡全力去做

例句
I **tried** starting up the computer, but it didn't work.
我試過將電腦開機，但沒有用。

Ron threw away all the junk food at his home and **tried** to eat more healthily.
榮恩扔掉家裡所有的垃圾食物，設法要吃得更健康一點。

5 go on +
- 動名詞 — 繼續做……
- to + 原形動詞 — 做完手邊之事接著去做……

例句
Although the other classmates took a rest, Ray **went on** dancing.
雖然其他同學都休息了，雷還是繼續跳舞。

After doing the dishes, Bruce **went on** to sweep the floor.
洗完碗後，布魯斯繼續掃地。

6 regret +
- 動名詞 — 後悔已做過……
- to + 原形動詞 — 很遺憾 / 抱歉要做……

註
「regret + to + 原形動詞」之原形動詞常用 say (說)、tell (告訴)、inform (告知)、announce (宣告) 等。

例句
My brother **regretted** making such a stupid mistake.
我弟弟很後悔曾犯下這樣愚蠢的錯誤。

I **regret** to say that I can't attend your birthday party.
很遺憾我得告訴你我不能參加你的生日派對。

7 mean +
- 動名詞 — 意味著 / 結果是……
- to + 原形動詞 — 打算 / 計劃做……

例句
Being a professional pianist would **mean** practicing day and night.
成為一名專業鋼琴家意味著要一直練琴。

I **meant** to help Melissa mail a letter, but I forgot all about it.
我本要幫梅莉莎寄封信，但我完全忘了。

8 dread +
- 動名詞 — 怕做……
- to + 原形動詞 — 不敢做……

註
「dread + to + 原形動詞」之原形動詞常用 think (想)。

Hugo **dreaded** <u>talking</u> to the serious teacher.
雨果害怕跟那位嚴肅的老師說話。

I **dread** <u>to think</u> how much money we would have to borrow from the bank if we bought the house.
我不敢去想如果買了那棟房子，我們得向銀行借多少錢。

＼ 即時演練 ／

一、單選題

① The tennis player denied ＿＿＿＿＿＿＿＿＿ any illegal drugs.
(A) take (B) to take (C) taking (D) took

② The little boy's shoes need ＿＿＿＿＿＿＿＿＿.
(A) washing (B) wash (C) washed (D) be washed

③ Many people are tired of ＿＿＿＿＿＿＿＿＿ travel abroad during the lockdown aimed at controlling the serious disease.
(A) to be not able to (B) not to be able to
(C) being not able to (D) not being able to

④ Would you mind ＿＿＿＿＿＿＿＿＿ me the pepper, please?
(A) pass (B) passing (C) passed (D) to pass

⑤ I miss ＿＿＿＿＿＿＿＿＿ with my grandmother in the yard.
(A) chat (B) chatted (C) to chat (D) chatting

二、請圈選出正確的答案。

① I met my old friend and asked him whether he remembered (to play / playing) several tricks on me when we were young.

② Although the shy student suddenly forgot what to say, the teacher gave him a hint and encouraged him to go on (to speak / speaking).

③ Could we just stop (to have / having) some snacks? I really need to eat something since I didn't have time for breakfast.

④ I regretted (to shout / shouting) at my mother the other day; that's why I said sorry to her yesterday.

⑤ I meant (to clean / cleaning) the house this afternoon, but my best friend called me and we talked for hours.

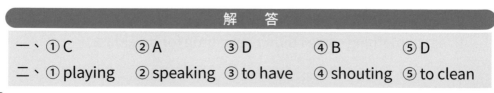

解　答

一、① C　　　② A　　　③ D　　　④ B　　　⑤ D

二、① playing　② speaking　③ to have　④ shouting　⑤ to clean

Chapter 11 動名詞

11-2 常見動名詞慣用語與句型

此類慣用語與句型在此概略分為三類： to + 動名詞 、 of + 動名詞 及
其他常見動名詞慣用語與句型 ：

1 to + 動名詞

❶ in addition to + 動名詞　　除……之外還做……
= besides + 動名詞

> 例句
> In addition to being a singer, Elmer is also the owner of several restaurants and drink shops.
> 艾爾馬除了是名歌手之外，還是好幾間餐館和飲料店的老闆。

❷ When it comes to + 動名詞　　談到做……

> 例句
> When it comes to looking after children, Herbert is always impatient.
> 說到照顧小孩，赫伯特總是很不耐煩。

❸ object to + 動名詞　　反對做……
= oppose + 動名詞
= be opposed to + 動名詞（★ 此處 opposed 是形容詞，表「反對的」）
= be against + 動名詞

> 例句
> I object to working in such a dangerous environment.
> = I oppose working in such a dangerous environment.
> = I'm opposed to working in such a dangerous environment.
> = I'm against working in such a dangerous environment.
> 我反對在如此危險的環境下工作。

❹ look forward to + 動名詞　　期盼做……

> 例句
> I'm looking forward to going to the amusement park next weekend.
> 我很期待下週末去遊樂園。

281

❺ devote oneself / one's life to + 動名詞 　　致力於做……
= devote one's time / attention / energy to + 動名詞
= be devoted to + 動名詞
= commit oneself to + 動名詞
= be committed to + 動名詞
= dedicate oneself / one's life to + 動名詞
= be dedicated to + 動名詞
= apply oneself / one's mind to + 動名詞

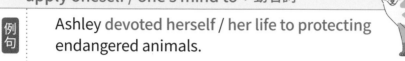

例句	Ashley devoted herself / her life to protecting endangered animals.
	= Ashley was devoted to protecting endangered animals. 艾希莉畢生致力於保護瀕臨絕種的動物。

❻ be / get accustomed to + 動名詞 　　習慣做……
= be / get used to + 動名詞
= adjust to + 動名詞

例句	My grandfather isn't accustomed to living in the city and thinks there is too much traffic. 我爺爺不習慣住在城市，他認為車太多了。

註	use 當「使用」之意時，其被動用法為：be used to + 原形動詞

例句	The money in this account is used to pay monthly fees such as the phone bill. 此帳戶中的錢是用來支付電話費等月費的。

❼ confess to + 動名詞 　　承認做……
= admit (to) + 動名詞
= own up to + 動名詞

例句	My boyfriend confessed to lying to me about his job. 我男朋友承認有關他的工作他都在對我撒謊。

❽ reaction to + 動名詞 　　對做……的反應

例句	Let's see the little girl's funny reaction to meeting her father's twin brother. 咱們且看一看這小女孩見到她爸爸的雙胞胎哥哥時的有趣反應。

9 devotion / dedication to + 動名詞　　專心致力於做⋯⋯

例句 The principal is greatly respected in part because of her enormous dedication to helping poor students.
這位校長之所以備受尊敬，部分原因是因她努力幫助貧困的學生。

10 come close / near to + 動名詞　　差一點做⋯⋯

例句 The couple came close to boarding the plane successfully.
這對情侶差一點就可以登機了。

11 with a view to + 動名詞　　為了做⋯⋯
= with an eye to + 動名詞
= for the purpose of + 動名詞
= in order to + 原形動詞
= so as to + 原形動詞

例句 The old houses were knocked down with a view to building a museum there.　拆掉這些老房子是為了在那裡蓋座博物館。

12 take to + 動名詞　　開始習慣做⋯⋯

例句 Erica has taken to exercising in the morning.
艾瑞卡已經習慣在早上運動。

2 of + 動名詞

1 instead of + 動名詞　　而不是做⋯⋯

例句 Jimmy went down the stairs instead of taking the elevator.
吉米走下樓梯，而沒有搭電梯。

2 dream of + 動名詞　　夢想⋯⋯；作夢⋯⋯

例句 Jim dreamed of being a pilot.
吉姆的夢想是成為一名機師。

3 make a point of + 動名詞　　重視做⋯⋯

例句 Gillian makes a point of reading her child a bedtime story every day.
吉莉恩很重視每天給她小孩讀床前故事。

4 make a habit / practice of + 動名詞　　養成做……的習慣 ★強調動作

例句
Ben has **made a habit of getting** up early.
班養成了早起的習慣。

5 be in the habit of + 動名詞　　有做……的習慣 ★強調事實

例句
Ben **is in the habit of getting** up early.
班有早起的習慣。

---

3 其他常見動名詞慣用語與句型

1 be busy + 動名詞　　忙於做……

例句
Andy **was busy replying** to customers' emails.
安迪正忙著回覆客戶的電子郵件。

2 What / How about + 動名詞?　　做……怎麼樣？

例句
How about going to the movies tomorrow?
明天去看電影如何？

3 feel like + 動名詞　　想做……
= would like to + 原形動詞

例句
Calvin got sick and doesn't **feel like eating** anything.
卡爾文病了，不想吃任何東西。

4 have trouble / difficulty + 動名詞　　做……(方面) 有困難
= have a hard time + 動名詞

例句
I **have trouble getting** along with Douglas.
我跟道格拉斯處不來。

5 have fun + 動名詞　　做……玩得很愉快

例句
I **had** lots of **fun hiking** with my friends last weekend.
上週末我和朋友去健行玩得很愉快。

284

6 cannot / can't help + 動名詞　　忍不住做……
= cannot / can't (help) but + 原形動詞

例句

Dana **couldn't help laughing** when she saw the little girl wearing her mom's shoes.

= Dana **couldn't (help) but laugh** when she saw the little girl wearing her mom's shoes.

黛娜看到小女孩穿著她媽媽的鞋子，忍不住笑了出來。

7 far from + 動名詞　　根本不……

例句

Far from helping ease his stomachache, the medicine actually made Greg feel more uncomfortable.

這藥不僅沒有幫葛瑞格緩解胃痛，反而讓他更不舒服。

8 insist on + 動名詞　　堅持做……

例句

The actress **insisted on having** a coffee from a store that was far away from here.

這女演員堅持要喝某家店的咖啡，而這家店離這裡很遠。

9 be worth + 動名詞　　值得做……

例句

The historic buildings in this city **are worth visiting** because many of them were built more than 200 years ago.

這座城市的歷史建築都值得一遊，因為很多都是兩百多年前建的。

10 do the + 動名詞　　做……

註

在此之動名詞常為 cooking（烹飪）、shopping（購物）、washing（洗衣服）、ironing（熨燙）等。

例句

It's my turn to **do the cooking** tomorrow.

明天輪到我煮飯了。

11 There is no + 動名詞　　不可能做……

例句

There is no negotiating with that stubborn woman.

和那頑固的女人沒得商量。

常見動名詞慣用語與句型

12 It / There is no use + 動名詞　　做……是沒有用的
= There is no sense in + 動名詞
= It is useless to + 原形動詞

 例句

It / There is no use complaining too much.
= There is no sense in complaining too much.
= It is useless to complain too much.
抱怨太多是沒用的。

＼ 即時演練 ／

單選題

① _____ being frustrated, Heidi encouraged herself and was determined to win the gold medal next time.
(A) According to　(B) Such as　　(C) Instead of　(D) As if

② I don't feel like _____ jogging this evening. Could we just take a walk?
(A) go　　　　　(B) going　　　(C) went　　　(D) to go

③ Larry's company had difficulty _____ a suitable manager.
(A) find　　　　　　　　　　　(B) found
(C) to be found　　　　　　　(D) finding

④ Jared objected _____ being charged for the damage, which was not caused by him.
(A) to　　　　　(B) with　　　　(C) on　　　(D) ×

⑤ Louis couldn't help but _____ by the sad story told by the old man.
(A) move　　　　(B) moved　　(C) be moved　(D) be moving

⑥ When it comes to _____ jokes, no one is better than Herman.
(A) tell　　　　(B) telling　　(C) be told　(D) told

⑦ Kirk dreamed _____ being chased by ghosts and started yelling, and his mother quickly woke him up.
(A) at   (B) with   (C) of   (D) on

⑧ Greta is used to _____ up late.
(A) stay   (B) staying   (C) stayed   (D) be stayed

⑨ Trust me. This food processor is worth _____ .
(A) owning   (B) owned   (C) own   (D) to own

⑩ Several new products are being created _____ a view to making the company more competitive.
(A) in   (B) at   (C) on   (D) with

11-2

常見動名詞慣用語與句型

解 答				
① C	② B	③ D	④ A	⑤ C
⑥ B	⑦ C	⑧ B	⑨ A	⑩ D

Notes

288

Chapter 12

不定詞

Chapter 12 不定詞

12-1 不定詞的作用一：擔任名詞的角色

不定詞為：**to + 原形動詞**，而當不定詞置於某些動詞後時，to 會省略。又不定詞（片語）的否定型如下：

 句型 **not + to + 原形動詞**

 例句 I told you **not to yell** at Grandfather. He's not deaf.
我跟你說過不要對爺爺大吼大叫。他沒有耳聾。

而不定詞（片語）的作用有三：擔任**名詞**、**形容詞**或**副詞**的角色。以下先介紹不定詞擔任名詞的角色時之功能及相關句型：

❶ 不定詞（片語）擔任名詞的角色之功能

此時不定詞（片語）可作主詞、受詞、主詞補語及受詞補語。

1 作主詞用

 例句 **To complete this task** will be very hard.
要完成這項任務會很困難。
★ 不定詞片語為句子的主詞。

2 作受詞用

 例句 I want **to visit Spain** one day.
我想有朝一日去西班牙玩。
★ 不定詞片語為及物動詞 want 的受詞。

3 作主詞補語用（對主詞做補充說明）

 例句 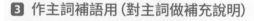 My wish is **to buy a house in that neighborhood**.

我的願望是在那一區買棟房子。
★ 不定詞片語對主詞 My wish 做補充說明。

4 作受詞補語用（對受詞做補充說明）

例句 My parents won't allow me to come home late.

我父母不准我晚回家。

★ 不定詞片語對受詞 me 做補充說明。

2 不定詞（片語）擔任名詞角色時之相關句型

1 To + 原形動詞 + 單數動詞 + ...

譯 做……是……

例句 To own this sports car is my dream.
擁有這臺跑車是我的夢想。

2 It is + 有關事物的形容詞（+ for + 名詞）+ to + 原形動詞
= To + 原形動詞 + is + 有關事物的形容詞（+ for + 名詞）

譯 （對……來說，）要……做……是很……的

註 此句型 It 為虛主詞，真正的主詞為「to + 原形動詞」。

例字 **常用於此類句型的形容詞為：**

important / crucial / vital（重要的）　useful（有用的）
necessary / essential（必需的）　possible（可能的）
convenient（方便的）　impossible（不可能的）
interesting（有趣的）　easy（容易的）
proper / appropriate（適當的）　difficult / hard（困難的）
natural（自然的）　urgent（緊急的）
traditional（傳統的）

例句 　It is important (for all of us) to attend the meeting tomorrow.
= To attend the meeting tomorrow is important (for all of us).
（對我們所有人來說，）參加明天的會議非常重要。

3 It is / was + 有關人本性的形容詞 + of + 人 + to + 原形動詞

譯 （某人）做……很……

註
1 此句型 It 為虛主詞，真正的主詞為「to + 原形動詞」。

例字 常用於此類句型的形容詞為：

nice / kind / good（好心的）　　　　wrong（不正當的）

polite（有禮的）　　　　　　　　　foolish / silly（愚蠢的）

wise（睿智的）　　　　　　　　　　rude（粗魯的）

clever / intelligent（聰明的）　　　careless（粗心的）

brave / bold（勇敢的）　　　　　　selfish（自私的）

loyal（忠心的）　　　　　　　　　naughty（頑皮的）

thoughtful / considerate（體貼的）　stingy（小氣的）

generous（寬宏大量的）　　　　　　greedy（貪心的）

 註 2 以上這些有關人本性的形容詞均可出現在「人 + be 動詞 + 有關人本性的形容詞」形成的句子中，即：

You are nice / polite / generous / selfish / greedy...

在「It is / was + 有關人本性的形容詞 + of + 人 + to + 原形動詞」的句構，一定要使用介詞 of，而非 for，即不可說：

It is very kind **for** you to help me move into the new house.（×）

例句 It is very kind **of** you **to help** me move into the new house.
你人真好，幫我搬家。

4 主詞 + 動詞 + to + 原形動詞

例字 以下動詞後常接不定詞（即 to + 原形動詞）：

wish（希望，想要）　　want（想要）　　　　　decide（決定）

hope（希望）　　　　　plan / intend（計劃）　expect（預計）

seem（似乎）　　　　　desire（渴望）

 例句 Lisa **seemed to get** very worried after hearing the news.
麗莎聽到這消息後似乎變得憂心忡忡。

5 主詞 + 動詞 + 受詞 + to + 原形動詞

例字 以下動詞後常接受詞（即名詞 / 代名詞）後，再接不定詞（即 to + 原形動詞）：

ask（要求）　　　　　　force（強迫）　　　　lead（促使）

order / tell（吩咐，命令）　warn（警告）　　　cause（導致）

allow（允許）　　　　　encourage（鼓勵）　　expect（預計）

 例句 Just **ask** one of the students **to erase** the words on the whiteboard.　就叫個學生來擦掉白板上的字就好。

註 **expect（預計）兩種用法皆可，即：**

主詞 + expect + $\begin{cases} \text{to + 原形動詞} \\ \text{受詞 + to + 原形動詞} \end{cases}$

 例句 I expect to finish this project within two months.
我預計兩個月內會完成這項專案。

We expect the profits to increase by 30% this year.
我們預計今年利潤會成長 30%。

6 主詞 + 動詞 + it + $\begin{cases} \text{形容詞} \\ \text{名詞} \end{cases}$ + to + 原形動詞

註 此句型 it 為虛受詞，真正的受詞為「to + 原形動詞」。

 例字 **常用於此類句型的動詞為：**

think / consider / feel（覺得，認為）　　　　make（使變成）

 例句 We think it necessary to help the victims of the flood as much as we can.　我們認為有必要來盡全力幫助洪水的災民。

I thought it a good idea to watch some English TV dramas to improve my listening skills.
我覺得看英文電視劇來改善我的聽力是個好主意。

7 不定詞省略 to：知覺動詞
知覺動詞指表示「看」、「聽」、「感覺」的動詞。
see（看見）　　　　watch（注意看）　　　　feel（感覺到）
hear（聽見）　　　　listen to（注意聽）
這些均為不完全及物動詞，補語有三種：

 句型一 主詞 + 知覺動詞 + 受詞 + 原形動詞
★ 強調已發生的事實

 例句 I saw Peter leave the office this afternoon.
今天下午我看到彼得離開辦公室了。

 句型二 主詞 + 知覺動詞 + 受詞 + 現在分詞
★ 強調正在發生的動作

 例句 I saw Peter leaving the office this afternoon.
今天下午我看到彼得正離開辦公室。

CH
12

12-1

不定詞的作用一：擔任名詞的角色

主詞 + 知覺動詞 + 受詞 + 過去分詞

★ 強調被動的動作，較少見

例句
On my way home, I saw a bleeding child rushed to the hospital.
在我回家的路上，我看到一個血流不止的小孩被緊急送往醫院。

8 不定詞省略 to：使役動詞（尤指 have、make、let）

主詞 + $\begin{Bmatrix} have \\ make \\ let \end{Bmatrix}$ + 受詞 + 原形動詞

譯 使 / 讓……做……

例句
I like to play with my 3-year-old niece because she always makes me laugh.
我喜歡和我三歲的姪女玩，因為她總是讓我發笑。

9 不定詞可省略 to：

All you have to / need to / can do is (to) + 原形動詞

= What you have to / need to / can do is (to) + 原形動詞

譯 你必須要 / 需要 / 能做的事是做……

例句
All you have to do is (to) sign this paper.
你要做的就是簽這份文件。

10 不定詞可省略 to：

主詞 + help + 受詞 + (to) + 原形動詞

譯 幫……做……

例句
Would you help me (to) put the toys into the box?
你能幫我把玩具放進盒子嗎？

單選題

① My parents warned me _____ near the beach during ghost month.
(A) not go   (B) to not go   (C) do not go   (D) not to go

② Since it's impossible _____ everyone, just do what you think is right.
(A) please   (B) to please   (C) pleasing   (D) pleased

③ Claudia considered _____ important to set an example for her children.
(A) it   (B) this   (C) that   (D) its

④ To listen to your child _____ also to love him.
(A) are   (B) be   (C) is   (D) were

⑤ All you have to do is just _____ a check by the items that you place in the box.
(A) put   (B) putting   (C) has put   (D) be put

⑥ Edith saw a man _____ a snack from the convenience store and told the clerk right away.
(A) stole   (B) steal   (C) stolen   (D) to steal

⑦ I helped the old lady _____ up the coins she dropped on the ground.
(A) picked   (B) picking   (C) pick   (D) be picked

⑧ It is very considerate _____ you to prepare a vegetarian meal for me.
(A) for   (B) with   (C) at   (D) of

CH 12

12-1

不定詞的作用一：擔任名詞的角色

解 答				
① D	② B	③ A	④ C	⑤ A
⑥ B	⑦ C	⑧ D		

Chapter 12　不定詞

12-2　不定詞的作用二：擔任形容詞的角色

不定詞（片語）除了作名詞外，還可作形容詞，此時不定詞（片語）的功能為修飾其前的**名詞**或**代名詞**，也可作**主詞補語**用。

① 修飾其前的名詞

句型	名詞 + to + 原形動詞
註	此類句型也可用形容詞子句來替換。
例句	I have no **friends** to help me now. = I have no **friends** that / who can help me now. 我現在沒有朋友可以幫我。 ★ 關係代名詞 that / who 為形容詞子句裡的主詞 I have lots of **homework** to do. = I have lots of **homework** that / which I must / should do.　我有很多功課要做。 ★ 關係代名詞 that / which 為形容詞子句裡及物動詞 do 的受詞

② 修飾其前的代名詞

句型	everything / everybody / everyone（每個事物 / 每個人） something / somebody / someone（某事物 / 某人） anything / anybody / anyone（任何事物 / 任何人） nothing / nobody / no one（沒有東西 / 沒有人） none（一點兒 / 個也沒） + to + 原形動詞
註	此類句型也可用形容詞子句來替換。

例句	I have **something** to tell you. = I have **something** that / which I must / should tell you.　我有話要告訴你。 ★ 關係代名詞 that / which 為此形容詞子句裡授與動詞 tell 的直接受詞

名詞 + to + 原形不及物動詞 + 介詞

說明

不定詞擔任形容詞的角色時，若其「to + 原形動詞」之原形動詞為不及物動詞，則此動詞之後的介詞不可省略，使不定詞之前的名詞作該介詞之受詞。

例句

Elmer wants to buy a house to live. (×)
Elmer wants to buy a house to live in. (○)

= Elmer wants to buy a house that / which he can live in.
= Elmer wants to buy a house in which he can live.
艾爾馬想買棟房子住。

Give me a chair to sit. (×)
Give me a chair to sit in. (○)

= Give me a chair that / which I can sit in.
= Give me a chair in which I can sit.
給我張椅子我要坐下來。

3 作主詞補語用 (對主詞做補充說明)

句型

主詞 + be 動詞 + to + 原形動詞

1 表「將會……」(= will) 或「預計會……」(= be going to)

例句

The mayor is to visit the local charities next week.

市長下週將造訪本地的慈善機構。

2 表「應該」(= should)

例句

You are not to eat here.

你不該在這裡吃東西。

3 表「可能」(= can)

例句 Few local people **are** to be seen in Rome during the summer vacation.
暑假期間很少會在羅馬看到當地人。

＼ 即時演練 ／

單選題

① The poor girl has no relatives _____.
    (A) relying   (B) relying on   (C) to rely   (D) to rely on

② Do you have anybody _____ to besides your parents?
    (A) talk   (B) talking   (C) to talk   (D) talked

③ The famous novelist _____ a speech at the hall next Friday.
    (A) is given   (B) is to give   (C) giving   (D) be to give

④ Douglas had lots of emails _____ today.
    (A) to reply   (B) to reply to   (C) replying   (D) replying to

⑤ I have something _____ in my bag. Do you want some?
    (A) to eat   (B) eat   (C) ate   (D) be eaten

解　答				
① D	② C	③ B	④ B	⑤ A

Chapter 12 　不定詞

12-3 　不定詞的作用三：擔任副詞的角色

❶ 不定詞（片語）擔任副詞的角色之功能

此時不定詞（片語）可修飾其前的動詞、形容詞、副詞或修飾整句。

❶ 修飾其前的動詞

例句	Yesterday Edward came to see my brother.

愛德華昨天來看我哥哥。　★ 不定詞片語修飾動詞 came。

❷ 修飾其前的形容詞

例句	I'm very sad to hear the bad news.

聽到這壞消息，我非常難過。　★ 不定詞片語修飾形容詞 sad。

❸ 修飾其前的副詞

例句	The hot chocolate is too hot to drink.

熱可可太燙了，還不能喝。　★ 不定詞片語修飾副詞 too。

❹ 修飾主要子句

例句	To tell you the truth, I don't really want to go to the party.

說實話，我並不想參加派對。　★ 不定詞片語修飾主要子句。

❷ 不定詞（片語）擔任副詞角色時之相關句型及慣用語

❶ (in order) to + 原形動詞
= so as to + 原形動詞
= with a view to + 動名詞
= with an eye to + 動名詞
= for the purpose of + 動名詞

譯	為了做……

例句
My mother exercises every day (in order) to keep fit.
= My mother exercises every day so as to keep fit.
= My mother exercises every day with a view to keeping fit.
= My mother exercises every day with an eye to keeping fit.
= My mother exercises every day for the purpose of keeping fit.
我媽媽每天運動以保持健康。

 註
此句型之否定型為：

in order not to + 原形動詞
= so as not to + 原形動詞

 例句
Dorothy got up early this morning in order not to be late for the important meeting.
= Dorothy got up early this morning so as not to be late for the important meeting.
為了重要的會議不要遲到，桃樂西今天早上很早起來。

2 主詞 + be 動詞 + 形容詞 + to + 原形動詞

 譯
……很……做……

 例字
常用於此類句型的形容詞有兩類：

1 與情緒相關的形容詞

happy / glad / pleased / delighted（高興的）

excited（興奮的）

amazed（感到驚奇的）

proud（自豪的）

surprised（驚訝的）

shocked（震驚的）

sorry（深感遺憾的 / 很難過的）

sad / unhappy（傷心的）

afraid（害怕的）

disappointed / upset（沮喪的）

2 其他形容詞

sure / certain（一定的）

willing（願意的）

ready（準備好的；願意的）

eager / anxious（渴望的）

right（對的，合乎道德的）

wrong（不對的，不道德的）

lucky（幸運的）

careful（小心的）

likely（可能的）

fortunate（幸運的）

reluctant（不情願的）

| 例句 | I'm proud to be your father.　身為你的父親，我感到非常自豪。
Clara is willing to do anything to make her child happy.
為了讓孩子開心，克拉拉願意做任何事。|

| ❸ 或 | 主詞 + be 動詞 + so + 形容詞 + as to + 原形動詞
主詞 + 動詞 + so + 副詞 + as to + 原形動詞 |

| 譯 | ……如此……以至於…… |

| 例句 | How can you be so ignorant as to ask the teacher how much he earns a month?　你怎麼會這麼無知去問老師一個月賺多少錢？
Some words, such as "all right," are misspelled so often as to become almost acceptable in two forms.（The other is "alright."）
有些字，如 all right，經常拼錯，頻繁到幾乎可以接受兩種拼法。
（另一種拼法為 alright。）|

| ❹ 或 | 主詞 + be 動詞 + 形容詞 + enough + to + 原形動詞
主詞 + 動詞 + 副詞 + enough + to + 原形動詞 |

| 譯 | ……夠……而可做…… |

| 註 | 此句型的形容詞／副詞必置於 enough 之前。|

| 例句 | Greta is wealthy enough to buy that expensive house, isn't she?
葛瑞塔很有錢，可以買下那棟昂貴的房子，不是嗎？
The company acted quickly enough to avoid more complaints from the customers.　此公司動作夠迅速，而避免了更多客訴。|

| ❺ 或 | 主詞 + be 動詞 + too + 形容詞 + to + 原形動詞
主詞 + 動詞 + too + 副詞 + to + 原形動詞 |

| 譯 | ……太……而無法從事…… |

| 例句 | You're still too young to make important decisions by yourself.
你還太年輕，還不能自己做重要的決定。
Haley worked too late to go to the movies with her friends.
海莉工作到太晚了，而沒有和朋友一起去看電影。|

| ❻ = | to tell (you) the truth　老實說
to be frank / honest (with you) |

| 例句 | To tell the truth, I don't trust your friend Ivan.
老實說，我並不信任你的朋友艾凡。|

7 needless to say 　　當然，不必 / 用說

例句 Needless to say, you're my everything. I love you the most.
不用說，你是我的一切。我最愛你了。

8 not to mention... 　　更不必說……
= not to mention the fact + that 子句
= to say nothing of...
= not to speak of...

例句 Jacob is good at playing the guitar and the violin, not to mention the piano. 　雅各擅長彈吉他和拉小提琴，彈鋼琴就更不用說了。

9 to be sure 　　肯定地，無可否認地

例句 Larry is bad-tempered, to be sure, but he is not calculating.
賴瑞脾氣當然很暴躁，但他沒有心機。

10 to put it another way 　　換句話說

例句 The elephant is still very young; to put it another way, it's still too early to set it free in the wild.
這隻大象還很小；換句話說，現在把牠野放還為時過早。

11 to do... justice 　　替……說句公道話，平心而論

例句 To do her justice, I think Kayla has done her best.
說句公道話，我認為凱拉已經盡力了。

12 sad / strange to say 　　真可惜 / 說來奇怪

例句 Sad to say, this historic building is not well preserved.
真可惜，這棟歷史建築物並沒有保存得很好。

13 To begin / start with, ... 　　首先，……
= First / Firstly, ...

例句 The trip was terrible. To begin with, there wasn't any hot water in the bathroom in the hotel.
這次旅行很糟。首先，旅館的浴室沒熱水。

14 To sum up, ... 　　總結來說，……
= To conclude / summarize, ...

例句 To sum up, the plan to increase taxes is a terrible idea.
總之，這項增稅計畫是個很糟的想法。

⑮ To top it all (off), ...　　更糟的是，……（= Even worse, ...）；
　　　　　　　　　　　　　　　更棒的是，……（= Even better, ...）

例句 Ronald broke up with his girlfriend last week. To top it all off, his company laid off several employees, including him.
羅納德上週和女友分手了。更糟的是，他公司解僱了包括他在內的幾名員工。

This is the most delicious apple pie I've ever had. To top it all off, it's on the house.
這是我吃過最好吃的蘋果派了。更棒的是，這派是餐廳免費招待的。

⑯ To make a long story short, ...　　長話短說，……

例句 I met Lindsay on my trip to Europe, and we both had a good time together. To make a long story short, we're getting married next month.
我在歐洲旅行時遇到了琳賽，我們一起度過了愉快的時光。長話短說，我們下個月就要結婚了。

⑰ so to speak　　可以這麼說，可謂

註 此不定詞慣用語尤指以有趣或特別的方式來講述某人／事物，因此並非從表面的字義上去理解。

例句 We're in the same boat, so to speak.
可以這麼說，我們現在面臨同樣的困境。

\ 即時演練 /

單選題

① Julia is training hard every day _____ make sure she can finish the marathon that will take place next month.
(A) as a result of　　　　　(B) in order to
(C) in addition to　　　　　(D) with a view to

② My daughter was very upset _____ that we can't go to the amusement park next weekend.
(A) to hear　　(B) hear　　(C) be heard　　(D) heard

③ I'm not so foolish _____ totally believe what the salesperson said.
(A) as of　　　　　(B) as if　　　　(C) as though　(D) as to

④ Samuel speaks Italian, French, and Japanese, _____ English.
(A) with regard to　　　　　(B) in spite of
(C) at the end of　　　　　(D) not to mention

⑤ Roger left his house early _____ get stuck in the traffic jam.
(A) not so as to　　　　　(B) so as not to
(C) in not order to　　　　　(D) not in order to

⑥ I believe our son is _____ to make the right decision by himself.
(A) mature enough　　　　　(B) enough mature
(C) such mature　　　　　(D) mature so

⑦ Stan failed the math test last week. _____ , his girlfriend broke up with him today.
(A) To begin with　　　　　(B) To make a long story short
(C) To put it another way　　　(D) To top it all off

⑧ The problem is _____ complicated to solve on our own. Maybe we should ask some experts for advice.
(A) so　　　　(B) such　　　　(C) too　　　　(D) enough

解　答				
① B	② A	③ D	④ D	⑤ B
⑥ A	⑦ D	⑧ C		

Chapter 12　不定詞

12-4　其他與不定詞相關的常見慣用語

以下列舉之常見慣用語皆使用不定詞並省略 to，如：

❶ do nothing but + 原形動詞　　除了……之外什麼也沒做，只做……

> **例句**　Samuel **did nothing but eat and sleep** yesterday.
> 薩姆爾昨天除了吃和睡之外，什麼也沒做。

❷ cannot / can't (help) but + 原形動詞　　忍不住……
= cannot / can't help + 動名詞

> **例句**　When his mother was singing his favorite song, the little boy **couldn't help but sing along** with her.
>
> = When his mother was singing his favorite song, the little boy **couldn't help singing along** with her.
> 當小男孩的媽媽在唱著他最喜歡的歌時，他就忍不住跟著她一起唱。

❸ would rather + 原形動詞 + than + 原形動詞　　寧願……也不願……

> **例句**　Although the convenience store was just around the corner, Tim **would rather ride** a scooter **than walk**.
> 雖然便利商店就在附近，但提姆寧願騎摩托車也不要走路去。

❹ had better + 原形動詞　　最好做……
= had best + 原形動詞（口語用法）

> **註1**　❶ 在此為 had，非 have。
> ❷ 此句型可縮寫成：
> 'd better + 原形動詞 = 'd best + 原形動詞（口語用法）

> **例句**　You **had better / best go to** the dentist's since you have had a toothache for several days.
>
> = You**'d better / best go to** the dentist's since you have had a toothache for several days.
> 因你牙痛好幾天了，你最好去看牙醫。

註 2 | 此句型之否定型為：
had better not + 原形動詞

 例句 | You **had better not eat** too much red meat.
你最好不要吃太多紅肉。

＼ 即時演練 ／

句子重組

① would rather / than go shopping / watch a movie / I

_____.

② better / go to bed / early / had / You

_____.

③ video games / did nothing / play / I / this afternoon / but

_____.

④ at night / had / drink coffee / not / You / better

_____.

⑤ help / cry loudly / but / Terry / couldn't

_____.

解 答

① I would rather watch a movie than go shopping
② You had better go to bed early
③ I did nothing but play video games this afternoon
④ You had better not drink coffee at night
⑤ Terry couldn't help but cry loudly

Chapter 13

名詞子句

Chapter 13　名詞子句

13-1　引導名詞子句的特定字

名詞子句是有「主詞 + 動詞」的子句,是一種從屬子句(即必須依附主要子句,無法單獨存在的子句),在句子中扮演名詞的角色。名詞子句常由下列三種特定字引導:

引導名詞子句的特定字	
從屬連接詞	that、whether、if
疑問詞	who、what、when、where、why、which、how
複合關係代名詞	what、whatever、whoever、whomever、whichever 等

以下分項闡述:

1 that 引導的名詞子句

 說明　that 引導名詞子句時,that 本身並無意義。

 例句　Paul thinks **that it is fine to eat fast food from time to time.**　保羅認為偶爾吃速食是沒問題的。

2 whether、if 引導的名詞子句

 說明　whether 或 if 引導名詞子句時,表「是否」,常與 or not 搭配使用。但 if 引導的名詞子句中,or not 僅能置於子句的句尾。句型如下:
- **1** whether (or not) + 主詞 + 動詞
- **2** whether / if + 主詞 + 動詞 + (or not)

 例句
The managers are discussing **whether (or not) they should hire Charles.**
= The managers are discussing **whether / if they should hire Charles (or not).**
主管們在討論是否要聘僱查爾斯。

I don't know **whether / if Lindsay has a boyfriend (or not).** (○)
I don't know **if Lindsay (or not) has a boyfriend.** (✕)
我不知道琳賽是否有男朋友。

3 疑問詞引導的名詞子句

疑問詞引導的名詞子句雖然是以疑問詞開頭，但句構不同於疑問句，而是應依照直述句的句構並保留時態、人稱的變化，如下：

1 有 be 動詞之句構：

疑問詞 + be 動詞 + 主詞 ？（疑問句）

→ 疑問詞 + 主詞 + be 動詞 （名詞子句）

2 有助動詞 will、must、can 等之句構：

疑問詞 + 助動詞 + 主詞 + 原形動詞 ？（疑問句）

→ 疑問詞 + 主詞 + 助動詞 + 原形動詞 （名詞子句）

3 有助動詞 do、does、did 的一般動詞之句構：

疑問詞 + do / does / did + 主詞 + 原形動詞 ？（疑問句）

→ 疑問詞 + 主詞 + 動詞 （名詞子句）

4 有 have、has、had 的助動詞之句構：

疑問詞 + have / has / had + 主詞 + 過去分詞 ？（疑問句）

→ 疑問詞 + 主詞 + have / has / had + 過去分詞 （名詞子句）

注意

疑問代名詞 who、what、which 在問句中作主詞時，變成名詞子句後則句構不變：

疑問詞（who / what / which）+ 動詞 ？（疑問句）

→ 疑問詞（who / what / which）+ 動詞 （名詞子句）

例句

What is her name?
→ I don't know what her name is.
我不知道她的名字。

How will we get to the airport?
→ We haven't decided how we will get to the airport. 我們還沒決定要怎麼去機場。

例句

Where does my brother work now?
→ I don't know **where my brother works** now.
我不知道我弟弟現在在哪裡工作。

How long has Tracy lived in Canada?
→ I'd like to know **how long Tracy** has lived in Canada.
我想知道崔西在加拿大住多久了。

Who went to the party last night?
→ Mom wants to know **who** went to the party last night.
媽媽想知道有誰參加了昨晚的派對。

❹ 複合關係代名詞引導的名詞子句

說明

複合關係代名詞除了 what 之外,可由關係代名詞後接 -ever 而成的。
常見的複合關係代名詞有下列幾種:

what(所……的東西)　　　　**whomever**(凡……的人)

whatever(……的任何東西)　　**whichever**(任何一個……)

whoever(凡……的人)

例句

What made me angry was the man's attitude.
讓我生氣的是那位男子的態度。

You can buy **whatever you want**.
你可以買任何你想要的東西。

Whoever owns that house must be rich.
那間房子的主人肯定很有錢。

 度補充

what 常見的用法

說明

what 可作疑問詞或複合關係代名詞,而 what 為疑問詞時又分疑問
代名詞與疑問形容詞:

	用法	意義
疑問代名詞	詢問事物、職業、身分等	表「什麼」
疑問形容詞	置於名詞前	表「什麼」
複合關係代名詞	意思等同於 the thing(s) that / which	表「所……的東西」

I wonder **what** Harry's plans are.
我好奇哈利的計畫是什麼。（what 為疑問代名詞）

I don't know **what** time it is.
我不知道現在幾點。
（what 為疑問形容詞，置於名詞 time 之前）

I can't believe **what** Ellen said.

= I can't believe **the thing(s) that** / **which** Ellen said.
我無法相信艾倫所說的。（what 為複合關係代名詞）

＼ 即時演練 ／

請選出下列畫線部分何者為名詞子句。

① At the party, Sally told all the guests that she is getting married.
     (A)   (B)   (C)

② When the news report revealed who the mysterious man was,
          (A)   (B)
everyone was surprised.
          (C)

③ The father quietly opened the door to see if his son was sleeping.
     (A)   (B)   (C)

④ David and I argued over whether we should move or not.
     (A)   (B)   (C)

⑤ Whoever gets the highest score will be the winner of this game.
          (A)   (B)   (C)

解　答

| ① C | ② B | ③ C | ④ C | ⑤ A |

13-2　名詞子句的功能

名詞子句在句子中具有下列四個功能：

名詞子句的功能	說明
作主詞	通常置於句首
作受詞	作及物動詞或介詞的受詞
作補語	作主詞補語或受詞補語
作同位語	常置 the fact、the news、the idea、the belief 等名詞後作其同位語

以下分項闡述：

❶ 名詞子句作主詞

名詞子句作主詞

 說明　除了 if 引導的名詞子句之外，其餘皆可作主詞。名詞子句作主詞時，其後應接單數動詞。

 例句　**That John is not happy with his job is obvious.**
約翰顯然對工作感到不滿意。

Whether the boss will agree to our plan is still unknown.
老闆是否會同意我們的計畫仍未知。

How the prisoner escaped remains a mystery.
這名犯人如何逃脫仍是個謎。

Whoever you bring to the party is fine by me.
不管你帶誰來參加派對，我都沒意見。

深度補充

虛主詞 it 代替名詞子句

說明
名詞子句作主詞時往往會造成主詞過長的現象，因此可使用虛主詞 it 代替，而被代替的名詞子句（真主詞）移至句尾。

例句
上方例句可改寫如下：

It is obvious **that John is not happy with his job.**

It is still unknown **whether the boss will agree to our plan.**

It remains a mystery **how the prisoner escaped.**

It is fine by me **whoever you bring to the party.**

❷ 名詞子句作受詞

❶ 名詞子句作及物動詞的受詞

說明
及物動詞的用意是將動作加諸於他人或他物，故及物動詞後須接受詞。一般而言，所有類型的名詞子句皆可作及物動詞的受詞。

例句
I know **that you can do it.** 我知道你做得到的。

Ted asked me **whether / if the story was true (or not).**
泰德問我這個故事是否為真。

Everyone wants to know **who the actor's new girlfriend is.** 大家都想知道這位演員的新女友是誰。

You are free to do **whatever you want.**
你想做什麼就做什麼。

❷ 名詞子句作介詞的受詞

說明
that 或 if 引導的名詞子句通常不可作介詞的受詞，其餘皆可作介詞的受詞。

例句
Katie is anxious <u>about</u> **whether she got the job (or not).**
凱蒂對於她是否有錄取那份工作感到很緊張。

Grandpa never speaks <u>of</u> **what he went through in the war.**
爺爺從未提起他在戰爭中經歷的事。

This painting will be sold <u>to</u> **whoever offers the most money.**
這幅畫將出售給開價最高的人。

CH
13

13-2

名詞子句的功能

313

❸ 名詞子句作補語

❶ 名詞子句作主詞補語

說明 主詞補語出現於「主詞 + 不完全不及物動詞 + 主詞補語」的句型中,用於補充說明句子的主詞。一般而言,所有類型的名詞子句皆可作主詞補語。

例句 My only worry is that I don't have enough money.
我唯一的擔憂是我的錢不夠。

The question is whether / if the two foreigners can communicate with each other.
問題是這兩位外國人是否能互相溝通。

A new computer was what Gina wanted for her birthday.
吉娜想要的生日禮物是一臺新的電腦。

❷ 名詞子句作受詞補語

說明 受詞補語出現於「主詞 + 不完全及物動詞 + 受詞 + 受詞補語」的句型中,用於補充說明句子的受詞。

例句 Years of experience made him what he is today.
多年的經驗成就了今天的他。

❹ 名詞子句作同位語

名詞子句作同位語

說明 **that** 引導的名詞子句常置下列名詞後作其同位語:

the fact (事實)   the belief (信念;信仰)
the news (新聞;消息)   the thought (想法)
the idea (主意;想法)   the rumor (謠言)

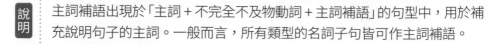

例句 The fact that Jenny is pregnant is still a secret.
珍妮懷孕的事仍是個祕密。

The news that the president was shot shocked everyone.
總統遭到槍擊的新聞令所有人感到震驚。

Julia doesn't like the idea that her son will move overseas.
茱莉亞不喜歡她兒子會搬到海外居住的這個想法。

 度補充

介詞 + the fact + that 子句

說明

上述提及 that 子句不可置介詞之後作其受詞。此情況之補救方法為：在介詞後加上 the fact，使 the fact 作該介詞之受詞，而 that 子句則成 the fact 的同位語。

例句

Ryan's teachers worry about <u>the fact</u> <u>that he is easily distracted</u>.
萊恩的老師很擔心他容易分心。

⑤ 名詞子句使用時的注意事項

① whether 不可被 if 取代的情形

說明

一般而言，whether 與 if 引導的名詞子句皆表示「是否」，可互相替換使用。但在下列情況下 whether 不可被 if 取代：
① 作主詞時　　　　　　　② 作介詞的受詞時

例句

If we should invite Kelly is not decided yet. (✕)
→ Whether we should invite Kelly is not decided yet. (○)
　我們是否該邀請凱莉還未決定。

We are talking about if we should cancel the event. (✕)
→ We are talking about whether we should cancel the event. (○)
　我們在討論是否該取消活動。

② that 可被省略的情形

說明

普遍認為，that 引導的名詞子句接在 say、think、know、hear、believe 等動詞後面作受詞時，可將連接詞 that 省略。此省略用法常見於非正式書寫或日常會話中。

注意

許多情況下，that 可否省略仍頗具爭議，故建議不確定時應保留 that。

例句

Jamie said (that) he will travel abroad soon.
傑米說他即將要出國旅遊。

I know (that) the little boy is lying.
我知道這位小男孩在說謊。

I can't believe (that) Gina is quitting her job.
我不敢相信吉娜要辭掉工作。

一、請勾選下列套色部分的正確功能。

① Erica couldn't remember where she had seen the man before.
☐ 主詞　　　☐ 受詞

② The thought that my parents are getting old makes me sad.
☐ 補語　　　☐ 同位語

③ The topic of my essay is whether working from home is effective.
☐ 受詞　　　☐ 補語

④ Whoever is responsible should take care of the problem.
☐ 主詞　　　☐ 同位語

二、單選題

① I will order _____ you recommend.
(A) that　　(B) whether　　(C) whatever　　(D) when

② We are angry about the fact _____ our trip was ruined.
(A) what　　(B) that　　(C) if　　(D) why

③ _____ the festival will be held depends on the weather.
(A) Whether　　(B) What　　(C) That　　(D) If

④ Years of training made the athlete _____ he is today.
(A) whether　　(B) that　　(C) when　　(D) what

⑤ You can attend the wedding with _____ you want.
(A) whoever　　(B) how　　(C) whether　　(D) that

解　答

一、① 受詞　　② 同位語　　③ 補語　　④ 主詞

二、① C　　② B　　③ A　　④ D　　⑤ A

Chapter 14

關係詞

Chapter 14 關係詞

14-1 關係代名詞

關係代名詞(如 who、which、that 等)的用法與連接詞相似,可用來引導形容詞子句。關係代名詞之前需有先行詞,即該關係代名詞所代替的字(常為名詞、代名詞等),而關係代名詞之後則引導形容詞子句。以下為關係代名詞之相關列表:

先行詞	主格	受格	所有格
人	who	who / whom	whose
動物或事物	which	which	whose / of which
整個句子	which	which	

以下分項介紹各個關係代名詞:

1 先行詞為「人」時

1 who 的用法

 說明
先行詞為「人」,且在形容詞子句中作主格時,應使用關係代名詞 who 來引導形容詞子句。

 例句
Debbie has a brother. He works in the hospital.

→ Debbie has a brother who works in the hospital.
　　　　　　　　　　　先行詞
黛比有個在醫院工作的哥哥。

2 whom 的用法

 說明
先行詞為「人」,且在形容詞子句中作受格(即為及物動詞或介詞的受詞)時,應使用關係代名詞 whom 來引導形容詞子句。

 例句
The man is Gail's uncle. You met him yesterday.

→ The man whom you met yesterday is Gail's uncle.
　　先行詞
你昨天見到的男子是蓋兒的舅舅。

深 度補充

先行詞為受格時使用 who 或 whom

說明　先行詞為「人」，且在形容詞子句中作受格時，應使用 whom 較為嚴謹。然而，非正式的日常生活中已普遍接受以 who 代表受格的用法，然而在正式場合或書寫時，通常仍使用 whom。

注意

關係代名詞作介詞受詞時，可分為下列兩種句構：

❶ 先行詞 + 介詞 + whom + 主詞 + 動詞

❷ 先行詞 + whom / who + 主詞 + 動詞 + 介詞

由上可知，形容詞子句中介詞後若為關係代名詞，此時只能使用 whom，不宜用 who。

例句

The man **whom** you met yesterday is Gail's uncle. (較正式)

= The man **who** you met yesterday is Gail's uncle. (較不正式)
你昨天見到的男子是蓋兒的舅舅。

Leah is someone **with whom** I enjoy working.

= Leah is someone **whom / who** I enjoy working **with**.
莉亞是我喜歡共事的人。

❸ whose 的用法

說明　關係代名詞所有格 whose 是用以代替人稱代名詞所有格 (如 his、her 等)，並引導形容詞子句。

例句

I have a friend. His name is Harry.

→ I have a friend **whose** name is Harry.
　　　　　　　先行詞
我有個叫哈利的朋友。

❷ 先行詞為「動物或事物」時

❶ which 的用法

說明　先行詞為「動物或事物」時，無論是主格或受格，皆使用關係代名詞 which 來引導形容詞子句。

CH 14

14-1

關係代名詞

319

作主格

Rex has <u>a dog</u>. <u>It</u> runs very fast.

→ Rex has <u>a dog</u> **which** runs very fast.
　　　　　先行詞

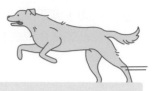

雷克斯有一隻跑很快的狗。

作受格

Amy is wearing <u>a dress</u>. Kimberly likes <u>it</u>.

→ Kimberly likes <u>the dress</u> **which** Amy is wearing.
　　　　　　　　　先行詞

金柏莉喜歡艾咪穿的洋裝。（which 作 is wearing 的受詞）

This is <u>the house</u>. Sam used to live in <u>the house</u>.

= This is <u>the house</u> **which** Sam used to live in.
　　　　　　　先行詞

這是山姆曾經住過的房子。（which 作 in 的受詞）

2 **whose 的用法**

除了代替人之外，關係代名詞所有格 whose 亦可用來代替動物或事物，此時可視為代替人稱代名詞所有格 its。代替動物或事物時，whose 可被 of which 取代，形成下列句構：

先行詞, the + 名詞 + of which + ...（★ 先行詞後必加逗點）

Roy bought <u>a new car</u>. I like <u>its</u> color very much.

→ Roy bought <u>a new car</u> **whose** color I like very much.
　　　　　　　　先行詞

= Roy bought <u>a new car</u>**, the** color **of which** I like very much.

羅伊買了一輛新車，我很喜歡它的顏色。

❸ 先行詞為整個句子時

which 的用法

關係代名詞 which 可用以代替整個句子，此時 which 之前必須置逗點。

例句

Kyle drank two cups of coffee this morning, which made him feel energetic.

凱爾今天早上喝了兩杯咖啡，使他精神百倍。

❹ 限定用法與非限定用法

❶ 限定用法

 說明

限定用法的形容詞子句所修飾的先行詞通常為非特定的，此時形容詞子句是用於為先行詞提供必要的資訊或用以界定範圍。限定用法中，關係代名詞之前不置逗號。

 例句

The book which I am reading is a romance novel.

我正在讀的書是愛情小說。

Lily has a friend who is a lawyer. 莉莉有個當律師的朋友。

❷ 非限定用法

 說明

非限定用法的形容詞子句所修飾的先行詞通常是特定的，如專有名詞（如 Ken、Italy）及獨特性名詞（如 father），此時形容詞子句是用於為先行詞補充額外的資訊，故即使省略也不會影響句意。非限定用法中，關係代名詞之前須搭配逗號使用。

 例句

Cheryl is engaged to Dave, who is ten years older than her.

雪瑞兒與戴夫訂婚了。戴夫比雪瑞兒大十歲。

The player lost the game, which was a surprise to everyone.

這名球員比賽輸了，這讓大家都感到訝異。

❺ 關係代名詞 that

(1) that 的用法

 說明

關係代名詞 that 可用以取代 who、whom 或 which，但僅能用於限定用法的形容詞子句中，且 that 之前不可有介詞。

 例句

The restaurant which we went to last night was good.
= The restaurant that we went to last night was good.
我們昨晚去的餐廳非常好。

CH
14

14-1

關係代名詞

例句 Our manager, that was on leave last week, will return to the office on Monday. (×，非限定用法不可使用 that)

→ Our manager, who was on leave last week, will return to the office on Monday. (○)
我們的主管上週請假，他會在週一回到辦公室。

．．．．．．．．．．．．．．．．．．．．．．．．．．．．．．．．．．．．．

We have many toys with that children can play.
(×，that 之前不可有介詞)

→ We have many toys with which children can play. (○)

= We have many toys that children can play with. (○)
我們有許多玩具供兒童遊玩。

---

(2) 僅能使用 that 的情況

1 先行詞有序數詞 (如 the first...、the last... 等) 時

 例句 The first person that finishes the race will win NT$500,000.
第一位完成比賽的人將贏得新臺幣五十萬。

The last movie that I watched was a horror film.
我上一部看的電影是恐怖片。

2 先行詞有最高級 (如 the best... 等) 時

 例句 Mr. Lee said George is the best student that he has ever taught.
李老師說喬治是他教過最好的學生。

This is the most expensive piece of jewelry that my mother owns.
這是我媽媽所有珠寶中最昂貴的一件。

3 先行詞前有 the only / very / same... 時

例句 Sarah is the only person in our company that can speak Japanese.　莎拉是公司裡唯一會講日文的人。

You are the very man that I want to see.　你正是我想見到的人。

Paul was working in the same department that I was in.
保羅工作隸屬的部門跟我相同。

4 先行詞為代名詞 all、any(thing)、every(thing)、some(thing)、no(thing)、none 等時

| 例句 | All **that** glitters is not gold.
閃閃發亮的東西未必全是金子。/ 虛有其表。—— 諺語 |

5 先行詞同時為「人」與「動物或事物」時

| 說明 | 關係代名詞前的先行詞有兩個,且兩個性質不一時,宜用 that 取代以避免混淆。 |

| 例句 | The rescue team could not find the man and the dog **that** fell into the river. 搜救團隊找不到掉進河裡的男子與狗。 |

6 形容詞子句中出現兩個關係代名詞時

| 說明 | 形容詞子句中若出現兩個關係代名詞,第二個關係代名詞通常應使用 that,以避免重複。 |

| 例句 | Sam broke up with his girlfriend, **which** is something **that** only a few people know.
山姆與他女友分手了,這是只有幾個人知道的事。 |

7 問句中引導的疑問詞為 who 或 which 時

| 說明 | 問句若是由 who 或 which 引導,句中的形容詞子句則應使用 that,以避免重複。 |

| 例句 | Who is the girl **that** is dancing over there?
在那裡跳舞的女孩是誰?
Which cake is the one **that** Patty made?
派蒂做的蛋糕是哪一個? |

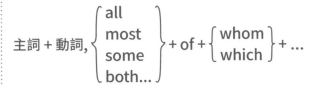

6 其他使用關係代名詞應注意事項

1 whom 與 which 的相關句型

| 句型 | 主詞 + 動詞, { all / most / some / both... } + of + { whom / which } + ... |

| 譯 | ……,他們全部 / 大部分 / 有些 / 兩個都…… |

| 說明 | 此句型的形容詞子句 (如 all of whom / which + ...) 之前必須加上逗點。 |

例句 Mr. Smith has three daughters, **all of whom** are still students.

史密斯先生有三位女兒，她們都還是學生。

Eva made some cookies, **some of which** are chocolate.

伊娃做了一些餅乾，其中有些是巧克力口味的。

2 關係代名詞的省略

 說明 在限定用法的形容詞子句中，若關係代名詞為及物動詞的受詞，則該關係代名詞可省略。此外，若該關係代名詞為介詞的受詞，須將該介詞移至形容詞子句的句尾，方能省略關係代名詞。換言之，若關係代名詞前有介詞，則不可省略。

 例句 Walter loves the food (which / that) the waiter recommended.
（此形容詞子句為限定用法，且關係代名詞 which 或 that 作動詞 recommended 的受詞，故可省略）
華特很喜歡服務生推薦的食物。

This is the hat **for which** Winnie paid NT$1,000.
（關係代名詞 which 前有介詞 for，故不可省略）

→ This is the hat (which / that) Winnie paid NT$1,000 **for**.
（此形容詞子句為限定用法，且關係代名詞 which 作介詞 for 的受詞，而 for 並非在 which 前，故可省略）
這是溫妮花新臺幣一千元買的帽子。

3 形容詞子句的動詞應與先行詞一致

 說明 由於關係代名詞是代替先行詞並引導形容詞子句，故形容詞子句中的動詞之人稱或數量須與先行詞一致。須注意的是，若先行詞為主要子句時，形容詞子句中的動詞一律採用單數。

 例句 Thomas only buys clothes which / that are white.
湯瑪斯只買白色的衣服。

Monica exercises on a daily basis, which is good for her health.
莫妮卡每天運動，這對她的健康有益。

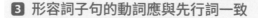

請圈選出正確的關係代名詞。

① Kent is a professional athlete (who / which) has won many awards.

② The person to (who / whom) we spoke was very friendly.

③ The artist, (whose / which) paintings are on exhibit now, will show up at the museum tomorrow morning.

④ Our new house, (which / who) we bought last month, has three bedrooms and two bathrooms.

⑤ The company, the name of (whose / which) was changed earlier this year, is growing bigger and bigger.

⑥ John has three projects due next week, (that / which) is making him feel stressed.

⑦ The money (whose / that) Sean earned was used to buy a new computer.

⑧ All (that / who) I want at the moment is some peace and quiet.

⑨ Jane has many pet dogs, most of (which / that) used to have no home.

⑩ London is the city in (× / which) Ned was born.

CH
14

14-1

關係代名詞

解 答				
① who	② whom	③ whose	④ which	⑤ which
⑥ which	⑦ that	⑧ that	⑨ which	⑩ which

Chapter 14 關係詞

14-2 複合關係代名詞

複合關係代名詞本身即由先行詞與關係代名詞結合而成，以下為常見的複合關係代名詞：

	複合關係代名詞	等同於	意思
代替人	whoever	anyone / the person who	（凡）……的人
	whomever	anyone / the person whom	（凡）……的人（★ 受格）
代替事物	whichever	any one that	兩者（含）以上任選一個……
代替事物	what	the thing(s) which	所……的事物
	whatever	anything that	凡……的事物

以下介紹複合關係代名詞的用法

1 複合關係代名詞前不置先行詞

 說明　複合關係代名詞本身即含有先行詞與關係代名詞，其中關係代名詞引導形容詞子句，修飾該先行詞。由此可知，複合關係代名詞前不須另置先行詞。

 例句
The person who stole the money should be punished.
　　先行詞　　who 引導的形容詞子句

= Whoever stole the money should be punished.
偷錢的人應該受罰。

Sally can buy anything that she likes on her birthday.
　　　　　　先行詞　　which 引導的形容詞子句

= Sally can buy whatever she likes on her birthday.
莎莉生日當天可以買任何她喜歡的東西。

2 複合關係代名詞可引導名詞子句

 說明 複合關係代名詞所引導的子句可視為名詞子句，在句中作主詞，也可作動詞／介詞之受詞。

例句 **作主詞**

What the mean girl said has affected me.

what 引導的名詞子句

那位尖酸刻薄的女孩說的話影響了我。

作動詞之受詞

There are two separate beds in our hotel room. You can choose **whichever** you want.

      whichever 引導的名詞子句

我們的飯店房間有兩張分開的床。你可以挑任何一個。

作介詞之受詞

The news media is interested in **whatever** the singer does.

        whatever 引導的名詞子句

新聞媒體對於這位歌手所做的一切都感興趣。

3 複合關係代名詞為主格或受格須視形容詞子句而定

 說明 上述提及，複合關係代名詞本身包含關係代名詞，而此關係代名詞又引導後面的形容詞子句。關係代名詞若在形容詞子句中為主詞，複合關係代名詞則亦採主格形；反之，關係代名詞若在形容詞子句中作受詞，複合關係代名詞則採受格形。

 例句 **作主格**

    The person **who** leaves last should close
          who 在形容詞子句中為主詞
    the door.

→ **Whoever** leaves last should close the door.
   whoever 亦為主格
   最後離開的人應該把門關上。

CH 14

14-2

複合關係代名詞

例句

作受格

You can give the flowers to **anyone** **whom** you like.

whom 在形容詞子句中為受詞

→ You can give the flowers to **whomever** you like.
　　　　whomever 亦為受格
你可以把花送給任何你喜歡的人。

 深 度補充

複合關係代名詞 vs 從屬連接詞

 說明

上述複合關係代名詞中，whoever、whichever 以及 whatever 亦可作從屬連接詞，引導副詞子句。其他類似的從屬連接詞包含 whenever、wherever、however 等，歸納如下：

從屬連接詞	等同於	意思
whoever	no matter who	無論是誰
whomever	no matter whom	無論是誰（★ 受格）
whichever	no matter which	無論哪個
whatever	no matter what	無論什麼
whenever	no matter when / every time that	無論何時；每當
wherever	no matter where	無論何地
however	no matter how	無論如何

此類從屬連接詞所引導的副詞子句可置主要子句之前或之後，修飾主要子句。

 例句

Whoever you ask, no one will be able to answer your question.
whoever 引導的副詞子句
不論你問誰，都沒人可以回答你的問題。

Whichever the boss chooses, we must accept his decision.
whichever 引導的副詞子句
無論老闆選擇哪個，我們必須接受他的決定。

Whatever happens, I will stand by you.
whatever 引導的副詞子句
無論發生什麼事情，我都會支持你。

 例句

 說明

Julia cries **whenever** she hears this song.

　　　　whenever 引導的副詞子句

每當茉莉亞聽到這首歌，她都會淚流滿面。

The little dog follows Owen **wherever** he goes.

　　　　　　　　wherever 引導的副詞子句

無論歐文走到哪，這隻小狗就跟到哪。

However long it takes, we have to finish this task.

however 引導的副詞子句

不論多久，我們都必須完成這項任務。

＼ 即時演練 ／

請圈選出正確的複合關係代名詞。

① (Whomever / Whoever) owns that sports car must be very rich.

② There are many tools here. You can use (whichever / whoever) you need.

③ The company will likely hire (whomever / whatever) you recommend.

④ No one believes (whichever / what) the little boy said.

⑤ Students can do (whatever / whoever) they want during lunch break.

解　答

① Whoever　② whichever　③ whomever　④ what　⑤ whatever

Chapter 14 關係詞

14-3 關係副詞

如同關係代名詞,關係副詞可引導形容詞子句,修飾其前的先行詞。基本上,關係副詞等同於「介詞 + 關係代名詞」。以下為常見的關係副詞:

關係副詞	等同於	表示
when	in / on / at / during + which	時間
where	in / on / at + which	地方 / 狀態
why	for which	理由 / 原因
how	in / by which (= the way)	方法 / 樣態

以下分項介紹各個關係副詞

❶ 常見的關係副詞

❶ when 的用法

說明

when 所引導的形容詞子句可用來修飾表時間的先行詞。

例句

I remember the day **on which** I first met John.
　　　　　先行詞

= I remember the day **when** I first met John.
我記得我跟約翰初次見面的那天。

❷ where 的用法

說明

where 所引導的形容詞子句可用來修飾表地點的先行詞。where 亦可用來修飾表狀態的先行詞,此時有「處於某種狀態 / 階段」的意思。

例句

表地方

This is the store **in which** I bought my new shoes.
　　　　　先行詞

= This is the store **where** I bought my new shoes.
我是在這間店購買我的新鞋。

表狀態

Grace is at the stage in her life **where** she has to decide what to
study.　　　　　　　先行詞
葛瑞絲目前處在得決定要攻讀什麼的人生階段。

❸ why 的用法

說明

why 所引導的形容詞子句僅可用來修飾表理由或原因的先行詞 the
reason。此時可省略 why，即 the reason 後直接置形容詞子句，但此
用法一般視為較不正式的用法。此外，亦可省略先行詞 the reason，此
時 why 所引導的子句為名詞子句。

注意

先行詞 the reason 若置句首作句子的主詞時，通常不省略 the reason。

例句

I don't know the reason <u>for which</u> Phil was fired.
　　　　　　先行詞

= I don't know the reason (why) Phil was fired.
　　　　　　　　　　形容詞子句

= I don't know why Phil was fired.
　　　　　　　名詞子句
我不知道菲爾被開除的原因。

The reason <u>for which</u> Lena is upset is a mystery to me.
　　　先行詞

= The reason (why) Lena is upset is a mystery to me.
　　　　　　　　形容詞子句
我不知道莉娜為何心情不好。

❹ how 的用法

說明

一般而言，可將 how 視為修飾先行詞 the way 以表示方法或樣態，但
how 與 the way 不可並用，應採用下列用法：

❶ the way 加上 (in which) 引導的形容詞子句。

❷ 省略 how，the way 後直接置形容詞子句。

❸ 省略 the way，視同以 how 引導名詞子句。

表方法

Please tell me the way (in which) you solved the problem.
<u>先行詞</u>

= Please tell me the way you solved the problem.
省略 how 的形容詞子句

= Please tell me how you solved the problem.
名詞子句
請告訴我你是如何解決此問題的。

表樣態

I don't like the way (in which) Kurt talks to people.
<u>先行詞</u>

= I don't like the way Kurt talks to people.
省略 how 的形容詞子句

= I don't like how Kurt talks to people.
名詞子句
我不喜歡科特跟別人講話的方式。

❷ 使用關係副詞應注意事項

❶ 限定用法與非限定用法

 同關係代名詞,限定用法(即關係代名詞之前不置逗號)是為先行詞提供必要的資訊或界定範圍;非限定用法(即關係代名詞之前搭配逗號使用)則是為先行詞補充額外的資訊。通常僅有 when 或 where 引導的子句才會出現非限定用法。

 Heather's grandfather died in <u>2020</u>, when her daughter was born.   先行詞
海瑟的爺爺在 2020 年過世,同年她女兒出生。

Justin plans to travel to <u>New York</u>, where he will stay for one week.   先行詞
賈斯汀計劃去紐約旅遊,他會在那裡待一週。

New York

❷ 省略先行詞

 因為有先行詞,故關係副詞所引導的子句為形容詞子句,用以修飾該先行詞。然而,在下列狀況中,可省略先行詞,此時該子句則視同名詞子句:

❶ 先行詞為主詞補語(即置 be 動詞之後)。

2 why 修飾其之前的先行詞 the reason 可省略。

3 how 修飾其之前的先行詞 the way 必須省略。

注意

上述 **1** 省略先行詞之情況，其省略的前提是說話者雙方或文章上下文已充分傳達所指之人、事、物為何。

例句

Sunday is the day <u>when</u> Oscar usually stays at home.
　　　　　　先行詞　　　　　　形容詞子句

→ Sunday is <u>when Oscar usually stays at home</u>.
　　　　　　　　　　名詞子句

星期日是奧斯卡通常待在家的時候。

This is the church <u>where</u> Nora and Ryan got
　　　　　先行詞　　　　　　　形容詞子句

married.

→ This is <u>where Nora and Ryan got married</u>.
　　　　　　　　名詞子句

諾拉與萊恩是在這 (間教堂) 結婚的。

(此句省略 the church 的前提應是說話者雙方或文章上下文已充分傳達所指的是哪一間教堂)

I can't figure out the reason <u>why</u> Polly won't talk to me.
　　　　　　　　　先行詞　　　　　　形容詞子句

→ I can't figure out <u>why Polly won't talk to me</u>.
　　　　　　　　　　　　名詞子句

我想不透為什麼波莉不跟我說話。

No one knows the way <u>how</u> the prisoner escaped. (×)
　　　　　　　先行詞　　　　　形容詞子句

→ No one knows <u>how the prisoner escaped</u>. (○)
　　　　　　　　　　　名詞子句

沒有人知道這名囚犯是如何逃獄的。

請圈選出正確的關係副詞。

① Trevor can't wait for the day (where / when) he moves into his new house.

② Our experiment has reached a stage (why / where) we only have to wait for the result.

③ Tanya remembers the way (× / how) her grandmother used to sing to her.

④ Last year, Rachel moved to Tokyo, (where / when) her sister lives.

⑤ Our manager wants to know the reason (how / why) Victor was late for work today.

解　答

| ① when | ② where | ③ × | ④ where | ⑤ why |

Chapter 14 關係詞

14-4 準關係代名詞

準關係代名詞共有三個： than 、 as 及 but ，通常是作連接詞用，但在某些情況下此三個準關係代名詞可同時具有連接詞與關係代名詞之特質，代替先行詞並引導子句，故稱準關係代名詞。

以下分項闡述準關係代名詞：

1 than 作準關係代名詞的用法

用於比較級句構

 說明
than 前有名詞作先行詞時，than 可表示該名詞，並在所引導的形容詞子句中作主詞、受詞或主詞補語。

 句型
than 作主詞
比較級 + 名詞 + than + 動詞
than 作受詞
比較級 + 名詞 + than + 主詞 + 動詞
than 為主詞補語
比較級 + 名詞 + than + 主詞 + be 動詞

 例句
Don't buy more things <u>than are necessary.</u>
　　　　　　　　　　　than 引導的形容詞子句
不要買超過需求的量。（此處 than 等於 than the things that，在形容詞子句中作主詞）

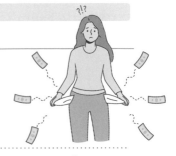

The buyer offered more money <u>than the seller expected.</u>
　　　　　　　　　　　　　than 引導的形容詞子句
買家的出價金額高於賣家的預期金額。（此處 than 等於 than the money that，在形容詞子句中作動詞 expected 的受詞）

Irene is a better singer <u>than you are.</u>
　　　　　　　　　　　than 引導的形容詞子句
艾琳是個比你更優秀的歌手。（此處 than 等於 than the singer that，在形容詞子句中作主詞補語）

335

2 as 作準關係代名詞的用法

1 表示「和……一樣的……；像……那樣 / 種的……」

說明 同 than 一樣，as 前有名詞作先行詞時，as 可表示該名詞，並在所引導的形容詞子句中作主詞、受詞或主詞補語。as 作準關係代名詞之用法，常出現於下列片語中：

1 as... as...　和……一樣的……

2 such... as...　像……那樣 / 種的……（★ 鮮少使用）

3 the same... as...　和……一樣的……

注意

as... as... 的句型中，第一個 as 為副詞，修飾其後的形容詞，第二個 as 即為準關係代名詞，引導其後的形容詞子句。

 as 為主詞

$$\left.\begin{array}{l} \text{as + 形容詞 + 名詞} \\ \text{such + 名詞} \\ \text{the same + 名詞} \end{array}\right\} \text{+ as + 動詞}$$

as 為受詞

$$\left.\begin{array}{l} \text{as + 形容詞 + 名詞} \\ \text{such + 名詞} \\ \text{the same + 名詞} \end{array}\right\} \text{+ as + 主詞 + 動詞}$$

as 為主詞補語

$$\left.\begin{array}{l} \text{as + 形容詞 + 名詞} \\ \text{such + 名詞} \\ \text{the same + 名詞} \end{array}\right\} \text{+ as + 主詞 + be 動詞}$$

 The prime minister is **as** brilliant a politician **as** ever lived.

　　　　　　　　　　　　　　　　　　as 引導的形容詞子句

這位首相是有史以來最傑出的政治家。

（此處 as 等於 as any politician that，在形容詞子句中作主詞）

You should read **such** books **as** will benefit you.

　　　　　　　　　　　　as 引導的形容詞子句

你應該讀那些對你有益的書。

（此處 as 等於 as the books that，在形容詞子句中作主詞）

Sean has **the same** <u>answer</u> **as** <u>is shown in the book</u>.
as 引導的形容詞子句

尚恩的答案與書中寫的是一樣的。

(此處 as 等於 as the answer that，在形容詞子句中作主詞)

Eddie gave the poor man **as** much <u>money</u> **as** <u>he had on him</u>.
as 引導的形容詞子句

艾迪把身上所有錢都給了這位窮苦的男子。

(此處 as 等於 as the money that，在形容詞子句中作動詞 had 的受詞)

Greg is wearing **the same** <u>clothes</u> **as** <u>Henry is wearing</u>.
as 引導的形容詞子句

葛瑞格穿的衣服跟亨利穿的一樣。(此處 as 等於 as the clothes that，在形容詞子句中作動詞 is wearing 的受詞)

Fiona is **as** <u>talented an actress</u> **as** <u>Denise is</u>.
as 引導的形容詞子句

費歐娜是位和丹妮絲一樣有才華的女演員。

(此處 as 等於 as the talented actress that，在形容詞子句中作主詞補語)

I have **the same** <u>car</u> **as** <u>this one (is)</u>.
as 引導的形容詞子句

我的車跟這輛車一樣。(此處 as 等於 as the car that，在形容詞子句中作主詞補語，通常會省略句尾的 be 動詞)

2 單獨使用

 說明　除了上述片語之外，as 亦可單獨用來引導子句並修飾主要子句。此時，as 代替整個主要子句，此時 as 表「如同……；以……的方式」。

 例句　**As** you can see, <u>our new product is very popular</u>.

如同您所見，本公司產品相當受歡迎。

<u>The writer's childhood affected his life greatly</u>, **as**

his stories show.

這名作家的童年深深地影響了他，可見於他的故事中。

❸ **but 作準關係代名詞的用法**

表示「沒有……不……」(★ 鮮少使用)

說明 **but 作準關係代名詞時，只用於下列句型：**

There is + 否定詞 + 名詞 + but... (★ but = who / which / that... not)

其中否定詞包含 no、not、little、few 等含有否定意味的
字詞。此句型中，but 表示其前的名詞，並在所引導的形容
詞子句中作主詞、受詞或主詞補語。

例句 There is no parent who / that does not care for their own children.
= There is no parent but cares for their own children.

but 引導的形容詞子句

沒有家長不關愛自己的孩子的。

\ 即時演練 /

句子重組

① more / than / food / needed / was
We bought _____.

② ever lived / as / a singer / as / great
Elvis was _____.

③ in / artificial ingredients / processed foods / such / are used / eat / as
Tom doesn't _____.

④ ordered / the same / as / I / food
Wendy ordered _____.

⑤ likes to watch / movie / but / Scott / no
There is _____.

解　答

① more food than was needed
② as great a singer as ever lived
③ eat such artificial ingredients as are used in processed foods
④ the same food as I ordered
⑤ no movie but Scott likes to watch

Chapter 15

句子中主詞動詞一致

Chapter 15 句子中主詞動詞一致

15-1 概述

❶ 主詞動詞一致性

動詞須依主詞的人稱及單複數形而來做變化,以下為簡要的分類整理:

人稱及普通名詞 時態	第一人稱:I(我) 　　　　　 we(我們) 第二人稱:you(你;妳;你們) 第三人稱:they(他們)	第三人稱:he(他) 　　　　　 she(她) 　　　　　 it(它)
	複數可數名詞	不可數名詞 單數可數名詞
現在簡單式動詞	原形動詞	動詞 + s / es
過去簡單式動詞	動詞 + ed	

以下詳述現在簡單式動詞加 s / es 等之規則,而過去簡單式動詞加 ed 之規則,
請參考 10-1 動詞變成過去分詞的規則。

❷ 現在簡單式動詞加 s / es 之規則

規則變化

❶ 一般動詞

說明	直接在字尾加 s 即可。
例字	look ▸ looks(看)　　　　　 work ▸ works(工作) borrow ▸ borrows(借)　　 attend ▸ attends(參加)

❷ 字尾為 ch(或 tch)、s(或 ss)、sh、x、z、o

說明	此時直接加 es。其中字尾為 s 或 z 時,要重複字尾再加 es。

例字	attach ▶ attaches (附上)	fix ▶ fixes (修理)
	watch ▶ watches (看)	quiz ▶ quizzes (提問)
	focus ▶ focuses / focusses (關注)	buzz ▶ buzzes (嗡嗡響)
	discuss ▶ discusses (討論)	do ▶ does (做)
	push ▶ pushes (推)	go ▶ goes (去)

3 字尾為「子音 + y」

說明	此時去掉 y，再加 ies。

例字	study ▶ studies (學習)	marry ▶ marries (結婚)
	try ▶ tries (嘗試)	carry ▶ carries (攜帶)

4 字尾為「母音 + y」

說明	此時直接在字尾加 s 即可。

例字	say ▶ says (說)	play ▶ plays (玩)
	pay ▶ pays (支付)	stay ▶ stays (停留)

不規則變化

說明	只有 have 及 be 動詞為不規則變化。

例字	have ▶ has (擁有)
	be ▶ is (是)

請更正套色方框內之動詞。

Every day my mom wake up at around 5:30 a.m. After she brush her teeth and wash her face, she go swimming. Then she usually have a large breakfast at home. After that, she go shopping at the traditional market and always buy fresh food for us. At noon, she just have a simple lunch. In the afternoon, she watch some TV dramas and take a nap. Then she pick up her granddaughter Cindy at school. After school, Cindy usually play on the swings or the slide in the park, and my mom just sit near her and relax. After coming home, my mom prepare a wonderful dinner for us. She love to see how satisfied we all be with her dishes.

解　答

Every day my mom wakes up at around 5:30 a.m. After she brushes her teeth and washes her face, she goes swimming. Then she usually has a large breakfast at home. After that, she goes shopping at the traditional market and always buys fresh food for us. At noon, she just has a simple lunch. In the afternoon, she watches some TV dramas and takes a nap. Then she picks up her granddaughter Cindy at school. After school, Cindy usually plays on the swings or the slide in the park, and my mom just sits near her and relaxes. After coming home, my mom prepares a wonderful dinner for us. She loves to see how satisfied we all are with her dishes.

Chapter 15 句子中主詞動詞一致

15-2 依主詞單複數決定動詞單複數

① 主詞為可數名詞或不可數名詞時

① 不可數名詞 + 單數動詞

例句　Money is important, but it can't buy everything.
錢很重要，但你不可能用錢來換取一切東西。

② 單數可數名詞 + 單數動詞

例句　That girl lives in the building across from the park.
那女孩住在公園對面的大樓。

③ 複數可數名詞 + 複數動詞

例句　Spices are very important in Indian cooking.
香料在印度料理中非常重要。

② 須使用單數動詞的情況

① much (很多)
little (幾乎沒有)
a little (一些)　　　　　　　　　　+ 不可數名詞 + 單數動詞
a large / small amount of (很多 / 少量)
a great / good deal of (很多)

例句　Much advice was given; it's up to Kelly to decide whether to take it.　意見已經給很多了；就由凱莉決定是否要接受這些意見了。

Little water was in the pond because it hadn't rained for months.
池塘裡幾乎沒什麼水，因為已好幾個月沒下雨了。

A little black pepper has been added to the soup.
湯已加了一點黑胡椒。

A large amount of rice is consumed in Asia every year.
= A great / good deal of rice is consumed in Asia every year.
亞洲人每年吃掉大量的米。

2 {each / every} + 單數可數名詞 + 單數動詞　　每一……

例句
Each / Every teacher has his or her style of teaching.
每個老師都有自己的教學風格。

3 {
everything / everybody / everyone （每個事物 / 每個人）
something / somebody / someone （某事物 / 某人）
anything / anybody / anyone （任何事物 / 任何人）
nothing / nobody / no one （沒有東西 / 沒有人）
} + 單數動詞

例句
Sir, everything you asked for is already there.
先生，您要的東西都已經在那裡了。

Mom, someone is singing on stage.
Could we go and watch her?
媽，有人在臺上唱歌。我們可以去看看嗎？

Does anyone want some coffee?　有人想喝咖啡嗎？

Nothing matters except my kids.　除了我的孩子外，什麼都不重要。

註
請注意 none（一點兒也沒；一個也沒）之用法：
none 代表不可數名詞時，其後接單數動詞；
none 代表複數可數名詞時，其後可接複數動詞。

例句
The children were very hungry, and since the meat was also delicious, soon none was left.
孩子都很餓，且因為肉也很美味，一下子就吃光了。

Poor John—he had invited several friends to his party, but none were present that day.
可憐的約翰，他邀請了幾個朋友來參加派對，但那天卻沒人來。

❸ 須使用複數動詞的情況

1 {
many（很多）
few（幾乎沒有）
a few（一些）
a large / small number of（很多 / 少量）
} + 複數可數名詞 + 複數動詞

344

例句
Many children in this poor country don't have the chance to receive an education.　這貧窮國家的很多小孩都沒有機會受教育。

Few people are interested in doing research in this field.
很少人有興趣研究這個領域。

The exam is very difficult; every year only a few people pass it.
此考試很難；每年只有少數幾人通過這考試。

A large number of children were playing on the beach.
很多小朋友在海灘上玩。（A large number of 視作形容詞，修飾主詞 children，children 為複數，故之後動詞採用複數 be 動詞 were。）

 註
「the number of + 複數可數名詞」是表「……的數量」，故 the number 做主詞，其後應接單數動詞，而非接複數動詞。

 例句
The number of this rare plant is decreasing.
此種稀有植物的數量正在減少。

② the + 形容詞 + 複數動詞

 說明
此常指「一群人」，常見的此類用法如下：

the poor	窮人（= poor people）
the rich	有錢人（= rich people）
the old	老人（= old people）
the young	年輕人（= young people）
the sick	生病的人（= sick people）
the blind	盲人（= blind people）
the deaf	聾人（= deaf people）
the homeless	無家可歸的人（= homeless people）
the dead	已過世的人（= dead people）

 例句
The rich in this area have strongly opposed the development plan.　此地區的有錢人強烈反對此發展計畫。

The homeless were also helped by the government during the spread of the serious disease.
在此嚴重疾病蔓延的期間，政府也幫助了無家可歸的人。

| some（一些）
a lot of（= lots of）（很多）
plenty of（很多）
all（全部）
none of（全無） | 不可數名詞 + 單數動詞

複數可數名詞 + 複數動詞

註 ❶ plenty of 勿寫成 a plenty of（即 plenty 之前不加 a）。
❷ 注意「none of + 複數可數名詞」之後除了可接單數動詞（較常使用），
也可接複數動詞。

 例句 Some furniture has been removed from the main bedroom.
一些傢俱已從主臥房搬走了。

Some students do very well under pressure.
有些學生在壓力下會表現得非常好。

A lot of / Lots of / Plenty of sugar has been added to the mung
bean soup. Don't add any more.
綠豆湯已加了很多糖。不要再加糖了。

A lot of / Lots of / Plenty of students are gathering there for a
grand parade.
很多學生正聚集在那裡準備參加一場大型的慶祝遊行。

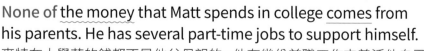

Don't worry. All the information about the project
has been stored on the cloud.
別擔心。有關此專案計畫的所有資料都已存在雲端上了。

The director said, "All performers have to take a
curtain call, so no one can leave early."
導演說：「所有演出者都要謝幕，誰都不能提早走。」

None of the money that Matt spends in college comes from
his parents. He has several part-time jobs to support himself.
麥特在大學花的錢都不是他父母親的。他有幾份兼職工作來養活他自己。

None of my friends dances / dance well.
我朋友沒一個跳舞跳得好。

2 There is + $\left\{\begin{array}{l}\text{不可數名詞} \\ \text{a(n)} + \text{單數可數名詞}\end{array}\right\}$

There are + 複數可數名詞

| 譯 | 有…… |

| 例句 | There's still some coffee in the mug.
馬克杯裡還有一些咖啡。

Dad, there is a stranger in front of our house.
Do you know him?
爸，我們家前面有個陌生人。你認識他嗎？

There are many beautiful flowers in Julie's backyard.
茉莉家的後院有很多漂亮的花。 |

3 Here is + $\left\{\begin{array}{l}\text{不可數名詞} \\ \text{a(n)} + \text{單數可數名詞}\end{array}\right\}$

Here are + 複數可數名詞

| 譯 | 給 (對方) ……，請 (對方) 看…… |

| 註 | 此句型之單數可數名詞前面除了可置不定冠詞 (a、an)，也可置定冠詞 (the) 及所有格 (如 my、his、her) 等。 |

| 例句 | Madam, here's your strawberry cake.
夫人，這是您的草莓蛋糕。

Here is a magazine for you to read while you wait.
這是本雜誌，供您在等候時閱讀。

Here are the documents you asked for.
這是您要的文件。 |

請圈選出正確的答案。

① Only (a little / a few) students think Mr. Taylor's class is interesting.

② (Have / Has) anything been done to settle the issue?

③ Look! There (is / are) a cat on the roof.

④ A large (amount / number) of information about the illness has been gathered so far.

⑤ According to the organization, plenty of food (have / has) been wasted so far this year.

⑥ Here (is / are) the books that I recommend you read.

⑦ Each student (have / has) the chance to perform on stage.

⑧ According to the news, the dead in the accident (was / were) all children.

解 答				
① a few	② Has	③ is	④ amount	⑤ has
⑥ are	⑦ has	⑧ were		

Chapter 15　句子中主詞動詞一致

15-3　特殊主詞

特殊主詞包括動名詞、不定詞片語、疑問詞引導的名詞片語、名詞子句、由連接詞連接之主詞等，茲分述如下：

(1) 動名詞 + 單數動詞

 例句
Exercising every day helps me reduce my stress levels.
每天運動有助於我減壓。

(2) 不定詞片語 + 單數動詞

 例句
To finish this project in two months is impossible.
要在兩個月內完成這專案計畫是不可能的。

(3) 疑問詞引導的名詞片語 + 單數動詞

 例句
When to tell Lucy the truth is really bothering me.
什麼時候要告訴露西真相真的很困擾我。

(4) 名詞子句 + 單數動詞

 例句
That the manager rejected the proposal is what I expected.
經理拒絕了這提案是在我的預料之內。

How the woman escaped from the prison is a mystery.
那女人是如何逃獄的還是個謎。

Whether you love me or not doesn't matter anymore.
你愛不愛我已經不重要了。

(5) 由連接詞連接之主詞 (亦請參考 9-2)

❶ both A and B + 複數動詞　　A 及 B 兩者都是……

 例句
Both Sean and Hillary like to go hiking.
尚恩和希拉蕊都喜歡健行。

2 {
A or Ⓑ (A 或 B)
either A or Ⓑ (A 或 B)
neither A nor Ⓑ (既非 A 也非 B)
not only A but also Ⓑ (不只 A 而且 B)
} + 動詞 (★ 依據 Ⓑ 做變化)

例句 (Either) some of my friends or <u>my boyfriend</u> <u>is</u> going to the beach with me next weekend.
我一些朋友或我男友下週末要和我一起去海灘。

Neither my brother **nor** <u>my two sisters</u> <u>enjoy</u> swimming.
我哥和我的兩個妹妹都不喜歡游泳。

Not only the basketball players **but also** <u>their coach</u> <u>was</u> crying tears of joy after winning the championship.
不只籃球員，連他們的教練都在奪冠後喜極而泣。

註 這些片語為疑問句時，則動詞依據 A 做變化。

例句 Are <u>you</u> **or** Mark going to attend the meeting tomorrow?
你或馬克明天會去開會嗎？

3 {
Ⓐ(,) along / together with B(,)
Ⓐ(,) as well as B(,)
} + 動詞 (★ 依據 Ⓐ 做變化)
除了 B 之外，A 還……；A 及 B

註 ❶ 以上這些片語義同於 in addition to。
❷ along / together with B 及 as well as B 的前後常加上逗點。

例句 The potato corn burger, **along with** the pizza, <u>is</u> among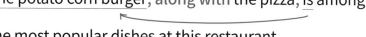

the most popular dishes at this restaurant.
除了披薩之外，馬鈴薯玉米漢堡也是這家餐廳最受歡迎的餐點。

<u>Ricky</u>, **as well as** some of his classmates, <u>wants</u> to go camping

next weekend.
瑞奇和他一些同學下週末想去露營。

單選題

① Neither my sister nor my parents _____ cheese.
　(A) likes　　　(B) liking　　(C) to like　　(D) like

② _____ Jeffery or his friends have time to help us move the furniture?
　(A) Has　　　(B) Does　　(C) Are　　(D) Is

③ That Taylor has lost so much weight really _____ me.
　(A) surprise　(B) surprising　(C) surprises　(D) to surprise

④ Teddy, as well as his two brothers, _____ going to work part-time in a restaurant during the summer vacation.
　(A) is　　　(B) are　　(C) be　　(D) were

⑤ Both my sister and I _____ mountain climbing a lot.
　(A) loves　　(B) love　　(C) loving　　(D) to love

解　答

| ① D | ② B | ③ C | ④ A | ⑤ B |

Notes

352

Chapter 16

被動語態

Chapter 16　被動語態

16-1　被動語態簡介

英文語態有兩種：主動語態與被動語態，只有及物動詞方可形成被動語態。前者如「喬摔破了花瓶」，後者如「花瓶被喬摔破了」。以下將分述被動語態如何形成、其使用時機，以及其 Wh- 問句：

❶ 主動語態如何形成被動語態

(1) 主詞 + 及物動詞 + 受詞：

主動：A + 及物動詞 + B

被動：B + be 動詞 + 過去分詞 + by + A

❶ 主動語態的受詞 B 變成被動語態的主詞。

❷ 主動語態的及物動詞改成：be 動詞 + 過去分詞。

（此時動詞的單複數形和時態變化，須依被動語態的主詞 B 而變。）

❸ 主動語態的主詞 A 置於被動語態的句尾，並在 A 之前加上介詞 by。

（by + A 可視情況省略。）

主動：The girl　drew　these pictures.

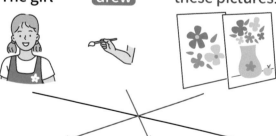

被動：These pictures　were drawn　by the girl.

這女孩畫了這些畫。/ 這些畫是由這女孩畫的。

註 1	可形成被動語態的一定是及物動詞，意即不及物動詞只有主動語態，無被動語態。
	但若「不及物動詞 + 介詞」，亦可形成被動語態。

例句

主動：The class stared at the new classmate.

被動：The new classmate was stared at by the class.

全班都盯著新同學看。/ 新同學被全班盯著看。

註 2	正式的被動語態為：be 動詞 + 過去分詞，口語的被動語態則為：get + 過去分詞，此時較常強調動作本身。

例句

Willy, guess what! I was just promoted. (正式)

= Willy, guess what! I just got promoted. (口語)

威利，猜猜看怎麼了！我剛升職了。

註 3	主動語態句型的主詞若為 someone（某人）、people（人們）等字，變成被動語態時，因施行動作者不明或為一般大眾，常省略 by someone / people。

例句

主動：Someone has stolen my purse.
　　有人偷了我的錢包。

被動：My purse has been stolen (by someone).
　　我的錢包被偷了。

主動：People should obey the law.
　　人們應守法。

被動：The law should be obeyed (by people).
　　法律應被（大家）遵守。

(2) 主動語態的主要動詞為進行式（即 be 動詞 + 現在分詞）時：

圖示

主動：A + be 動詞 + 現在分詞 + B

被動：B + be 動詞 + being + 過去分詞 + by + A

例句

主動：Sharon   is cleaning   the living room.

被動：The living room   is being cleaned   by Sharon.

雪倫正在清理客廳。／客廳正由雪倫在清理。

(3) 主動語態的主要動詞為完成式時：

圖示

主動：A +   have / has / had + 過去分詞   + B

被動：B +   have / has / had been + 過去分詞   + by + A

例句

主動：Kyle   has cooked   some dishes.

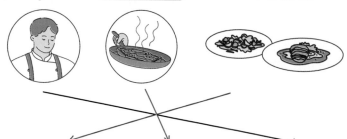

被動：Some dishes   have been cooked   by Kyle.

凱爾已煮了幾道菜。／幾道菜已由凱爾煮了。

356

(4) 主動語態為助動詞 (might/may/must/can/should/will 等) 接原形動詞時：

圖示

主動：A + might + 原形動詞 + B

被動：B + might be + 過去分詞 + by + A

例句

主動：Grandfather　might fix　the oven.

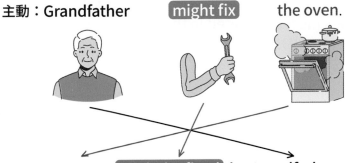

被動：The oven　might be fixed　by Grandfather.

爺爺也許會修這臺烤箱。/ 這臺烤箱也許由爺爺來修。

---

❷ **被動語態的使用時機**

1 強調接受動作者，或讀者 / 聽者對接受動作者較有興趣時。

例句

The park was built in 1952.

此公園建於 1952 年。

（此句強調「公園」，或讀者 / 聽者對此公園較有興趣，但對於誰建造此公園並不是很有興趣，因此句尾並無提及「by + 施行動作者」。）

2 強調動作或過程時。

例句

The children's reactions to the toys were recorded.

這些孩童對玩具的反應都被記錄了下來。

（強調「被記錄」的過程，誰記錄的並不重要，因此句尾無「by + 施行動作者」。）

CH
16

16-1

被動語態簡介

3 施行動作者不知為何人，或此並不重要，或要避免提及施行動作者時。

 例句

Hazel told me that she **was being followed** and that she needed help immediately. 海柔告訴我她被跟蹤了，立刻需要協助。
（海柔及說話者並不知道誰跟蹤她，因此句尾無「by + 施行動作者」。）

The papers must **be handed in** this Friday. 論文必須本週五交。
（說話者和聆聽者都知道要繳交文章的是學生，因此施行動作者是誰並不重要，所以句尾無「by students 或 by you」。）

I'm sorry, Luke; I didn't know you **got fired**.
很抱歉，路克，我不知道你被解僱了。（說話者不知道誰解僱了路克，或也想避免提及誰解僱了他，因此句尾無「by + 施行動作者」。）

4 對話或行文流暢用（即接受動作者為舊資訊，而施行動作者為新資訊時）。

 例句

M: These flowers are so beautiful.

W: Indeed. They **were planted** by my grandfather. He always likes to spend time in the garden.

男：這些花真美。

女：的確很美。它們是我祖父種的。他一直都很喜歡在花園裡消磨時光。
（男子提及花朵，女子就男子所提的花朵這舊資訊，再提供一些新資訊，即這些花是她爺爺種的。）

3 被動語態之 Wh- 問句

1 詢問接受動作者為何者時：

 說明

被動語態之 Wh- 問句要詢問接受動作者為何者時，被動語態肯定句中的接受動作者，依語意可改成：

1 Who 或 What。注意此時 Who 或 What 之後的動詞為單數動詞，而非複數動詞。

2 Which + 單數可數名詞（之後接單數動詞）。

3 Which + 複數可數名詞（之後接複數動詞）。

 例句

What **was drawn** by the girl? 這女孩畫了什麼？

或 Which picture **was drawn** by the girl? 哪一張畫是這女孩畫的？

或 Which pictures **were drawn** by the girl? 哪些畫是這女孩畫的？

What <u>is</u> being cleaned by Sally? 雪倫正在清理什麼？

What <u>has</u> been cooked by Kyle? 凱爾煮了什麼？
或 Which dish <u>has</u> been cooked by Kyle?
凱爾已煮了哪一道菜？
或 Which dishes <u>have</u> been cooked by Kyle?
凱爾已煮了哪幾道菜？

What <u>might</u> be fixed by Grandfather?
爺爺也許會修什麼？

Ken was hit by Bob at school yesterday.
→ Who <u>was</u> hit by Bob at school yesterday?
誰昨天在學校被鮑伯打了？

2 詢問施行動作者為何者時：

 被動語態之 Wh- 問句要詢問施行動作者為何者時，要將被動語態肯定句中的「by + 施行動作者」刪除後，在句首加上 By whom，且此時被動語態肯定句中的主詞和動詞（主要是 be 動詞、完成式助動詞 have / has / had 及助動詞 might / may / must / can 等）倒置以形成疑問句。

 By whom <u>were</u> these pictures <u>drawn</u>? 這些畫是誰畫的？
By whom <u>is</u> the meeting room <u>being cleaned</u>?
誰正在清理會議室？
By whom <u>have</u> some dishes <u>been cooked</u>? 誰煮了這幾道菜？
By whom <u>might</u> the oven <u>be fixed</u>? 誰也許會修這臺烤箱？
By whom <u>was</u> Ken hit at school yesterday?
肯昨天在學校被誰打了？

\ 即時演練 /

請將下列句子改成被動語態。

① The French architect built this church in 1925.

_____

② My husband cooks delicious meals every day.

_____

③ Mark must write an important message.

_____

④ Has someone fed the cat?

_____

⑤ My brother is making some donuts.

_____

⑥ Oliver has repaired the bicycle.

_____

⑦ Cindy had sent the letter before you called.

_____

⑧ Randy didn't wash the car.

_____

⑨ The maid hasn't cleaned the room.

_____

⑩ Does Lisa hold a party every month?

_____

解　答

① This church was built by the French architect in 1925.
② Delicious meals are cooked by my husband every day.
③ An important message must be written by Mark.
④ Has the cat been fed (by someone)?
⑤ Some donuts are being made by my brother.
⑥ The bicycle has been repaired by Oliver.
⑦ The letter had been sent by Cindy before you called.
⑧ The car wasn't washed by Randy.
⑨ The room hasn't been cleaned by the maid.
⑩ Is a party held by Lisa every month?

Chapter 16　被動語態

16-2　特殊動詞 / 句型之被動語態

此類包括知覺動詞、使役動詞、授予動詞、據說相關句型、祈使句等,茲分述如下:

❶ 知覺動詞（see、hear、feel 等）的被動語態

句型	A + be 動詞 + $\begin{Bmatrix} \text{seen} \\ \text{heard} \\ \text{felt} \end{Bmatrix}$ + $\begin{Bmatrix} \text{to + 原形動詞} \\ \text{動名詞} \end{Bmatrix}$ + (by + B)
譯	A 被 (B) 看 / 聽 / 感覺到……
例句	**主動**：Someone **saw** the politician <u>get</u> into a gray car and <u>leave</u> the businessman's house. （此處 get into 為原形動詞,表已發生的動作。） 有人看到那位政治人物上了灰色轎車,離開那商人的住處。
	被動：The politician **was seen** <u>to get</u> into a gray car and <u>leave</u> the businessman's house (by someone).（罕） 那位政治人物被看到上了灰色轎車,離開那商人的住處。
	主動：Someone **saw** the superstar <u>hugging</u> a girl last weekend. 上週末有人看到那位超級巨星正抱著一個女孩。
	被動：The superstar **was seen** <u>hugging</u> a girl (by someone) last weekend.　上周末那位超級巨星被 (人) 看到在抱著一個女孩。

❷ 使役動詞（make）的被動語態

句型	A + be 動詞 + made + to + 原形動詞 + (by + B)
譯	A 被 (B) 要求做……
例句	**主動**：The manager **made** Max <u>go</u> on a business trip to New York.
	被動：Max **was made** <u>to go</u> on a business trip to New York (by the manager).（罕）　麥克斯被 (經理) 要求去紐約出差。

註 使役動詞中，僅 make 用於被動語態；而 let 若用於被動語態，常以 allow 來替代。

 例句
主動：The guard **let** Kurt enter after he showed his identification.
= The guard **allowed** Kurt to enter after he showed his identification.

被動：Kurt **was let** to enter (by the guard) after he showed his identification.（×，無此用法）

Kurt **was allowed** to enter (by the guard) after he showed his identification.（○）
科特在出示身分證明後，警衛就允許他進入。

❸ 授予動詞（give、buy、send 等）的兩種被動語態

 句型
人 + be 動詞 + 授予動詞的過去分詞 + 物 + (by...)
= 物 + be 動詞 + 授予動詞的過去分詞 + 介詞 + 人 + (by...)

說明
授予動詞為可接兩個受詞的動詞，如 give（給予）主動語態的用法為：
give + 人 + 物
= give + 物 + to + 人

其中「人」為間接受詞，而「物」為直接受詞，因此授予動詞的被動語態有兩種：一種為以「人」為主詞的被動語態，另一種為以「物」為主詞的被動語態。

 例句
主動：The teacher gave Nancy a snack.
被動：Nancy was given a snack (by the teacher).
= A snack was given to Nancy (by the teacher).
有人（老師）給了南希零食。

❹ 表「據說」相關句型的兩種被動語態

 句型
It is said (that) + 主詞 + 動詞 + ...
= 主詞 + be 動詞 + said + to + 原形動詞 + ...

 譯
據說……

| 說明 | ❶ 在此是將「that + 主詞 + 動詞 + ...」改為被動語態。 |
| | ❷ 此句型的 said 也可替換成以下動詞，皆為相同的用法：reported（據報導）、believed（一般相信）、considered（一般認為）、expected（一般預期）、known（一般所知）等。 |

例句	主動：It is said (that) the pop singer has a son.
	被動：The pop singer is said to have a son.
	據說那位流行歌手有個兒子。

❺ 祈使句的被動語態

| 句型 | Let + 某人 / 物 + be + 過去分詞 + (by...) |

| 譯 | 讓……被…… |

| 說明 | ❶ 祈使句的主動語態強調請「對方」去做某事，而其被動語態則強調該動作要被執行，誰做並不是那麼重要。 |
| | ❷ 此句型的被動語態較正式，常用於書寫中，但不常用於口語中。 |

例句	主動：Release the boy.
	被動：Let the boy be released.
	釋放那男孩。

＼ 即時演練 ／

請將下列句子改成被動語態。

① My mother made my younger brother wash the windows.

_____

② Terry sent a birthday present to my sister.

_____

③ Someone heard the couple arguing with each other yesterday morning.

_____

④ Vince showed Lydia some old photos of the town.

_____

⑤ It is reported that the mayor strongly opposes the plan.

_____

⑥ Ladies and gentlemen, just pass the law.

_____

解　答

① My younger brother was made to wash the windows (by my mother). (罕)

② My sister was sent a birthday present (by Terry).

= A birthday present was sent to my sister (by Terry).

③ The couple was heard arguing with each other (by someone) yesterday morning.

④ Lydia was shown some old photos of the town (by Vince).

= Some old photos of the town were shown to Lydia (by Vince).

⑤ The mayor is reported to strongly oppose the plan.

⑥ Ladies and gentlemen, just let the law be passed.

★ 上列句中句尾 (by...) 實際寫作時一律要省略。

Chapter 17

比較句型

Chapter 17　比較句型

17-1　形容詞與副詞的比較級與最高級

比較句型是英文中使用頻率很高的句型，比較的概念來自於數量或程度上的差異，包括**原級比較**、**比較級**與**最高級**。

❶ 形容詞的原級比較、比較級與最高級

原級比較：數量或性質相等的比較

例句	Sue is **as tall as** Tom. 蘇和湯姆一樣高。

比較級：兩者之間數量或性質的比較

例句	Sue is **taller than** Leo. 蘇比李歐高。

最高級：三者以上數量或性質的比較

例句	Ted is **the tallest** student in the class. 泰德是班上最高的學生。

❷ 副詞的原級比較、比較級與最高級

原級比較：動作程度相等的比較

例句	Tina runs **as fast as** Ken. 蒂娜和肯跑得一樣快。

比較級：兩者之間動作程度的比較

例句	Tom runs **faster than** Abby. 湯姆跑得比艾比快。

最高級：三者以上動作程度的比較

例句	Gina ran **the fastest** in the running race. 吉娜在賽跑中跑得最快。

深 度補充

有些形容詞無比較級或最高級

說明 有些形容詞意義特殊或已表極限，故無比較級或最高級。

例字

round（圓形的）	excellent（極優秀的）	extreme（極度的）
dead（死的）	unique（獨一無二的）	favorite（最喜歡的）
final（最後的）	square（方形的）	empty（空的）
perfect（完美的）	entire（整個的）	superb（極好的）

❸ 如何形成形容詞或副詞的比較級與最高級

規則變化

以下就單音節、雙音節及三音節以上的形容詞或副詞，分述其比較級與最高級的變化規則：

(1) 單音節的形容詞或副詞

❶ 一般單音節的形容詞或副詞

規則
- 比較級：字尾加 er
- 最高級：字尾加 est

例字

原 級	比較級	最高級
broad（寬廣的）	broader	broadest
fast（快速地）	faster	fastest

❷ 字尾為 e

規則
- 比較級：字尾加 r
- 最高級：字尾加 st

例字

原 級	比較級	最高級
ripe（成熟的）	riper	ripest
safe（安全的）	safer	safest

❸ 字尾為「單一短母音 + 單子音」

規則
- 比較級：重複字尾加 er
- 最高級：重複字尾加 est

例字	原　級	比較級	最高級
	hot（熱的）	hotter	hottest
	sad（難過的）	sadder	saddest

4 字尾為「子音+y」

規則	• 比較級：去 y 改為 ier • 最高級：去 y 改為 iest		

例字	原　級	比較級	最高級
	dry（乾的）	drier	driest

5 字尾為「母音+y」

規則	• 比較級：字尾加 er • 最高級：字尾加 est		

註	在此「母音」是指發音為母音。

例字	原　級	比較級	最高級
	gray（灰色的）	grayer	grayest

(2) 雙音節的形容詞或副詞

1 字尾為 e

規則	• 比較級：字尾加 r • 最高級：字尾加 st		

例字	原　級	比較級	最高級
	simple（簡單的）	simpler	simplest
	gentle（溫和的）	gentler	gentlest

2 字尾為「子音+y」

規則	• 比較級：去 y 改為 ier • 最高級：去 y 改為 iest		

例字	原　級	比較級	最高級
	busy（忙碌的）	busier	busiest
	easy（容易的）	easier	easiest

❸ 其他大部分的雙音節字

規則	• 比較級：前面加 more • 最高級：前面加 most

例字	原　級	比較級	最高級
	famous（有名的）	more famous	most famous
	selfish（自私的）	more selfish	most selfish

註	有些雙音節形容詞的比較級與最高級可在字尾加 er / est，或也可在前面加 more / most：

friendly → { friendlier → { friendliest
（友善的）　{ more friendly 　{ most friendly

polite → { politer → { politest
（禮貌的）{ more polite 　{ most polite

(3) 三音節以上的形容詞或副詞

規則	• 比較級：前面加 more • 最高級：前面加 most

例字	原　級	比較級	最高級
	popular（受歡迎的）	more popular	most popular
	expensive（昂貴的）	more expensive	most expensive

不規則變化

原　級	比較級	最高級
good（好的） well（好地）	better（較好的 / 地）	best（最好的 / 地）
well（健康的）	better （身體健康逐漸好轉的）	best（身體最健康的） （★ 較少使用）
bad（壞的） badly（壞地） ill（生病的）	worse（更壞的 / 地）	worst（最壞的 / 地）
many（很多） much（很多）	more（更多的）	most（最多的）

little (少 / 小的)	less (較少的)	least (最少的)
old (老 / 舊的)	older (較老 / 舊的) (★ 規則變化) elder (較年長的)	oldest (最老 / 舊的) (★ 規則變化) eldest (最年長的)
far (遠的)	farther (較遠的) further (更遠的； 更進一步的)	farthest (最遠的) furthest (最遠的； 最大程度的)

＼ 即時演練 ／

請寫出下列形容詞或副詞的比較級與最高級。

比較級　　VS　　最高級

① thin _____ _____

② good _____ _____

③ close _____ _____

④ loud _____ _____

⑤ little _____ _____

⑥ early _____ _____

⑦ far _____ _____

⑧ ridiculous _____ _____

⑨ stable _____ _____

解　答

① thinner; thinnest　　② better; best

③ closer; closest　　④ louder; loudest

⑤ less; least　　⑥ earlier; earliest

⑦ farther; farthest 或 further; furthest

⑧ more ridiculous; most ridiculous

⑨ more stable; most stable

Chapter 17　比較句型

17-2　原級比較句型

原級比較用於描述兩個人/事/物的「性質或狀態的程度相同」。

1　原級比較基本句型

| A + 動詞 + as + ⎧ 形容詞 (+ 名詞) ⎫ + as + B + ⎧ be 動詞 ⎫ |
| ⎩ 副詞　　　　　⎭　　　　　　⎩ 助動詞 ⎭ |

譯	A 和 B 一樣……
說明	本句型中,第一個 as 是副詞,表「一樣地」,修飾之後的形容詞或副詞;第二個 as 是副詞連接詞,表「和」,引導副詞子句(即 B + be 動詞/助動詞),此副詞子句的句構須與主要子句(即 A + 動詞)一致,即:

1 主要子句使用 be 動詞時,第二個 as 之後的子句亦須用 be 動詞。

2 主要子句只有一般動詞時,第二個 as 之後的子句須依時態使用助動詞
do / does / did。

3 主要子句有一般助動詞時,第二個 as 之後的子句亦應有一般助動詞。

4 若第二個 as 之後的子句時態與主要子句相同時,「as +子句」可改為
「as + 名詞」,省略 be 動詞或助動詞。

例句	Rita is always **as busy as** a bee (is) at work. 麗塔上班時總是忙得不可開交。 Tim looked **as sad as** Ann (did) when he heard the bad news. 提姆聽到那壞消息時,看起來和安一樣難過。 Charlie will practice **as hard as** Gary (will). 查理會和蓋瑞一樣認真練習。

Tim　　Ann

註	若第二個 as 之後的子句時態與主要子句並不相同時,第二個 as 之後的子句不可改為「as + 名詞」,需使用「as + 子句」。
例句	The new tenant will pay **as much** rent **as** the others do now. 新房客付的租金會和其他人現在付的一樣多。

❷ 原級比較其他重要句型

---

❶ 倍數詞 + as + 形容詞 / 副詞 + as...

| 譯 | ……的……倍 |

| 例句 | This conference room is three times as large as the one on the first floor.　這間會議室是一樓那間的三倍大。

Edward's new car cost twice as much as mine.
愛德華的新車價格是我的兩倍。 |

---

❷ as many / much as + 數字 (+ 名詞)

| 譯 | 多達……的…… |

| 例句 | As many as five thousand people went to the popular singer's concert last night.
昨晚多達五千人去看那位人氣歌手的演唱會。

The sales have decreased by as much as 20% this quarter.
本季銷售量減少達百分之二十。 |

---

❸ 原級比較常見慣用語

---

❶ as + { 形容詞 (+ 名詞) / 副詞 } + as possible / as one can

| 譯 | 盡可能…… |

| 例句 | We should plant as many trees in the garden as possible.　我們應該盡量在花園裡多種些樹。

The teacher encouraged us to speak as much as we could in class.　老師鼓勵我們在上課時盡量多發言。 |

---

❷ as + 形容詞 / 副詞 + as can be

| 譯 | 極為…… |

| 例句 | If you think Jon was lying, you're as wrong as can be.
如果你覺得強在說謊,你就大錯特錯了。

John was as happy as could be to see his favorite band perform live.
約翰非常高興看到他最喜歡的樂團在現場演出。 |

3 as + 形容詞 / 副詞 + as ever

譯 一如往常地……

例句 Phoebe was **as** enthusiastic **as ever**;
she prepared lots of great dishes for dinner.
菲碧一如往常地熱情，晚餐準備了許多豐盛的菜餚。

Henry arrived at school **as** early **as ever** this morning.
亨利今天早上一如往常很早就到校。

4 as + 形容詞 + a(n) + 名詞 + as ever lived

譯 有史以來最……的……

例句 Marie Curie was **as** great **a** scientist **as ever lived**.
居禮夫人是有史以來最偉大的科學家之一。

Kobe Bryant was **as** excellent **a** basketball player **as ever lived**.
柯比‧布萊恩是有史以來最優秀的籃球員之一。

\ 即時演練 /

一、請根據中文提示完成下列句子，每格限填一字。

① 那場演講像電影《鐵達尼號》一樣長，我都快睡著了。
The lecture was ＿＿＿＿＿＿＿＿
＿＿＿＿＿＿＿＿＿ the movie *Titanic*. I almost fell asleep.

② 賴瑞可以跑得像其他選手一樣快。
Larry can run ＿＿＿＿＿＿＿ ＿＿＿＿＿＿＿
＿＿＿＿＿＿＿＿ the other competitors.

③ 新蓋的高速公路比舊的那條寬兩倍。
The newly-built highway is ＿＿＿＿＿＿＿ ＿＿＿＿＿＿＿
wide ＿＿＿＿＿＿＿＿ the old one.

④ 我們隊在十分鐘內輸給對手十分之多。
Our team lost ＿＿＿＿＿＿＿ ＿＿＿＿＿＿＿
＿＿＿＿＿＿＿＿ ten points to the other team within ten
minutes.

CH
17

17-2

原級比較句型

二、句子重組

① The businessman / rich / be / as / is / can / as

_____

② as / was / ever / curious / The student / as

_____

③ information / as / gathered / as / We / possible / much

_____

④ was / as / Albert Einstein / ever lived / as / distinguished / a physicist

_____

解　答

一、① as; long; as　　② as; fast / quickly; as

　　③ twice; as; as　　④ as; many; as

二、① The businessman is as rich as can be.

　　② The student was as curious as ever.

　　③ We gathered as much information as possible.

　　④ Albert Einstein was as distinguished a physicist as ever lived.

374

Chapter 17 　比較句型

17-3 　比較級句型

比較級用於兩者之間數量、性質或程度的比較。

❶ 比較級基本句型

---

1 **than 作連接詞**
A + be 動詞 + 形容詞比較級 + than + B + be 動詞
A + 一般動詞 + 副詞比較級 + than + B + do / does / did

譯	A 比 B 更……

| 例句 | Alex <u>is</u> more diligent than I am.　艾力克斯比我更勤勞。
　　　　　　　　　　　　連接詞

Daisy <u>studies</u> harder than I do.　黛西比我更用功。
　　　　　　　　　　　連接詞

Allen <u>arrived</u> home much earlier than his brother (<u>did</u>).
　　　　　　　　　　　　　　　連接詞
艾倫比他哥哥更早回家。 |

2 **than 作介詞**

說明	上列例句中，亦可將 than 作介詞，之後直接接名詞或人稱代名詞作受詞。

| 例句 | Alex <u>is</u> more diligent than me.　
　　　　　　　　　介詞 受詞
艾力克斯比我更勤勉。（此處 me 不可以 I 代替。）

Daisy <u>studies</u> harder than me.
　　　　　　　　介詞 受詞
黛西比我更用功。（此處 me 不可以 I 代替。）　Daisy

Allen <u>arrived</u> home much earlier than his brother.
　　　　　　　　　　　　介詞　　　受詞
艾倫比他哥哥更早回家。 |

CH
17

17-3

比較級句型

375

❷ 表「較少 (的)」之比較級句型

A + 動詞 + less + $\begin{cases} 形容詞 (+ 名詞) \\ 副詞 \\ 名詞 \end{cases}$ + than + B + $\begin{cases} be 動詞 \\ 助動詞 \end{cases}$

| 譯 | A 比 B 較不 / 較沒有…… |

| 例句 | The politician's son is less active in local politics than her.
這位政治家的兒子在參與當地政治活動上比她還不活躍。

The new model uses less fuel than the earlier one (does).
這款新車比前一代更不耗油。 |

❸ 相同與不同範圍的比較級句型

❶ 相同範圍

A + 動詞 + $\begin{cases} 形容詞比較級 \\ 副詞比較級 \end{cases}$ + than + $\begin{cases} any\ other + 單數可數名詞 \\ any(one) / any(thing)\ else \\ all\ the\ other + 複數可數名詞 \end{cases}$

| 譯 | A 比其他任何 / 所有……都…… |

| 說明 | ❶ 本句型中，A 與同範圍內其他人事物做比較，須將自己排除，因此須加 other 或 else。
❷ any other 之後加單數可數名詞，all the other 之後加複數可數名詞。 |

| 例句 | Ron is stronger than any other student in his class.
= Ron is stronger than anyone else in his class.
= Ron is stronger than all the other students in his class.
榮恩比他班上任何一個男生都強壯。 |

❷ 不同範圍

A + 動詞 + $\begin{cases} 形容詞比較級 \\ 副詞比較級 \end{cases}$ + than + $\begin{cases} any + 單數可數名詞 \\ anyone / anything \\ all\ the + 複數可數名詞 \end{cases}$

| 譯 | A 比任何 / 所有……都…… |

| 說明 | ❶ 本句型中，A 與不同範圍內的人事物做比較，不需將自己排除在外，因此不需加 other 或 else。
❷ any 之後加單數可數名詞，all the 之後加複數可數名詞。 |

例句	Tokyo is **bigger than any city** in Taiwan. = Tokyo is **bigger than all the cities** in Taiwan. 東京比臺灣任何城市都大。

❹ 比較級其他重要句型

❶ the + 形容詞或副詞比較級 + of the two (+ 名詞)

譯	兩者 (……) 中較……的

例句	The box on the left is **the heavier of the two**. 左邊的箱子是兩個之中比較重的。 George is **the more obedient of the two** boys in my family. 我家的兩個男生之中,喬治比較聽話。

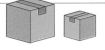

❷ 形容詞或副詞比較級 + and + 形容詞或副詞比較級

譯	越來越……

註	若形容詞或副詞比較級為「more + 形容詞 / 副詞」,則此句型為: **more and more** + 形容詞 / 副詞

例句	It's getting **hotter and hotter** these days. 最近天氣越來越熱了。 It's **more and more difficult** to find a parking space in this city. 在這個城市裡,要找到停車位越來越困難了。

❸ less and less + 形容詞 / 副詞

譯	越來越不……

例句	Somehow Noah is getting **less and less interested** in music. 不知怎的諾亞對音樂越來越不感興趣。

❹ The + { 形容詞比較級 (+ 名詞) / 副詞比較級 } + 主詞 + 動詞,

the + { 形容詞比較級 (+ 名詞) / 副詞比較級 } + 主詞 + 動詞

譯	……越……,……就越……

例句	**The more careful** you are, **the fewer** mistakes you'll make. 你越小心,犯的錯誤就會越少。

377

例句　The more Pat said, the angrier his wife became.　派特說得越多，他太太就越生氣。

5 倍數 + 形容詞或副詞比較級 + than...

譯　比……多……倍

註　倍數詞中，half 與 twice 只可用於原級比較的倍數句型 (見 17-2)，不可用於本句型。而於本句型中，若要敘述「(多)兩倍」，須用 two times。

例句　My sister's room is two times larger than mine.
我姐姐的房間比我大兩倍。

This train runs two times faster than the regular train.
這輛火車行駛的速度比一般火車快兩倍。

5 比較級的修飾法

形容詞或副詞的比較級可用下列程度副詞 (片語) 來修飾：

❶ even　　更加
❷ much / far　　……得多，非常……
= a lot
= a great deal
❸ a little　　有點
= a bit

例句　Time is even more valuable than money.

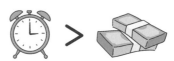

時間比金錢寶貴多了。

Owen spoke much more confidently in this
speech than he did last time.
歐文在這次演講中說話比上次有信心多了。

The test today was a little harder than
the last one.
今天的考試比上次難一點。

單選題

① Sara is more easy-going than her sisters _____.
   (A) do   (B) did   (C) are   (D) aren't

② Andy lost his job last month, so he's now spending _____ money than before.
   (A) little   (B) less   (C) the little   (D) the less

③ I can't believe that Jamie has changed; he treats people more politely _____ when I first met him.
   (A) than he did   (B) than he was
   (C) as he did   (D) as he was

④ Tammy's hair looks longer than that of _____ in her class.
   (A) any girl   (B) all the girls
   (C) any girl else   (D) any other girl

⑤ New York is bigger than _____ in Taiwan.
   (A) any city   (B) the cities
   (C) any other city   (D) all the other cities

⑥ There are two restaurants in this neighborhood. The Japanese one is _____ them.
   (A) more popular than   (B) the more popular of
   (C) most popular of   (D) the most popular of

⑦ The runners ran _____ when they got near the finish line.
   (A) fast and fast   (B) faster and faster
   (C) fastest and fastest   (D) more and more fast

⑧ _____ money Ted made, _____ he spent.
   (A) Much; much   (B) The much; the much
   (C) More; more   (D) The more; the more

⑨ This bridge is _____ the one over there.
    (A) as three times long as   (B) as long as three times
    (C) three times longer than   (D) longer than three times

⑩ Winnie arrived _____ later than Tom today.
    (A) very   (B) little   (C) even   (D) more

解　答

① C　理由　主要子句的動詞為肯定式 be 動詞 is，than (比) 引導的子句也須用肯定式 be 動詞，在此 her sisters (她姊姊們) 的 be 動詞為 are。

② B　理由　由 than (比) 可知空格本句為兩者之間比較的句型，因此空格應使用 little (少的) 之比較級 less (更少)。

③ A　理由　空格本句的動詞 treats (對待) 為現在式一般動詞，又由 more politely (更禮貌) 可知此為兩者之間比較的句型，因此應使用 than (比)，而 than 引導的子句依句意須採過去式，故空格須用助動詞 did。

④ D　理由　Tammy (塔米) 與班上其他女生在同一範圍內，比較時須將自己排除，故須加 other (其他的)。無 any girl else 的說法。

⑤ A　理由　紐約不在臺灣，故不須加 other (其他的)。

⑥ B　理由　「兩者之中較……的」須用以下句型：
the + 形容詞或副詞比較級 + of the two (+ 名詞)

⑦ B　理由　「形容詞或副詞比較級 + and + 形容詞或副詞比較級」表「越來越……」，fast (快地) 的比較級為 faster (更快地)。

⑧ D　理由　此句型為：

The + $\left\{\begin{array}{l}\text{形容詞比較級 (+ 名詞)}\\ \text{副詞比較級}\end{array}\right\}$ + 主詞 + 動詞,

the + $\left\{\begin{array}{l}\text{形容詞比較級 (+ 名詞)}\\ \text{副詞比較級}\end{array}\right\}$ + 主詞 + 動詞

表「越……，就越……」。

⑨ C　理由　「倍數 + 形容詞或副詞比較級 + than...」表「比……多……倍」。

⑩ C　理由　空格應置修飾比較級形容詞的副詞，如 even、much 等。

Chapter 17 比較句型

17-4 最高級句型

最高級用於三者以上數量、性質或程度的比較。

1 最高級基本句型

1

主詞 + 動詞 + the + {形容詞最高級 / 副詞最高級} + {of / among (all) + 複數可數名詞 / in / at + 地方}

=

主詞 + 動詞 + {形容詞比較級 / 副詞比較級} + than + {any (other) + 單數可數名詞 / all the (other) + 複數可數名詞}

譯	……在……之中最……

說明
❶ 形容詞或副詞的最高級前面通常會加 the，但部分副詞的最高級可省略 the，如：most、best。
❷ 第一個句型的「形容詞最高級」之後也可加上名詞。

例句
Taipei 101 is the tallest (building) of all in Taiwan.
= Taipei 101 is taller than any other (building) in Taiwan.
101 是臺灣最高的一棟建築物。

Mr. Chen is the most humorous among all the teachers.
= Mr. Chen is more humorous than any other teacher / than all the other teachers.
所有老師之中陳老師最幽默。

Willy dances (the) best among all the students.
威利是所有學生中跳舞跳最好的。

2 A + 動詞 + the + 形容詞最高級 (+ 名詞 / one) + (that) (+ B) + have / has ever + 過去分詞

譯	A 是 (B) 曾經……最……的

說明
本句型中，關係代名詞 that 引導形容詞子句，修飾前面的名詞，that 若作形容詞子句中動詞的受詞時可省略。

例句
This steak is the most delicious (that) I've ever had.
這牛排是我吃過最好吃的。

例句 This is the most vigorous debate (that) we've ever listened to.
這場辯論會是我們聽過最激烈的一場。

This is the greatest idea that has ever occurred to me.
這是我所想到過最棒的點子。

 表「最少」之最高級句型

主詞 + 動詞 + the least + $\left\{\begin{array}{l}\text{形容詞 (+ 名詞)}\\\text{副詞}\end{array}\right\}$

譯 ……是最不……的

例句 This island is the least polluted area in the country.
這個島是該國最不受汙染的地區。

The story is the least logical one I've ever heard.
這故事是我聽過最不合邏輯的故事。

 最高級其他重要用法

❶ be 動詞 + the last + 名詞 + $\left\{\begin{array}{l}\text{to + 原形動詞}\\\text{(that) (+ 主詞) + 動詞}\end{array}\right\}$

譯 是最不可能做……的……

註 本句型中，關係代名詞 that 引導形容詞子句，修飾前面的名詞，that
若作形容詞子句中動詞的受詞時可省略。

例句 As far as I know, Lily is the last person to tell lies.
= As far as I know, Lily is the last person that would tell lies /
tell a lie.
據我所知，莉莉是最不可能說謊的人。

Betraying his friends is the last thing (that) Victor would do.
背叛朋友是維克多最不可能做的事。

❷ the + 序數 (second, third...) + $\left\{\begin{array}{l}\text{形容詞最高級 (+ 名詞)}\\\text{副詞最高級}\end{array}\right\}$

譯 第二、三……

例
句

In this test, Bobby got the second highest score in the class.
這次考試，巴比的分數是全班第二高。

Keira ran the third fastest in the race.
琪拉在賽跑中跑第三快。

Keira

❹ 最高級的修飾法

形容詞或副詞的最高級可用下列程度副詞（片語）來修飾：

❶ by far　　大大地
❷ the very　　最，完全
❸ by far and away　　極，非常

例
句

I just watched by far the most exciting basketball game I've ever seen.
我剛在電視上看了一場刺激得不得了的籃球賽。

Heidi thought it was by far and away the worst interview she'd ever had.
海蒂覺得這是她參加過再糟糕不過的一次面試。

＼ 即時演練 ／

單選題

① Brenda is _____ of all the employees.
(A) very diligent
(B) more diligent
(C) the more diligent
(D) the most diligent

② The movie I saw last weekend is _____ I've ever seen.
(A) as scary as
(B) scarier than
(C) the scarier of
(D) the scariest

③ No one I know is politer than Ann. She's _____ person to say mean words like that.
(A) the very　　(B) the last　　(C) the least　　(D) the most

④ Only one student got 100 on the quiz. Jack got _____ score, 99.
    (A) the second high   (B) the second higher
    (C) the second highest   (D) the highest second

⑤ Pat is regarded as _____ the most hard-working player on our team.
    (A) a lot   (B) very   (C) even   (D) by far

解　答

① D 理由 由 of all... 得知本句為最高級句型。

② D 理由 空格後有 I've ever seen (我看過)，得知本句為最高級句型，故空格應填形容詞最高級。

③ B 理由 「the last + 名詞 + to + 原形動詞」表「是最不可能做……的……」。

④ C 理由 依句意得知空格應指「第二高」，句型為：the + 序數 + 形容詞最高級 (+ 名詞)。

⑤ D 理由 空格後有最高級形容詞 the most hard-working (最認真的)，故空格應置可修飾該形容詞的副詞如 by far 等。

Chapter 18

假設語氣

Chapter 18 假設語氣

18-1 if 條件句的假設語氣

假設語氣是一種虛擬語氣，用來表達想像或願望等，以下先介紹有關 if 條件句的假設語氣：

1 對現在或未來可能會發生的假設語氣

句型	If + 主詞 + 現在式動詞..., 主詞 + $\begin{cases} \text{will} \\ \text{can} \\ \text{may} \\ \text{shall} \end{cases}$ + 原形動詞...
說明	此時 if 子句只能用現在式動詞，不能用未來簡單式「will + 原形動詞」。
例句	**If** my mother **calls** again tomorrow, I **will visit** her right away. 如果我媽明天再打來，我馬上就去看她。 **If** you **are** tired, you **can take** a rest. 如果你累了，可以休息一下。

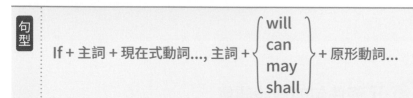

2 與現在事實相反的假設語氣（現在不太可能會發生）

句型	If + 主詞 + $\begin{cases} \text{過去式動詞} \\ \text{were} \end{cases}$ ..., 主詞 + $\begin{cases} \text{would} \\ \text{could} \\ \text{might} \\ \text{should} \end{cases}$ + 原形動詞...
說明	if 子句的 be 動詞不論任何人稱，一律用 were，不用 was。
例句	**If** Jerry **lived** near my home, we **could play** basketball together more often.　如果傑瑞住我家附近，我們就可以常常一起打籃球。 （但事實上傑瑞並不住在說話者家附近。） **If** I **were** rich, I **would buy** my parents a big house. 如果我很有錢，我會買棟大房子給我父母親。（但事實上說話者並不富有。）

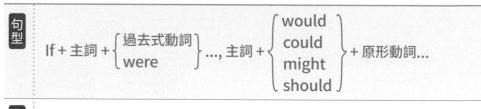

❸ 與過去事實相反的假設語氣（實際上過去並無發生）

句型

If + 主詞 + had + 過去分詞..., 主詞 + $\begin{cases} \text{would} \\ \text{could} \\ \text{might} \\ \text{should} \end{cases}$ + have + 過去分詞...

說明

此時 if 子句為過去完成式，主要子句為助動詞再加上現在完成式。

例句

If Flora **had been** here yesterday, the party **would have been** more fun.

如果芙羅拉昨天在這裡，派對會更好玩。

（但事實上芙蘿拉昨天並不在這裡。）

If Herman **had followed** my advice, he **might not have made** the mistake.

如果當時赫曼採納我的意見，他可能就不會犯這個錯了。

（但事實上赫曼並沒有採納說話者的意見。）

❹ 與未來事實相反的假設語氣（未來不太可能會發生）

句型

If + 主詞 + were to + 原形動詞..., 主詞 + $\begin{cases} \text{would} \\ \text{could} \\ \text{might} \\ \text{should} \end{cases}$ + 原形動詞...

說明

此時 if 子句的 be 動詞不論任何人稱，一律用 were，不用 was。

例句

If the sun **were to rise** in the west, I **would marry** you.

如果太陽從西邊升起，我就嫁給你。

（但事實上未來太陽並不會從西方升起，而是從東方升起。）

Louis is such a good student. If he **were to fail** the math exam next Tuesday, no one **might pass** it.

路易斯是個非常優異的學生。如果下週二的數學考試他都考不及格，那應該沒人會通過。

（但事實上路易斯下週的數學考試應會及格，因為他成績很優異。）

5 未來可能會偶然 / 意外發生的假設語氣

句型

If + 主詞 + should + 原形動詞..., 主詞 + $\begin{cases} \text{will} \\ \text{can} \\ \text{may} \\ \text{shall} \end{cases}$ + 原形動詞...

說明

1 此句型表「萬一……，……」，其中助動詞 will / can / may / shall 也可不使用。

2 主要子句（即「主詞 + will / can / may / shall + 原形動詞...」）也可使用祈使句（即以原形動詞起首的句子）。

例句

If this plan **should go** wrong, we **will have** to go ahead with Plan B.
萬一這個計畫出錯，我們得執行 B 計畫。

If anyone **should call** me, please **take** a message for me.
萬一有人打電話給我，請幫我留言。

 深 度補充

表真理、事實或習慣的 if 條件句

句型

If + 主詞 + 現在式動詞..., 主詞 + 現在式動詞...

說明

1 此時 if 可替換成 when，因為是條件許可就會發生某結果的情形。

2 if 子句和主要子句的時態可交替使用現在簡單 / 進行式、過去簡單 / 進行式等。

例句

If / When the temperature of a material **goes** down, the size of the material **decreases**.
如果某物的溫度下降，其尺寸會變小。（為真理）

If / When it **is** too hot, high-quality chocolate **melts**.
如果太熱，品質好的巧克力就會融化。（為事實）

If / When my mom **meets** the old lady, she always **chats** with her for a while.
如果我媽遇到那位老太太，她總和她聊天聊一會兒。（為習慣）

If / When the price of gasoline **is shooting** up, the prices of other things **are** in turn **going** up.
如果汽油價格飆升，那麼其他東西的價格也會隨之上漲。
（為事實）

I really miss the time when I played basketball at high school. For example, if / when our team **practiced** for a long time, our coach **treated** us to some delicious snacks or drinks.
我真的很懷念我高中打籃球的時候。例如，如果我們球隊練球練很久的話，教練會請我們吃好吃的點心和飲料。
（為過去的習慣）

Hannah always **went** in to buy a drink if / when she **was walking** past that café.
如果漢娜路過那家咖啡店，她總是進去買杯飲料。
（為過去的習慣）

❻ 混合的假設語氣

 說明 即時態不一致的假設語氣，如：

❶ if 子句與過去事實相反，使用過去完成式；主要子句與現在事實相反，使用「would / could / might / should + 原形動詞」。

❷ if 子句與現在事實相反，使用過去式；主要子句與過去事實相反，使用「would / could / might / should + have + 過去分詞」。

 例句 If I **hadn't eaten** ice cream yesterday, I **wouldn't feel** uncomfortable today.
如果我昨天沒吃冰淇淋，我今天就不會感到不舒服了。

If I **were** you, I **would have made** a different decision.
如果我是你，我當時會做出不同的決定。

不可說：

If I **had been** you, I **would have made** a different decision.
如果我當時是你，我會做出不同的決定。
（暗示我當時不是你，但現在我就是你。── 不合邏輯。）

CH 18

18-1

三、條件句的假設語氣

389

單選題

① Oh! Iris went to Italy yesterday. If she _____ here, she would be glad to see you.
(A) is   (B) are   (C) were   (D) did

② If the weather _____ good tomorrow, we will go hiking.
(A) is   (B) was   (C) were   (D) would be

③ If Gina _____ my life, I wouldn't be standing here and talking to you.
(A) doesn't save   (B) won't save
(C) hasn't saved   (D) hadn't saved

④ I would have gone to Martin's party if I _____ time. However, I was too busy then.
(A) have had   (B) had had
(C) had   (D) would have had

⑤ If the temperature drops below 4 degrees Celsius, lakes _____.
(A) would freeze (B) freeze   (C) had frozen (D) froze

⑥ If the typhoon _____ come tomorrow, the event will be put off.
(A) should   (B) would   (C) might   (D) could

⑦ If I _____ tomorrow, I would have no regrets.
(A) have died   (B) had died   (C) am to die   (D) were to die

⑧ If I _____ superpowers, I would put all the bad guys in prison.
(A) have   (B) have had   (C) had   (D) had had

⑨ Nobody told me you had moved house. If I had known your new address, I _____ to visit you.
(A) went   (B) would have gone
(C) would go   (D) will go

⑩ If cats _____ a human language, I would be happy to chat with them.
(A) have spoken   (B) speaks
(C) spoke   (D) could have spoken

解 答				
① C	② A	③ D	④ B	⑤ B
⑥ A	⑦ D	⑧ C	⑨ B	⑩ C

18-2 其他重要假設語氣

動詞 wish（希望）、連接詞 as if / though（彷彿）、表「要求」（如 demand、require）等的動詞及表「重要的 / 必需的」（如 important、necessary）等的形容詞等，均可形成假設語氣，茲分述如下：

① wish 希望

句型 1	主詞 + wish (that) { 主詞 + were / 過去式動詞 主詞 + could / would + 原形動詞 }
譯	……希望 / 但願（現在）……　（現在的事實並非如此）
說明	此句型表示現在不可能實現的願望。
例句	I really miss my boyfriend. I wish he were here. 我真的很想我男朋友。我真希望他在這裡。 （事實上說話者的男友並不在此處。） I wish I knew how to solve these math questions. 我希望我知道如何解這些數學題目。 （事實上說話者並不知道如何解這些題目。） The little boy wishes that he could turn anything into gold. 小男孩希望他能把任何東西都變成金子。 （事實上小男孩並無此特殊能力。）
句型 2	主詞 + wish (that) + 主詞 + had + 過去分詞
譯	……希望 / 但願（過去）……　（過去的事實並非如此）
說明	此句型表示過去不可能實現的願望。

例句	Kent **wishes that** he **had gone** to the movies with Erin. 肯特希望他當時有和艾琳一起去看電影。 （事實上肯特當時並沒有和艾琳一起去看電影。）	

註	wish 表「祝福」時，則與假設語氣無關，用法如下： **wish sb sth**　祝福某人……

例句	I **wish** you a merry Christmas / happy birthday. 祝你聖誕快樂 / 生日快樂。 Tony said goodbye to me and **wished** me luck. 湯尼跟我道別，並祝我好運。

 度補充

比較 wish 與 hope

	wish	hope
譯	希望	
區別	現在或過去不大可能實現的願望。	有可能實現的願望。
句型	**1** 表現在不大可能實現的願望： wish (that) + 主詞 + were / 過去式動詞 wish (that) + 主詞 + could / would + 原形動詞 **2** 表過去不大可能實現的願望： wish (that) + 主詞 + had + 過去分詞	hope (that) + 主詞 + 動詞 
例句	I wish I could fly. 但願我能飛。 （事實上說話者並無飛行能力。） Paul **wishes** he had finished his college education. 保羅希望他當時有讀完大學。 （事實上保羅大學並沒有畢業。）	I hope my boyfriend will give me some flowers on my birthday. 我希望我男友在我生日那天會送我 花。 （說話者的男友極有可能生日當天 會送她花。）

譯二	想要 (= want)	
區別	較客氣。	較直接。
句型	**wish to** + 原形動詞	**hope to** + 原形動詞
例句	Adam, Mr. Miller **wishes to talk to** you. 亞當，米勒老師想和你談一談。	Ned **hopes to move to** a bigger apartment next year. 奈德希望明年能搬到更大間的公寓住。

❷ as if / though　彷彿

句型1	主詞 + 動詞... + as if / though $\left\{ \begin{array}{l} 主詞 + were / 過去式動詞 \\ 主詞 + could / would + 原形動詞 \end{array} \right\}$
譯	……彷彿…… (現在)……
說明	as if / though 之後為與現在事實相反的假設。
例句	Kayla is acting **as if / though** she **were** a superstar. 凱拉表現得好像她是超級巨星一樣。 （事實上凱拉並不是巨星。） Nelly sounds **as if / though** she **knew** the president, but she has never met him before. 娜莉聽起來好像她跟總裁很熟，但她從未見過他。 （事實上娜莉並不熟識總裁。） Linda looks **as if / though** she **could eat** all the desserts in the bakery. 琳達看起來好像她可以吃掉這家麵包店的所有甜點。 （事實上琳達是不大可能吃掉麵包店的所有甜點。） 
句型2	主詞 + 動詞... + as if / though + 主詞 + had + 過去分詞
譯	……彷彿…… (過去)……

說明 as if / though 之後為與過去事實相反的假設。

 例句 Vince sounded **as if / though** he **had saved** the girl's life himself, but actually it was Doug who saved her.
文斯聽起來好像是他救了那女孩，但實際上是道格救了那女孩。
（事實上並不是文斯救了女孩。）

 註 as if / though 之後也可加上一般時態（即時態同 as if / though 之前的動詞），表示主詞真實的感受或看起來的樣子。

 例句 It **looks** **as if / though** it **is** going to thunder.　看起來好像要打雷了。
It **looked** **as if / though** it **was** going to thunder.
當時看起來好像要打雷了。

 3 表「要求」等的動詞

 句型 主詞 + ⎰ demand ⎱ (that) + 主詞 + (should) + 原形動詞
　　　　　　　⎱ suggest ⎰
　　　　　　　⎰ order ⎱

譯 ……要求 / 建議 / 命令……（應該）……

 說明
1 表要求、建議、命令等的動詞，其後 that 子句裡主詞之後應接助動詞 should，而 should 常予省略，直接使用原形動詞。

2 表要求、建議、命令等的動詞還包括：
require（要求，規定）　　　recommend（建議）
request（請求）　　　　　　propose（建議）
ask（請求）　　　　　　　　urge（力勸，敦促）
insist（堅持要求）

例句 The manager **demanded that** Tony **finish** the project on time.
經理要求湯尼按時完成此專案。

The boss **suggested that** the meeting **be** held on August 5th.
老闆建議八月五日開會。

The judge **ordered** an injury assessment report **be** handed in.
法官下令呈交驗傷報告。

395

④ 表「重要的 / 必需的」形容詞

句型	It is $\begin{Bmatrix} \text{important} \\ \text{necessary} \end{Bmatrix}$ (that) + 主詞 + (should) + 原形動詞
譯	……（應該）……是很重要 / 必需的
說明	**❶** 虛主詞 it 後加上表重要性等意思的形容詞，其後 that 子句裡主詞之後應接助動詞 should，而 should 常予省略，直接使用原形動詞。 **❷** 表重要性等意思的形容詞還包括： vital / crucial（至關重要的）　　imperative（極重要的；迫切的） essential（必要的）　　desirable（令人嚮往的）
例句	It is important / vital that your grandfather go to bed before 10 o'clock. 十點前你爺爺要上床睡覺是很重要的。 It is necessary that Walter go on a business trip to Italy next week. 華特下週必須去義大利出差。

＼ 即時演練 ／

單選題

① The doctor insisted that Jamie ＿＿＿＿＿＿ this kind of medicine every day.
(A) taking　　(B) to take　　(C) take　　(D) taken

② Ken wishes he ＿＿＿＿＿＿ abroad, but he is too busy.
(A) could go　　(B) go　　(C) can go　　(D) goes

③ Bob is just a part-time worker, but he talks as if he ＿＿＿＿＿＿ our boss.
(A) be　　(B) were　　(C) to be　　(D) been

④ It is important that Gary ＿＿＿＿＿＿ the meeting next Thursday.
(A) attending　　(B) attended　　(C) to attend　　(D) attend

⑤ Jill _____ that she can pass the French exam since she has been studying so hard for more than three months.
(A) orders　　　(B) wants　　　(C) hopes　　　(D) wishes

⑥ Iris didn't go to the party, but she does wish she _____ there.
(A) were　　　(B) had been　　(C) be　　　(D) has been

⑦ It is essential that each of you _____ a life jacket before you go aboard the ship.
(A) wore　　　(B) wearing　　(C) to wear　　(D) wear

⑧ Kirk is rather poor, but each month he spends a lot of money as if he _____ very rich.
(A) were　　　　(B) is　　　　(C) be　　　　(D) has been

⑨ The principal ordered that all the chairs in the hall _____ moved away.
(A) is　　　　(B) have been　(C) be　　　　(D) had been

⑩ Kyle just quarreled with Ida about an hour ago, but now he is acting as if nothing _____.
(A) happen　　　　　　　(B) had happened
(C) is happening　　　　　(D) to happen

解　答				
① C	② A	③ B	④ D	⑤ C
⑥ B	⑦ D	⑧ A	⑨ C	⑩ B

Notes

Chapter 19

倒裝句

Chapter 19　倒裝句

19-1　否定副詞（片語）在句首時的倒裝句

倒裝句是將句中某些詞類（大部分為主詞及動詞）倒置，而形成的特殊句型，常見

於書寫及文學作品中。以下介紹倒裝句常見的種類：

1 否定副詞（片語）在句首時的倒裝句。

2 「only + 副詞（片語 / 子句）」在句首時的倒裝句。

3 表地方的副詞在句首時的倒裝句。

4 so 或 such 在句首時的倒裝句。

5 假設語氣條件句的倒裝句。

6 so、neither 或 nor 引導的倒裝句。

7 讓步子句的倒裝句。

8 引用句後加上「某人說」等的倒裝句。

以下先介紹否定副詞（片語）在句首時的倒裝句：

此種倒裝句為句首有否定副詞（片語），如 never、no、not 等，基本句型如下：

句型	否定副詞（片語）+	be 動詞 + 主詞... 助動詞（can、will 等）+ 主詞 + 原形動詞... do / does / did + 主詞 + 原形動詞... 完成式助動詞 have / has / had + 主詞 + 過去分詞...

倒裝句

說明	**1** 若原句型為現在 / 過去簡單式的一般動詞（而非 be 動詞），形成倒裝句時，主詞之前應放置 do / does / did，再接「主詞 + 原形動詞」。 **2** 若原句型為完成式，形成倒裝句時，主詞之前應放置完成式助動詞 have / has / had，再接「主詞 + 過去分詞」。 **3** 以下為解說方便，補充句型中所提的倒裝句指的即是上述句型加號之後的結構（即主詞與動詞位置倒裝）。

接下來依意思分述有關否定副詞（片語）的倒裝句：

1 表「沒有」或「幾乎沒有」

never	從不
seldom / rarely	不常，很少
hardly / barely / scarcely	幾乎不
little	不多，很少
by no means	一點都不
= in no way	
= on no account	
= under no circumstances	

例句

Jerry will **never** play that boring game again.
→ **Never** will Jerry play that boring game again.
傑瑞再也不會玩那個無聊的遊戲了。

Martin **seldom** goes to the gym. He prefers to work out at home.
→ **Seldom** does Martin go to the gym. He prefers to work out at home.
馬丁很少去健身房。他比較喜歡在家健身。

Ken **hardly** slept last night.
→ **Hardly** did Ken sleep last night.
肯昨晚幾乎沒睡。

I have **barely** met such a strange person before.
→ **Barely** have I met such a strange person before.
我幾乎不曾遇過這麼奇怪的人。

I know **little** about this topic.
→ **Little** do I know about this topic.
我對這個主題所知甚少。

This problem is **by no means** easy to deal with.
→ **By no means** is this problem easy to deal with.
這問題絕不容易處理。

2 no longer 表「不再⋯⋯」

例句
Lance no longer wanted to talk to Laura.
→ No longer did Lance want to talk to Laura.
蘭斯不想再和蘿拉說話了。

3 nowhere 表「任何地方都不」

例句
This report does not list the sources anywhere.
→ Nowhere does this report list the sources.
此報告未在任何地方列出資料來源。

4 no sooner... than... 表「一⋯⋯就⋯⋯」

補充句型
No sooner + 倒裝句 + than + 子句

例句
The student had no sooner seen Ms. Clark than he ran away.
→ No sooner had the student seen Ms. Clark than he ran away.
那個學生一看到克拉克老師就跑走了。

5 not until... 表「直到⋯⋯才⋯⋯」

補充句型
Not until + $\left\{ \begin{array}{l} 某時間點 \\ 子句 \end{array} \right\}$ + 倒裝句

說明
此句型真正需要倒裝的是主要子句，而非 not until 所引導的副詞子句。

例句
Rick didn't arrive until 9:20 a.m.
→ Not until 9:20 a.m. did Rick arrive.
瑞克到早上九點二十分才到。

We didn't know the truth until Kelly told us.
→ Not until Kelly told us did we know the truth.
直到凱莉告訴我們，我們才知道真相。

6 **not only... but also...** 表「不只……而且……」

| 補充句型 | Not only + 倒裝句..., but + 主詞 ⎨ be 動詞 + (also)...
助動詞 + (also) + 原形動詞...
(also) + 動詞...
have / has / had + (also) + 過去分詞... |

説明 | not only 置句首時，之後的主要子句採倒裝句構，but 連接的主要子句不採倒裝，且 also 要置句中或予以省略。

例句

Lisa is **not only** beautiful **but** (also) kind.

→ **Not only** is Lisa beautiful, **but** she is (also) kind.
麗莎不僅美麗，而且也很親切。

Marge can **not only** sing sweetly **but also** dance very well.

→ **Not only** can Marge sing sweetly, **but** she can (also) dance very well.
瑪芝不僅歌聲甜美，舞也跳得很好。

Robin **not only** helped the orphans **but also** donated a lot of money to charity last year.

→ **Not only** did Robin help the orphans, **but** he (also) donated a lot of money to charity last year.
羅賓不僅幫助孤兒，而且去年也捐了很多錢給慈善機構。

Nora has **not only** finished her homework **but also** fed the dog.

→ **Not only** has Nora finished her homework, **but** she has (also) fed the dog.
諾拉不僅作業寫完了，狗也餵好了。

CH 19

19-1

否定副詞（片語）在句首時的倒裝句

\ 即時演練 /

請將下列句子改成倒裝句。

① My mother rarely has time to watch TV.

_____

② My grandfather has never yelled at my grandmother.

_____

③ Walter cannot play with his neighbors until he finishes mopping the floor.

_____

_____

④ Roy is not only handsome but also charming.

_____

⑤ We had no sooner started to play tennis than it began to rain.

_____

⑥ Paula no longer lives in the dormitory.

_____

⑦ I cannot find any books on this topic. (★用 nowhere 倒裝)

_____

⑧ My son not only did the laundry this morning but also cooked lunch for his younger sister.

_____

_____

解　答

① Rarely does my mother have time to watch TV.
② Never has my grandfather yelled at my grandmother.
③ Not until Walter finishes mopping the floor can he play with his neighbors.
④ Not only is Roy handsome, but he is (also) charming.
⑤ No sooner had we started to play tennis than it began to rain.
⑥ No longer does Paula live in the dormitory.
⑦ Nowhere can I find any books on this topic.
⑧ Not only did my son do the laundry this morning, but he (also) cooked lunch for his younger sister.

Chapter 19 倒裝句

19-2 「only + 副詞（片語／子句）」在句首時的倒裝句

這種倒裝句常見的句型如下：

❶ only then...

句型	Only then + 倒裝句　　直到那時才…… = Only at that time + 倒裝句
例句	I realized **only then** that my husband cheated on me.（劣） → **Only then** did I realize that my husband cheated on me.（佳） 　我直到那時才意識到我丈夫對我不忠。

❷ only + 介詞片語

句型	Only by / in / with... + 倒裝句　　只有透過／在／用……才……
例句	You can dance well **only by** practicing a lot. → **Only by** practicing a lot can you dance well. 　你只有透過大量練習才能把舞跳得好。 My dream can come true **only in** this city. → **Only in** this city can my dream come true. 　我的夢想只有在這座城市才能實現。 You can finish the task efficiently **only with** this software. → **Only with** this software can you finish the task efficiently. 　只有使用此軟體你才能有效地完成這個工作。

❸ only after...

句型	Only after / before / when 引導的副詞子句 + 倒裝句 只有在……之後才…… / 只有在……之前才…… / 只有當……才……
例句	The mother could take a rest **only after** the baby fell asleep. → **Only after** the baby fell asleep could the mother take a rest. 　只有等寶寶睡著了，那位媽媽才能休息。

「only＋副詞（片語／子句）」在句首時的倒裝句

例句 Mark told his daughter who her mother was **only before** he died.

→ **Only before** he died <u>did Mark tell</u> his daughter who her mother was.

馬克直到死前，才告訴他女兒她的母親是誰。

We made progress on the project **only when** Kyle helped us.

→ **Only when** Kyle helped us <u>did we make</u> progress on the project.

只有在凱爾的幫助下，我們才在此專案上有所進展。

註 after / before 亦可作介詞，故「Only after / before + 名詞」出現在句首時，之後的主要子句亦採倒裝句構。

例句 Sam realized the importance of seizing the day **only after** his grandmother's death.

→ **Only after** his grandmother's death <u>did Sam realize</u> the importance of seizing the day.

山姆直到祖母過世後才意識到活在當下是多麼的重要。

Nicole realized how much she loved Tony **only before** her departure for New York.

→ **Only before** her departure for New York <u>did Nicole realize</u> how much she loved Tony.

妮可直到她要去紐約之前才了解到她有多麼愛湯尼。

請將下列句子改成以 only 為開頭的倒裝句。

① I realized I was such an ungrateful guy only when I looked back on my childhood.

② The actress promised to star in the director's movie only after he visited her once again.

③ You can successfully make this special cake only with this key ingredient.

④ The boy realized only then how deeply his parents loved him.

解　答

① Only when I looked back on my childhood did I realize I was such an ungrateful guy.
② Only after he visited her once again did the actress promise to star in the director's movie.
= Only after the director visited the actress once again did she promise to star in his movie.
③ Only with this key ingredient can you successfully make this special cake.
④ Only then did the boy realize how deeply his parents loved him.

CH
19

19-2

「only + 副詞（片語／子句）」在句首時的倒裝句

19-3 表地方的副詞在句首時的倒裝句

這種倒裝句常見的句型如下：

 句型 地方副詞 (片語) + 不及物動詞 + 主詞

 說明
❶ be 動詞也為一種不及物動詞。
❷ 此句型的地方副詞 (片語) 如：here、there、on the table、by the window 等。
❸ 此倒裝句之主詞若為代名詞時，則不可倒裝。

 例句
Here comes my daughter. (= My daughter is arriving.)
我女兒來了。
Here she comes. (○)
Here comes she. (×)
她來了。

A: Could you pass me the pepper?
B: **Here you** are / go. / **There you** are / go.
A：你能把胡椒遞給我嗎？
B：給你。
(★ B 說 Here you are / go. 時，胡椒罐離 B 較近；而 B 說 There you are / go. 時，胡椒罐離 A 較近。)

Thousands of years ago, **there** lived a special tribe called Gaia.
幾千年前有個叫做蓋亞族的特殊部落。

The desserts Lydia made by herself were **on the table**.
→ **On the table** were the desserts Lydia made by herself.
桌上放著莉迪亞自己做的甜點。

A man in a suit stood **by the window**.
→ **By the window** stood a man in a suit.
窗邊站著一個穿西裝的男人。

句子重組

① our / comes / taxi / Here

_____ .

② are, / Cindy / There / you

_____ .

③ there / After the ceremony, / dinner party / follows / a

_____ .

④ in green / came / Into / a beautiful lady / the hall

_____ .

⑤ came / of / a lion / Out / the cave

_____ .

解　答

① Here comes our taxi
② There you are, Cindy
③ After the ceremony, there follows a dinner party
④ Into the hall came a beautiful lady in green
⑤ Out of the cave came a lion

Chapter 19 倒裝句

19-4 so 或 such 在句首時的倒裝句

 ① so 在句首時

句型	So + 形容詞 + be 動詞 + 主詞 + that 子句
	So + 副詞 + 助動詞（can、will 等）+ 主詞 + 原形動詞 + that 子句
	So + 副詞 + $\begin{Bmatrix} \text{do} \\ \text{does} \\ \text{did} \end{Bmatrix}$ + 主詞 + 原形動詞 + that 子句
	So + 副詞 + $\begin{Bmatrix} \text{have} \\ \text{has} \\ \text{had} \end{Bmatrix}$ + 主詞 + 過去分詞 + that 子句

 譯 如此……以致於……

 說明

1 so 後面為加形容詞，而非名詞。

2 若原句型為現在 / 過去簡單式的一般動詞（而非 be 動詞），形成此倒裝句時，主詞之前應放置 do / does / did，再接「主詞 + 原形動詞」。

3 若原句型為完成式，形成此倒裝句時，主詞之前應放置完成式助動詞 have / has / had，再接「主詞 + 過去分詞」。

 例句

Rex is so handsome that I have a crush on him.

→ So handsome is Rex that I have a crush on him.
雷克斯太帥了，帥到我超迷他的。

The little boy could dance so well that his parents decided to sign him up for dance classes.

→ So well could the little boy dance that his parents decided to sign him up for dance classes.
這小男孩跳舞跳得很好，所以他父母決定幫他報名舞蹈課。

Nora arrived **so late that** there were no seats left in the movie theater.

→ **So late** <u>did Nora arrive</u> **that** there were no seats left in the movie theater.
諾拉來得太晚了，所以電影院裡沒座位可坐了。

Zach's team has solved the problem **so successfully that** they deserve our respect.

→ **So successfully** <u>has Zach's team solved</u> the problem **that** they deserve our respect.
查克的團隊成功地解決了這個問題，所以他們應得到我們的尊重。

❷ such 在句首時

句型	Such（＋名詞）＋ be 動詞＋主詞＋ that 子句
	Such ＋名詞＋助動詞（can、will 等）＋主詞＋原形動詞＋ that 子句
	Such ＋名詞＋ $\begin{cases} do \\ does \\ did \end{cases}$ ＋主詞＋原形動詞＋ that 子句
	Such ＋名詞＋ $\begin{cases} have \\ has \\ had \end{cases}$ ＋主詞＋過去分詞＋ that 子句

 譯 如此……以致於……

 說明

❶ such 後面為加名詞（或是加「形容詞＋名詞」），不能只接形容詞而已；另外加的名詞若為單數可數名詞時，需加上不定冠詞 a 或 an，再加上此單數可數名詞。

❷ 此倒裝句型的主要動詞為 be 動詞時，such 後面也可依句意而不加名詞。

 例句

Patty is **such a lovely girl that** we all like her.

→ **Such a lovely girl** <u>is Patty</u> **that** we all like her.
派蒂是個非常親切友善的女孩，我們都很喜歡她。

The heat in the meeting room was such that many people started to sweat.

= The meeting room was so hot that many people started to sweat.

→ Such was the heat in the meeting room that many people started to sweat.
會議室裡很熱，所以很多人開始流汗。

The actor would play such an important role in the movie that he felt a lot of pressure.

→ Such an important role would the actor play in the movie that he felt a lot of pressure.
這演員將在此電影中扮演如此重要的角色，所以他覺得壓力很大。

Gina made such a delicious dinner that the children finished it quickly.

→ Such a delicious dinner did Gina make that the children finished it quickly.
吉娜做了一頓非常美味的晚餐，所以孩子們馬上就吃掉了。

Stan had done such a great job that the manager gave him a promotion.

→ Such a great job had Stan done that the manager gave him a promotion.
史坦做得很好，所以經理給他升職。

\ 即時演練 /

請將下列句子改成以 so 或 such 開頭的倒裝句。

① The boy sang the song so badly that many people covered their ears.

_____

_____

② Erica is such a talented musician that she can write a song in seconds.

_____

_____

③ The little girl was so excited that she couldn't sleep all night.

_____

_____

④ Gary made such a big mistake that Dorothy would never forgive him.

_____

_____

⑤ Fred has been studying so hard that his mother is worried about his health.

_____

_____

解　答

① So badly did the boy sing the song that many people covered their ears.
② Such a talented musician is Erica that she can write a song in seconds.
③ So excited was the little girl that she couldn't sleep all night.
④ Such a big mistake did Gary make that Dorothy would never forgive him.
⑤ So hard has Fred been studying that his mother is worried about his health.

Chapter 19 倒裝句

19-5 假設語氣條件句的倒裝句

這種倒裝句常見的句型如下：

1 假設語氣 if 條件句的動詞為 were 時

句型	Were + 主詞..., 主詞 + $\left\{\begin{array}{l} \text{would} \\ \text{could} \\ \text{might} \\ \text{should} \end{array}\right\}$ + 原形動詞
譯	若 (現在)⋯⋯，⋯⋯會 / 能 / 也許 / 應該⋯⋯
說明	此倒裝句型為與現在事實相反的假設語氣 (現在不太可能會發生)。
例句	If I **were** a boy, my mom would allow me to travel by myself. **Were** I a boy, my mom would allow me to travel by myself. 如果我是男生，我媽就會讓我獨自旅行了。

2 假設語氣 if 條件句的動詞為「had + 過去分詞」時

句型	Had + 主詞 + 過去分詞..., 主詞 + $\left\{\begin{array}{l} \text{would} \\ \text{could} \\ \text{might} \\ \text{should} \end{array}\right\}$ + have + 過去分詞...
譯	若 (當時)⋯⋯，⋯⋯會 / 能 / 也許 / 應該⋯⋯
說明	此倒裝句型為與過去事實相反的假設語氣 (實際上過去並無發生)。
例句	If you **had apologized** to your sister, she might have forgiven you. → **Had** <u>you</u> **apologized** to your sister, she might have forgiven you. 如果你當時向你姊姊道歉，她可能就會原諒你。

3 假設語氣 if 條件句的動詞為「should + 原形動詞」時

句型

$$Should + 主詞 + 原形動詞..., 主詞 + \begin{cases} will \\ can \\ may \\ shall \end{cases} + 原形動詞...$$

譯 （未來）萬一……，……會 / 能 / 也許 / 應該……

說明 主要子句（即「主詞 + will / can / may / shall + 原形動詞...」）也可使用祈使句（即以原形動詞起首的句子）。

例句
If a typhoon **should come**, stock your shelves with food and prepare flashlights.

→ **Should** a typhoon **come**, stock your shelves with food and prepare flashlights.

萬一颱風來了，在家裡的架上存滿食物並準備好手電筒。

＼ 即時演練 ／

請將下列句子改成倒裝句。

① If you had gone to bed early yesterday, you wouldn't have been late for school this morning.

_____

② If I were a bird, I would fly wherever I like.

_____

③ If an earthquake should happen, take cover under a table.

_____

④ If I had brought money with me, I could have bought the dress.

_____

解 答

① Had you gone to bed early yesterday, you wouldn't have been late for school this morning.
② Were I a bird, I would fly wherever I like.
③ Should an earthquake happen, take cover under a table.
④ Had I brought money with me, I could have bought the dress.

19-6 so、neither 或 nor 引導的倒裝句

這種倒裝句的句型如下：

1 so 引導的倒裝句

句型	肯定句, and so + { be 動詞 / 助動詞（can、will 等）/ do / does / did / 完成式助動詞 have / has / had } + 主詞

譯 ……，……也是。

說明

1 此處 so 是副詞，表「也」，故之前應置連接詞 and 以連接兩個主要子句。

2 so 之後動詞的變化需依其後面主詞的單複數來變化，而時態則依其前的肯定句而變。

例句

I'm from that city, and Jerry is, too.
→ I'm from that city, **and so** is Jerry.
我來自那個城市，傑瑞也是。

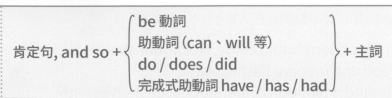

Gail can go to the party, and I can, too.
→ Gail can go to the party, **and so** can I.
蓋兒可以去參加那場派對，我也可以。

My parents enjoyed the show, and I did, too.
→ My parents enjoyed the show, **and so** did I.
我父母很喜歡這場演出，我也很喜歡。

I have finished my homework, and Rita has, too.
→ I have finished my homework, **and so** has Rita.
我已經寫完功課了，麗塔也是。

❷ neither 或 nor 引導的倒裝句

句型

否定句, $\left\{ \begin{array}{l} \text{and neither} \\ \text{nor} \end{array} \right\}$ + $\left\{ \begin{array}{l} \text{be 動詞} \\ \text{助動詞 (can、will 等)} \\ \text{do / does / did} \\ \text{完成式助動詞 have / has / had} \end{array} \right\}$ + 主詞

譯 ……，……也不是。

說明

❶ neither 是否定副詞，表「也不」，故之前應置連接詞 and 以連接兩個主要子句。而 nor 是連接詞，亦表「也不」，但其之前不得再置連接詞 and。

❷ neither 或 nor 之後動詞的變化需依其後面主詞的單複數來變化，而時態則依其前的否定句而變。

例句

This hamburger isn't delicious, and the fries aren't, either.
→ This hamburger isn't delicious, **and neither** <u>are the fries</u>.
= This hamburger isn't delicious, **nor** <u>are the fries</u>.
這漢堡不好吃，薯條也不好吃。

I won't join the tennis club, and Alan won't, either.
→ I won't join the tennis club, **and neither** <u>will Alan</u>.
= I won't join the tennis club, **nor** <u>will Alan</u>.
我不會加入網球社，艾倫也不會。

My brother doesn't like eggplant, and I don't, either.
→ My brother doesn't like eggplant, **and neither** <u>do I</u>.
= My brother doesn't like eggplant, **nor** <u>do I</u>.
我哥哥不喜歡茄子，我也不喜歡。

I haven't signed up for the class, and Paul hasn't, either.
→ I haven't signed up for the class, **and neither** <u>has Paul</u>.
= I haven't signed up for the class, **nor** <u>has Paul</u>.
我還沒報名這門課，保羅也還沒。

CH 19

19-6

so、neither 或 nor 引導的倒裝句

417

單選題

① I have two younger brothers, and _____.
(A) so is Cindy
(B) neither is Cindy
(C) so does Cindy
(D) neither does Cindy

② I'm really proud of you, and _____.
(A) so did your mother
(B) neither does your mother
(C) so does your mother
(D) so is your mother

③ Mandy doesn't like that TV drama, and _____.
(A) neither do I
(B) so do I
(C) neither am I
(D) so am I

④ Roger has eaten so many cookies, and _____.
(A) so I have   (B) so have I   (C) so I do   (D) so do I

⑤ I can't jump that high, _____.
(A) and Sean can so
(B) and Sean can't neither
(C) and so can Sean
(D) nor can Sean

⑥ I'm not hungry, and _____.
(A) so Peggy does
(B) so is Peggy
(C) nor does Peggy
(D) neither is Peggy

解　答				
① C	② D	③ A	④ B	⑤ D
⑥ D				

Chapter 19　倒裝句

19-7　讓步子句的倒裝句

讓步子句及其倒裝句的句型如下：

句型

原句型：

$\left\{ \begin{array}{l} \text{Although} \\ \text{Though} \end{array} \right\}$ + 主詞 + be 動詞 + 形容詞, 主詞 + 動詞...

$\left\{ \begin{array}{l} \text{Although} \\ \text{Though} \end{array} \right\}$ + 主詞 + 動詞 + 副詞,　　主詞 + 動詞...

倒裝句：

形容詞 + $\left\{ \begin{array}{l} \text{as} \\ \text{though} \end{array} \right\}$ + 主詞 + be 動詞, 主詞 + 動詞...

副詞 + $\left\{ \begin{array}{l} \text{as} \\ \text{though} \end{array} \right\}$ + 主詞 + 動詞,　　主詞 + 動詞...

譯　雖然 / 儘管……，……

說明　此倒裝句為將形容詞 / 副詞置於句首，although 改成 as / though（若原句型為 though 則繼續使用）。

例句

Although / Though Dan is handsome, he is not kind.
→ Handsome **as** / **though** Dan is, he is not kind.
雖然丹很帥，但他並不親切。

Although / Though Sam studied hard, he failed the final exam.
→ Hard **as** / **though** Sam studied, he failed the final exam.
雖然山姆很用功，但期末考卻沒過。

Although / Though Sid loves Roxanne very much, she dislikes him.
→ Much **as** Sid loves Roxanne, she dislikes him.
雖然席德很愛蘿珊，蘿珊卻不喜歡他。

（★ 倒裝句若為副詞 much 在句首時，其後常接 as，而非 though；且 very much 置句首時，very 一律省略。）

請將下列句子改成倒裝句。

① Although Willy was hungry, he had no money to buy any food.

_____

_____

② Although the little boy ran quickly, he still couldn't catch up with his elder sister.

_____

_____

③ Though my mother was tired, she still continued playing with her granddaughter.

_____

_____

④ Though Phil wanted to talk to Lena very much, he didn't have the courage.

_____

_____

解　答

① Hungry as / though Willy was, he had no money to buy any food.

② Quickly as / though the little boy ran, he still couldn't catch up with his elder sister.

③ Tired as / though my mother was, she still continued playing with her granddaughter.

④ Much as Phil wanted to talk to Lena, he didn't have the courage.

19-8 引用句後加上「某人說」等的倒裝句

這種倒裝句的動詞常為 say（說）、ask（問）、shout（大叫）等，其句型如下：

引文原以句點結尾時：

"引文," say 等動詞 + 主詞

引文原以驚嘆號結尾時：

"引文!" say 等動詞 + 主詞

引文原以問號結尾時：

"引文?" say 等動詞 + 主詞

譯

……說：「……。/ ！/ ？」

說明

1 此種倒裝句型的「say 等動詞 + 主詞」是置於引文之後，而非置於引文之前。

2 若引文原以句點結尾，置於雙引號之內時，應以逗號取代此句點，且此逗號須置於下引號（"）之前，不可置於下引號之後。

3 若引文原以驚嘆號 / 問號結尾，置於雙引號之內時，驚嘆號 / 問號仍置於下引號之前，不可置於下引號（"）之後。

例句

The woman in blue said, "This view is so beautiful."
→ "This view is so beautiful," the woman in blue said.
= "This view is so beautiful," said the woman in blue.
穿藍色衣服的女子說：「這景色真美。」

The policeman shouted, "Freeze!"
→ "Freeze!" the policeman shouted.
= "Freeze!" shouted the policeman.
警察喊道：「別動！」

The girl asked, "Have you seen my cell phone?"
→ "Have you seen my cell phone?" the girl asked.
= "Have you seen my cell phone?" asked the girl.
女孩問道：「你有看到我的手機嗎？」

請更正下列句子（包括標點符號等），並將雙引號之外的句子改成倒裝句。

① Shouted the woman, "Never call me again"!

_____

② "Why is Mom not in a good mood" ? my brother asked.

_____

③ The waiter said, "Here you are."

_____

④ "The papers must be handed in next Friday." the teacher said.

_____

解　答

① "Never call me again!" shouted the woman.

② "Why is Mom not in a good mood?" asked my brother.

③ "Here you are," said the waiter.

④ "The papers must be handed in next Friday," said the teacher.

Chapter 20

其他重要句型

20-1 祈使句

祈使句又可稱為「命令句」，用以表達邀請、勸告、請求、命令、警告、禁止等。形式則為使用主詞 you 並搭配原形動詞開頭，且 you 通常被省略。以下依不同用法介紹本句型：

❶ 肯定句

句型

一般動詞 / Be 動詞...
Let's + 原形動詞... (★ 較委婉)
Please + 原形動詞...
= 原形動詞..., please (★ 較委婉)

例句

Go to the party with me. 跟我一起參加派對。
Be here at 8 a.m. tomorrow. 明天八點到這裡。
Let's go to the party. 我們去參加派對吧。
Please go to the party with me.
= Go to the party with me, please.
請跟我一起參加派對。

 度補充

肯定祈使句加強語氣的用法

說明

肯定祈使句若要加強語氣，可在句首做以下變化：

Do + 原形動詞... 務必要……
Always + 原形動詞... 每次都要……
You + 原形動詞... 你 / 妳 / 你們……
Make sure + (that) 子句 確保……

例句

Do bring an umbrella with you. 務必要帶把傘出門。
Always check your answers twice. 每次都要檢查答案兩次。
You be quiet.
= **Do be** quiet.
你安靜 / 務必要安靜。

Make sure (that) you have enough gas before hitting the road.
上路前要確保有足夠的汽油。

② 否定句

 句型
Don't / Do not + 一般動詞 / be 動詞...
Let's not + 原形動詞... (★ 較委婉)
Please + don't + 原形動詞...
= Don't + 原形動詞..., please (★ 較委婉)

 例句
Don't panic when an earthquake strikes.
= Do not panic when an earthquake strikes.
地震發生時不要慌張。

Don't be a fair-weather friend.
別當個不願患難與共的朋友。

Let's not go to the movies tonight. I'm exhausted.
咱們今晚就別去看電影了吧。我累壞了。

Please don't slouch at the dinner table.
= Don't slouch at the dinner table, please.
坐在餐桌前，請別彎腰駝背。

 深 度補充

否定祈使句加強語氣的用法

 說明
否定祈使句若要加強語氣，可在句首做以下變化：

Don't you (ever) + 原形動詞...　　你 (永遠) 不准……
= Don't you + 原形動詞... (ever)
Never + 原形動詞...　　千萬不要……
Never ever + 原形動詞...　　永遠不准……
= Never + 原形動詞... + ever

 例句
Don't you ever lie to me again!
= Don't you lie to me ever again!
你永遠都不准再對我撒謊！

Never make a promise you can't keep.
別許下你無法實現的諾言。

CH
20

20-1

祈使句

425

例句

Never ever run a red light!
= Never run a red light ever!
永遠不准闖紅燈！

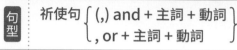

祈使句之後常與 and 或 or 開頭的子句連用，表示「……那麼 / 否則……」

句型

祈使句 $\left\{ \begin{array}{l} \text{(,) and + 主詞 + 動詞} \\ \text{, or + 主詞 + 動詞} \end{array} \right\}$

註

此句型 and 之前是否加逗點，可視 and 之後的句子是否太長等而定（若句子太長則加上逗點）；而 or 在此句型因為表「否則」，所以 or 之前必加逗點。

例句

Take a deep breath, and you'll feel relaxed.
深呼吸，那麼你就會覺得放鬆。

Don't jump on the bed, or you might fall.
不要在床上跳來跳去，否則你可能會摔傷的。

＼ 即時演練 ／

單選題

① ＿＿＿＿＿＿＿＿ your hand before you answer the question.
　(A) To raise　　(B) Raise　　(C) Raising　　(D) Be raising

② Please ＿＿＿＿＿＿＿＿ to work on time, or you'll be fired.
　(A) be getting　(B) to get　　(C) get　　(D) to getting

③ ＿＿＿＿＿＿＿＿ plant some flowers in the backyard.
　(選錯的一項)
　(A) Do　　(B) Let's　　(C) Always　　(D) Be

④ ＿＿＿＿＿＿＿＿ a good boy.
　(A) Be　　(B) Do　　(C) Let's　　(D) Always

⑤ Please ＿＿＿＿＿＿＿＿ bring any toys to school, Peter.
　(A) don't　　(B) not　　(C) that　　(D) ever

⑥ _____ run in the hallway. (選錯的一項)
(A) Let's not   (B) Not ever
(C) Never   (D) Don't you ever

⑦ Never _____ a backstabber, or you'll be despised.
(A) to be   (B) be ever   (C) be   (D) don't be

⑧ Don't drink too much beer, _____ you will get drunk.
(A) and   (B) or   (C) but   (D) yet

⑨ Take some medicine, _____ you'll feel better soon.
(A) and   (B) or   (C) but   (D) yet

⑩ _____ that you have enough money with you.
(A) Please   (B) Sure   (C) Let's   (D) Make sure

解　　答				
① B	② C	③ D	④ A	⑤ A
⑥ B	⑦ C	⑧ B	⑨ A	⑩ D

Chapter 20　其他重要句型

20-2　感歎句

感歎句用於加強語氣或表達較強烈的情緒，常用 What / How 開頭，並以驚歎號結尾。其用法分述如下：

❶ What 開頭的感歎句

	What + 名詞 + 主詞 + 動詞...!　　……多……的……啊！

❶ 此處 What 可視為形容詞，譯成「多麼的」，以供修飾其後的名詞。

❷ What 後的名詞若為與形容詞搭配的單數名詞，則需連同不定冠詞 a 或 an 一同放置 What 之後，如下：
What a(n) + 形容詞 + 單數名詞 + 主詞 + 動詞!
若為複數名詞或不可數名詞則寫為：
What + 形容詞 + 複數名詞 / 不可數名詞 + 主詞 + 動詞!

❸ 句子最後的「主詞 + 動詞」可以視情況省略。

❹ 將直述句改為 What 開頭的感歎句方法如下：
主詞 + 動詞（片語） + 名詞（片語）．

What + 名詞（片語） + 主詞 + 動詞（片語）!

直述句：It is a fantastic idea.
感歎句：What a fantastic idea (it is)!
　　　　多麼棒的主意啊！（an idea 為單數名詞）

直述句：They are passionate volunteers.
感歎句：What passionate volunteers (they are)!
　　　　（他們是）多麼熱情的一群志工啊！（volunteers 為複數名詞）

直述句：It is bad weather outside.
感歎句：What bad weather (it is) outside!
　　　　外面的天氣真糟糕啊！（weather 為不可數名詞）

② How 開頭的感歎句

| 句型 | How + 形容詞 / 副詞 + 主詞 + 動詞...!　　……多……啊！ |

說明

❶ 此處 How 可視為副詞，譯成「多麼地」，之後一定要加形容詞或副詞，以供修飾主詞或動作。

❷ 句子最後的「主詞 + 動詞」可以視情況省略。

❸ 將直述句改為 How 開頭的感歎句方法如下：

①　主詞　+　動詞 (片語)　+　形容詞 (片語).

　　How +　形容詞 (片語)　+　主詞　+　動詞 (片語)!

②　主詞　+　動詞 (片語)　+　副詞 (片語).

　　How +　副詞 (片語)　+　主詞　+　動詞 (片語)!

例句

直述句：The children are excited.
感歎句：How excited the children are!
　　　　這些孩子多麼興奮啊！

直述句：Eddie has become mature.
感歎句：How mature Eddie has become!
　　　　艾迪變得多麼懂事啊！

直述句：John gets annoyed easily.
感歎句：How easily John gets annoyed!
　　　　約翰多麼容易生氣啊！

CH
20

20-2

感歎句

 度補充

How 之後接非修飾主詞的形容詞時

說明

How 之後可接非修飾主詞的形容詞，而是接修飾其他單數可數名詞的形容詞；此時該名詞絕不能是複數名詞或不可數名詞。口語英文中已少用此表達方式。

句型

How + 形容詞 + a(n) + 單數名詞 + 主詞 + 動詞!

<table>
<tr><td rowspan="3">例
句</td><td colspan="2">How <u>incredible a teacher</u> Susan is! (○)</td></tr>
</table>

How incredible a teacher Susan is! (○)
= **What an incredible teacher** Susan is!
蘇珊是多麼出色的老師啊！(incredible 修飾單數可數名詞 a teacher)

How lazy students they are! (✕)
= **What lazy students** they are! (○)
他們是多麼懶惰的學生啊！(students 為複數名詞)

How good music it is! (✕)
= **What good music** it is! (○)
這音樂多麼動聽啊！(music 為不可數名詞)

\ **即時演練** /

一、單選題

① _____ it is to shop online!
(A) What conveniences   (B) What convenient
(C) How conveniently   (D) How convenient

② _____ terrible weather we are having!
(A) How   (B) What   (C) Much   (D) So

③ What _____ street!
(A) dirty   (B) a dirty   (C) dirty a   (D) be dirty

④ How _____ Ken walks!
(A) quick   (B) be quick   (C) quickly   (D) to quick

⑤ How important _____ !
(A) the notes are   (B) notes they are
(C) notes are they   (D) are the notes

二、請根據提示，將下列直述句改為感歎句。

① Life in big cities is busy.

How _____

② Dennis is an outstanding speaker.

What _____

③ Beethoven was a great musician.

How _____

三、翻譯

① 這房間還真大啊！（What...）

_____

② 這牛排還真美味！（How....）

_____

解　答

一、①D　　　②B　　　③B　　　④C　　　⑤A

二、① How busy life in big cities is!

　② What an outstanding speaker Dennis is!

　③ How great a musician Beethoven was!

三、① What a big room (it is)!

　② How tasty / delicious / yummy the steak is / was!

　 = How tasty / delicious / yummy this steak is!

Chapter 20　其他重要句型

20-3　反問句 / 附加問句

反問句也稱為「附加問句」(tag question)，為置於句末，其基本句型為「, be 動詞 / 助動詞 + 代名詞」(此句型之前要加逗點)，用於加強說話者的情緒，或者詢問對方的意見。其基本原則如下：

原則 1

敘述句為肯定時，反問句則為否定；敘述句為否定時，反問句則為肯定。

例句

Lia is tall, isn't she?　莉雅很高，不是嗎？
You don't like sports, do you?　你不喜歡運動，是嗎？

原則 2

句型基本原則 1

敘述句有 be 動詞時，以該 be 動詞形成反問句。

例句

Danny is a clever boy, isn't he?
丹尼是個聰明的男孩，不是嗎？

You weren't with Linda last night, were you?
你昨晚不是和琳達在一起，對嗎？

句型基本原則 2

敘述句有助動詞 (如 can、will 等或完成式助動詞 have / has / had) 時，以該助動詞形成反問句。

例句

You can't swim, can you?　你不會游泳，對嗎？

Katy has left the party, hasn't she?
凱蒂已經離開派對了，不是嗎？

We will leave for Taipei tomorrow, won't we?
我們明天就會出發前往臺北，不是嗎？

You should concentrate in class, shouldn't you?
你上課應該要專心，不是嗎？

句型基本原則 3

敘述句內為一般動詞時，應以主詞人稱及動詞時態判斷，以 do / does / did 形成反問句。

例句

The students love Mr. Wang, don't they?

學生們喜歡王老師，不是嗎？（主詞為第三人稱複數 the students，動詞 love 為現在式，故反問句需用 don't）

Alice went jogging this morning, didn't she?

艾莉絲今早去晨跑了，不是嗎？（主詞為第三人稱單數 Alice，動詞 went 為過去式，故反問句需用 didn't）

句型基本原則 4

前半為祈使句（或命令句）時，也就是以原形動詞開頭的句子時，不論肯定句或否定句，常用 will you 形成反問句。

例句

Open the door, will you?　開個門，好不好？

Don't let him go, will you?　別讓他走，好不好？

注意

若為以 Let's 為首的祈使句（或命令句），不論肯定句或否定句，反問句則用 shall we。

Let's get some milk on the way home, shall we?
咱們在回家的路上買些牛奶吧，好嗎？

Let's not turn the light off, shall we?　咱們不要關燈，好不好？

原則 3

反問句內只能使用「代名詞」。若為指示代名詞／形容詞 this、that 開頭的句子，反問句內一律用 it 代替；若為 these、those 開頭的句子，反問句內一律用 they 代替。

例句

Amy is a cat person, isn't she?
艾咪是位愛貓人士，不是嗎？

The Lins have gone abroad, haven't they?
林家人已經出國了，不是嗎？

This is not your fork, is it?
這不是你的叉子，對嗎？（This 為指示代名詞）

Those people are your friends, aren't they?
那些人是你的朋友，不是嗎？（Those 為指示形容詞）

注意

There is / are 開頭的敘述句中，因為 there 是副詞，所以反問句仍應使用 there。

There isn't much traffic today, is there?　今天交通並不繁忙，是嗎？

原則 4

否定的反問句中，not 可以與 be 動詞或助動詞合併，也可單獨置於句尾，但較罕見。

The sneakers are cheap, aren't they? (○)

= The sneakers are cheap, are they not? (罕)

= The sneakers are cheap, are not they? (✕)（代名詞不能置於句尾）
這雙運動鞋很便宜，對不對？

Joy went to school late, didn't she? (○)

= Joy went to school late, did she not? (罕)

= Joy went to school late, did not she? (✕)（代名詞不能置於句尾）
喬依上學遲到了，是不是？

 深 度補充

使用附加問句的特殊情況

說明 1
敘述句中帶有否定副詞或片語（如 little、few、never、hardly、rarely、no doubt、by no means 等）時，該敘述句視為否定句，因此反問句應為肯定句。

John has few friends, does he?　約翰幾乎沒有朋友，對不對？

Amanda is never angry, is she?　阿曼達沒有生氣過，對嗎？

Debby is no doubt the best singer today, is she?　　Debby
黛比絕對是現今最棒的歌手，是不是？

說明 2	敘述句中若用第一人稱單數的主詞 I 表示意見或觀點，後接 that 子句時，反問句則依 that 子句內的主詞及時態判斷。
例句	I think that <u>the engineers are</u> very intelligent, **aren't they**? 我認為這群工程師很聰明，不是嗎？ I don't think Eddie <u>will</u> apologize, **will** he? 我不認為艾迪會道歉，他會嗎？
說明 3	need、dare 除了當一般動詞使用外，也可當助動詞使用，若當助動詞時，使用原則同一般助動詞。
例句	Karen <u>needs</u> to do her homework, **doesn't she**? 凱倫得要做回家作業，對不對？（need 為一般動詞） The girl <u>need not</u> practice her speech today, **need she**? 這女孩今天不需要練習演講，對不對？（need 為助動詞） You <u>didn't dare</u> to watch the horror movie, **did you**? 你不敢看那部恐怖片，對嗎？（dare 為一般動詞） You <u>dare not</u> go near the haunted house, **dare you**? 你不敢走近那棟鬼屋，對嗎？（dare 為助動詞）

\ 即時演練 /

一、單選題

① They had to wait a long time to get into the restaurant, _____?
(A) don't they   (B) didn't they
(C) couldn't they   (D) shouldn't they

② Jimmy had very little to eat last night, _____ he?
(A) did   (B) had   (C) hasn't   (D) won't

③ Help me carry the bags, _____?
(A) shall we   (B) shall you   (C) don't you   (D) will you

④ Let's take a walk, _____?
(A) shall we   (B) will we   (C) will you   (D) won't you

⑤ That is the mug Ms. Lin gave you, _____?
   (A) didn't she   (B) isn't this   (C) isn't it   (D) didn't you

二、請填入正確的反問句

① I needn't bring my books here tomorrow, _____?

② Sean had finished his breakfast before you woke up this morning, _____?

③ I don't think these are your pencils, _____?

④ There aren't many employees in the company, _____?

⑤ Scott is rarely late for school, _____?

解　答

一、① B   ② A   ③ D   ④ A   ⑤ C

二、① need I   ② hadn't he   ③ are they   ④ are there   ⑤ is he

Chapter 20 　其他重要句型

20-4　間接問句

間接問句 (indirect question) 由直接問句變化而來，為**名詞子句**的一種，具有**名詞**的功用，以**疑問詞**開頭，其後再依規則做變化。

基本句型為：**疑問詞 + 主詞 +（助動詞）+ 動詞**

共通規則如下：

共通規則 1

疑問詞包含常見的 6W1H (what、where、when、why、who、which、how) 以及 if / whether。

> 例句
>
> I need to know **when Sophie will arrive**.
> 我得知道 Sophie 何時才會到。
>
> Would you tell me **whether you like the shirt**?
> 您能告訴我您是否喜歡這件襯衫嗎？

共通規則 2

疑問詞之後必定先接主詞，再接句子剩下的部分。若有助動詞 do、does、did，則刪除並將動詞做適當變化，其他形式的助動詞則一律保留。

> 例句
>
> 直接問句：Where will you go after the party?
>
> 間接問句：Let me know where you will go after the party.
> 　　　　　告訴我派對結束之後你要去哪裡。
>
> 直接問句：What did Amy do just now?
>
> 間接問句：I need to know what Amy did just now.
> 　　　　　我得知道艾咪剛剛做了什麼事。

共通規則 3

間接問句視為名詞，句末的標點符號以主句判斷。

例句 Do you know why Luna cried?

你知道為什麼露娜哭嗎？

I wonder if Ted will show up later.

我想知道泰德晚點會不會出現。

句型變化規則如下：

規則 1

直接問句內的動詞為 be 動詞時：

句型變化　直接問句：疑問詞 + be 動詞 + 主詞...

間接問句：疑問詞 + 主詞 + be 動詞...

例句　直接問句：How are you?

間接問句：I just want to know how you are.
我只想知道你過得好不好。

直接問句：What is the secret club like?

間接問句：I'm wondering what the secret club is like.
我想知道該祕密社團是什麼樣子。

規則 2-1

直接問句內的動詞為一般動詞，且使用助動詞 do、does、did 時：

句型變化　直接問句：疑問詞 + do / does / did + 主詞 + 原形動詞...

間接問句：疑問詞 + 主詞 + 原形動詞...

例句　直接問句：What did you buy?

間接問句：Tell me what you bought.
告訴我你買了什麼。

直接問句：Where **did you go**?

間接問句：I want to know **where you went**.
　　　　　我想知道你去哪裡了。

規則 2-2

直接問句內的動詞為一般原形動詞，且使用助動詞 will、must、can 等時：

直接問句：疑問詞 + 助動詞 + 主詞 + 原形動詞...

間接問句：疑問詞 + 主詞 + 助動詞 + 原形動詞...

直接問句：What **should we do**?

間接問句：I wonder **what we should do**.
　　　　　我想知道我們該怎麼做。

規則 2-3

直接問句內有 have、has、had 的助動詞時：

直接問句：疑問詞 + **have** / **has** / **had** + 主詞 + 過去分詞...

間接問句：疑問詞 + 主詞 + **have** / **has** / **had** + 過去分詞...

直接問句：Where **has Jim gone**?

間接問句：Tell me **where Jim has gone**.
　　　　　告訴我吉姆去哪了。

規則 3

直接問句為 Yes / No 問句時，轉為間接問句時疑問詞應使用 whether / if。
（whether / if 也可與 or not 合用，詳細用法請見 13-1。）

1 直接問句內的動詞為 be 動詞時：
直接問句：be 動詞 + 主詞...

間接問句：whether / if + 主詞 + be 動詞...

2 直接問句內的動詞為一般動詞，且使用助動詞 do、does、did 時：

直接問句：**Do / Does / Did** + 主詞 + 原形動詞...

間接問句：**whether / if** + 主詞 + 助動詞 + 動詞...

注意

助動詞為 do、does、did 時，變化方法同本節所述之規則 2-1。

3 直接問句內的動詞為一般原形動詞，且使用助動詞 will、must、can 等時：

直接問句：**助動詞** + 主詞 + 原形動詞...

間接問句：**whether / if** + 主詞 + 助動詞 + 原形動詞...

4 直接問句內有 have、has、had 的助動詞時：

直接問句：**Have / Has / Had** + 主詞 + 過去分詞...

間接問句：**whether / if** + 主詞 + have / has / had + 過去分詞...

直接問句：**Is Peggy** a student?

間接問句：Tell me **whether Peggy is** a student.
告訴我佩姬是不是學生。

直接問句：**Did Mr. Lee like** my painting?

間接問句：I'd like to know **whether Mr. Lee liked** my painting.
我想知道李老師喜不喜歡我的畫。

直接問句：**Will Ben go** to the beach?

間接問句：Do you know **if Ben will go** to the beach?
你知道班會不會去海灘嗎？

直接問句：**Has Willy passed** the exam?

間接問句：I don't know **whether Willy has passed** the exam.
我不知道威利是否有通過考試了。

規則 4

疑問代名詞 who、what、which 在問句中作主詞時,變成間接問句不需倒裝。

直接問句:who / what / which + 動詞...?

↓

間接問句:who / what / which + 動詞...

直接問句:Who bought the drink?

間接問句:Tell me who bought the drink.
告訴我是誰買飲料的?

直接問句:Which woman is the shortest?

間接問句:I want to know which woman is the shortest.
我想知道哪位女士最矮。

＼ 即時演練 ／

一、單選題

① I'd like to know _____ to school.
  (A) you will go when   (B) when will you go
  (C) when you will go   (D) when go you will

② Mom wants to know _____ from the supermarket.
  (A) what bought you   (B) what you bought
  (C) you bought what   (D) you did buy what

③ Would you tell me _____ this morning?
  (A) where were you   (B) you were where
  (C) were you where   (D) where you were

④ No one knows _____ .
  (A) where your bag is   (B) where is your bag
  (C) your bag is where   (D) is where your bag

⑤ We all wondered if _____ .
  (A) would things work out (B) things would work out
  (C) would work out things (D) things work out would

① { What year did you graduate from college?
    { Please tell me.

_____

② { Can you answer this question?
    { Would you tell me?

_____

③ { What happened to Claire?
    { We all want to know.

_____

解　答

一、 ① C　　　　② B　　　　③ D　　　　④ A　　　　⑤ B

二、 ① Please tell me what year you graduated from college.

　　 ② Would you tell me if / whether you can answer this question?

　　 ③ We all want to know what happened to Claire.

附錄 1　不規則動詞

A-A-A 型（三態相同）			
原形	過去式	過去分詞	中譯
bet	bet	bet	打賭
burst	burst	burst	（使）爆裂
cost	cost	cost	價錢為
cast	cast	cast	扔，拋；施（咒）
cut	cut	cut	切
fit	fit（美）/ fitted	fit（美）/ fitted	適合
hit	hit	hit	打
hurt	hurt	hurt	使……受傷；痛
let	let	let	讓
put	put	put	放，置
read	read [rɛd]	read [rɛd]	閱讀
rid	rid	rid	使……擺脫
set	set	set	放
shut	shut	shut	關上
quit	quit	quit	辭（工作）
spit	spit（美）/ spat	spit（美）/ spat	吐（口水）
split	split	split	（使）斷裂
spread	spread	spread	攤開
upset	upset	upset	使難過

A-A-B 型（動詞原形和過去式相同）			
原形	過去式	過去分詞	中譯
beat	beat	beaten / beat	打

443

原形	過去式	過去分詞	中譯
lay	laid	laid	放置
say	said	said	說
pay	paid	paid	支付
sell	sold	sold	賣
tell	told	told	告訴
catch	caught	caught	抓住
teach	taught	taught	教
buy	bought	bought	買
bring	brought	brought	帶來
fight	fought	fought	打仗
seek	sought	sought	尋找
think	thought	thought	認為
have / has	had	had	有
hear	heard	heard	聽見
make	made	made	做
build	built	built	建造
lend	lent	lent	借 (錢)
send	sent	sent	寄
bend	bent	bent	彎腰
spend	spent	spent	花 (錢)
light	lit / lighted	lit / lighted	照亮
sit	sat	sat	坐
shoot	shot	shot	開槍
lose	lost	lost	輸掉
win	won	won	贏
hold	held	held	拿著
burn	burnt / burned	burnt / burned	燃燒

A-B-B 型 (過去式和過去分詞相同)

444

dream	dreamt [drɛmt] / dreamed	dreamt / dreamed	做夢
meet	met	met	遇見
feed	fed	fed	餵；養
bleed	bled	bled	流血
breed	bred	bred	飼養
flee	fled	fled	逃離
feel	felt	felt	感覺
keep	kept	kept	(使)保持
weep	wept	wept	哭泣
sweep	swept	swept	打掃
sleep	slept	slept	睡覺
creep	crept	crept	悄悄移動
lead	led	led	領導
deal	dealt	dealt	做生意
leave	left	left	離開
mean	meant	meant	意思是
stand	stood	stood	站立
understand	understood	understood	明白
find	found	found	找到
bind	bound	bound	捆綁
grind	ground	ground	磨碎
hang	hung	hung	懸掛
spin	spun	spun	(使)旋轉
sting	stung	stung	刺，叮
swing	swung	swung	(使)搖擺
dig	dug	dug	挖，掘
stick	stuck	stuck	黏住
strike	struck	struck	打，擊

A-B-A 型（現在式和過去分詞相同）			
原形	過去式	過去分詞	中譯
run	ran	run	跑
come	came	come	來
become	became	become	變成
overcome	overcame	overcome	克服

A-B-C 型（三態不相同）			
原形	過去式	過去分詞	中譯
drink	drank	drunk	喝
ring	rang	rung	（鈴）作響
sing	sang	sung	唱（歌）
sink	sank	sunk	（使）下沉
shrink	shrank / shrunk	shrunk	縮小
swim	swam	swum	游泳
begin	began	begun	開始
break	broke	broken	打破
speak	spoke	spoken	說話
steal	stole	stolen	偷
choose	chose	chosen	選擇
freeze	froze	frozen	（使）凍結
wake	woke	woken	醒來
awake	awoke	awoken	醒來
weave	wove	woven	織（布）
take	took	taken	拿
mistake	mistook	mistaken	搞錯
shake	shook	shaken	搖動
bite	bit	bitten	咬
hide	hid	hidden	隱藏

446

bear	bore	borne	忍受
tear	tore	torn	(被)撕開
wear	wore	worn	穿;戴
swear	swore	sworn	發誓
ride	rode	ridden	騎(馬)
rise	rose	risen	上升
arise	arose	arisen	發生;出現
drive	drove	driven	開車
write	wrote	written	寫
know	knew	known	知道
grow	grew	grown	生長
throw	threw	thrown	丟,扔
draw	drew	drawn	畫
blow	blew	blown	(風)吹
fly	flew	flown	飛
show	showed	shown	顯示
see	saw	seen	看見
sew	sewed	sewn / sewed	縫
sow	sowed	sown / sowed	播(種)
give	gave	given	給予
forgive	forgave	forgiven	原諒
get	got	gotten / got (英)	得到
forget	forgot	forgotten	忘記
eat	ate	eaten	吃
fall	fell	fallen	落下
go	went	gone	去
lie	lay	lain	躺
do, does	did	done	做
be (am, is, are)	was, were	been	是

附錄 **2** 易混淆動詞

以下就 外觀相似的動詞 及 意思相似的動詞 分別舉例說明：

1 外觀相似的動詞

(1) lie 與 lay

lie

用法

1 *vi.* 躺；位於；在於（三態為：lie, lay, lain，現在分詞為 lying）
2 *vi.* 說謊（三態為：lie, lied, lied，現在分詞為 lying）

例句

Terry **lay** on the grass and took a nap there.
泰瑞躺在草地上小睡一會兒。
（此處 lay 為 lie 的過去式，表「躺」）

Joy **lied** about her age.
喬伊謊報了年齡。

lay

用法

vt. 放置 & *vi.* & *vt.* 下（蛋），產（卵）（三態為：lay, laid, laid，現在分詞為 laying）

例句

Please don't **lay** your books on this table.
請不要把你的書放在這張桌子上。（此處 lay 為原形動詞，表「放置」）

The hen didn't **lay** any eggs yesterday.
母雞昨天沒下蛋。（此處 lay 為原形動詞，表「下（蛋）」）

(2) sit、seat、set

sit

用法

vi. 坐；坐下（三態為：sit, sat, sat）

例句

We were **sitting** by the window.
我們坐在窗邊。（為主動用法）

seat

 用法 *vt.* 使就座；可容納 (三態為：seat, seated, seated)

 例句
We were **seated** by the window (by the waiter). (為被動用法)
= The waiter **seated** us by the window.
服務生安排我們坐窗戶旁的座位。

This theater **seats** almost 2,000 people.
這間劇院可容納將近兩千人。

set

 用法 *vt.* 放置；設定 (三態同形)

 例句
Julie **set** the vase on the table.
茱莉把花瓶擺在桌上。

Remember to **set** the alarm before you sleep.
睡前記得設鬧鐘。

(3) rise、arise、raise、arouse

rise

 用法 *vi.* (價格等) 上漲 / 增加；(太陽等) 升起；起身
(三態為：rise, rose, risen)

 例句
Prices keep **rising** these days.
最近物價不斷地上漲。

raise

 用法 *vt.* 增加 (價格等)；舉起；撫養；募 (款) (三態為：raise, raised, raised)

 例句
Many businesses have **raised** their prices recently.
近期許多商家都把售價提高了。

arise

 用法 *vi.* (問題、機會等) 出現，產生 (三態為：arise, arose, arisen)

Some problems **arose** when the boss was on leave.
老闆請假的期間出現了一些問題。

arouse

 vt. 引起，激發 (興趣、憤怒等)；喚醒
(三態為：arouse, aroused, aroused)

 The actor's behavior **aroused** a lot of interest from the media.
這名演員的行徑引起媒體極大的興趣。

(4) feel、fall、fail

feel

 vi. & *vt.* 感覺，感受；觸摸 (三態為：feel, felt, felt)

 I didn't **feel** any pain.
我沒有感到痛。

The nurse **felt** the sick boy's forehead.
護理師摸了摸這位生病的男孩的額頭。

fall

 vi. 跌倒；(氣溫等)下降；(雨 / 雪)降下
(三態為：fall, fell, fallen)

 Paula **fell** down and hurt her leg.
寶拉跌倒，傷了腿。

The temperature here could **fall** below zero
degrees in winter. 這裡的氣溫在冬天可能會降至零度以下。

fail

 vi. 失敗 & *vi.* & *vt.* (考試)不及格 (三態為：fail, failed, failed)

 Tina had wanted to win the game, but she **failed**.
提娜想要在比賽中獲勝，但她失敗了。

Walter didn't study hard, so he **failed** his test.
華特沒有用功讀書，所以他考試不及格。

(5) find 與 found

find

用法	*vt.* 發現；找到 (三態為：find, found, found)

例句	I can't **find** my cell phone. 我找不到我的手機。

found

用法	*vt.* 創辦，建立 (三態為：found, founded, founded)

例句	The company was **founded** in 2010. 這間公司是 2010 年創立的。

❷ 意思相似的動詞

(1) 表「說話，講話」的動詞：say、tell、talk、speak

說明	say、tell、talk 以及 speak 意思上皆與「說話，講話」相關，但它們的用法不盡相同，說明如下：

解說	
say	表示「說，講」
	常見片語或慣用語
	say hello / goodbye / thank you 問好 / 道別 / 道謝
	sb say + (that) 子句 某人說……
tell	表示「講，告訴」
	常見片語或慣用語
	tell a lie / a story / a joke / the truth 說謊 / 講故事 / 講笑話 / 說實話
	tell sb + (that) 子句 告訴某人……
	tell sb about sth 告訴某人某事

talk	表示「說話，談論」
	常見片語或慣用語
	talk to / with sb　與某人說話
	talk about...　談論……
speak	表示「說話，談論」
	常見片語或慣用語
	speak to / with sb　與某人說話
	speak about / of...　談論到……

比較

The teacher **said that** the boy is behaving well.
老師說這位男孩很乖。

The teacher **told** the boy's parents **that** he is behaving well.
老師對男孩的家長說他很乖。

The teacher wants to **talk to / with** the boy's parents.
= The teacher wants to **speak to / with** the boy's parents.
老師想跟這名男孩的家長談談。

Hannah **talked about** her new job last night.
= Hannah **spoke of** her new job last night.
漢娜昨晚提到她的新工作。

(2) 表「看」的動詞：see、watch、look at

see、watch 以及 look at 三者在中文中皆可譯成「看」，但三者在使用上意義不盡相同，說明如下：

解說	
see	指「無意地看」或「可以看見」
watch	指「(在一段時間內) 有意地看」，尤指有變化或移動的東西
look at	指「有意地看」，尤指靜止或無變化的東西

例句

I **saw** Nicole this morning.
我今天早上見到妮可。

We can **see** the beach from our hotel room.
從飯店房間望出去可以看到海灘。

My father **watches** the news every evening.
我爸爸每天晚上都會看新聞。

The couple sat on the beach and **watched** the sun go down.
這對情侶坐在海灘上，看著太陽西下。

The tourist is **looking at** the map.
這位觀光客在看地圖。

---

(3) 表「聽」的動詞：hear 與 listen to

說明

hear 與 listen to 在中文中皆可譯成「聽」，但兩者在使用上意義不盡相同，說明如下：

解說	
hear	指「無意地聽」、「被動地聽見」或「可以聽見」
listen to	指「有意地聽」

例句

I **heard** the singer's new song playing on the radio.
我聽到這位歌手的新歌在廣播電臺上播放。

I've **heard** about the good news.
我有聽說這個好消息。

The old man can't **hear** very well.
這位老先生聽不太清楚。

I'm **listening to** the singer's new song.
我在聽這位歌手的新歌。

(4) 表「穿、戴」的動詞：wear、put on、dress

說明

wear、put on 以及 dress 意思上皆與「穿，戴」相關，但三者在使用上意義不盡相同，說明如下：

	解說
wear	表示「穿著，戴著」（強調狀態）
put on	表示「穿上，戴上」（強調動作）
dress	為及物動詞，之後接人為受詞，表「為某人穿上衣服」（強調動作）；此字亦可採被動語態 be dressed in，但表「穿著」，等於 be wearing（強調狀態）。

例句

比較

You should wear a jacket today. It's pretty cold outside.
你今天應該穿外套。外面蠻冷的。（強調狀態）

You should put on a jacket. It's pretty cold outside.
你應該穿上外套。外面蠻冷的。（強調動作）

比較

George is wearing his uniform.
喬治穿著他的制服。（強調狀態）

George has put on his uniform.
喬治穿上了他的制服。（強調動作）

Help me dress the baby.
幫我為寶寶穿上衣服。（強調動作）

George is dressed in his uniform.
= George is wearing his uniform.
喬治穿著他的制服。（強調狀態）

454

(5) 表「借」的動詞：borrow 與 lend

 說明

borrow 與 lend 意思上皆與「借」相關，但它們的用法不盡相同，說明如下：

解說	
borrow	表示「借入」
	常見句型
	borrow + 事物 (+ from + 人)
lend	表示「借出」
	常見句型
	1 lend + 人 + 事物
	2 lend + 事物 (+ to + 人)

 例句

比較

Ken **borrowed** some money **from** Joe.　肯向喬借了一些錢。

Joe **lent** Ken some money.

= Joe **lent** some money **to** Ken.

喬借了一些錢給肯。

(6) 表「花費」的動詞：spend、take、cost

 說明

spend、take 以及 cost 意思上皆與「花費」相關，但三者在使用上意義不盡相同，說明如下：

解說	
spend	表示「花費 (金錢、時間)」
	常見句型
	1 人 + spend + 金錢 / 時間 + on...
	2 人 + spend + 金錢 / 時間 + 動名詞
take	表示「花費 (時間)」
	常見句型
	1 It takes (+ 人) + 時間 + to + 原形動詞
	2 事物 + takes (+ 人) + 時間

cost	表示「花費（金錢）」
	常見句型
	❶ It cost＋人＋金錢＋to＋原形動詞
	❷ 事物＋cost＋人＋金錢

I spent NT$1,000 on this bag.　我花了新臺幣一千元買這個包包。

= It cost me NT$1,000 to buy this bag.

= This bag cost me NT$1,000.
這個包包花了我新臺幣一千元。

比較

I spent five hours doing this job.
我花了五個小時做這份工作。（未必做完）

It took (me) five hours to finish this job.
這工作我花了五個小時才做完。（已做完）

This job took (me) five hours.
這工作花了我五個小時。（已做完）

---

(7) 表「攜帶」的動詞：take、bring、fetch、carry

take、bring、fetch 以及 carry 意思上皆與「攜帶」相關，但它們在使用上意義不盡相同，說明如下：

解說	
take	表示「帶去，拿去」，尤指從近處帶至遠處
bring	表示「帶來，拿來」，尤指從遠處帶至近處
fetch	表示「去取來，去拿來」，強調到某處取某物，並將其帶回
carry	表示「攜帶」，強調物品在身邊

Patty, could you take these books to Ricky?
派蒂，妳可以把這些書拿給瑞奇嗎？

Patty brought these books to Ricky.　派蒂把這些書拿給瑞奇。

Patty fetched some books for Ricky.　派蒂幫瑞奇拿了幾本書過來。

Vince carries some cash in his wallet.　文斯的錢包裡有一些現金。

(8) 表「擁有」的動詞：have、own、possess

have、own 以及 possess 意思上皆與「擁有」相關，但它們在使用上意義不盡相同，說明如下：

解說	
have	表示「有；(身上) 持有」，強調某人有某物，但不一定是法律上擁有該物品
own	表示「(合法) 擁有」，強調法律上擁有某物
possess	表示「擁有；(身上) 持有」，為較正式的用法

I don't **have** any money on me.　我身上沒有任何錢。

This house is not **owned** by the Smiths—they rent it.
這間房子不是史密斯一家人所有 —— 他們是用租的。

The man was arrested for **possessing** drugs.
這名男子因持有毒品而被捕。

(9) 表「回答」的動詞：answer 與 reply

answer 與 reply 意思上皆表「回答」，但它們的用法不盡相同，說明如下：

解說	
answer	表示「回答；應 (門)；接 (電話)」，可為不及物動詞或及物動詞
	常見片語或慣用語
	answer a question　回答問題
	answer the door　應門
	answer the phone　接電話
reply	表示「回答；回覆」，為不及物動詞，其後常接介詞 to 再加名詞
	常見片語或慣用語
	reply to a question　回覆問題
	reply to an email　回覆電子郵件

The shop assistant can answer your question.
店員可以回答你的問題。

The store has not replied to my question yet.
店家還沒回覆我的問題。

Notes

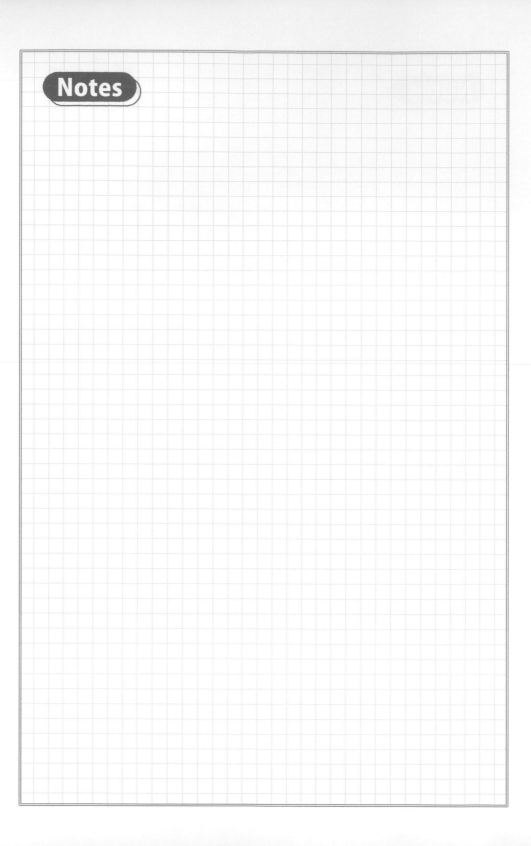

Notes

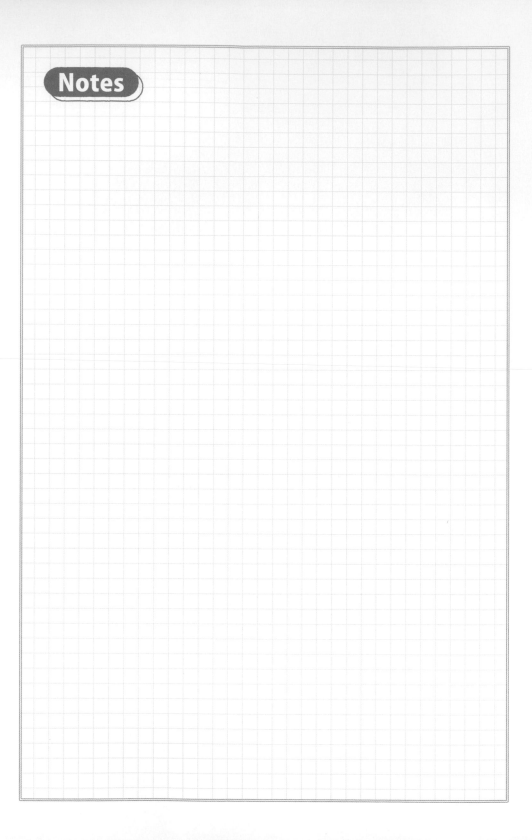

Notes

Notes

國家圖書館出版品預行編目（CIP）資料

賴世雄圖解英文法 / 賴世雄作. -- 初版. -- 臺北
市：常春藤數位出版股份有限公司, 2023.01
面；　公分. --（常春藤生活必讀系列；BA21）
ISBN 978-626-7225-12-7（平裝）
1. CST：英語　2. CST：語法
805.16　　　　　　　　　　111021147

常春藤生活必讀系列【BA21】 賴世雄圖解英文法

總 編 審	賴世雄
終　　審	賴世雄
執行編輯	許嘉華
編輯小組	鄭筠潔・黃莉婷・畢安安・魏宇姍・區光銳・Nick Roden
設計組長	王玥琦
封面設計	王玥琦
排版設計	王玥琦・王穎緁・林桂旭
法律顧問	北辰著作權事務所蕭雄淋律師
出 版 者	常春藤數位出版股份有限公司
地　　址	臺北市忠孝西路一段 33 號 5 樓
電　　話	(02) 2331-7600
傳　　真	(02) 2381-0918
網　　址	www.ivy.com.tw
電子信箱	service@ivy.com.tw
郵政劃撥	50463568
戶　　名	常春藤數位出版股份有限公司
定　　價	620 元

郵票黏貼處

100009 臺北市忠孝西路一段 33 號 5 樓

常春藤有聲出版股份有限公司　行政組　啟

常春藤　www.ivy.com.tw
愛上英語的第一站

 **讀者問卷【BA21】 賴世雄圖解英文法**

感謝您購買本書！為使我們對讀者的服務能夠更加完善，請您詳細填寫本問卷各欄後，寄回本公司或傳真至（02）2381-0918，**或掃描 QR Code 填寫線上問卷**，我們將於收到後七個工作天內贈送「常春藤網路書城熊贈點 50 點（一點＝一元，使用期限 90 天）」給您（每書每人限贈一次），也懇請您繼續支持。若有任何疑問，請儘速與客服人員聯絡，客服電話：（02）2331-7600 分機 11～13，謝謝您！

線上填寫
免郵寄最環保

姓　　名：＿＿＿＿＿＿＿＿＿＿　性別：＿＿＿＿　生日：＿＿＿＿年＿＿＿＿月＿＿＿＿日

聯絡電話：＿＿＿＿＿＿＿＿＿　**E-mail**：＿＿＿＿＿＿＿＿＿＿＿＿＿＿＿＿＿

聯絡地址：□□□□□□＿＿＿＿＿＿＿＿＿＿＿＿＿＿＿＿＿＿＿＿＿＿＿＿＿＿＿＿

＿＿＿＿＿＿＿＿＿＿＿＿＿＿＿＿＿＿＿＿＿＿＿＿＿＿＿＿＿＿＿＿＿＿＿＿＿＿

教育程度：□國小　□國中　□高中　□大專／大學　□研究所含以上

職　　業：**1** □學生

　　　　　2 社會人士：□工　□商　□服務業　□軍警公職　□教職　□其他＿＿＿＿＿＿＿

1 您從何處得知本書：□書店　□常春藤網路書城　□FB／IG／Line@ 社群平臺推薦
　　□學校購買　□親友推薦　□常春藤雜誌　□其他＿＿＿＿＿＿＿＿＿＿＿＿＿＿＿＿

2 您購得本書的管道：□書店　□常春藤網路書城　□博客來　□其他＿＿＿＿＿＿＿＿

3 最滿意本書的特點依序是(限定三項)：□試題演練　□內容　□編排方式　□印刷
　　□封面　□售價　□信任品牌　□其他＿＿＿＿＿＿＿＿＿＿＿＿＿＿＿＿＿＿＿＿

4 您對本書建議改進的三點依序是：□無（都很滿意）□試題演練　□內容　□編排方式
　　□印刷　□封面　□售價　□其他＿＿＿＿＿＿＿＿＿＿＿＿＿＿＿＿＿＿＿＿＿＿
　　原因：＿＿＿＿＿＿＿＿＿＿＿＿＿＿＿＿＿＿＿＿＿＿＿＿＿＿＿＿＿＿＿＿＿＿
　　對本書的其他建議：＿＿＿＿＿＿＿＿＿＿＿＿＿＿＿＿＿＿＿＿＿＿＿＿＿＿＿＿

5 希望我們出版哪些主題的書籍：＿＿＿＿＿＿＿＿＿＿＿＿＿＿＿＿＿＿＿＿＿＿＿

6 若您發現本書誤植的部分，請告知在：書籍第＿＿＿＿＿＿＿頁，第＿＿＿＿＿＿＿行
　　有錯誤的部分是：＿＿＿＿＿＿＿＿＿＿＿＿＿＿＿＿＿＿＿＿＿＿＿＿＿＿＿＿＿

7 對我們的其他建議：＿＿＿＿＿＿＿＿＿＿＿＿＿＿＿＿＿＿＿＿＿＿＿＿＿＿＿＿

感謝您寶貴的意見，您的支持是我們的動力！　常春藤網路書城 www.ivy.com.tw